Praise for

VICKI BRADLEY

'A twisty thriller about the happiest day of your life
descending into a nightmare'

Claire McGowan, author of *The Other Wife*

'As pacy as it is puzzling, you'll change your mind end-
lessly about what you think has happened'

Heat

'A deliciously dark and twisted read'

***Woman* magazine**

'Will take you on a frantic ride'

Sun

'An intense thriller'

Bella

'Such a joy to read ... Definitely an author to watch!'

Sam Carrington, author of *I Dare You*

'Tense, layered and atmospheric ... I couldn't
put it down'

Fran Dorricott, author of *After the Eclipse*

Vicki Bradley splits her time between writing psychological suspense and drama novels and being a DC with the Met Police. Her first novel, *Before I Say I Do*, won the 2018 inaugural Write Here, Right Now open submissions competition run by Simon & Schuster UK, Darley Anderson Literary Agency and the Bradford Literature Festival. *Your Life or Mine*, the second thriller featuring DC Alana Loxton, can be read as a standalone.

To find out more, visit her website or follow her on Twitter.

www.vickibradleywriter.com

🐦 @vbradleywriter

Also by Vicki Bradley

Before I Say I Do

YOUR LIFE OR MINE

VICKI BRADLEY

**SIMON &
SCHUSTER**

London · New York · Sydney · Toronto · New Delhi

First published in Great Britain by Simon & Schuster UK Ltd, 2021

1 3 5 7 9 10 8 6 4 2

Simon & Schuster UK Ltd
1st Floor
222 Gray's Inn Road
London WC1X 8HB

Simon & Schuster Australia, Sydney
Simon & Schuster India, New Delhi

www.simonandschuster.co.uk
www.simonandschuster.com.au
www.simonandschuster.co.in

A CIP catalogue record for this book
is available from the British Library

Paperback ISBN: 978-1-4711-8526-7
eBook ISBN: 978-1-4711-8527-4
Audio ISBN: 978-1-3985-0056-3

Typeset in the UK by M Rules
Printed and bound in Great Britain by CPI Group (UK) Ltd,
Croydon, CR0 4YY

MIX
Paper from
responsible sources
FSC® C020471
FSC
www.fsc.org

For my twin sister, Alison.

Thank you for your sense of adventure,
love of life, humour, and drive.

For encouraging me to reach for the stars like you do.

And for always being there for me.

Prologue

She jolted awake. Kennington; her stop. She jumped up and scrambled to get off the tube. She made it just in time. The doors slid shut behind her and she laughed in relief. She'd only just caught the last tube and she didn't fancy having to walk all the way back to Kennington from Oval at this time of night.

She glanced left and right, suddenly aware that there might be other people on the platform, but there was no one.

It was just her.

As she headed towards the exit, she felt sluggish. She staggered to the escalators, steadying herself on the handrail and wishing she hadn't had that last cocktail. Why did she always have to have that extra one? And why had she bought them all shots? Still, how often did she get to see the girls? It had been a special occasion and she didn't have to be at work until her Monday night shift at 10pm.

She stumbled at the top of the escalator and clattered forward on her heels, catching herself before she fell. Her footfall echoed around the empty station. She paused for a second to get her bearings as Kennington underground station spun slowly around her.

It was deserted – not even any staff around – and she was grateful. She'd hate for anyone to see her like this.

She tucked her hair behind her ears, took a big breath and tried to focus. She tapped herself out of the barrier, nearly dropping her police oyster card in the process, and cursed herself. If she lost that, it would cause her a lot of grief at work.

She shivered as the outside winter air hit her and the muggy, stale warmth of the underground was left behind. She pulled her red coat tighter around her. The street outside was dark and the pavement shiny with recent rainfall. Just as well it had stopped; she'd left her brolly on the tube. There was a break in the clouds, revealing a full moon, which was never good for police. Burglars loved a full moon. When the moon was so bright it was like a strange pale daylight; they didn't have to announce their presence with torch light, instead relying on the moon's beams to guide them through unlocked windows.

She looked left and right down Braganza street, but there was no one, so she set off along the side road – not far. Her footfall echoed down the deserted pavement and she picked up her pace, aware of how late it had become. She took out her mobile and scrolled to Luke, but stopped herself before she pressed dial. She'd got into the habit of calling him on the way home; it made her feel safer. But she couldn't call him anymore.

She dropped her mobile back in her bag and sighed. Luke had been great when she'd first met him, so relaxed and could make her laugh easily, but after one too many drinks that all changed. His temper had scared her. She wouldn't call him, even though she missed the Luke she'd first met and having someone to call.

A man thirty metres away, on her side of the road,

snapped her out of her thoughts. He was walking towards her with purpose. She put him in his mid-thirties, his pace slow and steady, as if trying not to scare her. Never a good sign. She crossed the road – nice and relaxed, not showing any fear. They could smell it, she knew, and it galvanized the really bad ones.

She clutched her house keys inside her coat pocket as a weapon. She was too drunk to pose any real danger to him, but the sharp edges of the keys comforted her. They weren't sharp enough to penetrate skin, but if it came to it, they could do some real damage to someone's eyes.

The man glanced across the road at her but walked past, remaining on the opposite side. She released her tight hold on the keys as she checked behind her, but he'd turned the corner and was gone.

She re-crossed the road. She preferred this side. There were little front gardens with low walls – no looming hedges for someone to hide behind. The engine of a car hummed in the distance. Civilization. She was so close to home now – only a minute away.

There was a sudden thud to her right and she froze, rooted by fear. It had come from behind a bush in the garden next to her. She tightened her grip on her keys again, wishing she had a better weapon. Something scrabbled over the wall and darted away. She'd startled it. Her shoulders relaxed. Just a cat.

She tried to stifle a yawn, wondering if the kebab place around the corner from her flat would still be open. But it was past midnight and she didn't fancy the extra walk with no guarantee of food at the end. Cheese on toast when she got home would have to do.

She turned into her street and relaxed. Not far now and then she could take her heels off. The arches of her feet ached and she knew she'd have blisters. Vanity over practicality, but she'd wanted to look good, to give herself a boost. The break-up with Luke had been tough.

She took her keys out of her pocket and turned down the pathway into the small front garden. She glanced down, skimming through her keys until she located the key fob to the communal front door.

There was a sudden sharp pain to the back of her head. She felt herself falling forward, but too fast to put her hands out, and her jaw collided hard with the concrete doorstep. For a moment she was stunned, felt nothing at all, and then white-hot pain burnt along her jawline.

She tasted rusty blood in her mouth. Before she could scream, there were fingers pressing tight into her wind-pipe, closing off her airway as her attacker straddled her back. Her hands scrabbled at the enclosing fingers, but she couldn't pull them apart; they were vice-like and getting tighter. They felt rough, like Luke's. She tried to turn her head to see who was behind her, but the hands had her neck pinned to the floor.

She swung her elbow back uselessly towards her attacker, failing to get her arm back far enough, the weight on her back restraining her against the cold ground. Her jaw screamed at her, the pain intensifying, and she realized with startling clarity that she was dying.

She shouted out, but all that came out was a strangled gurgling. Her lungs felt like they were burning, and she clawed frantically at the hands.

For a moment she thought of her mother, tiny and small in her big armchair – how fragile she'd seemed on her last visit and how she'd promised herself she'd see her more often.

Her vision faded, the edges becoming blurred. She

couldn't die; she wasn't ready. Darkness seeped into her peripheral vision, slowly covering everything in black. She struggled harder, a last frantic effort, but her assailant's grip didn't budge.

She couldn't leave her mother; it would kill her.

The pain was so intense now, like white fire burning inside her chest. She wanted it to stop. Please stop. And then it did. The blackness was complete and there was nothing.

Chapter 1

'Alana, come sit next to me.' Jane beckoned Loxton to the seat next to her at the pub table. 'It's so great to see you. This is my first night out since I had Joseph.' She was positioned at the centre of the group of women, at the heart of them, which was fitting. She had kept them all together when they worked in the murder squad, arranging the social gatherings, checking up on them all. And they had become friends for life because of it.

Loxton obliged Jane, sitting next to her, although she would have preferred to be tucked away at the end of the table, where there was less chance of being asked any awkward questions by the others.

It had been two years since they'd all worked together in the murder squad, but they'd continued to have their regular meet-ups until recently. Partly it was down to Jane having a newborn, but Loxton knew it was her fault too. When she'd been demoted from the murder squad a few months back, she'd gone quiet. But Jane had been persistent and recent events had pressed the matter. Loxton owed Jane just about as much as she owed anyone, so for her sake she had swallowed her pride about her demotion and come along. She didn't want the group to drift apart, and she needed to talk about what had happened too.

All of Alana's memories came flooding back as she looked at the women sat around her. The old stories, carefully placed in their boxes, were bursting to come out.

Emma grinned at her, already halfway through her first glass of white wine, always ready for a party. 'It's so good to finally get us all together again. How have you been since I saw you a couple of months ago?'

'Settling into Southwark CID okay,' Loxton said, feeling her mood lightening, Emma's energy was infectious. The male waiter was hanging off Gabriella's every word as she asked him about the wine menu. He looked entranced by her Italian accent.

Despite her pain at seeing them all together, reminding her of everything she'd lost, it was still good to be back with them.

'Are any of the boys coming?' she asked Jane.

'No, I decided to keep it to just us girls this time, although I don't know where Sarah's got to. I didn't get a chance to talk to her. I had to leave a message with her grumpy sergeant. He probably didn't even pass it on.'

'Has she got a big case on?' Loxton asked.

'Her sergeant wouldn't say. Just said she was busy and wouldn't be able to make it. Weird guy.'

'What's his name?' It was unlikely Loxton would have heard of him, but as the years passed it was surprising how small the Metropolitan Police became.

'Steven Anson. Seemed a bit arrogant.' Jane shrugged and took a sip of her wine.

Loxton nodded and picked up the drinks menu. She had heard of him but never met him. He was a legend in the surveillance world. He worked in undercover operations, making her wonder what Sarah was up to these days. She realized with sadness that they'd lost touch. She'd seen Jane occasionally over the past few months and had kept up her regular coffee dates with Emma, but she hadn't seen the others for a while. Well, she thought, here was her chance to make amends.

'How's the murder squad going?' Loxton asked Gabriella.

'Not the same without all of you. There's a new inspector, DI Meyer, trying to throw his weight around, but he'll settle down.'

'That's all you need on top of the cuts,' Loxton said.

'What I need is a bottle of Prosecco,' Gabriella said. 'Tonight's a bit of a celebration and commiseration all in one. It's been too long.'

Loxton nodded. 'Sounds good.' She marvelled at how easy it was to fall back in with them all.

Loxton spotted Sarah coming into the bar at the same time as Sarah saw her. They had always been strangely in tune. Sarah nodded at her and hurried over, sitting down heavily as if she was carrying the world on her shoulders.

'Sorry I'm late,' Sarah said. 'It was tricky getting out of work, but this was too important to miss.' She looked gaunt, with grey shadows under her eyes poorly concealed by make-up. Her hair was tied up, and there were a couple of inches of dark roots showing through her normally immaculate blonde highlights. Despite Sarah's strong perfume, Loxton could smell unwashed bodies and grime, and she wondered if she was doing undercover work. Sarah was normally so glamorous, never seen without lipstick and mascara on.

'Your sergeant said you weren't going to make it,' Jane said, then paused for a moment. 'God, girl, you look a mess. I thought *I* looked rough after four months of maternity leave, but you look terrible.'

Sarah glared at her. 'Look, it's my new job role, okay? It's quite involved. Let's leave it at that.'

'What hours are they making you work?' Emma asked.

'Never mind that. Have they got you working down a *mine*?' Gabriella said, her eyes wide at the state of her friend. 'You don't look like you've seen the sun for years.'

'I can't talk about it,' she said with finality, shutting the conversation down. Sarah wouldn't look them in the eyes, instead picking up the wine menu and studying it.

So, she *was* working in undercover. Loxton didn't like it. It was dangerous work. She decided to leave it, though. She hadn't seen Sarah for months; who was she to start telling her what to do?

'We've got a bottle of fizz coming,' Gabriella said.

'Great.' Sarah put the menu down and her eyes met Loxton's. 'Alana, how are you? Long time no see after all that Alec Saunders shit. I heard he caused you some more bother a few months ago, too.' Sarah shook her head, her eyes kind, but Loxton didn't want to talk about it with any of them; she was still too embarrassed.

It was inevitable that Alec Saunders would be mentioned, she supposed. The journalist who had masqueraded as an A&E doctor and got into her bed. She'd trusted him, talked to him about her work, and he'd nodded along, telling her in turn about his 'critical patients'. But it had all been lies. He was a reporter trying to get a story about a domestic murder trial she was working on, and she'd been an idiot to believe he was a doctor.

He'd published what she'd told him, which caused enough confusion for the trial to be thrown out. She could have lost her job, but instead she'd been demoted from the murder squad and sent back to borough CID.

'I'm all right,' she said. 'Southwark CID is keeping

me busy and I've got good colleagues.' She smiled as she
thought of the team she was with now, of Kowalski and
the way he could make her laugh.

Sarah raised an eyebrow and smiled. 'Is there someone at work?'

'No one.' She shook her head, but Kowalski's pale blue
eyes came into her mind. He'd given her a spontaneous
pretend kiss in front of Alec Saunders a few months back,
but it hadn't meant anything to him; it was just to show
Saunders. Kowalski was her best friend at work; did she
really want to risk that? Wasn't it a cliché – not being able
to have a male best friend without it becoming romantic
and then, inevitably, everything falling apart?

The other women glanced at each other and then back
at her and, as if on cue, burst into laughter.

'What?' Loxton said, irritation in her voice.

'Sorry,' Jane said. 'You just got this dreamy look in your
eyes when you talked about work. It's so obvious.'

'There's no one,' Loxton said. 'You know I avoid dating
colleagues.'

'Seems you've forgotten that rule,' Gabriella said
with a smirk.

'Leave her alone,' Emma said. 'She's still taking her
time getting over that dickhead Alec. When you've had a
bad breakup you don't exactly leap straight into another
relationship. Ignore them, Alana.'

Emma looked sad for a moment and Loxton leaned
towards her to ask what she meant. It wasn't like Emma to
be so cautious about love; she was the hopeless romantic,
whereas the rest of them were more cynical. Police work
made you more wary of your fellow humans, but Emma
had always seemed immune to that, until now.

Loxton wondered what could have happened and why

Emma hadn't talked to her about it. That wasn't like her, to keep things bottled up; it was strange. Before Loxton could ask her, a waiter bustled over with the Prosecco and elaborately poured them out five glasses.

Sarah held up hers and the others followed. 'To new beginnings, ladies. To new loves. And to old friendships. Let's not wait so long to get together again.'

Loxton chinked glasses with them all and sipped the crisp, cold Prosecco gratefully.

Once they were settled, Jane looked at each of them in turn. 'So ... how are you all doing?' It was a general question, but Loxton knew she was talking about Edward Barratt. The serial killer who had been the last case they'd all worked on together two years ago. Emma and Sarah had left murder after that, needing a break from homicide and to get Barratt out of their heads.

Barratt had been the case that had tested them all. It was a unique time in Alana's career, when it was the right people, in the right place, at the right time. And they had stopped him with a single piece of hair that linked him to one of the scenes. He had been so careful – forensically so – and had never thought he'd get caught.

Barratt had sworn he would make them all pay. It was the best work any of them had ever done, but it had taken a piece of all of them, and she normally tried her best to forget about it. But tonight she couldn't. Someone had tried to break him out of Broadmoor Hospital three days ago.

'I'm not all right, really,' Loxton admitted, at last letting her guard down. She'd always been able to around these women. 'Who would try to get Barratt out? And it sounds like they nearly managed it.'

'He was found in the woods to the east of Broadmoor

Hospital. He'd made some good distance,' Gabriella said, sipping her drink. 'He's had quite the fan following since he's been in prison. There are a lot of freaks out there. I reckon it was probably one of them that helped him.'

Loxton shook her head in annoyance. 'Have they caught anyone?'

'The staff were clueless,' Gabriella said. 'Under-resourced and stretched to capacity. It's not their fault.'

'It was definitely an inside job,' Sarah said. 'Gabriella, you should look at all the new hospital staff first.'

'But how, in a maximum-security wing of Broadmoor, would a new staff member be trusted so quickly to be in that position?' Loxton said. 'Barratt's been in there for two years and hasn't exactly behaved.' She shuddered, remembering his killing spree over a year ago when he'd murdered three inmates and a guard.

'Do you think it was a mistake?' Jane asked. 'Barratt just seizing an opportunity?'

'It's possible,' Loxton said. 'Barratt was always assessing different scenarios – his mind never stops, but this seems too lucky even for him. He must have had help.'

'He probably charmed one of the guards,' Gabriella said. 'Remember that female guard being prosecuted for taking in drugs for a prisoner a few years back? Broadmoor Hospital is weirder than a prison. It's not just the inmates who lose their minds in there. And Barratt is the most intense man I've ever met.'

Loxton knew what she meant. Barratt's attention was all-consuming, like a snake's; mesmerizing and terrifying all at once. He had a way of getting under your skin and into your head that she couldn't help but admire. His victims – sex workers, often medicated with heroin – had never stood a chance against him.

'I heard they're putting him back in isolation, in the most secure part of the hospital,' Gabriella said.

'Well, that's something,' Jane replied, but she took a large swig of her drink, and Loxton noticed that she was glancing around the room, as if checking to make sure Barratt wasn't watching them.

'Let's get cocktails,' Emma said. 'I start nights on Monday, so I might as well make the most of my last bit of freedom.' She waved at the waiter, a grin lighting up her face.

Chapter 2

The noise was deafening: a cacophony of voices and the usual chaos of Southwark CID as officers rushed from one side of the room to the other.

Loxton walked over to Kowalski's desk. He was sat with a woman in a smart dress suit who was around Loxton's age, with long dark hair tied in a neat ponytail. Kowalski handed Loxton a coffee in a polystyrene cup and she took it gratefully.

'This is DC Lena Trawinska,' he said. 'We worked together in the Polish police quite a few years back. DCI Winter was looking for a profiler for the series of sexual assaults we've had these past two weeks and I suggested Lena. She's one of the best.'

Lena smiled at him and then leaned towards Loxton in a conspiratorial style. 'He's biased; don't listen to him. We met at police training school and I've got too much dirt on him. If you take me for a beer, I'll tell you everything, and how, when I met him, he couldn't even down a pint.'

Kowalski looked flustered and Loxton tried to hide her smile. It was strange to see him so easily wound up. Usually nothing bothered him.

'All right, Lena,' Kowalski said quickly. 'Loxton doesn't want to hear about that. She'd much rather hear your opinion on our sexual assault case from last night. Do you think it could be one of your series?'

Lena glanced down at the paperwork. 'I don't think so. My guy seems to be following a set pattern. It's always parks late at night, which suggests he works in the day-time. Your case happened at two in the afternoon on a cut-through to the high street. The description's slightly out too. But I'll keep it on the possible list. You never know.'

Kowalski sighed. 'I thought it might be another suspect. Just our luck we've got two of them.'

Loxton noticed Meera Patel in the corner of the office. Her face was pale and she hurriedly swiped away a tear. She must have had some bad news. Loxton would go over in a minute to talk to her.

Then Loxton frowned as she took another look around the entire office. Something was off. Detectives were frantically working, but it was more than the usual buzz of stress. Loxton felt a creeping sense of dread rising in her as she sensed the adrenaline rolling off the people around her. Southwark CID was usually chaotic, but this was something else.

'What's going on?' she asked Kowalski, motioning to the rest of her colleagues.

Kowalski glanced up from the paperwork and threw a cursory glance around the room. 'All hell's broken loose, but that's usual for this place, right?'

Lena frowned. 'I'd been told it was busy here, but this seems extreme.'

The noise around them had reached fever pitch. She could see a uniformed officer in a heated debate with her superior, DCI Winter.

Something was really wrong.

Voices rushed at her, but she couldn't make out what was going on. She walked over to DCI Winter and the uniformed officer, who were huddled together in the far corner of the office.

The uniformed officer looked stressed. 'The detective didn't show up for her night duty.'

And there it was. A police officer had gone missing. One of their own. Loxton felt the usual pulse of pain radiating in her temples. Too much caffeine and not enough sleep mixed with something sharper – dread, as she imagined the worst-case scenario, knowing that what you feared the most sometimes did come true.

Loxton prayed she didn't know whoever it was that had disappeared, but the police became a small world after you'd lived in it for ten years.

'Who is it?' Her voice was louder than she meant it to be and she felt her stomach clench as if in preparation for a blow.

The uniform stopped speaking. Winter turned to her. 'It's DC Emma Robins. She didn't arrive for the start of her shift with the Child Abuse Investigation Team last night at Camberwell police station.'

Kowalski and Lena had joined her and she saw Kowalski's face had paled. She closed her eyes for a moment and all she could see was Emma's infectious grin and the smattering of freckles across her nose.

'There's got to be a mistake,' Loxton said, lowering herself onto a chair as the world slid sideways, remembering with growing dismay the murder squad reunion two nights ago. All the girls back together.

'We completed a welfare check at her flat on Southwark Park Road at 3am but she wasn't there.' The uniform's face was grave. He was in his forties, had seen it all before, but not this. Not one of their own going missing. She could tell by his eyes – he was concerned, like they all were.

'That's not like Emma,' Loxton said. 'She's never not shown up for work. She doesn't just disappear.'

Some officers in the police were haphazard about turning up for their shifts, one too many the night before to block out another disturbing case or another disastrous failed relationship.

Sure, Emma liked to party, Loxton remembered her insisting on buying them all a round of shots on Saturday night. The way she could always keep a party going. But Emma was also hard working, determined and above everything else a team player. She wouldn't have left her night duty team short. Not unless it was serious. Loxton found herself thinking of the reason they had all met up in the first place. Barratt escaping from Broadmoor. But he was back in the hospital, she reminded herself. This couldn't be him.

'Are they checking the hospitals?' Kowalski asked, reaching for a phone.

'It was done last night,' Winter said. 'I've asked Patel to give it another go this morning and she'll be widening the search.' Loxton remembered Patel crying. She'd already been told. She probably knew Emma too.

'When did she go missing?' Loxton asked.

'We don't know that yet,' Winter said. 'She was last in work four days ago. We need to get a timeframe, find out who was the last person to see her.'

'I saw her on Saturday evening,' Loxton said, and Winter looked surprised. 'A few of us who used to work together in the murder squad had a reunion. We had a fair bit to drink, left around midnight and I watched her get the Northern Line southbound from Waterloo.' Loxton flinched as she remembered the last time she'd seen Emma, waving at her as the tube pulled away and then rushing for her own train. She remembered there was something strange about Emma that night. But what was it?

'Well, that's a start,' Winter said. 'We can work with that for CCTV parameters. Does she have a car?'

'She didn't when we worked in the murder squad.' Loxton logged on to a computer to check. 'No car registered at her home address.'

'Kowalski, I want you and Loxton to lead on this one,' Winter said. 'Emma lives in Southwark borough, so she's our missing person case.'

'Of course,' Kowalski said. 'We'll go and search Emma's flat, try to establish her contacts, where she might have gone.'

'I'll get someone else to take over this sexual assault,' Lena said. 'Don't worry about that.'

Loxton nodded gratefully. 'Sir, has anyone spoken to Emma's mum? They're close; she might know what's happened, although she's not been well recently.' Loxton remembered Emma saying her mum had started forgetting things, how it worried her. That she was going to look into a care home.

'We've not been able to contact her mother yet,' Winter said. 'The details we have on the system are wrong. When you search the flat, see if you can find correct ones. Forensics should be there shortly to meet you.'

'Is there anyone else listed as Emma's next of kin on her police record?' Loxton knew Emma was single at the moment. No significant other. She'd been complaining on their night out about reaching her thirties and not having met 'the one' yet. Loxton had told her being single was easier – no one else to worry about or to screw up your life.

'It was just her mum listed,' Winter replied. 'The residents at the mother's old address said they moved in about three months ago. We'll try the estate agents they bought the place through; they should have some details on where the mother went.' He glanced at his watch. 'They should be open soon.'

Hope rose in Loxton's chest. Perhaps Emma had had to rush off to help her mum and had been unable to get a message to work. It didn't sound like Emma – but, then, none of this did.

'I'll get a team together working on the CCTV from Waterloo and request cell siting of her mobile,' Winter said as he turned from them and began directing the detectives around him like it was just another case. Loxton marvelled at Winter's ability to carry on as normal, but then realized that she'd also gone into autopilot. It was easier that way, to focus on each next step, and to avoid remembering the missing person cases that she'd worked on that at first seemed innocuous but then turned quickly into tragedy.

Once Loxton and Kowalski were out of the busy CID office, Kowalski turned to her. 'Are you okay to lead on this?' he asked. 'Emma is your friend. You don't have to come with me. You can swap with Lena.'

'It's fine. I can handle it.' Loxton kept walking, refusing to let anything slow her down. She would work every hour she could to find her friend. Emma would do the same for her.

PART 1

EMMA

Chapter 3

Emma's home was a small, one-bed flat in a new build apartment block. Loxton and Kowalski had suited up in forensic coveralls, gloves and masks. She used the key that the uniform officer had given her to open the boarded-up front door, which they had forced to gain entrance a few hours earlier.

It felt strange to be in Emma's flat without hearing her voice, her laughter peeling through the rooms. Loxton had been here so many times before for dinner and drinks. Without Emma, the place looked dreary and cold.

There were no obvious signs of a disturbance, but something didn't feel right. The flat felt abandoned somehow. Emma's red coat was missing and there was no handbag lying around. No mobile either. It was as if Emma had never returned home after their night out.

'Got something,' Kowalski called to her from the bathroom. She followed his voice and saw he was going through Emma's bathroom cabinet. He pointed at a little pedal bin under the sink. Loxton examined the contents – a single blue toothbrush and a man's deodorant. 'Looks like a man stayed here recently,' Kowalski said. 'Did she have a boyfriend?'

Emma hadn't mentioned anyone the other night. Then

Loxton remembered what had seemed strange about her. She'd been cautious about Loxton getting into another relationship after Alec Saunders. Was this man a mistake that Emma didn't want people to know about? If only Loxton had asked Emma how she was doing. Why hadn't she asked?

Kowalski kept searching through the bathroom cabinet. He held up a packet of contraceptive pills, and then another with 'Fluoxetine' written on the box. The prescription labels said they had both been made out to Emma. Kowalski checked his mobile and looked surprised. 'Fluoxetine's an anti-depressant. Was Emma depressed?'

'She didn't say anything,' Loxton said, thinking that it was true – you never really knew what people were struggling with when they were back inside their own private worlds.

In the bedroom, they found condoms in the bedside drawer. 'Looks like there must have been a recent boyfriend,' Loxton said. 'We need to find out who he is.' She was confused that Emma hadn't mentioned anyone. She was usually so open; she never seemed to censor herself, often telling them all far too much information. She was the most honest person Loxton knew.

'There's got to be something here.' Kowalski rummaged through Emma's drawers and Loxton stood watching in dumb silence. This was a friend's home and here they were riffling through her belongings. It wasn't right.

Kowalski glanced at her and paused for a moment, pressing his lips together. Then he turned back to what he was doing and she forced herself to go over to the wardrobe. Time was ticking, and she knew every second counted.

On the inside of the wardrobe door were a few photos, Blu-Tacked on. There was one of Emma and Loxton and their old team, all laughing together at a Christmas party. Loxton remembered the rich dinner and, later, the aniseed shots.

She studied each photograph as if she would be able to see the clue to her friend's whereabouts within one.

Loxton spotted Emma's mum in one image, somewhere sunny, and she realized mother and daughter shared the same infectious grin. They were so alike.

She noticed a space where a photo had been taken down, remnants of Blu-Tac still visible. She walked over to the little wastepaper bin in the corner of the room and, sure enough, inside was a torn-up photograph. She crouched down next to the bin and picked up the two pieces, fitting them together.

It was a photo of Emma next to a handsome man in his thirties with short brown hair and dark brown eyes. He had his arm wrapped tight around Emma's waist and she was beaming at the camera. It looked like they were in a cocktail bar. Loxton didn't recognize him, but the photo looked recent. Emma was wearing her red winter coat.

Kowalski glanced down at Loxton and the photo. 'Is this the boyfriend?'

'Maybe an ex now by the looks of it.' They didn't have a name yet, but at least they had a photo of him. It was something.

Loxton called Patel. 'Meena, can you check Emma's phone records? See who her top three contacts were in the last month. Looks like she had a recent boyfriend. We don't have a name yet.'

'Will do,' Patel said. 'Hopefully his phone's on contract. I should be able to get you his name and address.'

'Thank you,' Loxton said. Why wouldn't Emma have mentioned this man? Perhaps the break-up had been too painful to talk about. Loxton felt a chill run down her spine as she looked at the man's smiling face, slightly distorted by the ripped edges.

She checked the rest of the wardrobe. It was full of clothes, as was the chest of drawers. It didn't look like Emma had packed to go anywhere; her wheelie suitcase was there, empty. Loxton riffled through the wardrobe again. She couldn't find a silver dress and heels anywhere. Or Emma's red coat. She looked inside the wash basket and washing machine in the kitchen.

'What is it?' Kowalski asked, following her into the kitchen.

'Emma was wearing a silver dress and heels on Saturday night, but they're not here. It means she probably never made it back home.'

Kowalski nodded. 'We'll call Winter if we haven't found them by the end of the search.'

They moved into the small living room and Kowalski held up Emma's passport after checking the sideboard. He looked worried.

'Where the hell *is* she?' Loxton asked, feeling a growing sense of unease. It was getting harder to pretend Emma had just gone away for a few days. 'And where are Forensics?'

'There's not much for them to do here,' Kowalski said. 'But they won't be long.'

'They can at least use luminol for any blood traces.' Loxton felt a surge of anger as they continued searching. Something didn't feel right about the flat, but she couldn't quite say what it was.

By the end of the search they knew for certain that Emma's red coat, silver dress and heels were missing; there was no mobile, purse or bank cards and her warrant card wasn't anywhere to be found. Emma's work laptop had been on her coffee table. She wouldn't have gone to her night shift without it. She would have needed it. From what they'd found so far, it looked like Emma had never made it back home on Saturday night.

Chapter 4

Loxton found an empty desk to sit at in the corner of the CID office, away from everyone else. She didn't relish making this call. 'Jane, it's Alana. I need to ask you about Emma.'

'Emma?' Loxton could hear the sound of a washing machine going and the low murmur of a TV in the background. 'Is she all right?' Jane's voice rose with concern. Police always imagined the worst; they came to expect it.

'She's gone missing.'

'What?' Jane sounded shocked.

'She didn't turn up for work and we're treating her as a missing person case. I'm the last known person to have seen her on Saturday night when she got on the underground at Waterloo and I don't think she ever made it home.'

'God.' Jane's voice was a whisper.

To hear her so worried made Loxton's stomach lurch. 'Do you know anything about a boyfriend?'

Jane paused for a second. 'There was a guy. She met him about six months ago. But then the little one came along and I've been out of it for the last few months. You're better off asking Gabriella; she even met him once.

She said he was good looking but a right arsehole and told Emma as much. They had a bit of a falling out over it apparently. Gabriella said he was controlling, always moaning about Emma being at work and not spending enough time with him. The other night was the first time I've been out since Joseph was born, so that's as much as I heard. But try Gabriella; she'll know more.'

'Thanks, Jane.'

'Let me know when you find her. I'll be stressing out about her being missing now, imagining all sorts.'

'I keep thinking of Barratt,' Loxton said. 'The escape attempt.'

'Don't start me thinking about him or I'll never sleep,' Jane said. 'This can't be him, he didn't really escape, remember. I hope Emma's okay.'

'Me too. I'd better go.' Loxton hung up and sighed. She felt bad worrying Jane, but she needed to know everything that had been going on in Emma's life just before she disappeared.

Loxton pulled up Gabriella's name and dialled her. The dial tone rang and she waited, but Gabriella didn't answer. Loxton didn't like it. She was probably in custody with a prisoner, her mobile on silent. She was always so busy, still working long hours in the murder squad.

After a while her voicemail picked up: 'This is DC Gabriella Caselli. Leave a message and I'll get back to you as soon as I can.'

'Gabriella, call me back as soon as you can. I need to talk to you urgently.' She hung up. They had to find this boyfriend.

Patel ran into the office, her eyes bright, clutching some paperwork. 'The phone company got back to me. I think I've got him.'

Kowalski rushed over to her. 'Great work. Who?'

'His name's Luke Pearce. They were calling each other about three times a day, back and forth, until about two weeks ago, when she stopped calling him or answering his calls. And then he started calling her about twenty times a day but never got through. He's been calling her like that ever since, but stopped suddenly on Saturday night.'

Why had he stopped around the time she went missing? 'Have you got his address?' Loxton asked.

'Not yet. The mobile's a pay-as-you-go phone, so he didn't have to register an address when he bought it. But I've found out where he works. Google has him listed as an employee of South London Logistics, it's a delivery company. You could try there while I look for his home address. It might take me a couple of hours. He hasn't come up on police databases, so he doesn't seem to have a record.'

'Thanks, Meera.' Loxton looked at the details of the company. South London Logistics and a local address not too far away.

'Let's get over there now,' Kowalski said.

She grabbed her coat. Luke Pearce's obsessive behaviour was worrying; the fact that he had suddenly stopped all communication, even more so.

The depot where Pearce worked was quiet; there were a few vans and lorries parked up, but no movement around them. Loxton parked several cars down the street and they watched for a few moments.

They got out of the car in silence and walked through the large open gates. The shutters were down on most of the garages but there were a few open at the far end. Kowalski nodded towards the office. 'This place is big. I'll ask the boss if Pearce is here and which garage he's in.'

'I'll stay here and make sure Pearce doesn't leave – if he's still here.'

'I won't be long,' Kowalski said. 'Call me if you see him.'

She stayed outside, keeping an eye on the open garages, but then she heard an engine roar to life from the garage at the far end. If it was Pearce, he was going to drive out of here before Kowalski got back.

'Get them to close the gate, Kowalski, ' Loxton called to him over the radio and sprinted towards the last garage, trying to be as quiet as she could, glancing into the open garages as she went. The place was deserted; the morning shift already out on deliveries.

As she leaned her head around the open shutter, she heard bangs towards the back of the dark hanger. She saw a Luton van parked up, nose outward, raring to go as the engine idled. She took another glance at the driver's seat to make sure no one was in it waiting to ram four tonnes of metal into her body.

The noises sounded as if someone were moving boxes. She crept to the end of the van and peeked around the corner.

Pearce dropped a box into the rear of the van and then turned towards her. He jumped, startled, as she stood there watching him.

'You scared the shit out of me.' He eyed her suspiciously. 'What are you doing here?'

'Looking for you.' She pulled out her warrant card. 'I'm DC Loxton. I need to ask you a few questions.'

'You here on your own?' Pearce glanced behind her to see if anyone else was there.

Loxton realized her mistake as Pearce's eyes darkened. 'A colleague's just outside.'

'You're bluffing.'

She pulled out her radio. 'Kowalski, he's here. The last garage. Close the gate.'

He eyed her up and then slid his left hand into the van, retrieving a metal crowbar. 'Are you guys supposed to go out on your own? It's not really safe, is it?'

Loxton felt her throat tighten and her breath shorten. She glanced at the crowbar and then back at his face. 'Put the crowbar down.'

He looked at the weapon. 'Depends if you're going to let me drive out of here or not.'

Her baton was in her shoulder belt, within easy reach; it would take a second to grab it. There was only half a metre between them, though, and she might not have a full second. She pressed her emergency button on her radio so Kowalski would know she was in trouble. They all would.

'You're not going to drive out of here, Luke.' She pulled out her baton in one swift movement and flicked it to extend, locked open. 'I need to ask you some questions. Put the crowbar down.'

He nodded at the same moment that he hurled the crowbar at her and sprinted around the van. She managed to lift her baton just in time and the crowbar clanged against it, knocking her backwards.

The engine throttled louder and she jumped back in case he tried to reverse into her. But the van sped forwards, swerving out of the garage and taking off a wing mirror in the process. She ran after it, watching as it sped towards the gates, which were slowly closing, Kowalski standing by the control panel. Pearce honked his horn angrily at him, the noise piercing the morning quiet, but the gates continued to close.

The reverse lights suddenly came on. Pearce was

reversing at speed towards her. She only just dodged out of the way in time before Pearce's van raced forwards again towards Kowalski and the gates, gaining momentum. Kowalski's eyes widened and he flung himself away as Pearce's van ploughed into the gates, a horrible grinding of metal as they were shunted towards the road.

Pearce's van reversed again and then shot forwards, forcing the gates open, the screech of the gates scratching along the van, hurting Loxton's ears. After a chaotic three-point turn, he sped off. Loxton rushed to Kowalski, who was still on the floor.

'I'm all right.' He stood up, his face shocked, and started running towards their car. 'Come on! I'll call it up on the radio, you drive.'

She jumped into the driver's seat, shoving the gear stick into first and hitting the accelerator. She turned right, giving chase. She could see Pearce's rear lights ahead although he'd made significant ground ahead of them.

Kowalski was barking directions down the radio and calling for other units. She put her foot down, hoping her car would be quicker down the narrow car-lined streets than Pearce's van.

Pearce turned left out of her view and she tried to keep calm as her fingers tightened on the steering wheel. It was dark in the gloomy winter morning, her headlights picking out the road ahead. She prayed that Pearce wouldn't hit anyone and wished she'd tried to strike him when she had the chance. Anything that happened now was her fault. She was already losing her edge on this case.

'This is MikeDelta2, we're coming up Burgess Park Road.' The officer's voice was steady and calm. Backup was on its way.

'He's heading your way. We're a few seconds behind,'

Kowalski said. 'He's already rammed through a gate and driven at officers; be careful.'

'Roger that.' The radio went quiet.

'Left or right?' Loxton asked as they neared a T-junction.

'Go right.' Kowalski craned his neck, trying to see around the corner. 'No – go left. He's gone left.'

She spun the car left, nearly losing traction. Then she spotted the white van ahead.

'MD2 here, we have eyeball,' the police officer said over the radio.

Loxton saw ahead the blue lights of the police van bouncing off the windows around her and Pearce's van screeching to a stop in front of it, his way blocked. Loxton drove straight behind Pearce's car, aware that giving him any room to pick up speed would risk Kowalski's and her lives. She touched her bonnet against his rear bumper and kept her foot above the accelerator.

One of the uniformed officers shouted at Pearce to get out of the van. There was a horrible silence. Everything seemed to still – everything except the blue light that was spinning on the van, casting an eerie light across the street.

'He could have a weapon on him,' Loxton said into the radio. 'He threw a crowbar at me. Approach with caution.'

'Roger that,' MD2 replied.

Pearce's driver door flew open and he was out, running as fast as he could past Loxton and Kowalski. Loxton threw the car into reverse and followed him down the road. The uniformed officers weren't far behind, giving chase on foot. Kowalski was relaying the events down the radio.

At the far end of the road another police car appeared, it's blue light spinning, its siren silent. Pearce had no choice but to run towards it and the two police officers got out of the car, ready and waiting.

They managed to tackle Pearce as he tried to dodge onto the pavement and get around them. Loxton braked and she was out of the car running towards the group. Pearce was throwing punches wildly at the officers and Loxton slammed her body into Pearce's, knocking him forwards. She felt him fall to the ground underneath her, and then Kowalski was beside her, the four of them pinning him to the ground.

'Stop struggling,' the police van driver shouted at Pearce as he knelt down next to the melee with his handcuffs out and slapped them on to one of Pearce's wrists. The remaining officer grabbed Pearce's other arm. The reassuring click of the handcuffs made Loxton realize she'd been holding her breath. They'd got him and no one had been hurt. She glanced at Kowalski, who was looking at her with an odd expression, his lips pressed together and a frown on his face.

Chapter 5

There'd been no obvious signs of a struggle or anything out of place at Pearce's flat. Forensics had gone over it and sent some traces of blood to the lab, but the result would take a few hours to come through. Pearce's BMW had been completely clean.

Loxton decided to try Gabriella again before she went into the interview with Pearce. She wanted to hear her friend's opinion of the man. He hadn't run for no reason. She went into a side room away from the main office.

'Hi, Alana, what's up?' There were voices and music and Loxton had to strain her ears to pick out Gabriella's voice. Loxton felt a rush of relief at finally getting hold of her.

'Are you in a bar? Can you go outside for a minute?'

'I can't hear you,' Gabriella shouted down the phone. 'I'm going outside.'

The noise was deafening, life happening in London on a Tuesday evening. Had that really been her, Emma and the others just a few days ago? She marvelled at how everything could change in a heartbeat.

'What's up?' Gabriella sounded cheerful, the alcohol working its magic.

'Emma's been missing since Saturday.'

'Since our night out? Oh my God, what happened to
her?' The voices in the background became quieter as
Gabriella moved further away from the bar.

'It looks like she didn't make it home.' Loxton tried to
keep her voice steady. 'Do you know anything about a
boyfriend, Gabbie?'

'Yeah, I met him once,' Gabriella said. 'His name was
Luke. He was a real dick. Started flirting with me when
Emma was in the toilets, wanted my number. I told him to
his face he was an arsehole and when Emma came back I
told her he was trying to get my number. We had a little
falling out about that. We'd been drinking. She said I was
jealous, so I left them to it. She was distant with me for a
while but I think she ended it a few weeks back.'

'Did you ever see him again?'

'No, never. He was weird though, Alana. I didn't like
him. Why, do you think he has something to do with
Emma going missing?'

'We're not sure yet.'

'Well, from what I saw, he's definitely someone to look
at closely.' Gabriella sounded worried, she hadn't said it,
but they both knew that two women a week were murdered by their partners.

'What about Barratt? Don't you think it's strange that
he tried to escape just last week? I'm worried this is about
him. That we're not safe.'

'Barratt's in Broadmoor.' Gabriella's voice hardened.
'This isn't him. I think it's that prick, her ex. I could tell he
had a nasty streak in him. Have you arrested him?'

'I'm about to interview him. Did Emma say anything to
you about him harassing her? Or hurting her?'

'No . . . No, she didn't. But he's that type. I'm sure he is.'

'Okay, thanks, Gabbie. Do me a favour and take care of yourself, okay? Can you get someone to pick you up? Maybe stay with friends for a few days?' Loxton didn't like the idea of Gabriella out in town. The winter evenings had drawn in and there weren't as many people out after all the partying of Christmas and the New Year. She already had one friend missing; she didn't want to lose another one too.

'I'll head home now. Don't worry, I'll be fine. Keep me updated.'

'I will,' she replied, and hung up.

'There you are,' Kowalski said, coming into the side room.

'I've just spoken to Gabriella Caselli. She's convinced that Pearce is no good and that he's got something to do with Emma's disappearance.'

'Anything concrete?' he asked.

'Not really. Just that he was a sleazebag and she got a bad feeling from him.'

Kowalski nodded. 'I know what she means; there's something about him.'

Loxton walked towards the door but Kowalski put his arm out. 'Just a minute,' he said. 'I need to talk to you.'

With a sinking feeling, she turned back to him.

'Are you okay?' he asked.

'I'm fine,' she lied.

He pulled a frustrated face at her. 'You shouldn't have approached Pearce on your own; you could have got hurt.'

Loxton knew he was right; going after Pearce in the garage on her own *had* been reckless, but instead she said, 'There was no time and I didn't want him getting away.' She didn't want Kowalski to know how much she was struggling. She needed to find out what had happened to

Emma at any cost, to make up for leaving her on her own on Saturday night.

'You should have waited for me. We're a team. You're not alone in this.' Kowalski failed to keep his voice steady. She could see he was worried about her.

'It was a split-second decision. We got him, didn't we? Another minute and he would have driven out of there and disappeared.'

Kowalski hesitated before speaking. 'This case is too personal for you.'

Was he going to talk to Winter, insist she be taken off the case? She couldn't have that. 'It was a bit close, but we got him. That's what matters.' She left the room.

He followed her. 'I just don't want you getting hurt, that's all. Emma going missing, it's just made me think how anything could happen to any one of us.'

She kept walking, not turning back to him, wanting the conversation to be over. Kowalski was rattled and she didn't want him to see that she was too. She felt on edge all the time, like someone was watching her, waiting for her to make a mistake. She was normally so sure of herself, of her place in the world as a protector, hunting out dangerous people and stopping them. But with Emma being missing, everything was suddenly the wrong way around.

Pearce's eyes were bloodshot and there were deep shadows under them. His solicitor, in contrast, sat stiffly next to him with his pen poised above his notes.

'Why did you throw a crowbar at me and make off in your van when I tried to talk to you?' she asked.

'I didn't throw the crowbar at you; it was more towards the floor.' Pearce looked nervously at his solicitor. 'I ran because I just panicked. I can't explain it any more than that. I've had a bad time with the police before.'

'You weren't running because of what you'd done to Emma?' Loxton stared at him.

He shifted uncomfortably in his seat. 'I haven't done anything to Emma. I had a bad time in the Czech Republic last year with the police there. They can be pretty brutal. I thought you were going to be the same.'

'What happened in the Czech Republic?' Loxton asked. Pearce had come back clean. No arrests. What had they missed?

'I got arrested six months ago in Prague.' He shrugged at her. 'I got into a fight.'

'That's not come through yet, but it will. Tell me about this fight.'

Pearce looked crestfallen that he'd brought it up. 'It was with my ex. It was a shit holiday. We were arguing, she was drinking too much. She was driving me mad. On the way to the hotel I pushed her and a local went ballistic, got the cops involved. I was arrested over nothing. They beat the crap out of me at the station. I thought I was going to die. And then they gave me a caution and we had to fly home. We broke up a few weeks later.'

'Did you have a fight like that with Emma?' Loxton asked, trying to keep her voice steady.

'No, nothing like that. Emma and me are great.' Pearce kept eye contact with her.

'When did you last see Emma?' Loxton asked.

'I haven't seen her for a couple of weeks. She's been busy at work and with her mum.'

'You don't seem worried that she's missing,' Kowalski said.

'Worried? Should I be? She's independent, always doing

what she likes.' He shrugged at them. 'She's probably gone off with some of her girlfriends for a spa getaway or something like that. Half the time I can never get hold of her.'

'She didn't show up for work last night,' Loxton said. 'Does that sound like Emma to you?'

'I don't really know much about her work.' He rubbed at his hand as if it was bothering him. Loxton noticed the knuckles on his left hand were grazed, as if he'd fallen over or been in a fight. 'She didn't like talking about work to me, although she always seemed to be there. Maybe she got pissed off with it and decided to have a break?'

Loxton was appalled that Emma had been seeing this guy. Sure, he fit the picture of what Emma liked – big muscles, brown eyes, handsome – but Pearce had a temper and was impulsive. Had he hurt Emma?

'Can you give me a list of her friends?' Loxton asked.

'Don't you lot know? I only met a couple of them once. They were all police officers. I don't remember their names. We've only been dating for a few months.'

'Can you tell us what you've been doing since Saturday at around 10pm?' Loxton asked.

'Saturday? Christ. Well, I had a few beers with my mates in town. We were in Shoreditch, at the Bedlam bar at one point, after that it's a bit of a blur. I got a night bus home, but I can't remember what time – I was wasted. Sunday, I was hungover – the day was a complete write-off. Then Sunday evening I went down my local for a couple of beers. I was at work from 7am on Monday, out all day on deliveries. I finished quite late, past 7pm. I left the van at work and drove my car home. I grabbed a drive-through at McDonald's and then drove back to my flat in Bromley. Then I walked to my local for more beers and then went home.'

Loxton was amazed at the detail. As if it was rehearsed. Kowalski threw her a brief glance that told her he thought the same.

'What time did you get home last night?' she asked.

'Just before 11pm. Got myself a bit of a hangover today, that's why I was late in.' He rubbed his eyes and sighed. 'Look, I'm in the shit with the boss already. You guys haven't exactly helped with that. Can I go now?'

'How did you get the grazes on your knuckles?'

He looked taken aback for a moment and gazed down at his hands, as if seeing the scratches for the first time. 'Oh, that. I was loading the van yesterday and almost knocked a stack of boxes over. Ended up scraping my knuckles on the brick wall when I was stopping them from toppling over.'

'Did anyone see you have this accident?'

'No, I was in there on my own. But you can see it's scabbed over, it's an old graze.' He held his hand out, as if that proved the injury was an accident and not caused by punching something with force.

'Did you hit Emma? Is that how you got those injuries?'

Pearce looked at his solicitor, shocked. 'I told you, I scraped them on the wall. I haven't seen Emma for a few weeks.'

Loxton tried to contain her cold fury. This man may have wiped her friend out of existence. He could have reduced Emma to a memory. And when Emma's mother was dead, when most of her colleagues had moved on, lost other people, forgotten their old friend, then Emma Robins wouldn't even be a memory anymore.

'Are you and Emma still together?' Loxton thought of the torn photo in Emma's flat.

'Yes.' Luke looked defensive, anger flashing in his eyes for a moment, but he managed to gain control of himself.

'We're just focusing on work, that's all. And her mother got worse recently, dementia or something. Emma was talking about setting up carers. She was busy with that.'

'Forensics are checking your flat and car. What do you think they'll find?'

'Nothing. It's a waste of your time. My boss is going to do his nut with you lot swarming all over my car at work. He'll already be pissed off that I got nicked there. And the neighbours are going to think I'm a criminal if you have people in forensic suits coming in and out of my flat.'

'Let's worry about your girlfriend being missing for now, shall we?' Loxton said. 'When did you last speak to Emma?'

'I don't know. She'd been so busy recently. A few days ago.'

'Luke, we know Emma stopped calling a few weeks ago.'

Pearce's eyes darkened. 'You've been checking my phone? Are you lot even allowed to do that? Okay, we had a few issues, a bit of a row a few weeks back. I told her she wasn't putting enough effort into our relationship. But we were sorting it out.'

'She hasn't returned your calls for two weeks, Luke. That doesn't sound like you were sorting it out.'

He shook his head, waved his hand dismissively at her, as if he could brush her words aside. 'All couples have problems. We were just going through a rocky patch. She just needed some time, that's all.'

'Why did you stop calling on Saturday night? The night it looks as if she went missing?'

'Like I said, I was out with the lads on Saturday and then I had the hangover from hell. And I finally figured that Emma needed some space and time. I thought I'd wait for her to call me.'

'Are you finished, officers?' the solicitor said in his rich velvet voice. 'I fear we're about to start going around in circles and I'm sure you're both very busy searching for this missing detective.'

Kowalski nodded at Loxton. They weren't going to get anything else out of Pearce. He was sticking to his story, refusing to budge.

'We're done for now; I'm terminating this interview.' Kowalski hit the stop button on the digital recorder. 'But he'll have to stay in until we have the results back from the forensic team.'

Loxton didn't know if Pearce was responsible for Emma's disappearance, but she didn't like the way he talked about her in the past tense.

Chapter 6

Loxton tried not to feel disheartened as she walked back into Walworth CID office with a sandwich she'd grabbed from the local Tesco while they waited for Pearce's record from Prague to come through.

The samples from Pearce's flat had been traces of his own blood, nothing significant. She didn't know whether to be relieved or frustrated. She didn't like him, though, or the way he'd tried to make off when they'd gone to speak to him. He had an aggressive impulsive streak and she prayed Emma hadn't been on the receiving end of it.

Loxton felt tired and hungry as she went over to Kowalski's desk. He was tucking into a Big Mac.

'How are you not overweight?' she asked, pulling open the wrapper on her chicken salad sandwich. The noise of the CID office washed over her as the detectives around her worked through dinner.

'The gym,' he said, and took another bite out of his burger.

'What's that?' she asked, pointing at an unopened letter sat on his desk.

He glanced at it, as if noticing it for the first time. 'Just some post I hadn't picked up yet. They were moaning at me to get it.'

'It could be important,' Loxton said. 'Maybe about the case.' She tucked into her sandwich.

'I doubt it,' Kowalski said. 'It's from HR. Probably some training I haven't done.' He rolled his eyes but then saw the look of concern on her face.

'All right, I'll open it.' He wiped his fingers on a napkin and ripped open the letter. He scanned it quickly and swallowed once, his eyes full of surprise.

'Problem?' She nodded towards the letter.

'No ... no problem.' He looked up at her. 'I got the sergeant's promotion.'

'That's great news.' She smiled, pleased. She hadn't known he'd applied.

'I've got to put down my five choices for boroughs I'd like to work on, but it says nothing's guaranteed.' He avoided looking at her, studying the letter instead. 'I'm not allowed to put Southwark down. They've got enough detective sergeants here.'

Loxton's throat tightened and she didn't trust herself to speak. Instead she nodded, then sipped some water. She couldn't imagine not working with Kowalski, even though they'd only been partners for a few months. She felt sadness rise inside her at the thought of him leaving.

'Well done, Dominik. You'll be a great sergeant.' She'd always thought that by the time she'd hit thirty she'd have been promoted, but her career had taken a painful nosedive thanks to Saunders, and she didn't know when it was going to get back on track. Now, on top of all that, she was going to lose Kowalski.

'The Czech police have sent over what they have of

Pearce's arrest in Prague,' Lena called to them as she headed over.

Kowalski glanced at his screen and Loxton saw the email was in his inbox. He looked relieved to have a distraction and clicked on it. 'They've attached CCTV footage.'

Lena joined them, a notepad and pen ready in her hands. They all instinctively leaned nearer to Kowalski's screen as he clicked on the video attachment. A grainy, black-and-white image played of a woman walking down the road, obviously intoxicated. It was night, the streetlamps throwing an eerie grey light over the scene. The woman kept turning around to shout at a man who was following her. It was Pearce. He walked with purpose as she stumbled onwards. She waved her arms in the air, seemingly exasperated, and staggered along the deserted pavement. He didn't say a word back.

At her next shout, however, he rushed forward, throwing a punch into her face. She toppled backwards, landing on the floor hard as her legs gave way.

Pearce checked left and right and then dragged her up by her throat, walking her backwards into the doorway of a closed shop where he punched her again and again on the side of her head. She could barely stand up now, her arms flailing as she tried to ward off his blows. Loxton felt sick and put her hand over her mouth.

Another punch and she seemed to lose consciousness, her head lolling forward, and then Pearce's attention was drawn away. A man was running towards them, shouting. Pearce let go of the woman's neck, putting his hands up in a gesture of innocence. The woman had slumped to the ground. The men argued. Moments later, white strobing lights appeared and the police pulled up.

Loxton's stomach twisted and she gripped the table edge

hard to steady herself. *How* had Emma fallen for this man? Then again, she thought, Loxton had believed every lie Alec Saunders had told her.

Loxton closed her eyes, willing away the image of the woman being savagely beaten in Prague, but it played on repeat in her head. The rage rose in her like an illness, all-consuming. At least Barratt had attacked strangers; Pearce attacked the women he was meant to care for and love. There was something much darker about a loved one turning on you, the person who was meant to support and protect you, destroying everything you had believed in.

'This changes things,' Lena said. 'Pearce is definitely capable of hurting DC Robins. In fact, I'd say it's likely that he has. Perhaps he went too far this time?'

'We need to charge him,' Loxton said.

'Charge him with what?' Kowalski turned to look up at her. 'There's just no evidence. It's not enough that he's her ex-boyfriend and was violent to a girlfriend in the past. His flat and car have come back clean. There's nothing to suggest he's ever threatened Emma or that he was the last person with her. At the moment that's you, Alana. Pearce is claiming he hasn't seen her for a couple of weeks and we've got nothing to prove him wrong. Absolutely nothing. Not a single CCTV frame, text message or a witness who might have seen him with her in the last few weeks.' Kowalski shook his head in annoyance.

'Well, then we need to look harder,' Loxton snapped.

'He's given us an alibi for the days when Emma might have gone missing that we need to check out,' Kowalski said. 'And if Pearce and Emma had an altercation, maybe she's gone off on her own to get away from him. To think.'

'She would have told me if she was just going away,' Loxton said, although Emma hadn't told her about Pearce,

or the anti-depressant pills. 'There've been no transactions
on her bank cards, no calls on her mobile. She didn't show
up to work and she's not at her home. The non-police
friends that we've got hold of don't know where she is
either. Her mother's care home has confirmed she hasn't
visited her mother since Friday. *Something's happened
to her.* Look at him.' She pointed at the screen, her voice
rising, but she didn't care. 'He's an animal.'

'This *is* concerning,' Lena said, looking worried.

'We need something more and we don't have it right
now.' Kowalski looked sadder than Loxton had ever seen
him. 'We'll keep looking. We'll find her. We just can't lose
faith, okay?'

'I'm sorry,' Loxton said. 'I don't mean to shout at you.
She was my friend.'

'I know she was.' Kowalski squeezed her shoulder. 'I know.'

Loxton dropped her gaze. She'd used the past tense, and
neither Kowalski nor Lena had corrected her.

Chapter 7

Loxton knew she should try to catch a few hours' sleep, but she couldn't still her racing mind. She hated the fact that they'd had to bail Pearce. His alibis had backed up his account to an extent, but when he'd got off the night bus on Saturday night at 11pm he could have gone anywhere. She turned on the news for something to break the silence and her own thoughts.

Photographs of Emma smiling brightly into the camera flashed onto the screen as the news reporter explained she'd been missing since Saturday night. The presenter talked about a dedicated officer, whose family was desperate to get her back. Loxton felt the tears rolling down her cheeks and wiped them away with her shaking hands. What use was crying? It wasn't going to help Emma.

She was jolted out of her thoughts by her mobile ringing. She tried to calm her breathing before answering, her voice a croak. 'Jane?'

'Are you watching the news? I can't believe Emma's really missing. I thought she would have turned up by now.'

'I can't believe it's happening either.' Loxton tried to keep her voice steady.

'God, we were only with her on Saturday evening. I just keep thinking of Emma's mother. What's the latest?'

Loxton hesitated, not trusting herself to speak for a moment. Once she felt her voice was under control, she answered. 'It might be the ex, but I'm not sure. I've got a bad feeling about this one, Jane.'

There was the noise of a baby crying and a child screaming 'Mummy!'

'Just a minute, sweetheart. Why are you out of bed? A bad feeling, Alana? You know I don't like your bad feelings.' Jane was struggling to keep the anxiety out of her own voice.

'I don't know, ignore me.' The cries for 'Mummy' intensified and Loxton added, 'Sounds like you've got your hands full.'

'You're right. Look, I'd better go. Give everyone my love at work. And keep me updated, will you? I know I'm on maternity leave, but I want to know what's going on. If I think of anything, I'll call you.'

'Please do. And, Jane ...' Loxton paused. She didn't want to say it, but she couldn't not. 'Be careful, just in case this is Barratt.'

The baby's cries rose to a steady wail. '*Shit*,' Jane said. 'Do you really think this could be something to do with the murder team and Barratt?'

'Mummy, you swore,' a little voice complained.

'Aaron, go back to bed, it's late. Now.' Jane's voice was low and menacing. Loxton heard the mumbled complaint grow fainter.

'I don't know,' Loxton said. 'There's nothing leaping out, except his recent escape attempt, but I just have this bad feeling.'

'Well, I've always trusted your bad feelings, as much

as I don't like them. It's okay, darling, Mummy's here. I'll talk to Ben. We're due a holiday, and I fancy getting away for a few weeks.'

'Great, and take care of yourself.' Loxton felt some of the tightness from her shoulders release.

'You too.' It sounded like Jane was cradling the mobile between her head and shoulder. She would be holding little Joseph in her arms, trying to calm him.

The phone rang out. She stared at it for a moment and then called Sarah. After a few minutes, it clicked through to her voicemail.

'It's Alana. I know you're busy, but give me a call as soon as you can.'

Pearce was right, it was difficult to get hold of police officers when you needed to. In this instance it was probably for the best, though. She didn't want to ruin Sarah's sleep. She would call her again first thing in the morning. She felt a need to keep tabs on her old team, to make sure they were safe.

She placed her mobile on the coffee table as the news presenter talked about police efforts, saying that everything was being thrown into the investigation. She felt overwhelmingly tired but at the same time jittery and she knew she'd struggle to sleep tonight. She wanted to go for a run, to shake off the stress, but it was dark and she didn't want to risk it.

Not tonight.

Loxton got up and walked to the bathroom. She'd have a quick shower and then crawl into bed. Tomorrow was going to be hectic and she should at least try to sleep. She turned the shower on and undressed. Her muscles ached. Once she got into the shower, she raised the water pressure up a notch to ease her knotted shoulders and neck.

As the tension released, she heard a noise over the running water and she froze. Someone was in her flat. Her heart pounded in her chest. She left the water running and stepped quietly out of the shower, grabbing a towel and wrapping it tight around herself. She searched for her mobile through the steam but remembered she'd left it in the living room. She heard footsteps moving to the kitchen.

She tried to calm her breathing as she crept out of the bathroom and down the corridor into the living room. Her mobile was where she'd left it on the coffee table and she grabbed it, moving over to the front door where she kept an umbrella stand and a metal baseball bat.

Her hand stretched for the bat as she dialled 999.

'Alana, are you all right in there?' Kowalski called from near the bathroom.

Relief coursed through her body and she cancelled the call before it connected. 'Dominik?' She could smell take-away pizza wafting from the kitchen.

He strode into the living room, confused. 'Are you all right?' he asked.

'I'm fine. What the hell are you doing in my flat?' She still felt uneasy and irritated, stood there with her hair dripping and the towel wrapped around her, one hand clutching her mobile and the other holding a baseball bat.

'I text you, I've brought pizza,' Kowalski said. 'I knocked but you didn't answer and then I realized the door was slightly ajar.'

'The door was open?' She frowned, turning to stare at it.

'Only off the latch, but it made me worried, so I came in. You must not have shut it properly.'

She shook her head. That wasn't like her. She never made mistakes like that; she was always double checking. 'Are you sure?'

'How the hell else did I get in here?' he asked. 'I can't walk through doors. Look, I'll get the pizza ready and you ... go get ready.' His face flushed slightly.

'I won't be long,' she said, flustered. She checked the door was closed properly and dropped the baseball bat back in the umbrella stand. He raised his eyebrows but didn't say anything, just shook his head and smiled in relief.

'You had me worried,' he said, and went into the kitchen. She returned to the bathroom to turn off the shower and dress and to try to steady her shaking hands.

When she got to the kitchen, Kowalski had arranged two greasy boxes on the table. 'I couldn't settle this evening and I guessed you couldn't either, so I thought pizza would be nice. Pepperoni, chicken barbecue, or share?'

'Share.' She pulled out plates and a knife. 'Thanks for stopping by, but maybe next time call ahead.' The words came out sharper than she intended.

'It's a good job I did come over; that door could have been open all night. I just figured you could do with a little company. I know I could. Emma going missing must be hard for you.'

She cut the pizzas into slices and dished them out for them both. 'It's hard for everyone,' she said. 'Most people in Southwark know her. When you've been in as long as we have, everyone knows everyone.'

Kowalski nodded and started to devour a slice. 'God, I needed this.' He waved the pizza slice at her.

They sat in silence for a while, eating until they were full. He wiped his mouth with some kitchen roll and then ripped a fresh sheet off to wipe her chin. 'Just a splodge,' he said.

She smiled despite herself and got up to pour them a glass of red; she'd need something to help her sleep.

'I hate this,' he said. 'I can't bear thinking about what Pearce has done to Emma.'

'I keep hoping there's been some mistake, that she'll turn up,' Loxton said, not believing it herself.

'God, I hope so,' Dominik said. 'I think Pearce has done something, though.'

'It might not be Pearce,' Loxton said. She couldn't help thinking of the coincidental timing of Barratt's near-successful escape attempt from Broadmoor.

'Who else?' Kowalski said.

She felt herself going cold. 'She's a police officer. We end up with plenty of people who have grudges. Dangerous grudges.'

'Go on,' he said.

'This is going to sound crazy, but Emma worked on Edward Barratt when she was in the murder squad. He threatened to get his revenge on the female detectives who locked him up. Last week he tried to escape from Broadmoor, but they caught him within the hour.'

'Then it can't be him.' Kowalski frowned at her, confused. 'He was inside when she went missing.'

'I'm sorry, I'm just tired,' she said, realizing that she was exhausted. 'And I don't know, I've always been paranoid about Barratt, never quite feeling like I'm finished with him. That one day he'll make real on his threat.'

'Trust me,' Kowalski said. 'We've all got cases like that. Don't worry, we'll find Emma. I promise.' He gave her arm a quick squeeze. He got up and put his coat on. 'I'd best get going.'

She wanted to ask him to stay; the idea of being alone scared her, but it was a bad idea. Her emotions were getting the better of her – and the wine.

'Thanks for the pizza,' she said.

'Any time,' he said. 'I know you forget to eat when these big cases start.' Then his face fell as he remembered that it was Emma he was talking about.

Once he left, she put the latch on and made sure she double locked the door. She couldn't afford to make silly mistakes; Emma needed her to stay focused.

As she turned back to her small flat, it seemed darker with Kowalski gone, silence and shadows playing tricks on her mind. She went back to the sofa and poured herself another glass of red. She knew she wouldn't sleep tonight, nor any night until Emma was found.

Chapter 8

Emma felt groggy, as if she were still drunk, and her head throbbed. She blinked rapidly but she couldn't see anything. There was no light. It was the type of dark that you never got in London. Had she gone blind? She let out a sob into the darkness.

Her arms were stiff and sore, stretched behind her back at an odd angle. She tried to move them, but her wrists were tied with what felt like plastic cables. She opened and closed her fingers and felt the pins and needles burn through them. She tried to twist them so she could reach the cable, but whoever had secured her knew what they were doing. She realized her ankles were the same, bound together tight.

It was hopeless.

She wasn't getting out of here until someone released her. She blinked again in the gloom, expecting her eyes to have adjusted, but there was still just blackness. She'd never known anything like it. She tried to steady her breathing, to quell the panic inside her, so that she could concentrate. She could hear something – quiet, but there all the same. Drip, drip, drip. *Rhythmic. Where the hell was she?*

The stench of the place was overpowering. Like gutters on a hot summer day or bins in a heatwave. She wrinkled her nose in disgust. She could smell something oily mixed with rubbish, too. Was she near a refuse site? A scrapyard?

She thought of her mother, how scared she'd be that Emma hadn't turned up for her daily visits. That was if her mother had been having good days. If not, then she wouldn't even remember Emma existed.

Work must have realized she was missing by now. She had no idea how much time had passed, but it felt as if she'd been tied up here for days. Her throat was parched and she was starving.

She tried to recall again what had happened on Saturday night, after she'd left the bar, but it was patchy at best. Too much booze. Why did she always have to drink so much? She remembered getting off the tube, how she had thought there had been a man following her – or did she just walk past him? She shook her head, trying to clear the fogginess, and the sharp pain dug into her brain again.

Then she remembered the crack to the back of her head, the hands around her throat. Trying to say Luke's name, to get him to stop. Her heart froze as she thought of him. She was in serious trouble. She'd seen something in him. A vicious streak she recognized from certain suspects at work.

She put her head back against the cold stone. She hadn't told anyone about Luke's nasty side. She'd been too embarrassed that she'd fallen for his apparent charm and good looks. So when he'd hit her, she'd ended it and not spoken to him again, and she hadn't reported him. She was a police officer and she feared that her judgement would be questioned. She was supposed to be able to sort out the criminals from the victims. And she hadn't wanted pitying looks from colleagues.

Right now, however, she needed to get a grip, or she was going to die here. Her hands and ankles might not be free, she might not be able to see anything, but she could move. She didn't seem to be tied to anything. She could at least try to see if there was a way out. She shuffled forward, her progress painfully slow, but she pushed the thought aside. That type of thinking wouldn't save her. At least she was doing something and it gave her hope.

Just as she was starting to make some headway, something froze her to the spot. She could hear footsteps in the darkness, growing louder. Someone was coming.

Chapter 9

Loxton hung up the CID phone and sighed in frustration. She still couldn't get hold of Sarah and it worried her. She'd been trying all morning and had left several messages with Sarah's team to pass on the message that Emma was missing, but all they'd said was that she was out of the office and wouldn't be able to call back right away.

Loxton suspected Sarah was in the middle of an undercover operation, oblivious of Emma's disappearance. At least Sarah would have a team backing her up, making sure she was safe. Nothing could happen to her while she was on the operation.

She sent another email to Sarah's work address and sighed. She thought about Barratt again, always her mind looping back to him. She decided not to bother Winter with it yet. Kowalski had been right; Barratt was in solitary confinement in Broadmoor – this couldn't be anything to do with him. Still, she felt unsettled. His final words to her echoed in her ears: *'This isn't over. It'll never be over. I'll make you all pay.'* She closed her eyes for a moment and tried to focus.

Pearce was the obvious suspect. She prayed Emma

hadn't become one of the two women killed every week in the UK by a partner or ex-partner.

Kowalski dropped himself into the seat next to her and took a sip of the takeaway latte she'd brought in. 'Forensics have just told me that they think we didn't find anything in Pearce's car because he got it professionally cleaned. Some of the chemicals they lifted have come back as sophisticated cleaning products that hospitals use to sterilize operating theatres.'

'Surely they would have found something if he'd used his car.' She couldn't quite bring herself to say, 'to move the body'.

'Not according to them. The car was forensically cleaned. The company he took it to knew exactly what they were doing.'

'What car company was it?' she asked.

'Well, it's less a car company than an outfit under the arches in Peckham. Tony's Auto Repair Garage. Barely paid any tax last year, they seem to be running at a loss, yet Tony bought himself a four-bed detached house a couple of years back and has no problem keeping up with the sizeable mortgage payments. The ANPR shows Pearce's BMW in the area at 2am and it disappears for a good couple of hours.'

'Isn't that quite a jump to think that he went in there?' Loxton said.

'Not really. He used his debit cards to withdraw a thousand quid from a cash machine three minutes' walk away from Tony's at five to two in the morning on Sunday. Three years back the garage was involved with forensically cleaning a car that was suspected of a drive-by shooting. With a bit of persuasion they did the right thing and told us what they knew, off the record. It was a breakthrough for the case.'

'You can't beat local knowledge,' Loxton said. 'Let's go and pay them a visit.' She was glad they were getting somewhere, but she didn't like where they were headed. If Pearce had taken his car to this garage, what evidence was he forensically trying to hide?

Tony's Auto Repair Garage was as Loxton expected. Nestled under the archway, a faded sign above read: '*Car cleaning and repair jobs at great prices*'.

A car mechanic was tinkering with an old Ford Focus. When he spotted them, he stood up, the wrench still in his hand. He glanced at Loxton and Kowalski, a frown furrowing his brow. 'Yeah?'

'We're looking for the manager?' Loxton asked.

'He's not here.' He tapped the wrench in his open palm.

'Perhaps you could help?' She showed him her warrant card and watched as he straightened up, his frown deepening.

'Probably not,' he grumbled. 'I'm pretty busy here.'

'Can you tell us what work was done to a BMW, index LY19 AXM, on Saturday night.'

'I didn't do any work on a Beemer.' His eyes narrowed.

'Can you show us your diary?'

He brightened visibly. 'Sure. I can do that.' He walked them through to an office which resembled a cupboard. Inside was a table, a chair and an old computer. He opened up a faded red leather-bound ledger and flicked through the pages. 'It's not here.'

She leaned over and turned the book around so she could read the handwriting. There was barely anything in the diary, including the old Ford Focus he'd been working on outside. 'Any CCTV?'

He smiled at her. 'Nope. Too expensive.'

Kowalski took a step up to him. 'Too expensive? With the prices you're charging? I really doubt that. Look, jerk, this is an investigation into a missing cop. You'd better cooperate or you're going to have half of Southwark police looking into your business. Off the record, what work did you do on the black BMW?'

The man wiped his forearm across his sweating forehead. 'Missing cop? I saw that on the news.'

'We know someone here worked on the BMW,' Loxton said. 'The owner paid one thousand pounds cash for the work. We've got CCTV.' Loxton decided not to mention that the CCTV was just of Pearce taking the cash out.

The mechanic's face fell.

'We can arrest you.' Loxton shrugged, hoping he believed her threat. 'It's up to you.'

'I never talk to the police.' The mechanic crossed his arms in front of his chest.

'This time you might have to,' Loxton said. 'A female police officer has gone missing.' Loxton felt herself holding her breath as she waited for him to explode.

The mechanic seemed to consider for a moment, glancing at his knuckles and then at them. 'Fuck him, he was a twat anyway. He came in with his BMW on Saturday night. It had a dent in the front bonnet and the windscreen was smashed, so I fixed it up for him. He said it needed a clean inside and out. There was smashed glass everywhere. Plenty of people need that sort of thing after a little accident.'

'At two in the morning?' Kowalski stared at him.

'Accidents can happen anytime.' The man shrugged.

'Did you see any blood? The missing officer is my friend.' Loxton asked, her heart thundering in her chest. She imagined Emma's blood trickling out of her mouth as she lay motionless on a tarmac road.

'He said he'd hit a cat.' The mechanic paused for a moment, trying to work out whether what he said would come back to haunt him later. His voice softened. 'Maybe there was a little on the bonnet.'

'Let's get forensics to check the garage out now,' Loxton said to Kowalski.

'You can't do that. Tony will kill me,' the mechanic said, alarmed. 'I told you what you wanted to know. I thought we had a deal?'

'The deal was I don't arrest you; I never said I wouldn't search the garage,' Loxton snapped back, and she moved away from him and turned to Kowalski. 'I'll have Winter get a search warrant for the garage authorized now.'

Kowalski nodded, his face grave, realizing what the blood on Pearce's bonnet might mean for Emma. Had he hit her with his car?

Chapter 10

Loxton was scrolling through the CCTV around Emma's flat one more time, just in case they'd missed Pearce's BMW the first time round. It wasn't likely, but she needed to be doing something while they waited for the lab results to come back from the forensic search of Tony's garage.

Loxton was startled by Lena sitting down next to her, obviously too transfixed on the screen in front of her. Lena was holding a bundle of papers in her hand. 'Sorry, I didn't mean to scare you,' Lena said apologetically.

'It's okay, I was just checking the CCTV again.' Loxton frowned at the blurry images on her screen.

'I can see that. You were lost to the world. But you've been working flat out for a couple of days now; you should go home. Getting exhausted isn't going to help Emma.' Lena smiled at Loxton with warm eyes, but Loxton could see she had something.

'You didn't come over here to tell me to go home. Come on, what have you got?' Loxton felt the tiredness fall away as a fizz of adrenaline replaced it.

'As you requested, all the unsolved hit and runs involving cars in the last two weeks in all the southern boroughs of London. Not as many as you'd think. There's three here which I've put at the top that will be of special interest. Witnesses or CCTV indicate a car the same size and type as Pearce's BMW.'

Loxton leafed through the pages. The one she kept getting drawn back to was an Uber Eats motorcyclist who'd been hit on Saturday evening, around midnight, on the way to a delivery. The description of the driver was of a white male in his thirties with short brown hair. But the witnesses were contradictory; it had been dark, and a couple had insisted the driver had black hair and was in his twenties. They'd all agreed he'd been driving a dark-coloured BMW, though.

'I thought you'd want to look at that one. It's not too far from Emma's flat and it happened on Saturday around midnight. The motorcyclist was hit head on. The rider's at St Thomas hospital.'

'Is he all right?'

'No, I'm afraid not. He's in a coma. But forensics are going to compare the paint from Pearce's BMW against the car that caused this accident and the other ones where they have samples. It's going to take a little while, I'm afraid.'

'Thanks for helping. You don't need to, though. You're here to work on the sexual assault series.'

'I've got a running profile for that case and there's a whole team on it. I want to help with this. I have the time.'

'Well, we could use the help,' Loxton admitted. She glanced down at the notes she'd been making, realizing they didn't make much sense. *Where are you Emma?* was repeated on the page several times. She screwed the paper up into a tight ball, throwing it onto the table in front of her.

'Come on, we're getting out of here,' Lena said. 'Tomorrow morning's going to be busy when these results come back, and I'm exhausted and starving.'

'You go ahead; I won't stay much longer. I'll just check the CCTV one more time.' Loxton clicked onto the footage again.

'You're not a machine and you've been over that already,' Lena said. 'The team are going to check it again tomorrow. It's not all on you. You need to go home, get some rest.'

'You go ahead. This won't take long.' The truth was Loxton couldn't bear the idea of going home. Being alone in her flat, knowing Emma was missing, was too much. Lena seemed to read her mind.

'I saw a Chinese around the corner. Kowalski told me it stays open late,' Lena said. 'We can have some food, a quick drink, and then we'll both be able to get a few hours' sleep before we need to be back here in the morning.'

Loxton's head felt fuggy and she was struggling to focus her eyes. The images on the screen had become grainy and blurred. She barely knew Lena, but even Lena could see that Loxton was breaking. She needed to hide it better or she would be taken off the case. Loxton had been the last known person to see Emma alive and she couldn't help blaming herself. If she'd have gone with her, made sure she'd got home okay, maybe none of this would have happened.

Lena picked up the screwed-up ball of paper. 'If I get that in the bin over there, we're going to get something to eat and then go home. If I miss, I'll stay and help you go through the CCTV, *again*.'

Loxton glanced at the small wastepaper bin. It was a good four metres away. 'Good luck,' she said.

Lena smiled and tossed the paper ball into the air.

Loxton watched with amazement as it landed straight in the middle of the bin. A perfect shot.

'I played basketball at school.' Lena grinned. 'And I was on the police team in Poland. You never stood a chance.' She pulled their coats off the stand, handing Loxton hers.

The Chinese was almost empty, except for one guy on his own in his early twenties, halfway through his meal.

It was late, nearly 11pm, but the greasy food smelt good and she ordered beef and egg fried rice and a Tsingtao beer. Lena ordered a spicy noodle chicken dish and the same beer, which the waiter brought them as they waited for their food.

'How are you holding up?' Lena asked.

'I don't know.' Loxton realized she hadn't talked about it; she'd just gone straight into police mode; the need to talk suddenly felt overwhelming. 'It's surreal. I keep thinking that it can't be happening. That Emma's going to call me any minute, tell me she's okay and that there's been a silly mistake.'

Lena nodded. 'I remember having to work on a case where a colleague had been stabbed on duty. It was awful. It wasn't just seeing him hurt – vulnerable; it was realizing that we were *all* vulnerable. That at any moment we could be the one on life support in a hospital bed.'

Loxton nodded. She didn't feel prepared for this. It was like she was struggling in the deep end, being pulled under, while her friends around her were already drowning. Their only suspect was on bail, because without a body or any evidence that foul play had occurred, they hadn't been able to charge him.

Lena took a sip of beer. 'You know, no one would blame you if you wanted to step back. I know it's not my place, and I can see that you disagree, but I just feel someone has to say it. There are plenty of people working on the case. You don't have to put yourself through this. Everyone would understand.'

'Did Dominik put you up to this?' Loxton hadn't meant to sound so harsh, but then she couldn't believe Kowalski had talked about her to Lena.

Lena put her hands up. 'Okay, guilty as charged. But it's only because he cares about you. And I know I've only just met you, but I like you, Alana. And any friend of Dominik's is a friend of mine. He's just trying to look out for you, that's all.'

Loxton wanted to ask if Lena and Kowalski were an item, but it was none of her business. Still, she found herself irrationally irritated with her. She knew she was just trying to help, and so was Kowalski, but somehow it felt like a betrayal. Loxton blamed her tiredness for making everything worse.

'I appreciate the concern,' she managed. 'But I'm fine. I'd feel terrible not being involved.'

'I thought you'd say that; I'd be the same,' Lena said. 'But you've got to look after yourself. You can't work twenty-four seven. There's a whole team working on this, and we're all in this together. You're not alone, is what I mean. It's not all on you.'

Loxton nodded, too tired to argue and knowing it wouldn't do any good. Lena couldn't understand. It was Emma – *Loxton's* friend out there, not anyone Lena knew. Gone.

The waiter placed their food in front of them. Loxton was surprised by how hungry she was until she realized that the last thing she'd eaten was a sandwich for lunch. She tucked in gratefully with chopsticks and had to admit to herself that Lena was right. She was no good to anyone if she couldn't think straight.

She sipped the crisp beer and felt her body relax.

'This is tasty,' Lena said.

Loxton smiled. 'It's one of our favourites. I mean ... Dominik loves it here.' It sounded odd when she said it out loud. She felt a pang of guilt that she was here with someone else, and almost laughed at herself.

'How is Dominik?' Lena asked. 'I haven't seen him for a couple of years. I've been in the UK for four months working as a profiler and I hadn't got around to meeting up with him until now. We're always so busy with this job, aren't we?'

Loxton felt a wave of relief. Perhaps Lena and Kowalski weren't as close as she thought. 'Dominik's good. He's just been told he's being put forward for promotion.'

'That's great,' Lena said. 'That'll be good for him.'

'He deserves it,' Loxton agreed. 'He works hard.'

'I guess you'll miss him?' Lena asked. 'You two seem very close.'

'We've only been working together for a few months. I'll miss him, but people move on. That's what the police is like.' Loxton found it easy to say the words, but she didn't feel them at all. She couldn't imagine not working with Kowalski and wondered whether they would see each other still, or lose touch like he and Lena apparently had.

'You know it's strange to think how much he's changed from when I met him in police training school,' Lena said. 'His accent is almost like yours now. He's only been here five years but he barely sounds Polish. It's incredible.'

Loxton nodded, having never really noticed. She could always detect Kowalski's Polish accent but then, compared to Lena, she supposed he did sound more like a Londoner.

'He's always been like that,' Lena sighed. 'Trying to fit in. Always feeling like an outsider. We were both born in small farming villages. Both desperate to get away from it all, to see the bright lights of Krakow or Warsaw. And we made it as far as Krakow at least, both joining the police at the same time. And years later he came here for even brighter lights. It happens to a lot of people away from home. To fit in, they have to shed their old skin, like a piece of clothing that no longer suits them. You're smiling?'

'I'm sorry, you've just gone into profiler mode,' Loxton said. 'It's fascinating to watch but a little scary. It might be me next.'

Lena laughed, her whole face lighting up. 'I must stop doing that. I sound like a ... a duck. Is that what you call it?'

'A duck?' Loxton paused. 'Oh, I think you mean "quack". We call it a quack.'

Lena laughed and Loxton joined her.

'I meant one of them,' Lena said, smiling. 'English sayings can be so funny. And I'm sorry. I just haven't seen him for so long and here I am pulling him to pieces in front of you. Please, ignore me – I'm tired, and when I'm tired, I talk too much and it's usually rubbish. Also, I don't normally drink.' She held the bottle up that was nearly empty.

'It's fine, don't worry.' Loxton smiled. She admired Lena. Her mind never stopped; she was always trying to work people out. It was a good skill to have in their line of work.

Lena finished off her noodles and downed the last of her beer. 'We'd better get going; we need to be back in at seven.'

Loxton didn't want to go home, but Lena was right: she had to try to sleep, even if it meant more nightmares. For a moment she thought about asking Lena if she wanted another beer, but then pushed the thought away. She was surprised by how much she didn't want to be alone; normally it didn't bother her.

'I'm going to the underground,' Loxton said.

'I'm grabbing a cab,' Lena yawned. 'See you in the morning – and take care of yourself.'

'I will,' Loxton said. She left the restaurant and walked the short distance to the Elephant and Castle underground station. In the station she couldn't shake the feeling that there was someone there. Following her. She cursed herself for not getting a cab.

She stopped on the platform, quiet at this hour, letting one tube go past and then another. But everybody who walked onto the platform boarded the first tube that came along. She was being paranoid and chided herself as she got onto the next tube.

All the same, she couldn't stop checking the passengers near her, looking for anything out of place. She couldn't ignore that feeling of being watched, like an itch she couldn't scratch. Always there, persistent and urgent.

Chapter 11

'Couldn't sleep either?' Kowalski asked her as she walked into Walworth CID.

'I got a bit of sleep,' she said. She'd woken up early and couldn't get back to sleep, her mind racing.

A call came out on the radio. 'Body found in Camberwell Police Station. Any unit to attend? Witness on scene is Polish and will need a translator,' the operator said.

'We can attend,' Loxton responded. 'We're five minutes away and we have an officer who can speak Polish.' She glanced at Kowalski, who nodded.

'Received, assigning you. Witness is still on the site. She's the police station's cleaner. She wasn't making much sense. The alleged body is an adult female. Sit rep once you get there.'

'Understood, over and out,' Loxton said.

She stared at Kowalski with growing dread. A body in Camberwell Police Station. That station was usually empty outside of office hours. And Emma worked in Camberwell.

The station was eerily quiet. It had been unmanned over-night for several years and had been marked for closure.

There wasn't a living soul around as Loxton used her warrant card to open the electronic gate and Kowalski drove into the yard to park. Loxton scanned the area. Everything seemed in order. She had to swipe her warrant card to unlock the entrance door into the police station.

The cleaner was waiting inside the entrance, her face grey and her hands visibly shaking as she twisted a cloth in them. Kowalski showed her his warrant card and spoke to her gently in Polish. She looked relieved and reached for his hand, grabbing hold of it tight. She pointed down the corridor, her voice shrill and panicked as she replied to him.

'She's going to show us where the body is,' Kowalski said. They followed her through the corridors and up some stairs into the main office. Each step Loxton took felt like she was walking towards the executioner's chair. She dreaded what she would see.

The office seemed normal, chairs in front of desks, nothing out of place. The cleaner had stayed by the door, too frightened to come in, and Loxton glanced back at her. She was muttering to herself quietly as if in prayer. She pointed towards the far corner, but she wouldn't look in that direction.

Loxton walked towards it, her senses heightening. She saw a small window to her right and through it she could see a waning moon, hanging in the black sky.

She saw nothing out of the ordinary until she was almost on top of the body. It was slumped in the corner, sat with its back against the wall. You could walk most of the office and not spot it sat on the floor between the two desks. Its legs were outstretched, arms hanging limply to the sides. The head was leaning backwards. The body was a woman's and she was naked. Loxton leaned in to take a closer look at the face.

It was Emma.

Loxton shook her head. Nothing was in her brain. Just white noise. She kept shaking it, trying to dislodge the scene in front of her.

Kowalski crouched next to the body and touched the neck with his gloved hand for a full minute. 'No pulse.' His face was pale. His eyes met Loxton's but all she could do was carry on shaking her head.

'It is Emma, isn't it?' Kowalski asked, his voice urgent. 'I haven't seen her for years and she looks – different.'

'It's ... it's Emma.' Loxton's voice jarred in her throat. Emma's face was swollen and tinged blue, making her look strange. Her slim face and infectious smile gone forever.

'Alana, are you sure?' Kowalski leaned closer to Loxton, his voice soothing, as if he were talking to a lost child.

'Yes. Yes, it's her. This is insane. I just ... I just don't understand who would do this.' Loxton waved her hand towards the body, slumped like a drunk fallen asleep against a wall. But it wasn't a body. It was *Emma*, her old friend.

The cleaning woman was howling now from the other side of the office. Loxton had forgotten she was there, but her anguish came crashing into Loxton's head, along with the horror of what was happening. The woman was wringing her hands now, pulling at them viciously, as if they were burning her. The cloth was dropped on the floor, forgotten.

Loxton had seen hundreds of bodies and violent deaths, but she knew this sight would haunt her until her dying day.

'I'll check for a preliminary cause of death.' Kowalski said. 'May I?'

Loxton nodded, unable to speak.

Kowalski crouched next to Emma. He put his hands on either side of her head and came so close to her face that for a moment Loxton was sure he was going to kiss her. But he was peering into her eyes.

'I've seen this before.' Kowalski leaned backwards and looked up at Loxton. 'The capillaries in her eyes have burst.' He gently felt her neck and moved her head from side to side. 'Strangulation. And with some serious force. Her windpipe's been crushed.'

Loxton shook her head in amazement. Whoever had done this was strong.

Kowalski stood up.

The Polish woman became more hysterical and she began to shout, *'Szymański! Szymański!'*

'What's she saying?' Loxton asked Kowalski.

'It more or less translates as "it's terrible".' Kowalski paused, frowning in confusion. 'She's not making much sense. Let me talk to her, see if she saw anything.' Kowalski went over to the cleaner and tried to calm her. The cleaner's voice burnt into Loxton's synapses, the animal panic of it, as if she were in danger herself.

Loxton crouched next to Emma. 'Who did this to you?' she asked, knowing that Emma couldn't answer her back.

Loxton scanned the body carefully, looking for any signs of defensive wounds, but there were none. There were burn marks on her wrists, as if something had been rubbing against them. And then Loxton saw something in Emma's hand.

Loxton put on her own gloves before carefully retrieving whatever it was she was clutching. Even though Loxton's fingers were covered in blue plastic, she shivered when she peeled Emma's fingers apart to retrieve the object. The fingers were creaky in protest and cold to the touch where she'd instinctively expected them to be warm.

She looked up at Kowalski. 'Rigor mortis is setting in.'

'What?' Kowalski turned from the cleaner and came over frowning. 'But that means she only died in the last twelve hours. She's been missing since Saturday.'

'Whoever took her must have kept her alive,' Loxton said. 'And then they placed her here.' What had Emma endured before her death, alone and terrified? Not completely alone, though; *someone* had been there with her.

Loxton held up the piece of paper that she'd found and read the printed-out words:

'This has been a long time coming for Emma, the lying whore. Back off Alana or you'll be next. The war's started.'

Loxton looked at Kowalski in horror.

Kowalski stared at the paper, clearly shocked. 'He's named you in the note?'

Loxton nodded, speechless.

'Pearce is playing some sick game.' Kowalski frowned in anger. 'He knows you're leading the missing person case with me. He's insane.'

She couldn't believe Pearce was capable of this. This didn't feel like a crime of passion; it felt planned. The locked gates had still been intact, with CCTV trained on them. The entrance door had been locked. How would Pearce have got Emma over the six-foot brick perimeter wall and then inside the police station without anyone noticing? She felt bile rising up her throat as she thought of someone capable of pulling this off *and* who wanted Emma dead. *Edward Barratt.* But he was in Broadmoor; it was madness to think it was him, so she kept her thoughts to herself. 'But how could Pearce have got her in here?' she asked instead.

'I don't know, but somehow he has.'

'I don't think this is Pearce,' she said, but Kowalski didn't look convinced. 'Maybe her body has been placed here for a reason. The note said she was a *"lying whore"*. This might be a suspect she's dealt with trying to get revenge.'

'Or it could be Pearce thinking that she'd met someone else. Perhaps a police officer,' Kowalski said. 'Jealously can make people do crazy things. Though I don't like that you're warned off by name.'

'I'll keep the baseball bat by my bed,' she said.

'Good.' His face serious for once. 'And don't open your door unless you know who it is. You so much as hear a weird noise you call 999 and then you call me. I can be at your place in twenty minutes.'

'I will. I promise. But I'll be fine.' She needed Kowalski to back her up. Winter wouldn't want her near the case after seeing this note, but he might just listen to Kowalski.

He nodded roughly at her. 'We'll put special measures on your address and mobile so any calls will go straight to the top of the 999 queue. I'm calling forensics and then Winter. The cleaner's going to need to make a statement.'

'Whoever did this knew Camberwell station well,' Loxton said. 'They managed to get in without setting off any alarms or leaving any sign of a break-in. It could have been a police officer. They wouldn't set off an alarm.'

'A police officer?' Kowalski glanced at Emma's body and then back at Loxton in amazement. 'There's no way a police officer did that.'

'I hope you're right,' Loxton said. But this felt deeply personal to the police. The killer had wanted intimacy, to see the life ebb from Emma's eyes slowly. Not to miss a single moment. And he wanted the body to be found at a police station. He wanted to terrify them, but all she felt was anger.

Chapter 12

Dr Reynolds arrived in his forensic suit. 'Where is she?' he asked.

Loxton and Kowalski had put their own suits on and led him to where Emma was sitting.

'I'll do a preliminary examination now,' Reynolds said. 'Then the post-mortem will be tomorrow.'

Loxton nodded and watched as he knelt down next to Emma, taking photographs. He carefully inspected her wrists and ankles, drawn to the red marks. Then he examined the rest of her in silence, while Loxton and Kowalski waited.

'These are consistent with being bound by ropes,' Reynolds said as he studied the red marks. 'Have you found any ropes?'

'No,' Loxton said.

'So the killer's taken them.' He frowned and looked closer at the burn marks. 'The way the lesions are on the body suggests she was bound with sharper restraints at some point and also with ropes. I'm guessing the killer took the ropes off the body to avoid any forensic evidence being found.'

'He's forensically aware?' Loxton said.

'Exceptionally.' Reynolds shook his head in amazement. 'Almost medically so.'

'This isn't Pearce,' she said to Kowalski, trying to convince him.

Reynolds raised his eyebrows.

'The ex-boyfriend,' Kowalski said, a puzzled frown on his face.

'Bruising to the outer thighs.' Reynolds continued his examination. 'Signs of severe trauma to the vestibule.'

'What does that mean?' Kowalski asked, his voice strained as he glared at the pathologist.

Loxton pressed her lips together. She didn't trust herself to speak.

'The trauma suggests that she's been raped.' Reynolds didn't look up. 'I'll know for sure when I've conducted the post-mortem and taken swabs for trace evidence. Any clothes found?'

Loxton wanted to scream, but she wouldn't. Winter would send her home if he found out. 'We haven't seen any clothes yet.'

Reynolds nodded and started taking photos, the harsh light blinding Loxton's eyes momentarily.

Emma's head was turned towards Loxton at a painful angle. She wanted to put it right, but clasped her hands together to prevent herself from reaching out. Emma would never feel anything again.

Kowalski strode angrily outside as Reynolds glanced at Loxton, his eyes normally clinical, now full of pain. He raised his eyebrows as if to ask if she wanted to leave. She looked down at Emma's face and shook her head. She had to stay. Her friend needed her.

Reynolds moved through the crime scene analysis

systematically and she followed his lead. Once it was done, Reynolds turned off his recorder.

'I think the killer is left-handed. It's a hunch, and I won't be able to include it in my final report, but I've noted that the left side of the windpipe has more trauma. That really isn't enough to make a scientific conclusion about the killer, though, so I'm telling you off the record.'

'It's something,' she said.

'It might be nothing. Perhaps the way the killer was kneeling, putting more weight on the left side. Don't assume anything.'

'Understood,' she said.

'And, Alana ... I'm sorry. I know this is hard for you, losing a friend, and for Dominik.'

She nodded, wondering why he thought it was hard for Dominik. Perhaps he simply meant that Emma was one of them. That they weren't immune.

'How's he holding up?' Reynolds asked.

Loxton wondered what Reynolds was getting at. 'He's okay, I think. Why do you ask?'

'He and Emma used to be together.' Reynolds tilted his head at her; he must have seen the shock on her face.

'I didn't know. Dominik didn't say.' Loxton tried to hide the hurt she felt. It shouldn't matter that Emma and Kowalski had dated, but somehow it did. And it was strange that he'd made out he didn't really know Emma.

'It was years ago – when they first worked on Southwark CID. I've been here a long time myself. Longer than anyone else on this borough probably.'

'If I'd have known,' she said, 'I wouldn't have let him come with me.'

'I don't think anyone could have stopped him.' Reynolds covered Emma gently with a sheet, almost as if he were tucking her up in bed. 'Kowalski wants to fix everything, like we all do. But some things are too broken to be fixed. And just because we can't fix them, that doesn't make it our fault.' His eyes held hers for a moment.

She nodded, her throat constricting as she tried to keep it together. It didn't matter what Reynolds said; she'd let Emma down.

Loxton found Kowalski in the Camberwell CCTV room. He was scrolling through the past few hours of footage, checking each camera for anything unusual.

She didn't know how to begin, but she needed to ask Kowalski about Emma. Now seemed as good a time as any. At least they were alone.

'You didn't tell me that you'd been in a relationship with Emma.' Loxton couldn't completely hide the hurt in her voice. It felt strange that he'd dated her friend.

Kowalski looked shocked momentarily. 'That was five years ago, Alana. It feels like a lifetime ago now.'

'You should have said.'

'I want to work on this case and get justice for Emma just like you. If it had been me found in Camberwell station, I'd want the best investigating my murder and I'd be glad if it was you or Emma. Not some stranger. People who cared about me, who would put everything on hold until they found out who did this and made them pay.'

'I feel the same,' Loxton admitted.

'I loved Emma but work got in the way. We were tired all the time, on different shift patterns. The job won out like it always does, which is why police officer relationships never work out.'

She nodded for him to go on but felt a strange disappointment that he thought that way.

'We stayed friends and sometimes I wondered what

would have happened if we'd tried harder, but she went off to the murder squad and I stayed here. We lost touch. That's all there is to it.'

Loxton wasn't sure Kowalski was being honest with himself. The way he'd stormed off when Reynolds had examined Emma's body, she thought he was feeling it more than he wanted to admit. 'You know you can tell me things, right? We're a team.'

'I know that, but there's nothing to tell. You were the last person to see her alive. She was your friend. I haven't seen Emma for years.'

She nodded and turned to the CCTV.

'This is when everyone's out last night,' Kowalski said. They watched helplessly as the Child Abuse Investigation Team detectives left the building at the end of their shift around 21:57 hours.

Then there was no movement until they saw the cleaner arrive at 05:35, swiping herself in and the door shutting behind her.

Kowalski sped through the CCTV one last time up to when she and Kowalski arrived in their car. He shook his head in confusion. 'I thought we'd see something on here.'

There were blind spots around the perimeter wall of the car park and building. The CCTV was only on the car entrance gate and the entrance door and fire exits. It was possible the killer had scaled a wall and got in through a window, but how could they have without anyone hearing or seeing anything, and leaving no trace behind? And with a body? Camberwell station was surrounded by residential houses and was in the middle of Camberwell Green, a busy area even in the early hours.

'They must have got lucky. Maybe someone didn't close a lower ground window properly?' Loxton said.

'The cleaner said everything was secure when she got here and she seems to be right.' Kowalski shook his head in confusion. 'Forensics are checking everything, but you know what police stations are like. Even if the killer wasn't wearing gloves, there'll be hundreds of fingerprints and DNA profiles all over the place corrupting the evidence. The cleaner's only paid to do the bare minimum.'

Loxton shivered at the thought of someone being able to gain access, pose Emma's body, and not leave a single trace behind for them to hold on to. 'Still think it was Pearce?' she asked.

'Who else?' But Kowalski didn't look as sure.

Loxton thought of Barratt again. It was his style, leaving the body in a special place, on display to cause the most shock possible.

'Edward Barratt,' she replied. 'Even the way Emma is positioned, sat upright and naked, it reminds me of his first murder victim.'

Kowalski stared at her like she was mad. 'You said he was in Broadmoor when she went missing? It doesn't make sense.'

'It's a stretch, but just hear me out,' Loxton said. 'Emma worked on the Barratt case with me. He threatened us all when he started to lose the trial. Not just once, but consistently. He tried to get his lawyers to investigate us, suggested we were corrupt and had planted evidence. The judge didn't have any of it, but even he was shocked at the way Barratt behaved in trial and he'd dealt with a lot of murderers in his time. It was bizarre how Barratt became transfixed on us all, trying to put us on trial rather than worry about his own defence. He hated the fact that women had caught him, he couldn't let it go.' She thought she'd left Barratt in the past. She thought they all had.

'Okay,' Kowalski said, nodding at her. 'If you think it might be linked, that's good enough for me. I'll get hold of Winter. He'll want to hear this.'

'Thank you,' she said, relieved that Kowalski was at least willing to listen.

DCI Winter had arrived on the scene with a DI Meyer from homicide. They listened carefully to Loxton's and Kowalski's update.

'Let's get the ex-boyfriend in again,' Meyer said. 'He's our prime suspect.'

'I don't think he is,' Loxton said. 'The way Emma's been murdered, it's just like an Edward Barratt killing.'

Meyer frowned. '*The* Edward Barratt? The serial killer who raped and murdered sex workers? I'm not following you. He's in Broadmoor Hospital. Has been for a couple of years.'

'Except he escaped just before all this started, a week ago today. They caught him before he got very far, but he was missing for an hour and was picked up a few miles from the grounds.'

'Looks like he was trying to run to freedom, but there was no one waiting on the outside to pick him up,' Winter said.

'He's back inside on maximum security and is in complete isolation,' Loxton said. 'But what worries me is who he spoke to in that hour he was missing. What he arranged. He managed to get into the woods to the east of Broadmoor Hospital. Once they found him, they stopped looking, but who else was there?'

'But what's he got to do with Emma Robins being murdered if he's been in Broadmoor for the past week?' Winter stared at her intently.

'Emma was one of the DCs who locked him up,' Loxton said. 'There were five female detectives: Emma Robins, Jane Edison, Sarah Taylor, Gabriella Caselli and me. There were other officers on the team, male officers, but Barratt only ever threatened us. He vowed to get the five of us back, said it was only a matter of time. He hated women. It was pathological. His MO for killing the sex workers was similar to the way Emma died. It's uncanny. Raped and then crushed windpipe. Even the rope marks look the same.'

'That's quite a common MO for serial killers, though,' Meyer said. 'You should know that having been on the murder squad.'

Winter frowned. 'What else?'

Loxton felt her hands go clammy. 'All his victims were females in their late twenties to early thirties. They were all sex workers. He would leave the bodies in strange places – public places, for the police to find. And he would leave typed notes with the body. As the investigation went on, he addressed them to the investigating officers – first Emma, then Sarah, Gabriella, Jane and me. Emma is dead. I've warned the others, but I haven't been able to get hold of Sarah.'

Meyer shook his head in disbelief. 'Pearce makes more sense as a suspect. Not some serial killer who's been locked up for years. Emma must have told him about the case, so he's copied the details. That's all.'

'Can you get a comparison done on the notes and this new one?' Winter said to Loxton, ignoring Meyer. 'See if the style of language is the same as Barratt's notes. If it is, it would suggest a copycat. And see if DC Robins had anything to do with Barratt recently. Any correspondence. Any new threats.'

Loxton nodded, jotting the actions down.

'I'll get hold of Sarah Taylor,' Winter said. 'I'll speak to her boss. You're saying she's the only one that doesn't know what's happened to Emma?'

Loxton nodded.

'Then I'll tell her and her boss to be on their guard just in case.'

'I haven't got time to listen to this.' Meyer turned to Winter. 'Waste *your* resources on it but not mine. I'm getting Pearce arrested.' He left the room, calling to one of his detectives.

Winter shook his head as he watched the young DI leave. 'He's convinced it's Pearce, but that type of thinking is dangerous in this job.'

'Can we check that Barratt is still inside?' Loxton asked, hearing the strain in her own voice, louder than normal. Now that she'd discussed her theory out loud, the need to make sure Barratt was safe behind bars was overwhelming.

'From what you've said, he won't be able to break out again anytime soon,' Kowalski said. 'But I'll check now.' He squeezed her shoulder and made the call. As soon as he was off the phone, she asked him, 'Is he still inside?'

'Yes, in maximum security.' Loxton's own relief was mirrored on Kowalski's face. 'The hospital assured me he hasn't stepped foot outside since his recent escape attempt. He's in solitary confinement and they've changed his guards. There's no way this is him in person. They'll inform DCI Winter if there's any change in his status or if they find anyone responsible for helping him. Of course, it could still be one of his fan base acting on his behalf.'

Barratt having a fanbase willing to act on his behalf made her feel sick. She tried to reassure herself that in around ninety percent of murder cases the suspect was someone you were close to, like an ex-partner – like Luke Pearce. But if you were a police officer, working long hours in homicide, sometimes the people you knew the best were your suspects, as you learnt everything you could about them. And Barratt had been obsessed with them during the trial, adamant that he would one day get his revenge on all of them.

Chapter 13

Loxton left Kowalski at Camberwell station to head back to Walworth with the CCTV. But before she set off she knew she needed to tell the others about Emma. It was worrying her that Barratt had recently tried to escape, even if DCI Winter and DI Meyer didn't see it. The others needed to know what had happened. Somehow, even contemplating telling them made it feel more real.

She picked up her phone and called Jane first.

'Just a minute, Joseph's asleep.' She heard Jane close a door and it sounded like she was going downstairs.

'Shoot.'

'It's about Emma. I'm so sorry, Jane, I've got to give you the worst news. She's been murdered.'

There was silence on the other end of the phone.

'She'd been left inside Camberwell Police Station.'

'Oh God,' Jane said. 'Was it really her?'

'Yes. I was first on scene. Look, I don't know who did it, but it doesn't feel like a domestic to me anymore. It feels more like a Barratt killing to me.'

'Poor Emma,' Jane said. 'What did we miss back then?

Was there someone else involved as well as Barratt? Someone we didn't know about?'

'I don't know.' Loxton had thought the same thing. They'd assumed Barratt had been working alone, but now someone had tried to break him out of prison and Emma was dead. If the two were related, someone was working on Barratt's behalf to exact revenge. But who?

'I don't know, but can you get out of town? Take Ben and your boys and just go. I don't want to scare you, but this is bad, Jane.'

'I'll talk to Ben. We'll leave today. I won't take no for an answer.'

'Thank you. I'm sorry. If anything changes I'll call you, okay? Keep an eye on the media too.'

Loxton hung up and sat staring at her mobile for a few moments, shell-shocked.

She tried calling Sarah with a shaking hand, but it just rang out. Again. It made her nervous. But she told herself it was just that Sarah was working undercover, that was all. Then she called Gabriella.

'Hi, Alana, everything okay?' Gabriella answered.

'I'm so sorry. It's about Emma. It's bad news, I'm afraid.'

'Shit, is she all right?'

'She was found a couple of hours ago, in Camberwell station. She's been murdered.'

'God,' Gabriella said. 'Are you sure it's her?'

'I saw her myself, Gabriella. I'm sorry.'

There was a shaking sob and then Loxton heard Gabriella take a breath in, letting it out slowly. 'I'm okay. I'm fine,' she said, sounding anything but fine. 'You're arresting the boyfriend again, right?'

'He's a suspect, but I'm not sure he's got anything to do with it, Gabbie. There was a note and I was mentioned in it. So was Emma. I think this could be to do with Barratt.'

'Alana, you need to let Barratt go. It's got nothing to do with him. Focus on the boyfriend, for Emma's sake. I told her he was no good. It was him; I just know it.'

'I've told Jane to get out of town for a bit. To be safe. Do you think you could take some time off?'

'You expect me to run away? Are you joking? You're not running, so why should I? I want to find out who did this to her just as much as you do. I work on the murder squad. I can ask to be assigned to Emma's case.'

'Okay, just, seeing her like that has shook me up, Gabbie. It was just like a Barratt murder.' Loxton tried to hold the tears back.

'You can't protect everyone, Alana. And you don't have to. We can take care of ourselves. Thanks for calling me. God, *Emma*. How could this have happened? She was the sweetest.'

Loxton felt an overwhelming sadness. 'I wouldn't believe it if I hadn't seen her for myself. Be careful.'

'You too. And don't worry, I can handle myself.' Gabriella hung up but it made Loxton uneasy that Gabriella was so fixated on Pearce. She knew, though, that once Gabriella made her mind up, there was no changing it.

She dialled Sarah's number again but there was still no answer. She needed her to know what was going on. She drove the twenty minutes to Sarah's flat. It had been a while since she'd been here, maybe two Christmases ago for their usual get-together. She parked outside, just behind Sarah's red Mazda.

Sarah's windows were all in darkness. Loxton let herself into the communal entrance using her fire door key and made her way up to the third floor. The block seemed

deserted, but she could hear the rhythmical banging
of some dance music coming from one of the flats. She
reached Sarah's door and knocked hard. There was no
answer, as she'd suspected, so she tried the handle, but the
door was locked.

Loxton tried Sarah's mobile again and listened at the
door. It wasn't ringing from inside the flat. She crouched
down, opened the letterbox and peered into the dark,
using her mobile's torch to light up the floor inside. She
saw a pile of letters scattered on the doormat. Sarah hadn't
been here for some time. Loxton didn't like it.

A shiver ran down her spine and she suddenly got the
feeling she was being watched. As she turned her head, she
saw a man standing right behind her.

'Trying to get hold of Sarah?' the man asked. She
jumped up and her back was against Sarah's door he was
stood so close. The man was tanned, with rough stubble
and gelled hair. He was wearing designer charcoal jeans
and a tight black T shirt. He looked like he'd just walked
off stage at a rock concert.

'Who are you?' How had he crept up on her like that?
She was normally so aware of her surroundings. She
inched her hand towards her baton and hoped he wouldn't
notice. The corridor was deserted but if she screamed, the
residents might come out to help her.

'I'm DS Steve Anson, Sarah's sergeant. We'd best go
inside her flat to speak.'

He leaned past Loxton and unlocked the door. She
watched him walk inside as if he owned the place and she
checked either side of her and followed him in.

'Have you got your warrant card?' she asked.

He smiled at her. 'You're overly cautious, aren't you?'
He pulled out his warrant card and showed her.

She felt herself relax slightly as she closed the front door behind her.

'I'm DC Alana Loxton. I need to speak to Sarah.'

'I know who you are. You've called the office before.' Anson walked into the living room and went over to a large tropical fish tank, scattering some flakes on the surface. 'She's undercover on a sex trafficking operation and she's meant to check in every hour but she hasn't.'

Loxton couldn't stop the growing dread she felt. 'When did she last check in?'

'Twenty-four hours ago.' He stared at her, as if defying her to say anything.

'And you obviously can't ask the guys she's with where she's gone?'

'I'm not blowing her cover just because she hasn't been able to get us a message for a day. It happens. Not often, but it does happen. Why are you trying to get hold of her?'

'A friend of hers has died.'

'I'm sorry to hear that. Who passed away?' Anson sat down on a sofa and motioned for her to take a seat, so she sat on an armchair opposite him.

'I'd rather speak to her myself.'

'That's not going to happen. What's the friend's name? I'll tell her.'

'The friend is DC Emma Robins. She's been murdered. We need to speak to Sarah, find out when she last spoke to her. If Emma told her about any concerns or about anything unusual happening.'

'It'll have to wait. She's been on this op since Sunday night, so she probably won't be able to help you anyway.'

Loxton was beginning to dislike Anson. 'Can you just get hold of her? This is serious. I need to know she's okay.'

'I'm not going to do anything rash just because you've got a nervous disposition.' He stared at her like she was mad.

'How long's the operation been running?'

Anson looked as uncomfortable as she was about sharing information. 'A year, but this is strictly between us.'

She nodded. 'How have you lost her?'

'We know where she is; she's not lost. It's a warehouse lockout they've been operating out of. We have a few devices in there and she's able to send clicks back to tell us she's okay.'

'Has she ever been out of contact for this long before?'

Anson scratched the back of his neck lazily. 'No. But the equipment isn't perfect. Look, we should probably give it another day. I'll get a source in, we can confirm she's fine and you can stop panicking.'

'An officer's dead.' Loxton tried to keep her voice steady but failed. 'Sarah might not have a day if something's happened to her.'

'I hear you, but I heard about this officer's murder on the radio coming over here. It sounded like a domestic. The ex is the prime suspect. Sarah isn't involved in any of that. I know it's sadder than normal to us because it's a police officer, but we could screw up this whole operation if we're not careful, and for nothing.'

Loxton didn't like his priorities. He seemed more obsessed with his operation's success than his own officer's welfare. She didn't fancy Sarah's chances if it was up to Anson.

'I don't think it was the ex.' Loxton surprised herself by saying it with such confidence to someone she'd only just met. 'Look, I worked with Sarah on the murder squad on the Edward Barratt serial killer case. There were five of us. Five females, that is. And now, one of us is dead. The killer always said he'd get us back. He hated women. He never threatened the male DCs. I have a bad feeling DC Emma Robins's murder is somehow connected to Barratt.'

'Wow. You've got one keen imagination. Unfortunately, I haven't got time for wild theories.'

'It's not a wild theory. The ex has got an alibi and is denying any involvement. And I saw Emma's murder. It was exactly like a Barratt murder; it was like I was back there investigating him. Sarah going missing might be a coincidence, but can we really take that chance?'

Anson looked away and for a moment Loxton thought she saw concern flash across his face. It was quickly replaced by his usual relaxed look; almost like a defence mechanism, she thought. 'Sarah's talked highly of you in the past. Said I should get you on the team when a place comes up. I know this other detective was your friend and this is hard for you, but you need to control your emotions. And after dealing with Barratt you're bound to be suffering a little PTSD. Your friend's murder is a domestic.'

'This *isn't* a domestic, trust me,' she said, knowing Anson had no reason to trust her. 'This feels like Barratt. He escaped from Broadmoor Hospital last week. They caught him within the hour, but I think someone tried to help him. We need to make sure Sarah's safe. If something's happened to her and you didn't act, then you won't be able to live with yourself. I was the last person to see Emma alive on Saturday night. If I'd done something differently ...' Loxton stared at him, her hands balled into fists. She wasn't going to let anything happen to another friend.

'Take it easy,' he said but he didn't look so sure himself now. 'Look, I don't like that someone tried to break him out. I can ask my boss for authority to interrupt the operation, but if this is all for nothing this isn't going to help your career or mine. And I'll make sure everyone knows it was your concerns that called it off.'

Anson was a legend in the surveillance world. People respected him. He could make things hard for her if she turned out to be wrong.

He tilted his head, waiting. 'Are you still so sure you want to fuck up my operation for your hunch?'

'Call off your operation.'

Anson shook his head in annoyance. 'For fuck's sake. Okay, have it your way. I'll get it authorized. I'll start the arrest phase, but it's going to take me a few hours to get everything in place and signed off by the bosses. It's not the sort of place you just turn up to, either. These guys have guns on the premises. I'll get Sarah arrested just like everyone else, to protect her cover. Most of them will get bail so there's a chance she might be able to carry on in her undercover role. Obviously this is all need-to-know. This doesn't go anywhere else.'

'I'll need to tell DCI Winter at the very least and I'd expect to be involved. After all, it's my career that's on the line as well as yours.' Loxton folded her arms in front of her chest.

'Fine, you're welcome to be part of the arrest team. Just let us do the talking and don't fuck it up for us. Do you know how many women they've trafficked? We suspect it's in the hundreds. We've spent thousands on this op. Sarah's going to be pissed off that we messed this op up by panicking over some imagined threat.'

'Let's hope she's furious and you're telling me "I told you so",' Loxton said, praying that he was right.

PART 2

SARAH

Chapter 14

Earlier on Thursday 27 January, 05:05

Sarah wrapped her coat tighter around her and took another drag of her cigarette, trying to control her shaking hand. She had a few minutes alone in the small, enclosed courtyard. The nicotine was good and she exhaled slowly, blowing the smoke up towards the winter sky.

This job was getting too much. She could see how desperate the men with the guns were. One wrong move and their retribution would be both brutal and swift. She was struggling to keep them from turning vicious on the 'workers'. Her role as a madam here was becoming impossible. It was her job to keep the girls in line and collect the money. But money was going missing and a lot more besides.

She'd seen a henchman almost beaten to death in front of her for losing one of the 'workers'. The missing woman had been a stunner, in her early twenties, and in a different life she would have been a model. Having being born into poverty in a war-torn country, however, she'd become a commodity – and a valuable one at that. The unfortunate henchman had fallen for her, hard, and now the girl had somehow gone 'missing', causing the others to panic, because she could bring the police crashing down on them all.

The embers of her cigarette glowed brighter as she neared the end. She needed to get a message to Anson, and quick, but all three clickers had broken. That couldn't be a coincidence; someone must have tampered with them. Which meant they knew there was a mole. But did they know it was her yet?

Things were getting heated in the warehouse and tempers were frayed. It was liable to get serious fast and she was scared for the workers. If shots were fired and they didn't move out of the way quick enough, they could become collateral damage. At the rate things were going, Sarah might join them.

She dropped the cigarette butt onto the floor and stamped out the glowing ember. As she did so, she noticed something was out of place. The old, rusted manhole in the courtyard, which didn't seem to have been moved for a millennium, was now open.

She stepped closer. The covering had been shoved to the side.

The gang transported the workers out of the side door near the back and into waiting vans in the alleyway. She'd never seen anyone use this manhole before.

She glanced behind her and then leaned over to peer down into it, but there was just a black hole which seemed to go on forever. She wondered briefly if the wayward henchman had been killed after all and dropped down here. She hadn't seen him for a couple of hours.

Her eyes adjusted to the gloom. It was pitch black, but she could make out a ladder leading down. She wrinkled her nose as the smell of sewers wafted up. Had Anson started the arrest phase early? They'd never talked *about coming up from the sewers; it would be too dangerous. They'd be trapped like rats in a pipe if something went wrong.*

She glanced to her left and right. Anson would have got word to her, surely – unless they'd heard about the henchman and decided to act immediately. And she'd been out of contact for a day now.

She stepped away from the dizzying drop at the exact moment that something hard came down on top of her skull, nearly knocking her out. She staggered forwards towards the hole unable to stop, the world losing focus, and felt her assailant grab the back of her coat and drag her away from the drop before she fell into it. But that was where the kindness ended. A second blow knocked her out.

The only sign of what had happened to her was a spattering of tiny drops of blood on the wall from where the side of her cheek had split. And then it started to rain. A fine drizzle from the overcast grey sky.

Chapter 15

In the darkness of the early morning Loxton struggled to make out the shapes of the police snipers. It was as if they had melded into the outlying roofs surrounding the warehouse. Ahead of her were parked four battered white builders' vans.

The vans were filled with firearms officers, all poised to go in at Anson's command. Loxton waited nervously with Kowalski in their car further back down the road. The sky was black and the only sound was the drumming of the relentless rain on the car roof.

The special ops radio crackled and then Anson's voice broke through the calm.

'Go, go, go.'

Kowalski and Loxton glanced at each other, her nerves reflected in his eyes. The firearms officers slipped out of their vans, silent as tigers, and made their way to the warehouse ground-floor windows and door. They waited. Nothing stirred.

Two firearms officers soundlessly counted to three, and then smashed the windows at the same time, throwing in smoke grenades before moving away. A third officer hit a side door with the red metal enforcer. After three hits he stepped back, exhausted, and another officer seamlessly took his place. On the fourth attempt the door buckled inwards.

'Police, freeze,' shouted the firearms officers as they rushed inside, brandishing their rifles. The whole operation to get inside had taken around ten seconds.

Loxton strained her ears, but all she could hear was shouting. There was no gunfire and she breathed out a sigh of relief. After a few minutes an officer's voice came through on the radio. 'Area secure. All suspects contained.'

'Second phase, go, go, go,' Anson barked down the radio. Loxton swung open her car door and rushed forward with Kowalski right beside her. The smell of chemical smoke and uncleaned bodies hit her as she raced through the door. Grey smoke was everywhere, and she struggled to see where she was going. Kowalski kept to her side as they moved forward into the large open space.

She could see people on the floor through the smoke with firearms officers stood over them. She moved swiftly through the bodies, glancing at their faces, searching for Sarah. There were women huddled together in skimpy dresses, a few teenage girls among them. They looked dirty and thin, their faces gaunt, but it was their eyes that shocked Loxton. There was no fear in them, only defiance. This raid was just another thing for them to suffer; they didn't see it as their salvation.

She climbed up the metal stairs, still searching for Sarah. There were a few women who looked at odds with the rest, dressed in casual warm clothing. They were clean, their faces healthy, their eyes watchful. None of them was Sarah, though.

Anson came over to her, shook his head briefly and

gestured her to the side, away from prying ears. 'She's not fucking here.' She could see fear in his eyes. 'We're going be stuck here for a while dealing with this lot. If we find anything out, I'll let you know, but I doubt anyone's going to talk. They never do. What's happened to her?'

'I don't know, but we'll find her.' Loxton prayed Sarah had left the warehouse when she couldn't make contact, that she was safe and about to call Anson. She imagined Sarah giving her merry hell later for cutting the operation short and embarrassing her in front of her team, but Loxton knew that was just a fantasy. Something was really wrong.

She glanced out of the large grimy window and across the sprawling concrete industrial estate. Emma was dead and now Sarah was officially missing. Taken while in the middle of a surveillance operation, right under the noses of her colleagues. These guys were meant to be the best. She should have been safe.

Loxton closed her eyes. Sarah was out there somewhere, and she was in trouble. Loxton had to find her before something terrible happened to her too. This was Barratt's work; she knew he was somehow behind this. He was coming good on his promise of exacting revenge on the women who had put him away.

It felt like she was the one being hunted now, and she didn't know how to make it stop.

Chapter 16

'Loxton, the briefing's in ten minutes,' Kowalski said as he gathered up their notes and headed to Walworth CID office.

'I'll be there,' she said. 'I just need to call the others. They need to know Sarah's missing.'

'Okay, but don't let DI Meyer see you doing that; he likes to be in complete control and he'll think you're going behind his back.'

'They need to know now,' Loxton snapped. 'I'll be there in a minute.'

'Okay,' Kowalski said gently and walked out of the side room towards the bustling CID office. She saw him make an effort to hold his head up high, to try to instil confidence in the others when despair was setting into the team.

She closed the door behind him and pulled out her mobile. Her worst nightmare was coming true and now she had to warn Jane and Gabriella. She couldn't believe what was happening. It made her furious to think someone would do this, and seemingly with such ease.

'Gabriella, Sarah Taylor's officially missing.'

'I've just heard. They're saying she was on an undercover

operation. How would anyone even know where she was to abduct her? Someone in the police is leaking information to an organized crime group.'

'Or it's a police officer with access to everything,' Loxton said. 'Emma was found in Camberwell station. And Sarah was in the middle of an op. Whoever's doing this knows how we work.' It sounded absurd when Loxton said it out loud. But how could someone be doing this otherwise?

'Christ, I hope you're wrong. I'm trying to get put on the case, but my boss is pulling his face. Will you keep me updated?'

'Of course. And if you hear anything your end, call me, too.'

'How's Jane holding up?'

'She's taken an impromptu holiday; I don't know where. I'll give her a call now and tell her to get rid of her mobile and then move somewhere else. You should do the same.'

'I've told you, I'm not going to run away. Whoever's doing this needs to be stopped.'

'I feel the same,' Loxton agreed.

'Why hasn't Jane gone into police protection?' Gabriella asked.

'I didn't think that it was safe if this is somehow an inside job. And no one's mentioned it here. I'd rather she just went off grid.'

'Got you,' Gabriella said. 'My DI is saying here that Emma's murder and Sarah's abduction are separate incidents. They think Emma was killed by her boyfriend and your team missed some important evidence at the beginning that proves it. And they think Sarah's identity was compromised in the undercover op and she's been kidnapped. There are a few of that gang on remand, so whoever's taken her might demand the remand cases get dropped in exchange for Sarah's life.'

'They're wrong,' Loxton said, angry that Meyer was still treating the cases as separate incidents. The cases were linked, and if Meyer couldn't see it, then the killer could operate freely. 'We haven't missed anything on Emma's case. And Sarah's good – how was she compromised? There've been no demands.'

'I just thought I'd give you a heads up of what's being said here – it must be coming from Meyer.'

'This feels like Barratt,' Loxton said.

'Not Barratt again, Alana.' Gabriella sounded exasperated. 'He's been inside for the last two years. Forget about him. I'll try to get assigned to the case. Call me if there's anything new.'

'I will.' Loxton hung up.

She scrolled through her recent calls, hitting Jane's name. 'It's Alana, how are you doing?'

'Terrible,' Jane said, her voice heavy with exhaustion. 'Ben's in a mood with me. He had to take sick leave because there's a big work thing he's had to miss. We're hiding out in a cottage and he's terrified that work will find out so we're barely going out. He's already moaning that this is a waste of time, that I'm being ridiculous and paranoid. He thinks I've got postnatal depression.'

'We're not being paranoid,' Loxton said. 'Sarah's gone missing. She disappeared from an undercover operation and no one knows how it happened.'

'Shit.' Jane's voice was strained. 'What the fuck is going on?'

'I don't know, but it could be an inside job. You both need to get rid of your phones and move location today.'

'You're kidding me. Ben is never going to get rid of his mobile.'

'Please, Jane. This is serious. Don't tell anyone where you're going. Especially no one in the police.'

'You're scaring me.'

'We should be scared,' Loxton said. 'Emma is dead and Sarah's missing. Look, we just need to be careful.'

'What about you? Gabriella?'

'We're staying to work on the cases. That's our best chance. The murder squad are treating Emma's murder and Sarah's disappearance as separate incidents at the moment. But I know they must be linked to Barratt somehow.'

'So no protection for me, then?' Jane sighed.

'It might not be safe anyway. They took Sarah from the middle of an undercover operation. Whoever took her walked right in without being detected and managed to stroll right out again with her.'

'Okay, I'll do what you say. How am I going to contact you?'

'I'll be keeping my mobile, but don't call me; that will give your location away. Watch the news. Don't call anyone.'

'Alana, take care of yourself.'

'I will.' Loxton hung up. She shivered in the air-conditioned room. Even being in the police station didn't feel safe. She pocketed her mobile and hurried to the CID office.

Everyone was waiting for her it seemed. Meyer and Winter were stood at the front of the room while Kowalski sat in the front row, a seat empty beside him. He looked relieved when he saw her.

'There you are, Loxton,' Winter said. 'It's been decided that Meyer's team will run DC Emma Robins's murder.

We will be keeping DC Sarah Taylor's disappearance and work with her undercover unit on that. Can you give us all your handover?'

'Of course, sir.' Loxton stood next to Winter and avoided Meyer's scowl. She looked at the Southwark officers seated in front of her. The usual upbeat attitude was gone. Even Kowalski looked despondent.

'The preliminary findings are that Emma was raped and strangled, her windpipe crushed. Dr Reynolds speculated that the killer may be left-handed, but that's not something we can use evidentially. Pearce is right-handed. And I don't believe Pearce murdered Emma. The MO doesn't match the domestic violence profile. And now Sarah is missing. I believe the two incidents are linked by Edward Barratt.' Meyer bristled; she was going off topic. She saw the Southwark detectives lean in closer to listen, nodding their heads. The murder squad detectives murmured their dissent, one shaking their head and another giving her a pitying look.

Meyer stepped forward. 'Yes, we're all aware of your theories, DC Loxton. But to ensure we don't miss anything, we're going to treat Robins's murder and Sarah Taylor's disappearance as two separate cases until the evidence suggests otherwise. I understand that this is emotional for you Southwark officers, but you need to keep your heads and not get carried away. One officer has been murdered and the evidence points to her ex-boyfriend. Another has disappeared on a covert operation, her communication equipment having been tampered with, which suggests her cover was blown and the organized crime group she infiltrated is to blame. They once both worked at Southwark and then the murder squad. That's not a link; that's a coincidence. We don't want any more mistakes.'

'Mistakes?' Winter frowned at Meyer's suggestion.

'During the post-mortem, the pathologist, Dr Reynolds, found DNA on Emma Robins's neck,' Meyer said. 'Imagine our excitement.'

A shiver went through the room, everyone waiting for him to finish.

'A hit came back on the DNA database. It came back as DC Dominik Kowalski, the officer who found the body.' Meyer turned his cold disappointed stare on Kowalski, who coloured with embarrassment.

'But I was wearing gloves.' Kowalski threw Loxton a confused look.

'We were both wearing masks and double gloves,' Loxton said, remembering Kowalski inspecting Emma's neck. But mistakes like this could still happen, she knew. Pulling on the gloves carelessly or being panicked could lead to DNA getting on the outside of the glove, which then could transfer to the surface being examined. But she thought Kowalski had been careful.

'We wasted time and money analysing that sample,' Meyer said, ignoring them both. 'And, worse, it could have corrupted any of the killer's DNA that may have been there first. Your team is too close, Winter. It's understandable. And they're not trained to the standard my detectives are. So you stick with the missing person cases and we'll take the murders.'

Winter glared at Meyer and for a moment Loxton thought he might swing for him, but he seemed to remember where he was as his eyes fell on the seated officers watching him. He turned back to Meyer. 'There won't be any other mistakes, I guarantee it.'

'Good,' Meyer said. 'Don't let the personal nature of these cases get to any of you. Remain professional.'

'Emma's murder *is* personal,' Lena said from the back of the room and stood up. 'The note said, *"the war's started"*, didn't it? It mentioned Emma and Alana by name. Can't you see what's happening? It isn't a domestic.'

'I don't need to hear your profiling "theories" about serial killers again, DC Trawinska,' Meyer said. 'Please, sit down. Of course we need to keep an open mind at all times, but we also need to follow the evidence or risk missing something chasing wild theories. The note also said, *"lying whore"*, which points to Emma being killed by someone she knew intimately. Like Pearce. Barratt is in Broadmoor; it's got nothing to do with him. There's the unlikely possibility that Pearce is somehow linked to Sarah's disappearance. If Emma confided in Sarah about his harassment, asked her for help, then Pearce could have gone looking for Sarah to warn her to stay out of it. DC Loxton, in your report you stated that Emma and Sarah were friends. That they were both at the Saturday night reunion when Emma was last seen. Maybe Pearce followed Emma there and saw you all together. Maybe he followed Sarah and compromised her operation without even knowing it. It doesn't matter. Pearce isn't the one who has taken Sarah. Someone else has, and you need to find them while there's still time.'

'But what if it's the same person?' Loxton said.

'The job we do is dangerous, especially undercover work, and sometimes things go wrong. DC Taylor was working with very dangerous individuals. DS Anson is leading the search for her and I know he'd be grateful if your team could help him.' Meyer glanced at DCI Winter.

'I've already spoken with DS Anson and we've agreed to work together on Sarah's case,' Winter said.

'What about the press?' Kowalski asked. 'Emma Robins's murder has made the national news.'

'We might have to release a press statement that another detective's gone missing if it gets leaked,' Winter said. 'But we need to keep Sarah's identity confidential; that can't go out into the public domain. It might put her in more danger. We'd better get hold of Covert now, see what they advise with the press.'

The briefing was dismissed, and Loxton and Kowalski joined Lena, who was stood at the back of the room.

'They're making a mistake,' Lena said. 'But DI Meyer won't listen to me. You're right, Alana. Luke Pearce didn't kill DC Robins; it isn't a domestic murder. It's too meticulous; almost like someone is on a mission. Something bigger is going on.'

'I'll fill you in on the Barratt murders,' Loxton said, relieved that she had Kowalski and Lena on her side.

Chapter 17

Loxton put her key in her front door and was about to take off the dead lock when the door swung inwards. It pushed open easily. It had been left slightly ajar. Again. She reached for her baton but realized she'd left it in her locker, like she did every time she went home from work.

She pulled out her mobile while she tried to remember if she'd locked her flat this morning, or had she forgotten again in her rush to get to the warehouse stakeout? She was always so careful, but then it had happened the evening Kowalski brought pizzas round too.

Still, something felt wrong. She dialled 999 and crept into her hallway. The flat was in darkness, just like she'd left it. She peered into the shadows in her hallway, her hand stretching to the umbrella stand. She could see only blackness. She felt the reassuring metal of the bat handle and gently slid it out of the stand, trying not to make a sound.

She strained her ears but there was nothing. She held the bat high, ready to swing. She crept forward. There was no one in the bathroom, so she moved to her bedroom. No one there either, the bed still unmade.

Everything was exactly as she'd left it. Nothing disturbed. Perhaps she *had* forgotten to lock the door. It could have been open like that all day without anyone noticing or caring. She'd been so tired – working long hours, dealing with Pearce and finding Emma's body. The case was taking its toll.

She padded slowly to the living room, finding it in darkness too.

'You should be more careful.' The man's voice came from her left. She felt her blood go cold.

She flicked on her living room light and stared at Anson, who was sat in her armchair, his face pale.

'What the fuck are you doing here?' She didn't know what weird power game he was playing, but she wasn't going to be part of it.

'Your door was left ajar. I thought something had happened to you so I came in to check you were okay but you weren't here. No one was. It was creepy as fuck. I figured I'd wait for you, make sure no one weird was hanging around waiting for you to come home. If anyone else did come in, I was going to give them a surprise.' His eyes met hers, and she saw they were red-rimmed, as if he'd been crying or drinking heavily.

Loxton couldn't believe he was in her flat. She threw a betrayed look at her front door. There was no sign of a break-in. The lock was still intact and working fine. Had she left the door open or had someone got in somehow?

'Why are you here?' she asked firmly.

'Sarah's been officially reported missing in the line of duty. I need to find her. You seem to know more than anyone else. Tell me everything.'

'And you couldn't do this at the station?'

'I don't trust anyone at the station. Do you? Whoever

is doing this managed to drop a body off in Camberwell without raising a single eyebrow. And then they're able to infiltrate a police operation, sabotage the equipment and magically disappear our undercover officer away without a single person noticing. Come on. It's got to be someone in the police or at least someone that has access to everything.'

Loxton glanced at Anson warily. She had thought it herself so many times in the past few days, but she couldn't help noticing that Anson looked rather unhinged. But, then, if he wanted to hurt her, he would have done it already.

'I need a drink.' She went into the kitchen and stashed her baseball bat in a cupboard.

'I'll have red,' he called after her.

She poured them two large glasses of Merlot. She didn't know whether to throw it at him or hand it to him. She reluctantly decided on the latter.

'So, how long have you and Sarah been sleeping together?' She sat on the sofa opposite him.

He looked momentarily surprised, and then anger flashed briefly in his eyes. 'That's none of your business.'

'You walk into my flat uninvited and you don't want to get personal?' she asked.

'I was making sure you were all right. You should thank me.' He paused for a moment and then sighed. 'We've been together five months. What does it matter?'

'I just want to try to understand this,' she said. He sat on the edge of her armchair, his face angry and scared all at the same time.

'I have to find her.' Anson looked desperate.

She paused a moment, wondering whether to try to convince Anson about Barratt. He hadn't believed her theory before; he was arrogant like Meyer. 'I still think it's to do with Edward Barratt.'

'Shit.' He knocked back the red wine and Loxton realized he was already drunk. 'You need to go and see Barratt. Find out what the fuck's been going on.'

She'd been afraid of this, but she'd known it was coming as soon as Sarah had gone missing. 'I know.'

'When you've seen him, you tell me everything you find out from that creature. I'll try all the sources I know, cover the organized crime angle and ask about Barratt. *Someone* knows what the fuck's going on and where Sarah is.'

'Anson, don't do anything ... illegal.'

'Don't worry, Loxton. I won't involve you. You just focus on Barratt. I'll see what the underworld knows.'

If he was perfectly okay with breaking into a police officer's home out of hours, Loxton dreaded to think what he'd do to criminals to find out what he wanted.

'Anson, I'm sorry.' She knew police relationships could be intense. Spending every day together, death on the periphery at times. It must have been all-consuming, and now Sarah was gone.

'Sarah talked very highly of you. She said you had a knack for solving murder cases. She said you couldn't switch off; whatever the question was, you would always be rolling it over in your mind, looking at every angle. She wished you'd kept in contact more. Kept telling me I should get you on the team while I could, before you went back to murder or for promotion.'

Loxton could imagine Sarah trying to help her out like that. 'We'll find her.' She wouldn't stop until she had. She envisaged Sarah being kept somewhere dark, perhaps another disused warehouse. She dreaded to think what would happen to her if they didn't find her soon.

Anson stood up and put the empty glass down on her coffee table. 'I want to know any developments the minute you do.'

'I'll call you when I can.' Loxton didn't like this, but what choice did she have? She watched him leave, but at the door he stopped and looked back at her.

'Loxton, be careful. This isn't going to end well for anyone.'

'I know,' she said and double-locked the door the moment he was gone. She put the chain across and then rested her forehead against the solid oak door. She shivered at the thought that Anson had caught her unawares like that, but perhaps she should be grateful it was him waiting for her. She couldn't shake the feeling that someone else had been in here before him.

She walked around her flat more carefully, trying to see if anything had been moved, anything taken. Everything seemed to be in order, but then she noticed that her book-case looked different somehow. She went to the middle shelf, checking between the books for her diary, which she kept hidden in between two large tedious police manuals. It was there, but it wasn't pushed to the very back, which is where she always kept it. She took it out and leafed through the pages. It looked the same, but somehow it wasn't hers anymore, it felt like someone else had been reading it.

It wasn't safe to stay in her flat anymore. She would get a hotel room. She headed to her bedroom to pack, taking her diary with her. She wasn't going to sleep here tonight or any other night soon. Anson had scared her. Perhaps that had been his intention all along. Well, it had worked. She wasn't going to let herself become the next victim.

PART 3

GABRIELLA

Chapter 18

Gabriella came to and realized she was being tossed from side to side in a car trunk. The streetlight seeped through the glass tail lights and tiny gaps in the seals of the boot. It was hard to see, but already her eyes were adjusting to the gloom.

Her head hurt and she felt sick and groggy, like when you wake from a hangover. But this was much worse.

How had she got here? For a moment she had no idea. Then it came back to her. She'd been walking home after work. There'd been a scream, barely audible from an alleyway to her side. Probably a fox, but her instincts had kicked in, so she'd run down it to take a look, imagining a woman in distress.

She'd taken her mobile out of her pocket as she ran. She'd pulled up short, hanging back to assess the situation, rather than blindly running into danger. She hadn't seen anyone, not even a fox. And then she'd spotted it. A mobile in the middle of the alleyway. The noise had been coming from there, human and animal at the same time. At that moment she realized how stupid she'd been. Loxton had warned her.

She'd stabbed frantically at her phone, trying to dial 999 and seeing Rosa's name on her screen as she spun around, but it was too late. That was all she could remember. That screaming voice and her own rising with it. And then this, whatever this was. Her head was swimming and it wasn't just the motion of the car. She probably had a low-level concussion, but she was awake at least.

She thought of Rosa, worried sick alone at the flat. She had to get out of this for her. She was all Rosa had left in the world, now that both their parents were dead.

She looked around her for some chance of escape. Beside her was a heavy sports bag. Next to it was a dark grey satchel, which was tied loosely, and if she craned her neck she could see gleaming metal. It was a chef's professional knife set. She'd seen them on cookery programmes.

She let out a low moan of despair, muffled by the gag tied tightly around her mouth. It wasn't loose. Salvation was so close, if she could just reach a knife, but her hands were bound behind her back to her ankles and these knots weren't coming undone.

The blood supply to her hands and feet had been compromised and they had gone numb and tingly. If she could roll over to the knives she doubted if her hands would work well enough that she wouldn't just end up cutting her own fingers off by mistake.

She wondered if her attacker had left the knives partly on display on purpose. To torture her before the real pain began. She craned her neck towards the sports bag, half undone, and saw more metals objects that looked like surgical instruments. She began to panic as she imagined what they were for. Her breathing became short and desperate. If she didn't calm down, she'd hyperventilate and pass out.

She decided to focus on the knife set. That was her best chance. This lunatic was going to kill her, she was sure of that. Barratt must have arranged it, to exact his promised revenge at last, to kill her like one of his victims. She shivered, reliving finding them again. They'd been kept tied up in the tunnels and abused until he'd eventually tired of them and choked them to death.

That wasn't going to happen to her. Her only chance was to free herself with one of those knives and then strike when they opened the boot up. She tried to roll over, so her back was nearer to the knives, her tied hands behind her within reaching distance.

But she couldn't turn.

Something was holding her back. She craned her neck to look over her shoulder and saw that she'd been tied to a metal hook on the side of the boot. She wouldn't be able to roll over. With her hands and feet tied behind her, all she could do was stare at the knives helplessly.

She howled in rage and frustration. And then she screamed for help. But the gag muffled her voice. The car speeding along the road drowned out more of it. And the loud bass music did the rest.

Chapter 19

Loxton and Kowalski were in the CID office trawling through the CCTV around the warehouse where Sarah had gone missing. There was lots of movement, vans and lorries coming out of the industrial estate at all hours of the day. She noted down registration plates for the team to follow up on, but it was proving to be a mammoth task.

Meyer came into the office, his face clouded.

'What's wrong?' she asked.

'The blood traces found at Tony's Garage have come back.'

Loxton felt as if her heart had stopped as she waited for him to speak.

'It's Nathan Marshall's. He's the Uber motorcyclist in a coma who was hit last Saturday around midnight.'

'That pretty much puts Pearce in the clear,' she said. 'He must have hit Marshall and then driven over to Tony's Garage.'

'Maybe Emma was with him,' Meyer said. 'Or he drove to her house asking for her help and she wanted to turn him in to the police. An altercation happened . . .' He was grasping at straws and he must know it, Loxton thought. The timing was too tight.

Winter rushed into the office. 'Another detective's been reported missing,' he said. 'DC Gabriella Caselli. Her sister has just called it in.'

Loxton's stomach knotted in dread. *Gabriella*.

'I need to get Pearce arrested for this hit and run,' Meyer said.

'We'll go and take the full missing person report from Gabriella's sister,' she said, looking at Kowalski, who was already gathering his things to go with her.

'I thought you'd want to,' Winter said, handing her a printout of the 999 call. 'Here's what we have so far. That's three officers now from the Barratt case, Loxton. Looks like you were right. It could be a Barratt copycat seeking revenge against the team who locked him away. Be careful. Kowalski's not to leave your side.'

'I won't,' he said.

'You two lead on it for now. DI Meyer, do you need a hand with Pearce?'

'No, I've got that covered,' Meyer said. 'Keep me informed of this other detective going missing. I might have been looking at this wrong.'

Loxton and Kowalski headed to the car.

'Oh God. Poor Rosa,' Kowalski said when they were alone. His face had gone grey.

'You know Gabriella?' she asked.

He nodded. 'We were good friends when she used to work in Southwark. I haven't seen her since she was promoted to murder. I can't believe this is happening.' He struggled to keep the anger out of his voice.

'I don't know what to do anymore.' Loxton covered

her face with her hands as a wave of grief rose and then smashed into her. She felt like she couldn't breathe.

Kowalski wrapped his arms around her and gave her a tight hug. 'It's going to be all right; we can do this.'

When she felt in control again, she moved her hands and looked up at him.

'I'll drive.' He held out his hand.

She nodded, passed him the keys and pressed her lips together to stop from screaming.

Gabriella Caselli. She had been the bravest of them. Never taking no for an answer, she was tenacious and as fiery as they came.

Emma dead and both Sarah and Gabriella missing, all of them linked to Barratt. It had to be something to do with him. Her old team were being taken one by one. And it would soon be her turn; she was sure of that. Unless she could stop it.

Gabriella rented a ground-floor maisonette with her sister, Rosa. It was large and spacious but somehow had a temporary air, every wall painted magnolia, nothing hanging on them.

Rosa was fresh out of university and had just started working in the charity sector. She was shaking so much she spilt the tea she had insisted on making for them. She left her own untouched, instead repeatedly tucking her long wavy black hair behind her ears. She tried to make things normal, to hold on to something comforting, but there was no comfort anymore.

'Tell me why you think Gabriella has gone missing.' Loxton vaguely recognized Rosa and then realized they had met at Gabriella's thirtieth two years ago. A group of them had gone to a swanky cocktail bar on a rooftop overlooking Trafalgar Square where they watched the sunset and the twinkling lights of the city come on. Loxton remembered champagne cocktails and nearly missing the last tube home. And laughing so hard that she'd cried.

'She's not answering her mobile.' Rosa's voice was so quiet that Loxton had to lean forward to hear her.

'For how long?' Loxton asked.

'She's not checked her WhatsApp since ten thirty last night. And she's not returning my calls. I know it seems strange, but she usually answers straight away. Or if not straight away, then she calls me back within the hour. She's so paranoid all the time; she likes to keep tabs on me, but especially since Emma Robins was murdered. She wanted me to stay with friends but I told her she was being ridiculous. I thought Emma's murder was a domestic.'

'What else has happened to make you worried?' Loxton asked. Rosa didn't seem to want to say. It was as if voicing her fear made it real. 'Please.'

'She . . . she left this horrible voicemail on my phone last night.' Rosa's voice was a whisper. Her gaze had drifted to her hands, which were shaking on her lap. 'It was like something was happening. I only listened to it twenty minutes ago when I tried to call her again for the tenth time. I never get voicemails; I've forgotten how to check them. But when I was trying to work out when I last spoke to her, I saw it. That's why I called 999.'

'Can we listen to it?' Loxton asked.

Rosa nodded and pulled out her mobile, putting it on speaker and dialling 121. She pressed play and screwed her eyes shut, her hands covering her ears. A piercing scream came from the mobile, like a fox late at night, the eerie wail high and long. Then the phone cut off.

'Is that the only voicemail?' Loxton asked gently, her own heart racing, her hands going clammy.

Rosa nodded, her bottom lip trembling, and Loxton was struck by how young she looked. Still a baby, only in her early twenties. Far too young for all of this.

Rosa tried to say something, but only a strangled noise came out. She gulped back some tears and tried again. 'She left the voicemail at quarter past eleven. I was out with friends. We had a few drinks. More than a few. I don't even remember how I got home. I was dead to the world. Then this morning I had the worst hangover ever and I was in such a rush to get to work. I had this charity fair weekend event I had to go to. I didn't see her in the morning, but I normally don't. She's usually gone before I wake up. Her shift starts ridiculously early.'

'At 7am,' Loxton said.

'When I got home this evening and she wasn't here I tried calling. She's meant to cook on a Saturday evening. It's our weekly routine, so that we spend some time together in the week, and she jokes it's so I get at least one decent meal. She's like a second mum to me.' Rosa flinched as she said the word 'mum'.

Loxton remembered Gabriella's mother had passed away just before Loxton had met her. It had happened when Rosa was only eighteen, a few years ago now. Gabriella had assumed the role of Rosa's mum – she was always talking about her, so proud of her little sister. Loxton had been a teenager when her own mother had died, and Gabriella had asked her for advice. Loxton remembered wishing she'd had a big sister like Gabriella, someone looking out for her, someone going through the same thing to help her.

'I thought maybe Gabriella had got stuck at work

again. A prisoner or something. When a murder breaks everything goes on halt. But normally she calls.'

'She's not been to work.' Loxton felt tears welling in her own eyes.

'I know she never turned up.' Rosa swallowed hard. 'I called the station first. They had her down to take a statement from a victim, but when they called the victim, she said Gabriella hadn't showed. That's not like Gabriella. Do you think that weird noise was an animal or the phone crashing or something?' Rosa looked desperate.

'Maybe. We don't know what's happened yet.' Loxton's heart was hammering in her chest. First Emma, then Sarah and now Gabriella. What the fuck was happening? She felt herself going cold and then hot, sickness swelling inside her.

'The whole station is working on this case, Rosa.' Kowalski leaned across and squeezed Rosa's hand, then leaned back.

'Please, Dominik, find her.' Rosa looked at Kowalski, her eyes pleading. She burst into tears.

'Don't you worry, kiddo,' he said. 'We're on it.'

'I saw on the news last night that another detective's gone missing.' Rosa started to shake violently now. 'Gabriella told me Emma's murder was a domestic. It couldn't be connected to Gabriella, could it? She wanted me to stay at a friend's, but all my stuff is here. She installed a video doorbell and a burglar alarm. She told me not to open the front door unless I knew who it was and to set the alarm even when I was in. Gabriella's dead, isn't she? Just like Emma.' Rosa's lower lip trembled as she tried to hold herself together for the answer.

'We don't know Gabriella's dead,' Loxton said. 'We're going to do everything we can to find her.' The words sounded hollow.

Rosa burst into tears and Kowalski pulled her into his

chest and held her there. He looked over at Loxton, her terror mirrored in his eyes.

They'd waited for a friend of Rosa's to come to the flat before they'd left her and now they sat in the car outside, both silent and lost in their own thoughts. Loxton's mind was whirring with possibilities but everything seemed to lead back to Barratt.

'I need to warn Jane,' she said. 'I told her to get rid of her mobile and to get out of London, but she's got to go into police protection.'

'Do you know where she is?' Kowalski asked.

'I have no idea. I told her not to tell anyone.'

'Maybe you were right and she's safer off where she is,' Kowalski said. 'We still have no idea who's behind this.'

Loxton nodded but hated the idea of Jane finding out from the news. She tried to call her mobile on the off chance, but it was switched off. At least Jane had taken her advice.

She called Winter and updated him on Gabriella's disappearance and told him that she couldn't get hold of Jane.

'That's three now from the Barratt team,' Winter said. 'Leave Jane Edison to me. I'll get a team working on it. We'll track her down and get her and her family into police protection.'

'Thank you, sir,' Loxton said, feeling hopeful that they'd be able to find her.

'Pearce has been arrested. He'll be interviewed about the hit and run and Emma Robins's murder, but I really don't think he's involved. Alana, I want you and Kowalski to go and see Barratt in Broadmoor. I've arranged it for Monday morning; they won't allow visitors at the weekend.' Winter sounded annoyed.

'I'll see if I can get him to talk,' Loxton said. The idea of facing Barratt made her heart race, but she needed to find out what he knew.

'He's now at suspect status along with anyone associated with him,' Winter said. 'I want to know who his followers are on social media, who's on his email list. Anyone and everyone who's had contact with him and especially visited him. And how staff think he briefly escaped.'

'We'll collect his letters for review too,' she said.

'And take Lena with you,' Winter said. 'Her insight might be useful. The more officers with you at the moment, Alana, the better.' He hung up.

Loxton didn't like the strain in his voice. She felt like her time on the case was running out and it wouldn't be long before he pulled her off it. And then she'd be helpless to stop the killer, instead waiting for her time to come.

Chapter 20

Loxton watched the guard unlock the elaborate security doors while she, Kowalski and Lena waited to be allowed onto Barratt's wing. She felt her chest tighten in dread at the thought of meeting Barratt again. Kowalski, apparently sensing her unease, put his hand on Loxton's shoulder briefly. 'We're with you all the way.'

Loxton nodded; she didn't trust herself to speak.

'I'm sorry it has to be you, Alana.' Lena sighed. 'But Barratt is more likely to let something slip if he sees you. There's a connection there, and he may not be able to help himself if he is involved.'

'You mean he might not be able to stop himself from taunting me?' Barratt had a sadistic and twisted mind – one she thought she'd never have to deal with again.

'Exactly.' Lena nodded. 'If you don't want to do this, Dominik and I will talk to him. You can wait out here.'

'No, I'll do it,' Loxton said. 'You're right. He always said he wanted to see each one of us in the ground before him. If he's involved, Barratt won't be able to stop himself from gloating. This could work.'

As Loxton walked down the wing, she felt like a

sacrificial offering to the murder gods, and she didn't like it one bit, but there was no other option. No one knew Barratt better than her.

Barratt's cell was at the end of a long, empty corridor, hidden in the basement of the high-security hospital. It was made entirely of glass except for the solid steel door and was like nothing she'd ever seen before.

'Barratt, you've got visitors.' The guard was well-built and in his thirties. His eyes were alert and flitted around everything, constantly checking and reviewing for anything out of place.

There was no movement from inside until they were a few metres away, and then Barratt stepped towards them from behind the metal door to study them through the thick wall of toughened glass.

'Edward, remember me?' Loxton asked.

The man had lost weight and his skin was sallow. His hair was to his shoulders and he had a beard hiding his once handsome jawline. Solitary confinement had been hard on him. He squinted at her, as if trying to remember, then a smile spread across his face.

'I've not seen a woman in months. And now I've got two beautiful women at once; it's a dream come true. You haven't aged at all, Alana.' His eyes wandered over her face and down her body. 'And look at those curves.'

'This isn't a social visit,' she said. 'I need your help.' She hoped playing to his ego would work.

'I'm not really in a state to help anyone.' He motioned at his surroundings. 'They never have time to talk to me, only to torment me. I thought he was winding me up when he said I had visitors. They do that every few months – insist someone's coming to see me and then no one ever does.'

'We're here and we want to talk.' She couldn't gauge

his mood. She'd spent so many hours in the past trying to work out what drove him, before she'd even known who he was, and even after spending days interviewing him, he was still a mystery to her.

'Yes, you're here, but are you real?' He put his hands against the glass, his breath clouding the cold surface, obscuring his face in mist. When it cleared, he was studying her again with his cold eyes. He scanned the glass, as if looking for a way through that he might have missed. 'If only I could touch you to be sure. I imagine things, you see.'

Kowalski threw Loxton a look, his eyes widening for a split second. He mouthed 'bat shit crazy' at her. Lena glared at him.

'Edward, we're real,' Loxton said. 'These are my colleagues, Dominik Kowalski and Lena Trawinska. Lena's a police profiler. As I said, we really need your help.'

Barratt glanced at Kowalski and then his gaze fell onto Lena. He frowned. She seemed to stiffen under his gaze. 'You're a police profiler. That's interesting. Can you come a little closer?'

Lena shook her head at him and smiled. 'You can see me just fine from here.'

'Don't you want to come closer?' He leaned towards her. 'Aren't I fascinating to you? You're very fascinating to me. You're not what I expected.' He tilted his head at her.

'I read your prison file on the way here,' Lena said. 'It says you were inspired by the serial killer Krystian Szymański. Is that true?'

'Reading up on me?' Barratt eyed her warily. 'I feel at a disadvantage.'

Loxton frowned. She'd heard the name Szymański before, but couldn't think where. It hadn't come up in

Barratt's trial, but perhaps while he had been languishing in Broadmoor he'd told his psychiatrist about how his killing spree had started. She'd heard he was trying to write a memoir about his life, but the prison had been keen to put a stop to that. No one wanted to give him a platform. There were plenty of ill people out there looking for inspiration and a leader.

'Krystian Szymański targeted female tourists. You targeted female sex workers. Why was that?'

Barratt laughed. 'Isn't it in my file? I believe they describe me as impulsive and prone to violence without considering the consequences. The truth is that I had a rather unfortunate incident with a sex worker. She was most unpleasant in the way she addressed me.'

'But why did you continue?' Lena asked. 'You might have got away with it if you'd stopped at one.'

'I suppose you could say I got a taste for it. And anyway, it didn't really do any harm; those women weren't living anyway. They were like the walking dead. Get a hit, come down, desperately strive for the next hit. On and on. The joke is they'd probably all have died of overdoses by now anyway and yet I'm still here serving time for their untimely deaths.'

Loxton could see Lena was intrigued, but she felt they were getting off track and their audience with Barratt wasn't long.

'Edward, we're here because you seem to have a copycat,' Loxton said.

'A copycat?' Barratt moved away from the glass a fraction and the vapour evaporated.

'Do you know anything about that?' she asked.

'Me?' He placed his hand on his heart with fake sincerity. 'This is the first I'm hearing about it. It's nothing to do with me.' He smiled at her again and she swore he was trying to conceal a smirk.

'It might be one of your fan base,' she said.

'Fan base?' He shook his head at her in bewilderment. 'What fan base?'

'You have quite a following. They write to you a lot.' Had Barratt lost his mind in here? He'd had such a sharp one. It was a shame in a strange way.

'I hardly get any letters.' He frowned and the old rage stirred in his eyes. 'Only ever from my solicitor and a well-meaning prison charity that does nothing.'

Loxton glanced backwards towards the guard. He wouldn't meet her eye.

'You fucking toad!' Barratt smashed his fists into the glass, his temper exploding. 'I know you lot put excrement in my food. I can taste it! You fucking wanker. Just wait until I get to you!'

'Can you give us a moment?' she asked the guard over Barratt's abuse.

'I'm not supposed to, not after the stunt he pulled recently.' The guard didn't take his eyes off Barratt.

'Please,' Loxton said. 'This is important.'

The guard studied her for a moment as if assessing whether he could trust her. 'Okay, but he won't help you. Everything he says is a lie. Don't trust a word. You've got five minutes and then I'm coming back.' The guard strode off.

'Edward, if you help us, we could help you.'

'You could get me out of solitary confinement?' Barratt's eyes looked desperate. This was new.

'You're too high risk, you know that.' She shook her head at him. 'You tried to escape less than two weeks ago.'

He rolled his eyes at her. 'A few lousy days and they can

treat me like this forever. Everyone has bad days. I didn't even get past the woods.'

'We might be able to get visits reinstated. Get some of this fan base seeing you weekly?' He never could resist when his ego was being massaged – even when he was clever enough to work out what she was doing, and he was *always* clever enough.

His eyes lit up and he smiled at her. 'I've missed you. I want a change of guards too. All women. And I never want to see that macho arsehole's face again. I've been looking at his face on and off for six months now.'

'I can speak to the governor,' she said.

'And they say Broadmoor's not a prison but a hospital.' He shook his head.

'This will only happen if you help us first.' She held his gaze. He was still the most powerful man she'd ever met. The way he looked at her, as if she was the only other living thing on the planet. As if he were a god who could either crush or save her.

'I want guarantees.' He stepped closer to the glass. Closer to her. 'From you. I don't trust those two.' His eyes flicked from Kowalski and Lena back to Loxton.

'I can't give you them today.' She was sweating. She could feel her shirt becoming damp.

'Well, in that case I can't help you today.' He shrugged sadly and turned away.

'Emma Robins is the victim.'

Edward eyed her suspiciously. 'DC Emma Robins?'

'Yes.' She was annoyed at herself for conceding that information so early, but with Barratt you could never win. He was stubborn. All you could do was try to cajole. Humiliation and pain usually turned him on to your way of thinking.

Kowalski stepped forward, his face almost touching the glass. 'Was this you, Barratt?' he asked, his voice a low growl.

Barratt stepped back, surprised, and for a moment Loxton was sure he looked alarmed. Then he laughed. 'If this was anything to do with me, which would be impressive even for me seeing as I'm trapped in here incommunicado, do you really think I'd tell you? Alana, get your dog on a chain or I won't say another word.'

Loxton glanced at Kowalski, in her head pleading with him to back off. Kowalski shook his head but stood his ground.

'Have a think about it,' Loxton said. 'I'll leave you the case file. We'll come back tomorrow. I should have finalized everything by then.'

'I don't believe you,' he said, his eyes narrowing.

'I'm being straight with you here.' She pressed her lips together in frustration. All this time and she'd never told him a single lie, but still he was suspicious.

'Answer me one question and it's a deal,' he said.

'I'll try,' she replied.

He motioned for her to move forwards to the hatch. 'I don't want your henchman and his girlfriend hearing.'

'I don't like this,' Lena muttered to Kowalski.

'Alana, don't go near that wicket.' Kowalski stared at her, the concern obvious in his eyes.

'No deal then.' Barratt smirked at Kowalski, as if Kowalski had made a mistake.

'Can you both just give us a minute?' Loxton asked. 'I won't open it.'

'I don't want you on your own with him,' Kowalski said.

'Scared, Kowalski?' Barratt stepped towards Kowalski. 'You should be.'

'I'm not scared of you.' Kowalski stepped closer to the glass.

'Dominik, I'll only be a minute,' Loxton said.

Lena shook her head, but Kowalski hesitated for a moment, looking at Loxton, and then nodded. 'Come on, Lena. We'll be just over here, Alana.' He walked briskly up the corridor with Lena following him, then he turned and stood by the door facing her and Barratt.

Loxton realized Kowalski wasn't going to take his eyes off her. It hurt that he didn't trust her not to open the hatch. But he was right. If he hadn't been there, she probably would have taken the risk for Sarah's and Gabriella's sake.

She moved nearer to the glass. 'Ask away,' she said.

'Which was your favourite murder? Come on, in your whole career you must have had a favourite. The standout one. I did.'

'I'm not like you,' she said.

'You're alive, aren't you?' He frowned at her. 'We're predators, you and me. We like to hunt.'

'I want to protect people.'

He laughed. 'You crack me up. You want to know the thing we have in common? You and me, we like the thrill of the chase, and we don't care who gets hurt along the way. Neither of us like people. We know that they're all just overhyped animals, capable of unspeakable horrors when they think no one's watching.'

'Do we have a deal?'

'No.' He snapped the word out, angry. 'Not until you admit you're like me.'

She hated his power games. It always came down to this. He wanted to control her. 'I'm drawn to murder investigations.'

'Was I your favourite case?'

She thought for a second. 'You scared me the most. Catching you was the pinnacle of my career. I don't think I'll ever better that.'

A slow smile spread across his face. 'Which one of my victims was your favourite? I have one. I know I shouldn't. I should love them all the same. But it would be a lie.'

She shook her head at him.

'Come on.' His voice was so quiet she wasn't sure if she'd heard him right. 'I won't tell anyone if you don't. I'll take it to my grave.'

'The last one. That was your best work.' She hated herself.

'Snap.' He slapped the glass hard at the same time and startled her. 'You have a deal, Alana.'

She took a moment to recover herself. 'I'll pass the file to the guard and he'll give it to you. Tomorrow you can tell me your thoughts.'

'Tomorrow I'll play the role you've assigned me. But who knows? Maybe one day you'll get to play the role I assign you. Just like Emma Robins did.' He stroked the glass, running his hand down it, smiling at her.

'Did you have something to do with this, Edward?' She stepped closer to the glass. 'You've got nothing to lose. They can't do anything else to you. Why not just tell me? Don't you want me to know?' She prayed his desire to show off would make him let something slip.

'I merely meant that I told Emma she'd get what was coming to her and it turns out I was right. That's all.'

'Who tried to get you out of here?' she said.

He smiled at her. 'Now that would be telling.'

'So there *was* someone else?' she asked.

A flash of anger crossed Barratt's face but was quickly

replaced by indifference. 'I didn't say there was anyone else. I acted alone. I'll have a look at your file and tell you what I think, but it won't help you. You're not going to be able to stop it. The wolves are out of the cage now and they're coming for you.'

She forced herself to turn away and not to react to his bait. She walked down the corridor, refusing to look back at him, but it was like turning her back on a grinning tiger. She wanted to know where he was at all times.

Chapter 21

The hotel Loxton and Kowalski found for the night was cheap and functional and on the outskirts of town. Loxton hoped it was far out enough that the night revellers wouldn't be coming back after the nightclubs kicked them out.

Lena had travelled back to London with all of Barratt's letters. Loxton wanted to get her and the team researching the senders straight away, to see if any of them seemed like a likely candidate to be avenging Barratt by murdering Emma and abducting Sarah and Gabriella. If Loxton didn't know better, she'd think Barratt had spooked Lena.

'We could drive back to London now too,' Kowalski said. 'It's only forty miles away.'

'Winter wants me out of harm's way.' Loxton sighed. 'That's why he sent us here.'

Kowalski shook his head. 'If he wants you out of harm's way, he should have sent you abroad. This guy isn't going to stop.'

'I know that.' Her voice was sharp. She didn't need him reminding her.

'I won't let anything happen to you,' Kowalski said, his eyes full of concern.

'What shall we get for dinner?' She changed the subject, not wanting to dwell on Barratt any longer tonight.

'Room service?' He passed her the menu from the coffee table. 'I don't feel like eating out.'

'I was hoping you'd say that.' She scanned the menu, seeing a salmon salad and thinking a side of chips would go well.

'Alana, I don't mean this in the wrong way, but can you do me a favour?' He looked serious.

'Sure,' she said, putting the menu down.

'Can I sleep in your room tonight? I won't sleep otherwise, knowing you're on your own.' Kowalski was rattled. Barratt always knew how to get under someone's skin.

'I'll use the internal chain as well as lock the door and I'll keep my baton by my bed. I'll be fine.'

'Please, just listen. Barratt was right. I am scared. The idea of losing you ...' He wouldn't look at her. 'I'll sleep on the sofa.' He patted the sofa he was sat on.

She didn't want him to mother her, but she had to admit she didn't really want to be on her own either. 'All right, but if you snore, you're out.'

He grinned at her. 'Done. I'll just grab a few things from my room. Can you order me a steak and chips? Medium rare.'

She rolled her eyes at him. 'If this is just so you can order the most expensive meal and charge it to my room, I won't be happy.'

'I'll be two seconds.' The door banged behind him.

She was alone. Her skin prickled and she realized she hadn't checked the room before he'd gone. She got up, leaving the open menu on the bed, and walked towards the tall curtains. She looked behind them, but there was no one there, only her own reflection in the dark glass. She looked on edge; her eyes alert and focused.

She turned to the bathroom. The air con in the room whirred above her. She grabbed the handle and pulled the door open. The small room appeared empty. She pulled the shower curtain back. No one. There was a rap at the door. Her body tightened.

'It's me,' Kowalski called.

She closed her eyes for a second, relief flooding her system. She let him in. He had his suitcase with him. 'You know it's only one night, right?'

'It was just quicker to grab the bag.' He dumped it in the corner and then inspected the minibar. 'I don't know about you, but I could really do with a beer right now.'

'You're paying for half of this, just so you know.' She took the beer he offered her, and he clinked bottles with her.

'Here's to Edward Barratt,' Kowalski said. 'May he rot in hell.'

'Cheers to that.' She took a swig from her bottle.

Chapter 22

'It looks like a copycat to me.' Barratt leafed through the notes. He was surrounded by the redacted copies of the file, which he'd spread out all around him. It looked like he'd been obsessing over it all night. 'Not as good as me, admittedly, but copies never are. Still, I admire his handiwork. Leaving Emma in the police station – inspired, if not a bit obvious. And the note. It's beautiful.'

'Anything new you can offer?' Kowalski asked. 'I mean, something you've come up with yourself, and we've not just fed you.'

'Your boyfriend's jealous,' Edward grinned at Loxton. 'Should he be? Do we have something going on here?' He let his eyes travel down her body. She'd picked a high-neck shirt and trouser suit to shield herself, but his gaze still bothered her. She knew he only did it to rattle her.

'We need anything you can tell us today,' she said. 'This is serious. I can't give you what you want if you don't meet me halfway.'

'Okay, okay.' Barratt put his hands up in surrender. 'Is that for me?'

Loxton nodded. 'You need to stand at the back of your room and face the wall.'

Barratt tutted but his eyes lingered on the bag.

'Back wall,' she said again.

'There's no trust in the world anymore.' He did as he was told.

She shoved the McDonald's breakfast bag through the hatch and slammed it shut, just as Barratt sprinted towards the hatch, his hand whipping towards her, trying to grab her, but she snatched hers back with plenty of time.

'Thank you for this.' He took the bag from the hatch and his eyes gleamed at her. She realized she'd just been very lucky.

'Fucking hell, Barratt. What the fuck?' Kowalski was by her side, pulling her away. Loxton shuddered at her stupidity. She knew better and berated herself for the slip.

Barratt carried his McDonald's back to where he'd been sitting earlier in his nest of paperwork, the incident already forgotten for him. Loxton wouldn't forget so easily, her heart racing at the thought of what he might have done. She glanced at her fingers and then back at Barratt.

'Where's the profiler gone? I liked her.' Barratt asked between mouthfuls of a hash brown. 'There was something about her.'

'She had to get back to London. Sorry to disappoint you,' Kowalski said.

'Tetchy, Mr Policeman. How many girlfriends have you got?' He put his hands up as if to placate Kowalski and then carried on tucking into his breakfast. 'God, this is good. It's been a while since I've eaten anything but prison food. You could have got me something more special than a McDonald's breakfast, though, Alana.' He dripped brown sauce onto the papers scattered around him on the floor. 'Emma raped and murdered, and Sarah and Gabriella missing. They hadn't worked together for two years, their only time together a few golden years on the murder team where they got lucky and caught me. The MO used to kill Emma Robins is very similar to mine, I'll give you that. Even a note with the body talking about war and naming Emma and you.'

Loxton nodded.

He sipped some coffee from a polystyrene cup. 'That does sound like something I'd write if I was in a temper. I stored my bodies in the disused train tunnels. Have you checked there?'

'We're checking. Cadaver and blood dogs are being put though the lines,' Loxton said. 'But there's a lot of work going on in the underground and new lines are being put in. The CCTV is much better too. Someone would have noticed.'

He bit into his egg muffin. 'Delicious. You definitely brought this in, didn't you?'

Loxton nodded.

'Good. If Turner had got his hands on it, he would have put mouse droppings in it for sure. He's an animal. Disgusting how he treats other human beings.'

Loxton tried not to rise to the taunt, but as she watched Barratt, she wasn't sure he was goading her. He meant it.

'We're wasting time here,' Kowalski said to Loxton. 'He doesn't have a clue; he's just fucking with us.'

'Can't use the train tunnels as it's too risky, but he needs to replicate me as much possible,' Edward shifted through the paperwork, ignoring Kowalski. 'Tried the sewers yet?'

'No.' Kowalski said. 'That's quite a jump.'

'It's what I'd do.' Edward shrugged and took another large bite out of his egg muffin. 'Nearest geographically that you can get and aesthetically similar if he's trying to capture the atmosphere of my kills. Dark, cold, dripping tunnels. And it may be how he got Emma Robins's body into the police station.'

'What do you mean?' she asked.

'Big old public buildings like police stations and hospitals have extra-large sewage access points, because they have a lot more use. Hundreds of people using them daily. Blockages can happen. Easier for maintenance work to take place on public service properties; no private residents refusing access. If he's using the sewers, then he might have brought her body up through a sewerage access point.'

'But there was no smell,' Kowalski said.

'And no forensics either?' Barratt asked.

Kowalski shook his head reluctantly.

'He would have cleaned her meticulously at the crime scene. And I mean *meticulously*.'

'He has a point,' Loxton said, trying to ignore Barratt talking about Emma's murder like it was a job to be admired. 'We'll check that out.' Loxton thought of the marks on Emma's body that looked like she'd be bound up with multiple ropes. Maybe they'd been used to lower her into and pull her up from the sewers.

'When do I get my visits reinstated and my letters?' Barratt asked.

'Not until this is finished,' Kowalski said. 'If it's one of your new friends, we don't want you giving them ideas.'

'You could be missing a crucial lead keeping me cooped up here with no one to talk to.' Barratt finished the last piece of muffin and smacked his lips together, satisfied.

'I don't think so,' Kowalski said. Loxton knew he was keen to get away from Barratt. She was too.

'Any other insights?' Loxton asked.

'There's only two women left for him to target, if you're right that he's avenging me. How is Jane?'

'You don't need to worry about that.' Was he bluffing or did he know something?

'*You* do though, Alana. You're on the list.'

'Thank you for reminding me, I'd completely forgotten,' she said.

'I hope he cuts you up nice. I would love to see that. You were always my favourite, you see. Do you think he knows that? Do you think he'll leave you until last? Make you watch all the others get butchered first? Each killing's going to get worse. More depraved, as you'd put it. Just like I did. Until the finale.' He stood up and moved in front of her, the glass the only thing separating them.

'I didn't know I was your favourite,' she said.

'Come, come, Alana, don't be modest. I've never been shy about that. If I were him, I'd leave you until last. You're the dessert. You know you shouldn't, it won't be good for you, but you can't help yourself anyway. That old sweet tooth gets the better of you.'

Kowalski stepped forward and slammed his hand against the glass. Barratt didn't even flinch. Kowalski turned to Loxton. 'Are we done here? We've wasted nearly a whole day on this prick, and all we've achieved so far is giving him a McDonald's breakfast and listened to his malicious bullshit. He doesn't know anything. Let's get out of here and leave him in his cage to rot.'

Loxton was surprised by Kowalski's outburst in front of Barratt. He was losing his cool. She stared into Barratt's eyes. She got the feeling he was holding back.

'Is that it, Edward? Is that all you've got to share? Is DC Kowalski right and you don't know anything?' She waited a moment, not shifting her gaze from his eyes.

'That's all I'm sharing for now. Try the sewers. You won't be disappointed.' He smiled. 'Oh, and, Dominik, you won't be able to save her. Don't beat yourself up about it, okay. It's too late. He's coming for her.'

Kowalski moved towards the hatch and opened it. 'Feeling brave in there? You'd better hope you get to stay in there, because if you ever set foot outside, I'll kill you.'

Loxton grabbed Kowalski's arm, pulling him away from the hatch.

Barratt hadn't moved. 'Easy to taunt a man locked in a glass cage. Not so easy to catch a killer. I'm glad you're afraid, Dominik. You should be.'

'You know who this is, don't you?' Loxton narrowed her eyes at Barratt.

He smirked at her. 'That's why you're my favourite. You always were a clever girl. Who do you think tried to get me out of prison?'

'This is pointless.' Kowalski shook his head. 'Turner was right. He's full of bullshit and fucking psychobabble. He's making it up. DI Meyer said this was a waste of time.'

'You're not going to tell me, are you?' she said to Barratt. 'You're enjoying this too much.'

'I want him to turn you into a shivering, quaking mess, as you watch your friends die and it's just you left. I want you to piss yourself in fear as you cower before the first cut. He's going to slice you up into tiny little pieces for what you've done to me. For what you've done to both of us.' He turned away from her. His power game over. He'd shown the cards he'd wanted to, and now he wasn't playing anymore.

'What do you mean, "both of us"?' she asked. 'Who are you talking about?'

Barratt ignored her, facing the back of his cell.

'Barratt, who the *fuck* is doing this?' she shouted, desperate for him to tell her. 'They're making you look like an amateur.' She tried to goad him into saying something, but he stayed resolutely facing the wall. Their audience with him was at an end. He'd told her just enough to make her believe he knew something. Enough to taunt her.

Loxton and Kowalski sat in the car in the bleak prison car park. There was no other living soul around, and the grey clouds above them seemed to hang lower in the sky than normal.

'Are you all right?' Loxton asked Kowalski.

'I'm fine, he's just something else.' Kowalski's face was rigid with rage and Loxton reminded herself that Kowalski had been Emma's lover and Gabriella's friend. Although he pretended he was okay, he clearly wasn't.

'Sorry, I should have warned you better. I lost it too.' She hated to admit that she'd let Barratt get to her. Emotions never helped anything, and she needed to get a hold of it, because if Winter realized how on edge she was, he'd take her off the case. And then she'd be powerless to do anything.

'Let's get out of here,' Kowalski said, throwing an uneasy glance around the car park. Loxton had never seen him so anxious.

'Best update Winter first,' she said and put her mobile on speakerphone. 'Sir, we didn't get a lot out of Barratt and it could all be rubbish. But he said that whoever tried to break him out of prison was responsible. He suggested the killer would be using the sewers. And he said the killing was revenge for both of us. I don't know what he meant by that. There might have been more than one person involved in the Barratt murders.' She relaxed a little, feeling Barratt's grip fading.

'We'll start letting his mail through and monitoring his responses,' Winter said. 'I'll reinstate his calls, but make sure someone's listening and recording them all. Visiting's a bit trickier. There's a waiting list to see him, and from the checks we've done so far, no one's standing out. But there's still quite a few to get through. Lena's working on it.'

'This one's clever,' Loxton said. 'He won't have left a link that obvious behind.'

'I've got the team going through every correspondence Barratt's ever had while he's been inside, and I'll get them to look at the prison staff too. He's had hundreds of letters since he's been in there. And the guard, Turner, admitted that since he was posted to guard him, he's been binning most of the letters and not letting Barratt see them.'

'It could just be a game Barratt is playing to waste our time,' Kowalski said.

'Maybe, but we can't take that chance,' Winter sounded tired. 'We'll go through the sewer schematics of London, but it's like a city in its own right. We'll start at Camberwell. I think he's right, though, the police station does have one near the outhouse for the bins and it's not covered by CCTV. And there was an access point at the warehouse Sarah disappeared from.'

She thought for a moment. 'When he said "both of us", maybe he meant that he didn't work alone on his murders. Maybe there were two of them? We never thought so, but we could have been wrong. During the investigation he came up as a loner. No family or friends.'

'He has his fan base now,' Kowalski said. 'Do you think he was referring to one of them?'

'Maybe,' she said, although it didn't feel right. Then again, she thought, nothing felt right about this case.

'I'll let Lena know and tell her to really focus on the fan

base, with the hypothesis that it might be a group working together,' Winter said. 'If that is the case, it's going to be hard to identify them. It's rare, but not impossible, to get psychopaths working together, and thanks to the internet it's easier for them to find each other than ever before. And we should review Barratt's associates at the time he was active. Maybe an old friend has decided to get revenge on his behalf. Someone you didn't identify at the time.'

'But why now?' Loxton asked.

'Maybe they were in prison themselves,' Kowalski said. 'Or lying low after the trial. Let's get back to London and focus on people he knew who have only just got out.'

Loxton hated the idea that they'd missed something when they'd been investigating Barratt's murders. That there could have been another person involved, maybe someone she'd spoken to at the time, but she'd missed the signs and Emma's life was the price.

Chapter 23

When Loxton and Kowalski got back to the office, they found Lena with stacks of letters around her. She was sorting them into three piles: high-risk, medium-risk and low-risk. Loxton glanced at the high-risk pile; it was already five case files high.

'Are there really that many dangerous people to go through already?' Kowalski asked.

Lena looked up. 'I'm afraid so. Turns out a lot of people wanting to visit a serial killer aren't as wholesome as you'd think.'

'Good point,' Kowalski said, sitting next to her and absently leafing through the letters.

'I've been going through Barratt's psych reports from Broadmoor Hospital,' Lena said. 'After two years there are already quite a lot. He told his psychiatrist that Krystian Szymański was his main inspiration.'

'What sort of profile are we looking at here for the current killer?' Loxton asked.

'Assuming this is a serial killer?' Lena said. 'At the moment we only have one murder, so it's hard to make a profile from that. This is just a preliminary sketch, but from the nature of the attack on Emma Robins and the control the killer showed afterwards, I'd say he's not an impulsive person. So probably more mature, in his thirties and disgruntled with life. The way the killer stored her body and then managed to deposit it in Camberwell station, avoiding all the CCTV cameras and not leaving any forensics behind, keeping her alive, the brutal rape and strangulation – I'm thinking ex-military. Probably saw significant combat and is suffering from serious PTSD. He's fallen from grace. Maybe works in some sort of on/off manual labour now and lives alone. He's had plenty of space and time to plan this killing and carry it out. He must have stored her somewhere secure and secluded and he was hiding her for a few days without detection. A derelict building would be perfect. Perhaps he's now in construction?'

'Not the sewers like Barratt thought?' Loxton asked.

'Possibly, but Emma's body was clean,' Lena said. 'And it sounds like Barratt is involved in this in some way. He would try to lead us astray. If the killer works in construction or maintenance of some sort, he would know of some abandoned buildings in London. It would explain how he knew to get past Camberwell Police Station's CCTV cameras if he knows building schematics. How to break inside without leaving any trace. Maybe he's even been involved in some work there in the past? Knew the layout? Has there been any new work done?'

'I can find that out about Camberwell,' Kowalski said. 'And I've briefed POLSA search teams about the sewers. They're going to take dogs down, but obviously it's a challenging environment for them, and it's going to take a long time. It's a huge area.'

'I'm betting on the sewers,' Loxton said. 'I don't think Barratt could help himself; he wanted us to know that he's got insider information. His weakness is showing off. Giving us a real lead would confirm his involvement without us being able to do anything about it. As you say, the sewer system is huge.'

'I'll find out if any maintenance has been done at Camberwell recently and brief the POLSA team.' Kowalski stood up. 'You work on the profile with Lena. Let's keep Winter in the loop. We're getting somewhere.'

Loxton nodded, but found herself wondering if they *were* getting anywhere. If she'd pushed Barratt harder somehow, could she have got more out of him? Had she missed an opportunity to help her friends?

Loxton admired Lena's work ethic. They'd been working on the profile for hours, looking at Emma's murder and reviewing the Barratt murders. Trying to see the pattern.

'The more I look at this,' Lena said, 'the more I think Emma's murder is closer to a Szymański killing than a Barratt killing.'

'You mentioned Szymański when we saw Barratt.'

'Yes, he appears to have been Barratt's inspiration, according to the psych reports.' Lena sighed. 'Krystian Szymański was the worst Polish serial killer in modern times. Not many people will say that name out loud out of respect for the victims. And because people are afraid. He caused complete panic when he was active. Targeted female tourists in Poland and women in the tourist industry. Raped and then strangled them to the point that their windpipes were crushed, just like Barratt. Left handwritten notes at the scene taunting investigators. Never any forensics. The body stored somewhere and then placed in an iconic location. In Szymański's case, he left them in popular tourist spots. All women in their twenties, their whole lives ahead of them. People stopped coming to certain parts of Poland where he was operating. Communities struggled without the tourism revenue. He wanted to have maximum impact. Like this killer leaving Emma in a police station. His murders got more vicious as he continued. He started using knives to mutilate the bodies after he'd strangled them to death.'

Loxton closed her eyes for a moment, thinking of her missing friends. 'He sounds awful – and at least he was well named,' Loxton said, finally remembering where she had heard the name before. The cleaner had been shouting '*Szymański*' over and over again when she and Kowalski had found Emma's body.

'What do you mean?' Lena asked.

'Szymański means "terrible" in Polish,' Loxton said, remembering what Kowalski had told her.

Lena shook her head in confusion. 'No, it doesn't. It's just a surname. It has no meaning.'

'Really?'

'Why did you think that?' Lena asked.

'I must have got confused, or perhaps it got lost in translation.' She needed to think. Kowalski had misled her. Why? The cleaner had seen the body and had clearly recognized it as a Szymański killing. And Kowalski hadn't told her.

'Are you all right?' Lena asked.

'I'm just tired, that's all.' It was a lie, of course, but she needed to understand what was going on before she involved anyone else. What was Kowalski playing at? He had probably assumed it was a coincidence. These killers were inspired by similar things – popular culture, films and books even. It was probably nothing more than that.

'Did they catch Szymański?' she asked.

'Yes, we did,' Lena said. 'I was actually on the team that caught him. So was Dominik. It was Dominik who was instrumental. Szymański had alibis for some of the murders, but Dominik wouldn't give up on the idea that he was the suspect. He persuaded the lead investigator to search Szymański's house again after another killing and they found a microscopic piece of the victim's skin in the plug in the shower. Without Dominik's persistence, Szymański might have managed to get away with it for longer. Dominik was always adamant it was him.'

'Dominik?' Loxton was surprised. He'd never mentioned it. Sometimes it felt like he'd always been in the Met.

Lena nodded. 'It was a long time ago. Eight years now. Poland had never seen anything like it, and we were ill prepared. They had to put a task force together. We were new in the job, both desperate for some excitement. We didn't know what we were getting ourselves in for really. It was a nationwide search for the killer. Most officers got involved in one way or another.'

'He's still in prison, right?' Loxton asked.

'No,' Lena said. 'Actually he was murdered in prison a few months back. Another prisoner attacked him. Boiling water to the face and then stabbed in the neck.'

'That's strange timing,' Loxton said, and glanced at Lena, who looked pale. 'You look terrible. Are you all right?'

'It's just thinking about Szymański makes me feel ill,' Lena said. 'It brings it all back.'

'When did you last eat?' Loxton asked.

'Not since this morning. I'll go grab myself something from the shops. And some fresh air will help.'

'No problem,' Loxton said. She knew how Lena felt. She had the same response with Barratt; it could be physical at times.

Loxton picked up her mobile to give Kowalski a call. She wanted to ask him about why he'd told her Szymański meant 'terrible' now that she was on her own. But just as she was about to dial, Anson strolled into the office and sat on the chair next to her, putting his feet on her desk.

'Been looking for you,' he said.

'Have you never heard of a mobile phone?' Loxton held hers up for him to see.

Anson tilted his head at her in surprise. 'Have you never heard of a tapped phone? I don't trust them.'

'Well, perhaps I shouldn't. It seems you always know where I am anyway.'

Anson smiled at her, but there was no warmth in it. 'I have some bad news. I've tried all my sources and some that aren't officially sources.' He regarded his scuffed knuckles for a moment. 'They weren't all happy to see me. But none of that matters. Not a single one has any idea what went down in that warehouse or where Sarah's gone. They knew a girl had gone missing, that the Albanians weren't happy that she'd been taken, but none of them has any idea who took her.'

Loxton frowned. Usually sources would have something, even if it was just rumours. 'Not organized crime then,' she said.

He shook his head. 'It's like she vanished into thin air. The CCTV shows her going into the warehouse. She had communication with us from inside. And then she went silent. And then we stormed the place. There's no evidence of her leaving.'

'Maybe the Albanians realized she was undercover and carried her out.' Loxton didn't want to say 'in pieces', but she could see Anson had grasped her meaning from the look on his face.

'No.' Anson shook his head fiercely. 'They have no idea. Trust me. I've been monitoring them. Not one of them knows anything. This isn't to do with the organized crime world. This is something else.' He trailed off and she saw dread in his eyes. It was out of his area of expertise. He didn't know how to control it. Didn't know what to do. She knew how he felt.

'Barratt mentioned the sewers and there's an access point in the courtyard of the warehouse. We're sending POLSA through them. And we're looking into Barratt's fan base. We'll find out who's doing this. We'll stop them.'

Anson nodded roughly. 'Yes. Yes, we will.' He stood up. 'That's me done here tonight. I know a few more people I might try. I'll push the Barratt angle. Someone must know something. I'm not going to stop looking for her.'

'Me neither. Keep in touch.'

He nodded at her and headed out of the CID office. As he reached the door he turned around and caught her eye. 'Take care of yourself.'

'I will,' she said, but it felt like someone had walked on her grave. She usually told other people to take care, not the other way around.

Chapter 24

Loxton needed to talk to Kowalski about Szymański, but she couldn't find him anywhere in the police station and he wasn't answering his mobile. He'd probably gone over to McDonald's, knowing him.

She returned to the office and found Lena was back, poring over the reports of potential suspects that she'd compiled. 'He's got to be here somewhere,' Lena said.

The CID office phone rang and Loxton answered it.

'This is DI Whitcombe, night duty inspector.'

'Evening, sir. DC Loxton here, how can I help?'

'I'm trying to get hold of a DC Kowalski. He's actually just accessed his and your HR personal files on his laptop and it looks like he checked your home addresses. DCs normally don't have authority to do that, so I need to speak to him. Do you know why he's done that?'

Loxton's chest tightened. 'I've no idea, but are you sure? I've just looked for him and he's not in the building.' Loxton thought of Anson, who had left five minutes earlier, then dismissed the idea. He didn't need to check their personal records; somehow he'd already discovered where she lived.

'The alarm that's come through says the access was from the Walworth station secure Wi-Fi from the laptop registered to him. Someone could have hacked the system remotely or done it from his laptop. He's not answering his mobile. Get him to call me back when you get hold of him and his laptop. I'll call digital security now.' He hung up on her.

'Shit,' Loxton said, and then fear gripped her. 'Have you seen Dominik?'

Lena shook her head. 'Is he okay?'

Loxton checked Kowalski's desk and saw his laptop. She pressed a button on the laptop and, sure enough, Kowalski's locked screen came up.

'Someone's hacked into Dominik's laptop. I left the office empty for five minutes when I was looking for him. How long have you been back?'

'Just a couple of minutes before you walked in. I didn't see anyone on my way back into the building.'

'Shit, where the hell is he?' Someone else could be in the building and have accessed the files. She needed to know Kowalski was okay.

She ran up to the canteen, Lena following her. The door was open and she could hear someone inside. The smell of fries hit her, and Kowalski turned to look at her as she rushed in. He frowned when he saw her and Lena's faces.

'What's happened?' He stood up, looking around in alarm.

'Someone in this building has just accessed yours and my personal records,' Loxton said. 'They hacked into the system using your laptop and looked up our home addresses.'

'What the fuck?' Kowalski threw a furtive glance into the dark corners of the canteen. 'How have they done that? I left my laptop in the main office.'

'The office was empty for a few minutes,' Loxton said. 'It's meant to be impossible to hack into the HR system anyway.'

'Are they still in the building?' Kowalski asked.

Lena shook her head. 'We don't know.'

'Let's check the CCTV,' Loxton said. It was kept in a small office behind reception and they headed down the stairs together, all of them straining their ears for any sound of an intruder nearby.

Lena checked the security system. She frowned in confusion. 'The only people to have swiped in this evening are us and a DS Anson.'

'I saw Anson,' Loxton said. 'Did he swipe out?'

'Yeah, about seven minutes ago,' Lena said checking her watch. 'Looks like he didn't come back in.'

Kowalski had logged onto the CCTV and scrolled through the screens covering the entrances and car park, rewinding at speed. Nothing except the three of them and Anson. There was no CCTV in the main office or any of the other offices. If they'd managed to get in without getting picked up, they could be moving freely through the building without being detected.

'Could someone have gained access in the day and hidden themselves until the evening?' Lena asked.

'It's possible,' Loxton admitted. 'This place is big enough to hide a football team in it if you wanted to.'

'Or you could scale the wall around the car park at a CCTV blind spot and climb through an open window,' Kowalski said. 'But you'd have to know the station well to do that.'

Security was always poor in police stations. People were expected to try to break *out* of custody, not try to gain unauthorized access. There was nothing of real value for anyone to steal, only out-of-date computer equipment and tired-looking office furniture. Not a burglar's idea of heaven. And it was normally filled with police officers, although in recent years it was becoming more like a ghost ship what with all the cuts to staffing levels.

'Call it in, Lena,' Kowalski said. 'They're probably well gone, if they were ever here, and this isn't some online cyber hack, but we'll search the building just in case the bastard is still hiding somewhere. Loxton and I will start at the bottom floor in the middle and work our way down the corridors. When we hit the stairwells, we'll go up to the next floor and so on. Hopefully we'll force them onto the top floor, and they'll be stuck. Lena, I want you to watch the live CCTV feed, keep us updated if you see any movement. And lock the door behind you when we leave.'

'I will,' Lena said.

'The stairwells won't be covered when we're going down the corridors,' Loxton said. 'They might get past us.'

'It's the best we can do with the three of us, and the uniform will be on their way. They'll stop them at the outer perimeter,' Kowalski said.

Loxton sighed. She didn't like this.

'Once I call this in, this place will be crawling with police officers in less than two minutes,' Lena said, trying to reassure her, but Loxton knew just how long two minutes could be.

'Come on, Alana.' Kowalski was on his feet moving to the stairwell.

Lena gave Loxton a worried glance.

'We'll be fine, just make sure you lock this door.' Loxton followed Kowalski into the corridor.

Kowalski pushed the double doors open and they climbed the deserted stairs. It was eerily quiet, the only noise their footsteps and her own ragged breathing. She pulled out her baton and flicked it open. The cold metal gave her comfort. Kowalski drew his baton too.

She craned her neck so she could look up the entire stairwell, but she didn't see anyone. At the first floor she pushed open the doors as quietly as she could and checked each room on the left while Kowalski searched the offices on the right.

The robbery and burglary office normally held twenty officers and she systematically checked under the bank of desks, but there was no one there.

As she came out of the office, she heard the noise of a door closing quietly ahead of her and her heart rate sped up. The lights there were flickering on and she tried not to panic. She crept forward towards the noise, baton raised high.

The door in front of her opened a creak and she stopped as a large figure came out of the doorway.

'*Gówno*!' Kowalski said and stumbled backwards. 'God, you're quiet.'

'Sorry, I thought . . .' She lowered her baton, relieved that it was him. 'Let's try the next floor.'

At the end of the corridor she gently pushed open the double doors and Kowalski carefully closed them behind him. They waited and listened at the stairs but there was nothing. She looked down the stairwell and above her, straining her ears for the tiniest sound, but she was met with silence. If the person had ever been here, they'd either already left the building or had gone to ground, hiding in one of the offices upstairs.

On the second floor they repeated the same routine, finding no one in the canteen or offices. They climbed the final stairwell.

The top floor had smaller offices, not wide-open spaces

like the first and second floors. She rushed through her side, sure the perpetrator would be hiding behind a door waiting to attack her, but again there was no one. She closed her eyes for a brief second, relieved. She'd been convinced someone was still in the station.

Her heart stopped as a crash sounded behind her, down the corridor, and then she rushed towards the noise. She saw an upturned table in one of the offices Kowalski had searched and ran to the stairwell. Kowalski was clattering down it two steps at a time. She chased after him, her lungs bursting with the effort of trying to catch up. He smashed through the fire exit and out into the walled car park, Loxton a few seconds behind him.

'Which way?' she shouted as she caught up.

'I'll go left, you go right,' Kowalski shouted back. Before she could speak, he rushed to the car park's security door, pushing it open and running left. She ran out of the station car park and turned the other way, sprinting down the side street that led her onto the main road. Even past midnight the high street wasn't deserted. The few people walking along the pavements took no notice of her. She ran towards a nearby homeless person, slumped underneath a cash machine.

'Ted, has anyone come this way in the last few seconds?'

'Nah, love.' He shook his head. 'No one.'

'Are you sure?' Her voice was urgent and Ted sat up straighter. 'This is important.'

'I promise, love. I wouldn't lie to you, you're one of the nice ones.' His rheumy eyes locked onto hers.

She nodded. 'Thanks, Ted.'

She turned and ran back the way she'd come, pulling out her radio and calling up on the main Southwark channel. 'Anything, Kowalski?' she asked.

Kowalski's heavy breathing was the only response and she felt her stomach tighten in concern.

'No one,' he managed to reply. 'All units, they've left the police station. Search the nearby roads.'

'Any description?' A police operator asked.

'Dark clothing, athletic build, male. That's all I've got.' The disappointment in Kowalski's voice was palpable.

Loxton watched a police car sail past her with its headlights off. She met up with Kowalski outside the rear entrance. He shook his head at her, clearly annoyed with himself. 'They gave me the slip. You?'

'Ted says he didn't see anyone and I believe him. I didn't see them either so I can't help with a description.'

'They bolted from one of the offices. Nearly knocked me over with a table. They flew down the stairs and out the fire exit. They were so fast. It's like they knew the layout of the building. Maybe Lena's right; it must be someone who's got knowledge of police stations. I'll get forensics to have a look at the fire exit in case there are any prints on it.' They both knew the chances of getting anything off a door that was used by hundreds of people a week was beyond remote, but it was worth a try.

'Let's re-check the CCTV.' She shivered as she checked left and right before swiping her warrant card to get back into the car park, which was already being searched by uniform, officers shining torches under each car systematically.

Someone had managed to break into the police station. They'd looked at her and Kowalski's personal records. The thought made her feel sick with anger.

Lena was rewinding the CCTV footage as they came into the office.

'Are they on it?' Loxton asked.

Lena nodded, a grim expression on her face that Loxton couldn't read. 'Just when he runs out of the fire exit, we get an image of his back. It won't help with identification.'

'Play it anyway,' Kowalski said.

Lena hit play but she was staring at Kowalski.

Loxton watched the footage. A dark figure shot out of the fire exit, running full pelt. Kowalski right behind them, so close he could reach out and grab them, but he stumbled and lost ground. The suspect ran to the left, jumping onto a car bonnet and launching himself over the 6ft wall.

'How the hell?' Loxton gasped.

On the screen, Kowalski rushed to the back door and was out of it, Loxton right behind him.

'Why didn't you tell me he'd gone left?' Loxton asked.

'I wanted to cover both ways and there was no time to explain,' Kowalski said. 'He could have hidden behind a car until I'd run past him and then doubled back and gone right. I wanted to make sure both routes were covered.'

'You should have caught him,' Lena said, her voice irritated.

'I know I fucked up, Lena,' Kowalski said. 'You don't need to tell me.' He turned away from them and walked out of the office. Loxton wanted to go after him, but she decided to let him go.

Chapter 25

The next morning Loxton woke feeling exhausted, having struggled to sleep in the unfamiliar hotel bed and on edge after the break-in at the station. It felt strange not having been home for the last few days and knowing that she wouldn't be back for some time to come.

It was early, but she called Kowalski anyway. She needed to speak to him in private and she knew the office would be too busy. 'Dominik, how are you doing?'

'I didn't sleep too good. What about you?'

'Not great either. Look, I wanted to ask you something. When we went to the crime scene at Camberwell, the cleaner was shouting "Szymański". You told me that it meant "terrible" in Polish. But it's not a word. She was referring to Krystian Szymański.'

He sighed. 'If it had been an American cleaner, they would have been shouting "Bundy". Szymański's dead. I took the cleaner's statement; she didn't see anything. She was just hysterical.'

'No, she wasn't,' Loxton said. 'She was shouting "Szymański" over and over again because the MO of the killing was exactly the same as a Szymański killing. Which is why I was so convinced it was a Barratt killing, because he was inspired by Szymański.'

'Yes, it looked like a Szymański killing, but we're in England and Szymański died recently.' Kowalski struggled to keep the exasperation out of his voice. 'Plenty of serial killers rape and then strangle their victims to death. Like you say, Barratt does. The cleaner isn't an expert on murder scenes. Any violent thing she sees, it's Szymański. That's what fear will do to you. Look, I worked on the Szymański case. I didn't want to talk about it. Bad memories. I thought he was irrelevant. I thought I'd left him in Poland.'

'Well, you didn't. His name keeps coming up and I don't like it.'

'I'm sorry, I should have told you. I just couldn't accept Szymański had followed me here. He's the reason I left Poland.'

She'd never heard Kowalski's voice so haunted. 'What happened?'

'I was convinced there were two killers, that Szymański had an accomplice and that's how he'd managed to have some solid alibis for some of the later murders. He denied it, of course, but some of the evidence never quite fit for me. I thought it might be someone in the police, perhaps from the forensic team. The bosses wouldn't listen to me; they had their killer, but I couldn't let it go. They made things difficult for me. I was ruining their careers, you see. We'd caught the infamous killer, reassured the Polish people and the tourists that it was over, but I was spoiling their happy ending. I couldn't progress. In the end I had to leave Poland. I'd upset so many senior officers it didn't matter where I tried to go. London seemed like the best option.'

'So, possibly Szymański's partner is still out there.' She couldn't keep the annoyance out of her voice.

'It's been eight years and nothing. I was wrong.' But Kowalski sounded unsure.

'Szymański's only been dead a few months. Maybe that's what started this?' She wished he'd told her this earlier.

'*Gówno*,' Kowalski whispered.

She sighed. Taking it out on him wasn't helping. 'Look, I'll see you at work. Chances are it's a coincidence, but it's good to know about it.' She hung up. She'd thought she and Kowalski were a team, but it turned out he was keeping things back from her. Already distancing himself, knowing that he would be leaving Southwark.

She headed into Walworth station, nervous that Winter might take her off the case. Three detectives from her old team had been targeted and now her personal records had been accessed. But, then, so had Kowalski's. It didn't make sense. Could it be a journalist, paying police staff to try to find out about the investigators? The story was dominating the news feeds and she could imagine that they would stoop to such levels.

The office was busy. Lena was already in and Loxton could see she was excited about something from the way she was pacing, as if to sit still would halt the discovery. Kowalski walked in carrying three coffees in a holder and handed them out to her and Lena.

'Alana, I think we've got a possible.' Lena stabbed her finger at one of the files stacked around her. 'This guy stands out a mile from Barratt's fan base who tried to visit him. Kevin Harding. Complete loner. Obsessed with serial killers and then Edward Barratt becomes his favourite.'

'Go on,' Loxton said, picking up the file.

'Harding writes to Barratt the most frequently by far, almost every week, although we know that most of the letters never got through. The ones I've managed to get

hold of show that Harding was an avid admirer. He had
to resign from his last job four months ago as a hospital
cleaner for harassing female patients and following a
female doctor home twice. He recently applied to be a
cleaner at Broadmoor Hospital, but after a trial period
they turned him down; his behaviour was odd and he
was paying too much attention to security. That was a
few days after Barratt's escape. Before all that, he used to
have a contract as a cleaner for police stations. He used
to cover any of the cleaners who were sick, so he's had
access to most of the stations in south London over the
years. Probably Walworth and Camberwell. He's very
active in the Red Pill community on Reddit and even
some of the men on there have blocked him for having too
extreme views.'

'Red Pill community?' Loxton asked, unfamiliar
with the term.

'It's a place online where men go to express their views
of women and how feminism has gotten out of hand.
They discuss, and I quote, *"sexual strategy in a culture
increasingly lacking a positive identity for men"*. It's called
Red Pill after *The Matrix*. If you take the red pill with
them, you discover their terrifying reality that women are
subjugating men. There's a subset that goes even further,
believing women are biologically designed to be raped.'

'And your guy was blocked by some of these members
for being too extreme?' Loxton tried to contain her shock.

'Harding posted his top five pornographic snuff videos
of women and offered to share them with other members
if they messaged him privately.'

'How has he not been arrested?' Loxton asked.

'No one's reporting him. And no one's monitoring
the site. Even if they did, he's tried to be clever. Though

obviously not clever enough to stop *this* silly female from finding him.' Lena smiled. 'He's anonymous on the website and he's used the darknet and TOR, but he's not jumped enough IP addresses, so in reality he was quite easy to find.'

Loxton threw Kowalski an appreciative glance and he nodded back. 'Lena likes to study. She did a computer forensic course back in Poland. It's not fair, but she is cleverer than me. Proves those Red Pill Neanderthals wrong.'

Lena shrugged. 'I just liked learning while you liked partying, Dominik. And I worked in the forensic crime unit in Poland for a time and that was all about tracking criminals through the darknet.'

'We need to bring this Kevin Harding in,' Loxton said, desperately hoping Winter would let her remain part of the 'we'.

'He's currently unemployed after Broadmoor let him go and appears to have a lot of time on his hands,' Lena said. 'I've got his address from the Job Centre. He hasn't got a criminal record so we haven't got much on him. This is his online picture.' The image was of an athletic man wearing camouflage trousers and a green T-shirt. It looked as if the photo had been taken in an army barracks. Kowalski paused to take a closer look.

'Was he ever in the military?' Kowalski asked.

Lena shook her head. 'I've requested that information, but it's not come back yet.'

'Probably best if all three of us go,' Kowalski said.

Loxton didn't disagree and they all put on their covert stab vests and utility belts.

'Wait a second,' Winter said, coming out of his office. 'Kowalski and Loxton, you know I need to speak to you about last night's break-in.'

'Sir, we have a possible suspect,' Loxton said.

'I understand that, but, Loxton, this is getting too close for comfort.'

'I've been staying in a hotel since Friday under a false name,' Loxton said.

'That's good.' Winter nodded his approval. 'Kowalski, you should do the same. Put it through the Met expenses, both of you. And stay at the same hotel so you can go back together. I don't want Loxton out on her own.'

'No problem, sir,' Kowalski said. 'And we'll use anti-surveillance techniques to make sure we're not being followed.'

'Good. Forensics aren't hopeful that we'll get anything off Kowalski's laptop to identify the intruder. Let's face it, he was probably wearing gloves. The team are still trying to find Jane Edison and her family to place them into protection, but the Edisons are proving difficult to find. They've not turned on their mobiles or used their bank cards. No one seems to know where they've gone. Though if *we're* struggling, then anyone who means them harm is probably struggling too.'

'I told her to go to ground.' Loxton shook her head in frustration at the mistake.

'We'll find her, don't worry about that. And I want you to take a couple of murder detectives with you to arrest Harding to be safe.'

Loxton nodded, unable to argue with that. At least he was letting her go to Harding's arrest and carry on with the case. For now.

Kowalski banged on the flimsy door of Kevin Harding's flat while Loxton stayed back with Lena and the two murder detectives. Kowalski had been knocking for a couple of minutes, but there'd been no answer.

'Mr Harding, we're not going away,' Lena said through the letterbox. 'Open the door. We know you're in there.'

Loxton had heard him walk up to the door, probably to take a peek at them through his spyhole. She and the others had stood to the side, so he'd only seen Lena waiting outside, but still he was hesitant.

'We just want to talk to you,' Lena said in a friendly voice.

'I don't want to speak to you,' he said.

'Kevin, we have a warrant,' Lena said, changing tact. 'You need to let us in or we'll break down this door.'

Loxton heard him come to the door, pause for a moment, and then the welcome click of the Chubb lock being undone.

The group braced themselves for Harding to come out fighting, but he was eerily calm as he opened the door. He was not what she had been expecting. He was physically strong, but she also saw he was controlled and measured in every gesture that he made. He appraised them all in turn, as if sizing up his chances against each one of them. Perhaps he was ex-military, but if he was, how had he ended up as a cleaner?

'We're going to need to come in and do a search,' Kowalski said, stepping in front of Loxton and Lena. Kowalski blocked Loxton's view of Harding. She knew he was only trying to protect her, but it annoyed her all the same. She felt like she was being pushed out of the investigation.

Harding was startled when he saw Kowalski. 'What for?' he asked.

'We'll explain inside.' Kowalski moved forward, forcing Harding to step back.

'Fine.' Harding walked back into the shadows of his flat. They all filtered into the living room. Harding kept

eyeing Kowalski suspiciously. It was normal for a suspect to take a dislike to a particular officer, to find a
home for their agitation, but Harding seemed fixated on
Kowalski. Loxton glanced between them. 'Don't worry,
Mr Harding,' she said. 'He's with us. I'm DC Loxton, this
is DC Trawinska, DC Parry, DC Fletcher and he's DC
Kowalski.'

'I don't know why you've brought the muscle,' he complained. 'I'm not going to *do* anything. There doesn't need
to be five of you. What's all this about anyway?' He stayed
standing, his eyes moving between them all.

'Have you got any ID to confirm you are Kevin
Harding?' she asked.

He went to a side table and pulled out his driving licence
from a wallet. She checked the picture and jotted down
the licence number.

'Did you used to work at King's College Hospital as a
cleaner?' she asked.

Harding looked irritated suddenly, but also slightly
relieved. 'Yes, but the police have already talked to me
about that. I haven't gone back or spoken to her since I
got the first warning. It was a misunderstanding. She made
signals and then went weird on me. I left soon after that.'

'Just don't contact her, Mr Harding,' Loxton said.
'That's all that matters now.' It was good that he was put
at ease, irritated by what he thought was a police bureau-
cracy oversight, that they were repeating what had already
been done. He might be off his guard slightly.

She scanned the room. It was immaculate. His shoes
stored carefully on a shoe rack near the front door.
Everything was at right angles. There was no clutter. But
what piqued her interest was his book collection. The
shelves were neatly lined with books on serial killers. A

few were on Edward Barratt. Another name also jumped out at her: Krystian Szymański. She felt her heart beating harder in her chest.

'You're into your serial killers.' She kept her voice steady as she nodded at his collection.

He shrugged and looked at her carefully. 'I like psychology and I find them fascinating. I did a course on forensic criminality through the Open University.'

'Is that why you've been writing to Edward Barratt in prison?'

For a moment Harding looked nervous, but he had the intelligence to try to hide it. He shrugged at her. 'He's never written back. I was hoping he would answer a few questions for an essay I was writing for my course, but he never did. It was a bit naïve of me, really.'

'Tell me about your fascination with Barratt.' Lena stepped closer to Harding. 'Why him?'

'It was just for one of the modules.' Harding shrugged. 'I would have preferred to do it on Szymański, but he was murdered in prison a few months ago, and he lived and worked in Poland. I found Barratt through researching Szymański online. Barratt was inspired by Szymański. It's like a collaboration; when one falls, another takes up the baton.'

'But now Barratt's in prison, there's no one to take up the baton anymore, is there?' Lena said.

Harding tried to keep his features neutral, but Loxton saw the fire in his eyes for a brief moment. 'There'll always be someone to take up the baton. The war's never over.'

'So who do you think will take on the baton next?' Lena asked. 'You?'

'I don't mean literally.' He smiled at her. 'Just figuratively. There's always another serial killer. It's just a matter

of time. You people will always have a job, don't worry.
Are you going now?'

Something about Harding's dead blue eyes sent a cold
shiver through Loxton.

'We need to do a search to see if you were involved in
trying to break Barratt out of prison recently.' Loxton pro-
duced the Magistrate's search warrant that they'd obtained
on the way to his flat. 'You were a cleaner on a temporary
basis at the time. The court's given us permission.'

'I only got that job to help with my course. I wasn't
involved in any breakout attempt.' Harding snatched the
copy out of Loxton's hand. He studied it and then looked
back up at her, a scowl on his face. 'You lot make some
real jumps of the imagination, don't you? Do what you
like, you won't find anything.' He sat down heavily on
the sofa and Loxton was surprised. She'd expected more
of a fight.

'I need to search that first before we can just let you sit
there.' Lena moved towards Harding, who looked worried
for a moment, but he moved out of her way.

Suspects often tried to hide things when a search began
and Loxton wondered if Harding had left something concealed in the sofa. Loxton caught Lena's eye, who nodded
back and started a thorough search of it. Kowalski stepped
forward to help her and after five minutes they finished,
having found nothing. Lena motioned for Harding to
take a seat.

Harding shook his head, sitting back down. 'You won't
find anything.' But as they searched the living room, his
eyes followed them, watching their every move.

Lena came in from the kitchen. 'Mr Harding, why do
you need five mobiles?' Lena held up an evidence bag with
the phones inside.

'I just never get around to throwing them away when I get an upgrade. I should really.' He shrugged.

Kowalski came out of the kitchen and marched over to Harding. Loxton could tell by Kowalski's strained movements that he was angry. 'What's this, then?' Kowalski held up a piece of paper.

Loxton moved closer. The sheet had Kowalski's and Loxton's home addresses scrawled on it.

'What is it?' Harding glanced at Kowalski and Loxton, panic spreading across his face. 'I've never seen that before.'

'It was on top of your kitchen cupboards, tucked away at the back,' Kowalski said. 'If it's not yours, how did it get there?'

'I don't know.' Harding shook his head. 'I used to clean Walworth Police Station, but that was a few years back. Maybe it's some old paperwork from back then. Or maybe you put it there?' He pointed a finger at Kowalski. It was a good act, but Loxton had seen it all before. Suspects often cried police corruption when they were desperate.

'Kevin, you're under arrest for unauthorized access of a police computer under the Computer Misuse Act 1990 and burglary,' Kowalski said, giving him his rights.

Loxton glanced at Harding. He'd broken into Walworth and taken their information. What had he been planning to do with it? Loxton saw Harding in a new light, and she felt her chest tighten in concern as she took in his large frame and cold eyes. She shouldn't have come here. She should have stayed away. He could do some serious damage.

They didn't find anything else incriminating, but they took his laptop and phones anyway. Winter authorized a forensic team to check the flat, ordering forensic officers to use luminol to look for any traces of blood and to search for any evidence that any of the missing detectives had been in the flat.

The police activity arose the neighbours' interest, but none of them seemed to want to back up Harding, eyeing him suspiciously. Usually when someone was arrested from their home a neighbour would complain to the police or ask what was happening, but they stayed back, watching Harding warily in silence as he was taken away.

Chapter 26

The print-outs from Harding's laptop so far did not make for good reading. He was in contact with a man calling himself 'Szymański's Avenger' on social media. Their conversations were disturbing, centring around Szymański's Avenger's mission for the perfect kill.

The conversation cited times of war as step-ups in mankind's progression, naming the Cold War as the reason that humans made it to space. They both believed that through adversity man relied on his true nature and pushed the boundaries of what was possible to new levels. Survival of the fittest, nature's way, had been hampered by civilization.

Szymański's Avenger had praised Edward Barratt for continuing Szymański's original work and fantasized about breaking Barratt out of prison. Harding had been keen to assist and had successfully applied to start cleaning at Broadmoor Hospital. But no one could prove he'd been involved.

DCI Winter, DI Meyer and Lena were watching Harding's interview from the observation room so they could get the measure of him. Harding had opted for a solicitor, who occasionally mumbled that George Orwell's thought police did not exist yet in English law, and that it wasn't a crime to have peculiar opinions, even if they were rather distasteful.

Loxton tried to probe Harding for more information on Szymański's Avenger, but it was hard to get him to talk. He was agitated, his eyes flicking to the door and back to Kowalski.

'Who is Szymański's Avenger?' she asked again.

'I don't know his real name,' Harding said. 'We're just friends online. It's just chat. We're allowed to talk. It's freedom of expression; it's not illegal.' He glanced at his lawyer, who nodded back at him encouragingly like a proud coach.

'You've never spoken offline with this person?' Loxton asked.

'Only ever on the online forums.'

'We've got some of those chats.' She scanned the print-outs until she found the page which reminded her of the note in Emma's hand. 'What does "*the war's started*" mean?'

Harding looked surprised. 'How did you get them?'

'We can get on the darkweb too,' she said.

Harding sighed. 'He just told me that the war's started again. That one day I'll be called on to act.' A flicker of pride flashed across Harding's face that he tried to hide, and his solicitor looked concerned at the turn of the conversation.

'What war?' she asked. Harding seemed to know something, although he was skirting around it, and she tried to control her impatience.

'The war for men's independence.' Harding's voice got impatient. 'We've been cowed for too long, forced to adhere to liberals' pathetic ideologies. We shouldn't be ashamed of our masculinity. We're physically and mentally stronger than women, yet we're forced to step back and let them go first? That's not equality. That's slowing our species' progression. It's no wonder mental health issues are on the rise in men.'

'You're fighting that war on your own there,' Kowalski said. 'Most of us men live in the twenty-first century.'

'You're brainwashed,' Harding mumbled, but then went quiet. He still seemed wary of Kowalski, which struck Loxton as strange, as Harding was physically as big as Dominik. What did he have to be nervous of?

'Harding, you're not here to give us a lecture on your prehistoric ideology,' Loxton said. 'You're here to tell us what you know about Szymański's Avenger and breaking into Walworth Police Station.' She failed to keep the annoyance out of her voice. She needed to stop him waffling his bullshit and get him to answer their questions.

'I don't know anything.' Harding sounded less sure of himself now.

'Was it Szymański's Avenger that asked you to get our personal details?' Kowalski asked.

Harding flicked his gaze to his hands for a second. Fidgeted nervously. If Loxton wasn't too far off, Harding was scared of Szymański's Avenger. 'No,' he said reluctantly. 'No, that was all me.'

'Are you now saying that you *did* break into Walworth station?' Kowalski asked. Harding wouldn't meet Kowalski's eye; he seemed to be closing down to being questioned.

'Yes, it was me,' Harding said, his voice quieter, as he clearly realized the implications of admitting what he'd done.

'What were you going to do with our details?' Kowalski asked, barely able to keep the anger out of his voice.

'I don't know.' Harding shrugged. 'I just wanted to know more about you both. That's all. Loxton investigated Barratt and you investigated Szymański back in the day. You interested me, on a purely theoretical level. You're the people who caught them.'

Kowalski leaned nearer to Harding and glared at him. 'Kevin, that shit isn't going to work on us. What were you going to do with our details?'

Loxton studied Harding's face. He looked anxious, like he was being pushed into a corner he didn't want to be in.

He shrugged. 'I just wanted to see if I could break in and get your details. That's all. It was kind of a challenge. Like an Ironman or something. It was stupid, I see that now.'

'The court isn't going to believe that and neither do we,' Kowalski said. 'I think Szymański's Avenger wanted those details. Did you send them to him? We'll check your laptop.'

Harding met Kowalski's gaze but sweat beaded his forehead. 'It was just a game. I didn't know any policewomen had gone missing for real when I did it. I was just showing off to him, proving what I was capable of. We were just messing around. The police officers going missing have got nothing to do with us.'

'You should answer "No Comment" from now on,' the solicitor said, alarmed. The interview was taking an unexpected turn.

'What do you mean, "you didn't know any policewomen had gone missing for real"?' Loxton leaned closer to Harding. 'Is that something you and Szymański's Avenger discussed, making them go missing? Again, there's no point in lying; we'll see on your chat history on your computer.'

'Again, I advise you to go "No Comment",' the solicitor said.

Harding's shoulders dropped and he closed his eyes briefly. 'You're going to see it anyway. We were just messing around. Joking about what we'd do if we caught us a couple of girl coppers. I wasn't going to do it. Szymański's Avenger started the conversation, but it was just a fantasy, just locker-room chat. It wasn't real. We both knew that.'

The solicitor looked away from his client, a disgusted look on his face. He rearranged his features into concern and turned back to Harding. 'You need to answer "No Comment" from now on.'

'What did you say you'd do with the officers?' Loxton asked.

'I don't know.' Harding looked uncomfortable. 'Keep them alive for a few days, you know. Do what we wanted. Then kill them. But it wasn't real. At least for me it wasn't.' He swallowed nervously, watching the door again, as if he expected someone to burst through it and attack him.

'Where were you going to keep them?' Loxton asked.

Harding shrugged. 'I don't know. That's the tricky bit. Barratt kept his victims in the London underground railway tunnels. But with all the work going on now, that would be impossible. I used to work in the sewers, straight after the army. I joked that we'd keep them there, like the shits they were. But you wouldn't be able to do it. There's always work going on there. We were just messing around. If you look on the internet, there's loads of people talking shit. It doesn't mean anything, otherwise they'd all be getting arrested, right?'

Loxton hated to admit it, but without something more, he was right. It was all just internet chat and the behaviour of someone obsessed with serial killers and the officers who locked them up. Unless the technicians could find anything linking Harding to Emma, Sarah or Gabriella, or anything came up in his flat, it was looking likely that he'd only get charged with the minor burglary and misuse of a computer.

'Before, when we were searching your flat, you denied ever seeing the page with our addresses on,' Loxton said. 'You accused DC Kowalski here of planting it, but now you seem quite happy to accept it was you. Why is that?' Loxton tilted her head at Harding. Sometimes, when a suspect decided to admit to a crime so readily, it was because they were trying to hide something bigger.

Harding shrugged again. His voice was quieter than it had been when he said, 'I panicked in the flat, but there's no point in lying. You'll see it on the internet chat. I was only messing around by breaking into the police station, seeing if I still had it in me. I was in the army. SAS. I turned it into a mission. When you've been in the military, sometimes the lines of what's normal get blurred. It didn't seem like a big deal. Just a bit of a game to show Szymański's Avenger that I was who I said I was.'

'Come on,' Kowalski said. 'That's ridiculous. Nothing's come back on you yet. If you were in the army, what's your warrant number?'

'W524378,' Harding recited immediately. 'I was in the army. SAS intelligence. You'll find out soon enough. I got laid off a couple of years ago.'

'Another misunderstanding, like at the hospital?' Loxton asked.

'Yeah, another misunderstanding.' Harding folded his arms. 'That's all I can tell you. That's all there is to it. It's got nothing to do with these women going missing. I'm sorry that they have.'

'What were you doing on Saturday through to Monday night?' Loxton asked.

Harding closed his eyes briefly, realizing the trouble he was in. 'I didn't do much really. I was just in my flat watching TV. And I went online a lot. You can check my internet history, right? And my mobile's location. I'm unemployed at the moment. I've got no money. I don't do much but play *Call of Duty* and hang out on online forums.'

'Can you give us your passwords to your laptop and mobile?' she asked. 'To help us confirm your alibi that you were inside online?'

Harding looked nervous. 'I don't remember them.'

Loxton shook her head at him. 'That's not going to help your case.'

The solicitor glanced at Harding's face and saw the concern in his eyes. 'If you can't remember, you can't remember,' the solicitor said. 'You don't have to give them over.'

'What about last Wednesday evening? Can you remember whether you were anywhere near Camberwell Police Station?'

'Why would I go there? You can check the CCTV cameras; you won't see me there. I was nowhere near.'

They *hadn't* seen anyone there, that was the problem, and Harding's confidence made Loxton think that he knew that.

'We wouldn't find your fingerprints or DNA there, then, would we?' she asked.

'I did used to work there a few years ago,' he said. 'I was a cleaner.'

He was clever. 'And on Thursday, Friday and Saturday, where were you?'

'I've told you; I spend most of my time in my flat these

days. I might have gone to the shops at some point, maybe the off-licence down the road. But I was mostly inside. I've got nowhere to go. It's hard at the moment. But that doesn't mean … I've got nothing to do with those police officers going missing. I was in the army, for Christ's sake. I wouldn't hurt another officer.'

'But you'd fantasized about it with strangers online,' Loxton growled. She couldn't keep the hate out of her voice as her hands balled into fists. Harding stared at her in surprise and glanced at Kowalski.

'That'll do for now,' Kowalski said, throwing Loxton a warning look. 'We'll take a break, but we might need to ask you a few more questions. You won't be going anywhere just yet.'

Even the solicitor was looking at Loxton strangely, and she realized she'd overstepped the line. You were supposed to get suspects onside, try to get them to tell you things they didn't mean to, and she'd just blown it by losing her temper. She nodded abruptly at Harding, got up and left the room. She strode down the corridor and turned left, and as soon as she was out of view, she closed her eyes and tried to calm the shaking rage inside her. It was all-consuming and she couldn't stop it. She'd wanted to kill him. She needed to get a grip.

Loxton went back to the CID office to wait for Kowalski while he finished up in custody. The lab were struggling to hack into Harding's computer and mobile without his passwords, but they had prioritized it and were doing their best to see what was on there. They'd managed to access some of the chat, but the deleted data would take a few days. Of course, that was where the interesting stuff would be.

Loxton was so tired. Interviews always took something

out of her, but this one was different. The thought that Harding had acted out his fantasies on Emma and that Sarah and Gabriella were still out there was too much.

Kowalski came and sat next to her in the office. 'I'll type up the interview. We've got enough to charge him for the burglary and misuse of computers, but there isn't anywhere near enough to charge him for Emma's murder or Sarah's and Gabriella's disappearances. We're going to need something more. There's no offence yet for expressing unpleasant sexual fantasies, however sick.'

'There should be,' Loxton said. Kowalski couldn't understand; *he* wasn't the one who felt threatened. No one was going to kidnap and hurt *him*.

'Dominik, you need to tell me more about Szymański,' Loxton said. 'I need to know everything.'

Kowalski sighed and rubbed his temples. 'Every time a serial killer strikes in Britain, people bring up Jack the Ripper. In America, it's Charles Manson. Well, in Poland it's Krystian Szymański. These killers just become popular folklore. Harding's just come up with an imaginary second person to try to distract us. But you're right: if Harding is being inspired by Szymański, then it's helpful to know the background.'

'Thank you.' She needed to understand what Szymański's relevance was in all of this. If Harding was telling the truth, Szymański's Avenger was still out there.

Chapter 27

Lena looked at Loxton and Kowalski concerned. 'I don't like this. *Szymański's Avenger.* I thought I'd seen the last of Krystian Szymański when he died, but now there's this guy. I was at Szymański's funeral to make sure it really was that bastard they buried.' Lena shook her head.

'It was him, wasn't it?' Kowalski asked, for a moment looking unsure. Loxton realized that Szymański was Kowalski's Barratt. He hated to talk about him as much as Loxton did Barratt.

'It was him all right,' Lena said. 'There was an open coffin – not that anyone could pay their respects; the ceremony was closed to the public. Only family were allowed, but I was the only person there. Even his mother didn't turn up. She suffers with Alzheimer's, and I'd never normally say this, but it was a blessing for her. She lives in the past, way before she knew the truth about her only son.'

Loxton felt cold when she thought of Szymański's mother. What must it be like to find out that your child is a monster? There could be no worse pain.

'I'm not buying this Szymański's Avenger thing,' Kowalski said. 'It's either some troll on the internet who happens to have picked Szymański's surname as his tag and isn't relevant, or Harding's just made him up. Loxton's convinced the Szymański murders are relevant to our current case.'

'I think Alana's right, it's too much of a coincidence,' Lena said. 'And if Szymański is the inspiration for Emma's murder and these abductions, then there may be a specific pattern the killer's following motivated by the way Szymański murdered his victims. It might help us work out where he's been keeping the bodies.'

'Thank you,' Loxton said, glad Lena was taking her seriously, even if Kowalski wanted to dismiss it all. 'Has anything come back from the search of the sewers?'

'So far, nothing,' Kowalski said. 'But we'll keep looking, it's a massive area to cover.'

Lena opened up her laptop and showed them the profile she'd compiled at the time of the Szymański killings. It was eerily similar to the brief profile she'd made for Emma's murderer.

'Do you really think this is linked back to Szymański?' Kowalski said. 'I know I thought there was a second killer, but there were no further murders. Why would they come here?' His face was filled with concern.

'I don't know but perhaps the killer came here and worked with Barratt,' Lena said. 'And then when Barratt was put in prison they stopped again, preferring to work in a pair. But Szymański's death has prompted them to start up again. Someone did try to break Barratt out. And even the Polish cleaner recognized the signs of Szymański's work at Emma's crime scene.' Lena stared at Kowalski for a moment and he looked embarrassed that he hadn't brought Szymański up earlier.

'Can you see if your profile of the current killer matches Kevin Harding?' Kowalski asked.

'I thought you were against psychological profiling?' Loxton asked.

'At this point I'm desperate enough to try a psychic,' Kowalski said. 'And even to entertain the idea that this is linked to a dead Polish serial killer.'

Loxton nodded in agreement. The desperation was starting to get to her too.

'Let's get Harding charged for the police computer misuse and keep him in tonight, but I think he's our man for Emma's murder and the abductions.' Winter was stood with Loxton, Kowalski and Lena in the interview observation room, Harding on the other side of the two-way mirror, oblivious to their presence. 'I got a friend in the army to send me Harding's military background on the hurry up and its confirmed that he was SAS. He was dishonourably discharged for taking a firearm home and threatening his then girlfriend with it. He's lucky he didn't go to prison, but the military police dealt with it, and we know how they like to keep things in house. They blamed it on the action he'd seen in Afghanistan and severe post-traumatic stress disorder.'

'He fits your profile perfectly,' Kowalski said to Lena.

Loxton studied Harding through the two-way mirror. Harding was sat up straight, his eyes moving around the room, as if looking for weak points so that he could escape. 'We should keep an open mind, sir, like you told us to,' Loxton said. 'It could be this Szymański's Avenger. Harding seemed scared of him when we mentioned his name. I get the impression Harding was meant to take the fall, but when it's come to it, he's almost bottled it. He seems to be protecting Szymański's Avenger.'

'Harding fits the profile,' Lena said. 'Ex-military, PTSD,

previous violence against women and we have a link. He took your personal details off the police HR system. And he's worked in both Walworth and Camberwell police stations. He knows the layouts.'

'But why did he take Kowalski's details?' Loxton asked. 'That's what I don't understand. And it's too easy. He left us a breadcrumb trail; this killer wouldn't be that stupid.'

'Sometimes we get lucky,' Kowalski said. 'And you heard him in interview; he said he was interested in me because I helped put Szymański away. Sometimes they make a mistake and get sloppy.'

'I think Dominik and Lena are right, Alana,' Winter said. 'Szymański's Avenger is just some troll on the internet; there's plenty of them.' Winter shook his head. 'But I've got the tech guys trying to track down where he was posting from. They're trying to track his IP address, but it'll probably end up being dodgy cash only internet cafés who have no CCTV or somewhere abroad. What we do need is some more concrete evidence to prove Harding was responsible for Emma's murder and the abductions to get the courts to keep him in. Let's double check if there are any links between Luke Pearce and Kevin Harding,' Winter said.

Loxton felt sick thinking that Pearce had made contact with Emma simply to gain her trust, so he'd be able to kill her more easily in some sort of weird pact with Harding. It seemed far-fetched that there could be two people as evil as each other working together, but, then, serial killers had been known to work in pairs.

'I've already checked,' Lena said. 'There's nothing on their phones or social media profiles linking them, but they are both Red Pill members. I haven't actually seen any interaction between them on the site, but they could have deleted their chat room or used aliases. Then again, the site has twelve thousand members, so maybe they don't know each other at all and it's just a coincidence.'

'Harding claims he was at home when the detectives were taken,' Winter said. 'I want cell siting on all of his mobiles to see where he was, although we know he's tech savvy, so he might have left his mobiles at his flat to try to create a more solid alibi. We need to work fast if we're going to be able to find something that will definitely convince the courts he's the suspect. The way it stands now, there's a chance he'll get bailed by the court tomorrow morning.'

'He wouldn't get bailed in Poland.' Lena shook her head in annoyance.

'We'll go to the court tomorrow and try to convince them,' Loxton said. She felt a sense of dread that something bad would happen if Harding got out. She was sure he knew something about Emma's death, even if he wasn't the murderer.

They were getting closer, but not quickly enough.

Chapter 28

Loxton and Kowalski entered custody, which was eerily quiet. It was getting late, and all around them behind the closed cell doors suspects were sleeping. There was hardly any activity, just the custody sergeant sat behind his computer, flicking through the custody records making sure everything was running smoothly.

She glanced behind the sergeant and saw one of the custody staff, head back, fast asleep. She couldn't blame her; night shifts were hard, and they got progressively worse as the years crept up on you. She remembered hardly being affected in her twenties, but now, in her thirtieth year, long hours and nights were starting to bite.

'We need to charge Harding,' she said to the custody sergeant. 'Keep him in for court in the morning.'

'Sure thing. He's not asleep; he's having a chat with an officer. He's in cell twenty, right at the bottom of the corridor – as far away from the other prisoners as possible. I hate having ex-military in; they can be live wires and disrupt the others.'

Loxton frowned. 'An officer is having a chat with him?'

'Yeah, I've forgotten his name. It's fine; go through and

see if he's done. Then you can bring Harding here and I'll charge him for the computer thing.'

She hurried down the corridor, Kowalski following. As they turned the corner and went through another set of double doors, she heard a commotion at the end of the corridor. She threw Kowalski a look and they ran towards the noise. Cell 20's door was wide open. What the hell was going on? She heard a shout and the noise of punches being thrown.

She rushed through the door, lifting her fists, ready to strike. In the cramped cell she saw Harding and Anson fighting, and Anson wasn't winning.

'What the fuck?' Kowalski said.

Loxton rushed forward, pulling Anson away from Harding. 'What the hell are you doing?' she said.

'This prick knows where Sarah is, I just know it. He wouldn't fucking tell me.' Anson's nose looked broken.

Loxton glanced at Harding; Kowalski was just about holding him back. Harding's lip was cut, and he had the beginnings of a black eye.

'This is not how we do things,' Loxton said, pulling Anson out of the cell.

'This is one of our own, Alana. And that animal knows more than he's letting on.'

Loxton sighed and shook her head. 'What is wrong with you?'

'I love her. I thought she was your friend. We need to get him to talk. To give us something.'

'Not like this,' Loxton said, appalled.

'She's out there, somewhere.' Anson pointed out of the barred window. 'She could be dying of thirst for all we know, locked up somewhere alone, while this piece of shit is in here, safe and warm, moaning about the quality of the tea.'

Loxton led him away from the cell. 'This isn't the way, Anson.'

'I don't know shit about your girlfriend,' Harding called after Anson. 'You're a maniac. I want to complain. I've been assaulted.'

'All right, Harding,' Kowalski's voice was placating. 'I'll get the inspector down. You're safe now, okay.'

'Safe with *you* lot?' Harding was shouting. 'He tried to kill me. Look at my eye. You lot are supposed to make sure no harm comes to me when I'm in here, not attack me when I'm trapped in this cage, defenceless.'

Loxton glared at Anson. 'I'll have to report this. Harding will probably get bail in court tomorrow because of you. The courts will take one look at him, hear he was assaulted by a police officer in his cell and deem his life at risk if he stays in prison. They'll think another officer or prison guard might have a go at him. He goaded you into that.'

Anson spat some blood on the floor. 'If they think he's safer outside of prison then so be it. That makes my life easier. I don't give a shit about it. About this job. About any of it.' He waved his hand at the cell doors. 'This can all go to hell. What's the point of any of this, if we can't even keep our own safe? If I can't find Sarah?' He strode out of custody, slamming the door behind him, and the custody sergeant stiffened.

'What's going on?' he asked, seeing the blood on Loxton's shirt.

'There's been an incident,' Loxton said, her heart heavy. 'You need to double check the CCTV, but I think Anson's assaulted Harding in cell twenty.'

'Is Harding all right?' The custody sergeant looked panicked.

'You'd best get a doctor to check him out.'

'Fucking great,' the custody sergeant grumbled as he picked up the phone. 'It's not the seventies anymore. Christ, I'll probably lose my job for this. Anson just said he wanted a quick word. I thought it was part of his covert thing. I didn't ask any questions; I didn't even log him coming in. I'll get in the shit for this.'

'You weren't to know,' Loxton said, but she wasn't really listening. Instead she was thinking about Anson, frantic to get Sarah back, willing to risk anything. Loxton felt his desperation, but she couldn't cross lines like he was able to. Anson had become unhinged. Time was running out and she didn't know what he was capable of.

Chapter 29

Loxton smoothed her suit jacket and glanced at Kowalski. He looked as worried as she was, but as the knock resounded through the courtroom, he rearranged his features to one of calm confidence. She marvelled at the way he was able to put on a relaxed persona. Both of them were expecting the worst at Harding's bail hearing.

The judge came into the courtroom, her eyes sweeping across her domain, and then she sat. Something in the room seemed to release and everyone else sat down.

The judge listened dispassionately as the prosecution lawyer hinted at the police's belief that Harding was involved in the murder of a police officer and the disappearance of two other officers, but it became clear that the judge was in no mood for conjecture.

'I need evidence, Mr Morley. This court doesn't hear speculation and rumour. We deal in facts. Do you have any facts?'

Mr Morley shuffled through his papers and glanced back up. 'The police are still in the early stages of the investigation, Your Honour.'

The judge shook her head. 'It seems to me that this man

is at more risk from the police than they are from him.'
She raised her eyebrows and Loxton could see the fury in
them. A prisoner being attacked in a police station was a
very serious thing and the judge's eyes regarded her and
Kowalski with disgust. 'I see no alternative but to release
this man on bail for trial of the Misuse of Computer Act
and burglary. And he is bailed for the other matters too,
but if the Crown can't produce a stronger case than what
they've shown me so far, I'll be dismissing it at the next
hearing.' She nodded in Harding's direction. Harding tried
to hide his surprise and nodded back at her. The judge
stood up and everyone took to their feet as well as she
made her way slowly out of the courtroom.

Harding glanced warily across at Loxton and then
Kowalski, a frown on his face. Then he was led out of the
courtroom by two prison guards to speak with his defence
solicitor and be released.

Mr Morley gave Loxton and Kowalski an apologetic
shrug. 'It was always a long shot.'

'Thank you for trying,' Loxton said. She and Kowalski
left the court and hurried to their car.

'Don't look so worried,' Kowalski said when they were
safely inside the car and away from prying ears. 'The
surveillance officers will keep an eye on him. And who
knows? If he is involved then he might lead them to where
Sarah and Gabriella are being kept. He has to go and see
them at some point if it's him.'

'I just hope they don't lose him. Harding's ex-military.
He'll be surveillance-aware. And maybe he has someone
else helping him. This is risky.' She didn't like it. She'd
rather Harding was remanded, locked up tight where he
couldn't harm anyone else.

Anson was suspended now, but he'd got what he

wanted: Harding out in the open and rattled, with Anson's team right behind him. She felt like Anson had set the whole thing up and she was worried he wouldn't wait for Harding to lead the surveillance team to Sarah and Gabriella. Her concern was that Anson would go after Harding on his own, get him alone and try to beat information out of him on where Sarah was being hidden. And it might not go Anson's way, either he'd be killed or Harding would, and they'd be no nearer to finding Sarah and Gabriella.

Loxton and Kowalski drove straight from the court to Rosa Caselli's flat. She wanted to check Gabriella's sister was safe. Neither Loxton nor the team had been able to get hold of Jane, but at least she could try to protect Rosa. She owed it to Gabriella. Kowalski understood and had agreed to go with her.

Loxton knocked and heard someone come to the door. Before she had a chance to call out that it was her, Rosa had opened it, oblivious to any danger there might have been. She glanced at Loxton and Kowalski.

'Have you found Gabriella?' Rosa's eyes were desperate.

'Not yet,' Loxton said.

Rosa's shoulders dropped, her gaze falling to the floor in pure despair. She nodded to Loxton and Kowalski and led them into the living room.

The flat was a mess, nothing like when Loxton had first come to visit. The curtains were drawn and the air stale. Rosa trudged to her sofa, slumping back into the cream fabric. She drew her knees up to her chest, pulling a cushion in front of her and wrapping her arms around it as if she was in physical pain.

'Rosa, you need to be careful when you open the door. You need to keep the chain on.' Loxton glanced back at the flimsy flat door. It would only take a couple of kicks to break it open.

'Sorry, I forgot.' Rosa sighed heavily, as if Loxton's visit was another unwelcome distraction.

'I thought a friend was staying with you?' Loxton glanced around, but there was no evidence of anyone else living here.

'I want to be on my own.' Rosa was staring past Loxton, her mind clearly on something else.

'But it might not be safe for you here. Is there anyone you can stay with?' Loxton asked.

'I'm fine. I prefer being on my own,' Rosa said. 'Why are you here?' Loxton could tell Rosa didn't care anymore; fear had overwhelmed her. She clearly couldn't face a future without her sister and moving out of the flat was a step closer to accepting that new reality.

'We're here to let you know about your sister's missing person case. Luke Pearce is remanded in prison for sentencing for the road accident with the motorcyclist. He's on technical bail for Emma Robins's murder and is a possible suspect for your sister's disappearance.'

Rosa nodded dully. This wasn't news to her. Her eyes started to drift again.

'But there's another man,' Loxton continued. 'A Kevin Harding. He's been bailed for Emma Robins's murder and has been released this morning from court.'

'Kevin Harding?' Rosa's eye snapped onto Loxton, and for a brief moment Loxton saw her old friend's fire in her little sister's eyes. 'Who is he?'

'He's a bit of a loner,' Kowalski said. 'Ex-military. We're not sure if he is involved, but he's shown up as a suspect. The court can't keep him in; we don't have enough evidence.'

Kowalski's mobile began to ring. 'It's Winter. Look, I'll

be just outside the front door, but I need to update him on Harding and see if he can arrange protection for Rosa.'

Loxton nodded and watched Kowalski leave, closing the door carefully behind him.

'This is serious, Rosa. That's why I'm asking you, is there anywhere else you can stay right now until we arrange something?' Loxton asked.

'I don't want to go anywhere else. This is where Gabriella and I live together. This is where her things are. She might come back.' Rosa's eyes shone with tears, but she managed to hold them back.

'I know, but it's not safe here. What would Gabriella want you to do?' It was a cheap shot, but Loxton was desperate.

Rosa glared at her. 'She's missing, so how the hell should I know?' Colour appeared high on Rosa's cheeks. It was something. A sign of some fight still in her.

'I think you do know,' Loxton said, keeping her voice soft despite Rosa's rising anger. She couldn't back down. She had to push for Gabriella's sake.

'Where am I supposed to go? My friends all live in bed-sits with their boyfriends. There's no space.'

'We'll sort something out.'

'Maybe Dominik will let me stay at his?' Rosa said. Loxton knew Kowalski had said Gabriella had been a good friend, but she hadn't expected Rosa to know him well enough to stay at his place.

'You knew him before all this, right?' Loxton asked.

Rosa frowned, then shook her head, realizing Loxton's concern. 'It's not like that. He's like my brother. Him and Gabriella went out a few years back. It was just after my mum died. It was an intense time. They were good together. But it fizzled out. Gabriella was so sad after

Mum passed away. She wasn't in the right head space for a relationship.' Rosa looked upset as she said that.

'Did they get back together?' Loxton asked. She tried to hide the shock from her voice. She hadn't known Gabriella back then, her mum had died a couple of years before Loxton met her.

'No, but they stayed friends. He'd still come over for dinner a few times a year. I still got to see him then. But I haven't seen him for a few years. Gabriella got a serious boyfriend and Dominik kept his distance after that. She broke up with that loser, though, a year back, and I kept hoping maybe she'd get back together with Dominik. She said they were just friends and that was that. But she always looked sad when I asked her about him. Like he was the one that got away.'

Why had Kowalski told her that he and Gabriella were just close friends? Perhaps Kowalski was one of those men who was promiscuous but managed to keep it quiet. Loxton tried to keep her voice steady, surprised by how upset she was. 'I didn't realize the connection, sorry. Let's get you packed up, Rosa. You can't stay here; you're going to come with Dominik and me.'

Rosa sighed. 'You're as stubborn as Gabriella. Fine. Let me get a few things together. And a few of her things. She might need them, and she won't be able to come back here, will she?'

'I would offer you my place, but my flat isn't safe,' Loxton said. 'And you can't stay at Dominik's either, I'm afraid. Our addresses have been compromised.'

Rosa glanced at Loxton, a flash of fear crossing her face as the seriousness of her situation finally hit home. 'I'll call a couple of friends. Someone will put me up. I don't want police protection. I'd rather be with them.'

Loxton nodded. 'It's there if you need it.' She'd rather Rosa stayed with friends. She still couldn't shake the feeling that the police had been infiltrated in some way.

'Someone will put me up,' Rosa said and began searching the sofa until she found her mobile. 'Alana, do you think it *is* this Harding guy?'

'I don't know. And until we do know, we can't take any chances. I've got the car outside. We'll give you a lift, make sure no one follows us. But, Rosa, you can't come back here. Not for the time being. Make sure you pack everything you need. And we'll get you a new phone. You have to leave your one here. Do you understand?'

Rosa sighed. 'Fine, fine.' She bustled off to her bedroom. Loxton thought that being with other people might help Rosa with all of this.

Loxton felt a weight lift. At least Rosa would be safe for now. That was something she could do for Gabriella.

She thought of Kowalski. He had dated both Emma and Gabriella. The Met could be a small world; it wasn't that unusual. Still, the thought made her feel uneasy. He must be worried about being taken off the cases like she would inevitably be, but she'd told him about her connection – he should have given her the same consideration. This was all getting far too close to home.

Chapter 30

Loxton had hugged Rosa when she'd left her with her friends, making her promise she'd do as she'd said. No contact with anyone. She just had to wait. It hadn't sat well with Rosa.

There was a buzz of activity in the office as she returned. She could see Patel talking to Kowalski, but before she could head over her office phone rang and she picked it up automatically.

'Hello, Alana. How are you?' Edward Barratt's voice was calm but with a slight lift, as if he was holding back telling her some good news.

She froze momentarily, checking around her in case he was somehow stood nearby. She could almost feel his breath on the back of her neck as a chill ran down her spine. 'I'm very well, thank you. Did you have some new information?'

'Just a call to see how you were getting on,' he said. 'I'm allowed one call a week now, remember? And I thought I'd waste mine on you. I hope you're not too busy this evening?'

How had he known that she'd be here to pick up? Or was it just sheer luck? She glanced at her colleagues around her, paranoia getting the better of her. 'I feel honoured, Edward, but I am actually quite busy. So I'll have to go now, unless there's another reason you called?'

'I just wanted to make sure you were safe, what with everything going on,' Barratt said. 'That you're locking your front door nice and tight and the windows, too. Nefarious types are good at scaling walls and getting into first-floor flats, and there's plenty of old-style cat burglars about. Just be careful, okay? I wouldn't want something to happen to you when it's not your time yet.'

'How do you—?' Before she could finish, the disconnect tone was ringing in her ear. She felt her heart racing, adrenaline coursing through her body. Barratt had somehow known that her address was compromised. At least he didn't know she'd moved into a hotel. She took comfort from that.

She joined Patel and Kowalski, but she could see they were having some sort of disagreement.

'What's going on?' she asked.

'There was a 999 call while we were out,' Kowalski said. 'Some nut making out there's another body, but the uniform have checked it out and there was nothing. They even took the dogs through and sent the helicopter over. It's just a hoax.'

'Have you got the 999 call?' Loxton asked.

Patel nodded. 'It's here. I can play it for you.' She pulled up the audio digital file that the call centre had sent over and clicked on it. They waited in silence until the police operator's voice came on.

'Police, fire or ambulance?'

'Police.' The man's voice was distorted, strange and cold. There was no emotion; it was almost robotic.

'Putting you through,' the operator said.

There was a pause while the operator transferred him,

and Loxton strained her ears to listen for any background noise. But all she could hear was his breath, in and out. It was slow, measured – completely in control.

'Police, what's your emergency?' a man asked.

'There's a body in Dulwich Wood,' the robotic voice crackled.

'Are you with the body now, sir?' the operator asked.

'Yes. It's by the lake.'

'Is there anyone else there?' The operator was trying to keep his voice neutral, but this was not the type of call you got every day.

'The war's started,' the distorted voice replied.

'I'm sorry? What's your name, sir?'

'The war's started,' he repeated, then hung up.

The operator sighed heavily, obviously thinking it was a hoax, and ended the call a moment later.

'There's something odd about his voice,' Loxton said. 'It sounds like it's been scrambled through a voice distorter. That's a lot of trouble to go to just for a prank. And he quoted the note in Emma's hand. It could be Harding; he's tech savvy and he talked about a war.'

'"The war's started" is quite a common thing for people to say when they're pissed off,' Kowalski said. 'A teenager could probably distort their voice in five minutes on some app. I bet it's not hard to do. And Harding's being followed by a covert team, so it can't be him.'

'Barratt just called me. He didn't say anything exactly, but it was just his demeanour. He seemed to be gloating.'

'Shit, that's not good,' Kowalski said. 'Let's check Harding is still being followed.'

Loxton nodded and called Anson's team. They answered immediately. 'Hello, Jamie here.'

'It's Loxton. Have you got Harding in sight?'

'We're just trying to relocate him.'

'What?' She tried to keep her voice calm.

'He got on a bike and disappeared into an estate. We're waiting for him to resurface.'

'When did you lose him?'

'Over an hour ago.' He sounded embarrassed. 'But this can happen. We'll pick him back up again, don't worry.'

'Those estates are like rabbit warrens,' Loxton said. 'He could have dropped the bike in a flat, changed clothes and got out.'

'If he knows someone in here, then yes, he could have,' the man admitted. 'But he wouldn't have got past us in a change of clothing. He's just trying to wait us out.'

'Can't you track him with his court tag?'

'He took off his ankle tag with a hacksaw and left it in his flat. Look, when we pick him up again, I'll call you.'

She shook her head angrily. 'He's ex-SAS. You won't pick him up again.' She hung up. 'They've lost him. I don't like this.'

Loxton felt sick. Harding was out there. She was glad Rosa had gone to a friend's. Now if only she could warn Jane . . .

'Let's take another look at those woods,' Kowalski said. 'The uniform won't go back out there again. They think it's some teenagers having a laugh.'

'I really hope they're right,' Loxton said.

Kowalski swept his torch in a long arc through the tree branches in Dulwich Wood. 'There's nothing here. No one in their right mind would be able to come in here and dump a body. There are always people walking dogs. And then it's full of teenagers at night. Probably the same ones who called this crap in.'

'The killer left Emma's body in Camberwell station,' Loxton said. 'This would be easy for him. It's dark now. Maybe he's playing a game.' The woods were pitch black, the branches and grey clouds above them blocking out the anaemic light from the rising moon.

'It's just teenagers, Alana,' Kowalski said. 'The uniform didn't find anything earlier and they had the search dogs and the heat-seeking helicopter. We'll do one last walk through and then get out of here. We need to help them track down Harding.'

She nodded, hating to admit it, but Kowalski was right. There was nothing here. It was probably some kid messing about, just random chance that the caller had used the words from the note, or perhaps somehow that piece of evidence had been leaked. The idea that it was some police officer's son disturbed her, but teenagers could act out in the cruellest ways. He might have heard his mum or dad talking about the case and decided to play up.

They started walking through the wood again, but it was a massive area. Her hands and feet were freezing.

Then she heard a noise. Up ahead, towards the lake. Both she and Kowalski froze.

'Animal?' she whispered.

'Maybe,' Kowalski answered quietly.

There was a snap, as if someone had stepped on a broken branch just in the foliage ahead. A brief pause, and then a scrabbling noise from the shrubbery just out of sight.

Kowalski charged forward and she burst after him, barbed branches and the thorny undergrowth ripping at her, as if trying to hold her back.

Kowalski's torchlight bounced crazily off the trees and she was dazzled by its brightness. The gloom around her seemed to darken around them.

Kowalski was getting ahead of her as she struggled to keep up, chasing him through the foliage, which was becoming denser. A bunch of trees blocked her path, so she veered right, rushing around them, but she was yanked backwards and nearly pulled off her feet. She managed to catch herself before she fell over backwards and turned to face her assailant.

Her coat had caught on a thorny bush. She tugged frantically at the navy material until it was ripped free. Once she was facing forwards again, she realized she couldn't see Kowalski's torch beam anymore.

'Kowalski,' she called out, straining her ears in the dark. Nothing.

'Kowalski.' She waited another brief moment, but there was no reply.

She pulled out her torch, but the light was weaker; she could see barely a metre ahead of her.

She moved forward slower now, unable to run as she had before in the dim light. If she wasn't careful, she would twist her ankle or worse, and then she would be no good to Kowalski.

The trees were bunched together here, almost preventing her from struggling forward. Progress was slow, and all the while she strained her ears, trying to hear anything in the silent wood.

She was surprised at how jittery she felt. She had searched woods plenty of times. Chased after suspects with knives on her own. But here she was, alone in the dark, and she was scared. The trees were becoming sparser and through the thinning branches she could see glimpses of the shimmering lake.

She looked right along the shoreline, and then left in the opposite direction, but she couldn't see Kowalski's torch beam at all.

She pulled out her mobile and called him. On the fourth ring, he answered.

'Where are you?' she asked.

'I have no bloody idea. I lost whatever it was. It must have been an animal. It was so fast through the wood.'

'Where are you now? I'm on the shoreline facing the lake. I've got my torch on.' She waved the torch above her head.

'I can't see you. I'll head to the shoreline too, if I ever work out which damn way it is.' Kowalski's breathing was heavy after running. 'This was a terrible idea. I hate dark woods.'

'It's hard to believe we're still in London. I'll stay here and keep my torch on. Call me when you reach the lake.'

'Will do,' he said. 'The phone map's useless here. My blue dot just shows me floating in the lake. I'll call you in a minute; it can't be that hard to find.' He hung up and she was left in silence.

Loxton didn't like having her back to the wood, but then she needed to peer across the water and try to spot Kowalski's torchlight.

The thought struck her that the killer might have tricked them on purpose. Set up a diversion, while he operated somewhere else. That was the likely scenario. This was all just a distraction technique while he left another body at a closed police station.

There was a snap in the undergrowth behind her.

She spun around. It sounded too heavy to be a bird. Maybe a fox? She heard another snap and a scuffle through the leaves as something darted away from her. Smaller than a fox. She followed it anyway, her nerves rattled.

What if this wasn't a diversion at all? What if this was to lure her here? Barratt's call to ensure she'd come? Did the killer and Barratt know she would keep searching, even when it was past pointless and everyone else had given up? Loxton shivered. The killer could be here, waiting to snatch her right in the middle of their search efforts for Sarah and Gabriella.

She stopped.

There was a noise behind her now. She turned slowly. Something darted away again, the foliage left shaking in its wake. *It's nothing. Just an animal*, she told herself. A person would make more noise. Even still, she was nervous.

She needed to get back to Kowalski. She pulled out her mobile and called him again as she walked towards the shoreline. 'Kowalski, I don't like this.'

'What do you mean?'

She felt stupid just saying it out loud, but she persisted. 'What if this is a trap? Barratt's call to get me here and now the killer has separated us.'

There was silence on the other end of the phone. '*Gówno.* Alana, I'm nearly at the shoreline. Can you see my torch light? I'm going to start waving it, okay, so you know where I am. Get to the shoreline. I'll be with you in minutes.'

'Promise?' she said.

'Promise.' Kowalski's voice was loud, and she could tell he was running. 'And get your baton out.'

She drew it, wishing she had something more dangerous to protect herself with. The lake was in front of her, just through the trees, but she hesitated. The noise was coming from there now. She forced herself forwards. She hated the idea of waiting for the killer to come to her. No, she would go to him.

She charged through the trees and broke out onto the shoreline. As she did, the noise intensified to a crashing as little creatures darted away from her, too fast to say for sure what they were. The shape of them made her guess rats.

She scanned the area where they had been congregating and saw it. The body. Hair tangled with leaves and mud. Blonde hair. She trailed her gaze along the hair until she reached a forehead and then pale blue eyes. The soft white skin spattered with mud and blood.

Sarah.

She spun around, sweeping the treeline with her torch. He was near; she could feel him watching her. She screamed into the woods. An angry, guttural call. She felt the scream die but her rage only grew. She was going to find him. And when she did, she was going to kill him.

'Alana! Alana!' Kowalski shouted.

'Over here.' She waved her torchlight in his direction and watched him fight his way through the trees and undergrowth to join her. His face was ghostly in the pale light.

'Oh, Sarah,' he said when he saw her.

Sarah's face and hands hadn't been touched by the rats. Her body had only just been dumped. The killer was nearby.

Loxton pulled out her radio and called it in. 'Body found by the lake in Dulwich Wood, identified as missing detective Sarah Taylor. Suspect still in the area. There's only two of us here in the woods; we need backup. Send in a heat-seeking helicopter and dog units.'

'This is Control, sending requested units now.'

'We'll remain at the crime scene,' she said.

It felt like forever as they waited with the body in silence, but in reality it had been less than five minutes when she heard the distant sound of helicopter rotors.

'India 99 here. Sweeping the woods again, starting from the lake. Two still targets by the lake.'

Loxton heard the roar of the helicopter's rotors growing. The leaves in the treetops began to dance and the water of the lake rippled. The helicopter's light beam fell onto them.

'That's us,' Kowalski said. 'Don't come too close or you'll disturb the crime scene.'

The noise receded slightly and the leaves and lake stilled again. 'Roger that, confirmed that we have you. Targets ruled out. Beginning systematic sweep of area.'

Loxton watched as the helicopter moved away from them, moving directly east.

She looked down at Sarah and then at Kowalski. He looked as strung out as she was. She hadn't expected to find Sarah like this. She tried to hold back the tears, to keep a tight grip of her emotions. She needed to stay alert.

'From India 99. Moving target spotted. Following target.'

Her heart sped up. 'Where?' She could hear the helicopter further ahead and trained her eyes to the sky. There was the light.

She bolted forward through the bracken, not caring as it clawed at her hair and face.

'Wait!' Kowalski called after her, but she couldn't stop; she had to catch the killer. She had to stop all of this. She ran as hard as she could towards the noise of the helicopter.

'Moving target doubling back towards the lake. Headed in your direction.'

She carried on running forward, picking up a dirt trail that circled the lake, her hand tightening its grip on the baton.

The helicopter's rotors grew louder and louder.

'Any visual?' Kowalski asked over the radio.

'No visual, moving target using treeline for cover. Officer on the ground, head 90 degrees to your right.'

She turned right and followed their instructions. They were flushing it towards her.

'Target forty metres away from you. Target twenty metres away. Target ten metres away.'

She stopped and waited, planting her feet into the ground and raising her baton above her head ready to strike. The helicopter light was coming straight for her. She couldn't see because of the trees and bushes. She strained her eyes, and then suddenly there it was, to her right. Movement. And then it was on top of her, rushing past her as she swung for it, missing it by inches as it darted to the side.

A fox.

She stood breathless and exhausted, her heartbeat still racing.

'Sit rep?' Kowalski called as the helicopter moved after the fox.

'A fox,' she managed. 'Just a fox.'

'Moving target discounted,' India 99 said. 'Continuing sweep.'

Loxton felt the weight of the defeat upon her. There was no one in this wood but Kowalski, her and Sarah.

The killer was gone.

Chapter 31

As Loxton returned to the body, she could see Kowalski pacing through the branches, muttering to himself. She paused, concerned but curious in equal measures. She'd never seen him talk to himself before. The case was taking its toll on him as well her. Somehow it made her feel less alone.

A cold breeze rattled through the tree branches high above her, making her glance up, and Kowalski paused in his stride and also stared. Above them a few white lights trying hard to twinkle through the London haze in the black winter sky.

She moved forward, pushing through the lower branches, and joined him.

'He's toying with us.' Kowalski's face was miserable. 'We were so close to him.'

'I know.' She wanted to reach out and hug him, but she didn't dare, scared that they would both fall apart. The next few hours would be tough, and they couldn't afford to miss a single thing. The killer had been careful so far, but there was always a chance that there would be something that could change everything. Something that could end this madness.

Her mobile vibrated in her pocket and she felt her insides tighten as she saw Anson's name on the screen. Her eyes briefly met Kowalski's and he shook his head. There were no words that could convey what they felt in that moment.

'Anson, I'm so sorry. We've found Sarah. She's been murdered, like Emma.'

There was silence on the phone. She wondered for a moment if he'd heard her.

'Did she ... did she suffer?' His voice cracked and she could hear muffled sobs.

Loxton looked down at her old friend, whose face was twisted in agony, eyes bloodshot like the others, her neck at a strange angle.

'Yes. I'm so sorry.' Her phone went dead before she could say any more. Loxton ground her teeth to stop herself from screaming. How had it come to this?

Winter and Lena arrived just before Forensics. They discussed the cordon and Kowalski contacted Control, making sure the officers were in place to secure the area. There was a large section of the wood to cordon off, and the number of uniformed officers needed was staggering.

'We're keeping the late shift on to man the cordon,' Winter said. 'Forensics will start now, but they'll make slow progress until daylight.'

'I don't think he killed her here,' Loxton said. 'He brought her here afterwards.'

'How did he get her out of a surveillance operation without any of the surveillance officers even noticing she was gone?' Kowalski shook his head.

Loxton shuddered in the night air. Plucked from the middle of a busy established operation and then dropped here. And the killer had even called them, controlling their movements.

'I don't like this,' Winter said. 'And we still can't get hold of Jane Edison to take her into police protection. Still nothing on their mobiles or bank cards. We're putting out a media appeal for her to call us. Alana, you're going into police protection too. This one was too close. For now, Kowalski will stay with you. It'll take a couple of hours maximum to arrange.'

'Lena could be my protection officer,' Loxton said, trying to keep the desperation out of her voice. 'We could work on the profile together at my hotel. See if it's related.' She didn't want to go into protection, where she would be kept out of the loop, powerless to stop the killer.

'That would be helpful,' Lena said. If Lena was scared of being with Loxton while she was a target, she didn't show it.

'Lena, you're not a protection officer,' Winter said.

'Of course, sir,' Lena said, but she looked disappointed.

'Alana, you can't be involved in the investigation.' Winter paused, his face grave. 'Barratt called you to gloat. You're a target. I'm sending a team to talk to him again, but they won't get anywhere with him. The best I can do right now is get you out of harm's way. You must not talk to any of us when you go into protection. We have to assume that the killer has some way of accessing our information. We can't let the killer find you.' His gaze drifted down to Sarah. 'None of us would be able to live with the consequences. You need to go to a safe house, out of London. That's an order.'

'This killer is three steps ahead of us.' Loxton tried to control her voice. 'I'd be safer here with all of you than stranded in the middle of nowhere waiting for him to come. You saw how it turned out for Sarah. I don't want that to happen to me. If a covert operation couldn't keep her safe, then how is a protection officer meant to keep me safe? Our best chance is catching him before he gets to me.' Loxton was shocked at the strength of her own voice, but she couldn't bear the idea of sitting in a dingy flat with a stranger, waiting for the killer to come. She was rattled and she didn't care who knew. 'I need to be working on the profile with Lena. I know this case. I know the victims. I'm the only one who does.'

For the first time since she'd met him, she saw Winter's resolve waver for a moment. There was no manual for him to follow. No procedure. Any decision he made could be the wrong one and could be sentencing her to death. This might be the last time he spoke to her.

He shook his head. 'No, you're going back to the station with Kowalski and Lena and the protection officer will pick you up there. Stay within eyeshot of Kowalski or Lena. I don't want to hear another word about it. That's final.'

'We understand, sir,' Kowalski said. 'Don't worry, Alana. We've got you covered.'

Loxton wasn't sure that they did. The killer was coming for her and she was losing hope that her, Gabriella and Jane's fate would be any different.

Chapter 32

'Winter's making a mistake,' Loxton said. 'Dominik, can't you talk to him?' The idea of being protected, rather than protecting others, was terrifying for her. She was used to chasing killers to keep other people safe; she'd never had to run from one before.

Kowalski tried to keep his voice down as he paced up and down the meeting room at Walworth station. 'Maybe if Sarah and Gabriella had been in police protection this could have all been prevented. We can't make the same mistake again, Alana. This is your life we're talking about.'

'A protection officer won't make a difference. Sarah had a whole surveillance team. I'll be waiting to die.'

'You shouldn't have run off in the woods.' He stopped pacing. 'You're going to get yourself killed and I don't want to lose you.'

'You ran off first,' she complained. 'Look, we're used to chasing after suspects, not being hunted. I hate this.' Loxton tried to hold the tears of frustration and anger back.

'This case is too personal for you; it's clouded your mind.' He shook his head.

'This is getting too personal for *me*?' Loxton said, trying to keep her voice under control. 'You didn't tell me about your relationship with Emma *or* Gabriella and you told me Szymański meant something else in Polish when it's actually the serial killer who inspired Barratt. What the hell are you playing at?'

'So this is all my fault, is it?' Kowalski stared at her, his face hurt. He looked out of the window into the main CID office. He was probably worried about making a scene, she thought. Didn't want everyone knowing he was a ladies' man. He would be a sergeant soon. He needed to think about these things now.

'You should have told me,' she said. It hurt that he'd pushed her out. 'And about Gabriella. She wasn't just your friend; she was your ex-girlfriend. That's personal.' The words were out before she could stop them.

A pained expression crossed his face. 'What's got into you? That was all a long time ago. It's got nothing to do with all of this. The killer is targeting officers who worked on the Barratt case. This is a war on your old team.'

'Maybe, but you shouldn't be working on their cases either.' The conversation was taking a turn she didn't like, but she couldn't help herself now she'd started.

'I could have said the same to you at the start but I didn't,' he said. 'I haven't been close to Emma and Gabriella for years. Not like you. You were the last person to see Emma alive for God's sake.'

'Gabriella and Emma would want me working their cases. Would they want you to be? Seeing Emma like that?' She thought of Emma's naked body slumped in Camberwell – vulnerable, violated and broken.

Kowalski pressed his lips together, as if to stop himself from speaking, and closed his eyes for a moment. When he opened them, they were cold, staring into hers. 'I just want to find her killer. I owe Emma that. I cared about Emma and Gabriella. I could have married Emma if this job hadn't got in the way.'

'Two of the victims are your ex-lovers. That's more than a coincidence, don't you think? Unless you've slept with half the police force. You should have told me.'

'Most people know about the relationships, Loxton.' Kowalski glared at her. 'It's not a big secret. I didn't want to talk about it. If Winter wanted to take me off the cases, he would have. Emma and I stayed amicable; we didn't hate each other. We even worked together afterwards for a bit. Gabriella was a few years back. It lasted less than a year, but the romance fizzled out for both of us. We should never have got together; we were good friends, but there you go. I don't know what you're getting at and I don't want to hear it. I need some fresh air. Where's Lena? She can take over babysitting you.' He pulled on his coat.

'What about Sarah? Did you sleep with her, too?' She called after him.

He spun around. 'So what if I did years ago? What's that got to do with anything? People get to know each other at work, have relationships that sometimes don't work out. It's normal, Alana. We're not all as suspicious and untrusting as you.' He strode out of the side office as Lena came through the door.

'You look after her. I'm getting some air,' Kowalski said, not looking back at them and slamming the door on his way out. The glass in the frame shuddered. Lena glanced after him in surprise, nearly dropping the stack of take-away coffees she was carrying.

Loxton was left staring after him. She'd fucked up. Plenty of people had relationships with other officers. It wasn't uncommon when you spent every waking moment at work. The job consumed people. And after a decade in the police, you could soon find yourself working with ex-partners again, whether you liked it or not.

Why had she been so aggressive? Because he'd told her it was getting too personal for her, that she should come off the case. She thought he was her ally, but it felt like they were drifting apart, so she'd done what she always did. Lashed out. Pushed him away. She tried not to let the tears come. She was losing everyone around her and there was no one who could stop it.

Lena held out a coffee. 'This one's got sugar in it. Look, this is tough on all of us. It's really messing with all our heads. Whatever that was, it doesn't matter. It's the situation, okay?'

Loxton breathed deeply, trying to push down the tears, and nodded roughly at Lena.

Winter charged into the office. 'Where's Kowalski?'

'He just went out for a moment,' Lena said.

'Well, call him back in. It looks like Jane Edison has gone missing.'

'But she's been in hiding?' Loxton said, confused. 'We don't even know where she is.'

'There's been a call from a neighbour of Eileen Edison – Jane Edison's mother-in-law. She thinks Eileen's house has been burgled.'

'But Jane and her family are out of town,' Loxton said. 'They're not staying there. They know how serious this is.'

'Not according to the neighbour. Apparently they came back early this morning.'

'Why would they do that?' Loxton asked, the concern for her friend rising.

'Eileen was taken seriously ill last night. An ambulance

took her to hospital. The Edisons rushed back when they heard she'd been admitted; the husband wanted to see his mother before it was too late. Jane stayed in the mother-in-law's house with the children. We've just had a report from the hospital that Eileen was poisoned with anti-freeze.'

'Where are Jane and the children?' Loxton asked, her blood running cold.

'Police on scene say the children were upstairs asleep,' Winter said. 'But Jane is missing.'

Kowalski stumbled into the CID office, his face grey, his coat still on. 'I just heard about Jane. We'd better get over there now.'

Winter stared at Loxton like she was a liability that needed to be managed. 'The protection department are arranging an escort and a safe house but it's going to take them a couple of hours.'

'I'm safer with you and the team.' Loxton grabbed her coat, walking to the door and praying he wouldn't stop her. 'Better than staying here with just Lena waiting for the protection team to arrive. Walworth isn't safe.'

Winter shook his head in annoyance. 'Fine, but don't leave my side.'

PART 4

JANE

Chapter 33

There was no doubt: this was not a burglary. Jane Edison was missing, and she had not gone of her own accord. The house was in disarray. Loxton saw a smashed vase, glass pieces scattered across the living room carpet, the tulips wilting and trampled.

Books had fallen by the bookcase and there was a bright red bloody handprint on the wall to the side of the shelving, like a child had made a painting. There were blood marks on the bookshelves, too, as if someone had been trying to claw their way up them and get back onto their feet.

Loxton glanced upwards and, sure enough, she saw tiny spatters of blood on the ceiling. There wasn't enough for it to have been an artery cut, but she pictured the knife slicing upwards and cutting flesh, the blood on the tip of the blade being thrown upwards with the momentum.

Jane had put up a fight. Tried to keep on her feet, to get away, to follow her police training. But it had all been to no avail. She was nowhere to be seen.

Loxton felt dizzy and hot in her forensic suit, the mask making the air she breathed warm and heavy with her own carbon dioxide. She wanted to rip it off her face, take a breath of fresh air, but she knew better than to contaminate the scene.

Jane had always been so kind to Loxton, like an older sister. The one who took her under her wing when she first joined the murder squad. The one who kept calling after she'd left the team in disgrace. The one who never gave up on her. Always ready to listen and often able to give sound advice when Loxton or the others had any problems. But obviously not as good at listening to advice when given it. Jane and Ben were supposed to be incommunicado, but Jane had given Eileen a temporary number to call in case of an emergency. That was just like Jane, always looking out for other people.

She moved through the house. The front door was still eerily left ajar, as if someone had just popped out to put the bins out. Whoever had done this was as quick as lightning and so far, none of the neighbours spoken to had seen or heard anything.

Loxton moved to the kitchen and then the back door. It was closed, still locked apparently. There was one set of keys in the drawer, but Loxton made a mental note to ask Ben if any were missing. This killer was clever. He would want them checking for cars parked nearby the front of the house. Prioritizing house to house on the neighbours across the road. But if he'd gone out the back and climbed over some fences, then his vehicle could have been parked on a side road and the police would be looking in the wrong direction.

Kowalski came over and shook his head at her. She could only see his eyes, but there was fury in them. If only Jane had gone into police protection. Loxton had sent her away, but it had ended up with her being taken anyway, and Loxton knew she had let another friend be abducted when she should have protected her better.

A few doors down and Jane's children were being looked after by a police officer at a neighbour's house. They didn't have a clue why the police had woken them up and why Mummy still hadn't come to pick them up. All they knew was that they were allowed all the chocolate they could eat and to watch cartoons, even though it was really late. It was the best day ever.

It wouldn't stay that way.

'Do you think she's dead?' Kowalski's voice broke for a brief moment.

'Not yet,' Loxton said. 'I hope she's alive, and Gabriella too. He seems to be taunting us by keeping them alive, giving us a chance to save them. But where's he keeping them? Each body has been a message. Emma, to warn us that he was here, and that it was personal to the police. Sarah, to show us that none of us are safe, that he can pluck us from the middle of a police operation just like *that*.' She snapped her fingers in rage. She paused for a moment, trying to get a grip of herself before the emotion overtook completely. 'Gabriella was on her way home from the murder squad. Jane he's taken alive, just like the others. But I think he'll hold onto her longer, like he has been with Gabriella. He's playing with us. And he'll need to draw it out more to get the same excitement from it. With each hit the stimulus needs to be bigger.'

'So we've got some time to save them.' Kowalski looked at her and there was dread in his eyes. She was next on the list. The last one to be taken.

'A little. This time he came to a busy residential street. He's upping the risk for himself. He seems more confident he won't get caught.'

'Maybe he'll make a mistake,' Kowalski said.

Lena came over to them. 'I don't think he will. I'm not sure it was that risky. This is a detached house, with good solid walls. He struck after 9pm on Thursday night, when people are either out socializing or watching TV inside. The children were asleep and out of the way. It's dark outside. I bet he came and recced the house beforehand. Even timed Eileen's poisoning so she'd get worse around now.'

'Which fits your ex-military profile, Lena,' Kowalski said. 'And sounds like Kevin Harding to me.'

'Harding thinks he's on a mission to avenge Barratt and he won't stop until it's completed,' Lena said.

Kowalski shook his head and moved off towards the stairs. Lena watched him in silence and then turned to Loxton. 'He hates to get inside their minds. He prefers to hunt them like animals. As soon as he tries to understand them, he begins to see them as human, and for Dominik that's too much. He can't accept that they are anything like him.'

Loxton looked into Lena's eyes. 'How long did you work together?'

'Long enough to know murder isn't for Kowalski. It messes his head up. Too compassionate by half.'

Loxton nodded at Lena. 'I think you're right by the way. The killer feels justified in what he's doing. He's exacting revenge for Barratt. He's meticulous and careful. But if that's the case, then how can it be Harding? He left a trail leading us right to him. This Szymański's Avenger is more likely the killer, I'm sure of it. If we can identify him—'

'Harding is our suspect,' Lena said. 'He's made a few mistakes, granted, but not many. He still managed to get out on bail and now he's disappeared. Maybe Harding worked with Barratt on the original series? He's making mistakes on his own.'

'We always thought Barratt worked alone,' Loxton said. There'd been no evidence of him working with anyone else. Every killing the same. No deviations. No activity after he was locked up. Not until now, at least.'

'Whereas Kowalski has always been convinced Szymański worked as a pair, and I can see why he thought that,' Lena said. 'There were little inconsistencies with some of Szymański's murders, easily dismissed at the time, as no case is ever perfectly laid out. And after Szymański was put away there were no more murders; it all stopped. But now I'm seeing all this I'm starting to think Kowalski's instincts were right. The killings are so alike. I really think it's possible that Harding worked with Szymański, but then when he got caught Harding came to the UK and worked with Barratt. And when Szymański was murdered Harding decided to get Barratt out so they could work as a team again. Szymański and Harding are both ex-military. Maybe that's how they met.'

Loxton closed her eyes for a moment, the thought horrible. Kowalski did have a way of reading people. He'd had none of the training, scorned forensic psychology, but it was within him anyway. Instinctive.

'So, not a Barratt copycat, but one of the original Szymański killers that Barratt himself copied and maybe learnt from.' Loxton felt sweat trickle down her back and her hands were clammy in the gloves. 'But if that's true, why risk targeting Barratt's old police team? To up the ante?'

Lena's eyes met Loxton's. 'Exactly. And if he is one of the original killers, then he's been doing this for a very long time and getting away with it.'

Chapter 34

Loxton looked around the almost empty CID office. Even in the police station she no longer felt safe. In a way she was glad it was quiet here. Just Lena and a couple of officers working nearby, while she waited for the protection officer. Loxton had been sent Dr Reynolds's early examination notes on Sarah's body via email. It was hard reading. Her friend had endured a brutal death.

Again, there was clear evidence that she had been raped, but the killer had not left any trace DNA behind. It was incredible that he was so forensically aware. And it was frustrating. Predators like this were so rare. Normally they were compulsive, making some mistakes along the way. But this killer, despite escalating in violence, seemed to maintain a firm grip on himself and preserve his discipline to a faultless forensic level.

On a search of the woods another printed-out note had been found near Sarah's body. It had read, '*Too late for Sarah. Will you be too late for Gabriella?*'

Kevin Harding was a perfect candidate – almost too perfect. He fit the profile Lena had compiled, even down to the PTSD. The murders were calculated and must have been planned over a significant amount of time. It did fit someone with military experience. Someone with a hatred of the system, lashing out at authority in any way they could. And they'd had him and he'd got away.

Winter walked into the office. His face was grave, and Loxton saw that a firearms officer was following him. 'Alana, your protection officer is here.'

She closed her laptop down, knowing that she wouldn't be able to take it with her, wouldn't even be allowed to take a mobile with her.

The man nodded a hello at her. 'My name's Philip. I've been doing this for ten years and I'm going to keep you safe.'

'Thanks,' she said, trying not to sound ungrateful.

'I know this is weird, but we'll get through it. I've got the car outside.'

'We won't be able to have any contact after this,' Winter said. 'So take care of yourself, okay? And I'll see you on the other side.'

'Thanks, sir,' she said. Now was not the time to argue with him. 'Catch him for me.'

'We will,' Winter promised.

She followed the protection officer out of the office. She couldn't see Kowalski anywhere, but Lena caught her at the door. 'Alana, thank you so much for everything. We're going to stop him and then you'll be straight back with us,' she said.

'I know,' Loxton said.

'It's going to be so weird not being able to ring you about the case.' She shook her head.

'You don't need me,' Loxton said.

'You were the one who first realized this was a series. We *do* need you.'

Loxton smiled. 'I'll see you soon.'

'Take care of yourself.' Lena hugged her briefly and then stepped back.

'I will,' Loxton said.

'We've got to go,' Philip said.

Loxton glanced around the office one last time, watching the team working. She couldn't see Kowalski, but maybe it was for the best.

Chapter 35

It was so cold. Jane shivered in the dark. She couldn't see anything. Complete blackness that she'd never experienced in her life. Deadly silence surrounded her, broken only by the drip, drip *of something high above. There was water on the floor and the smell was bad. Like gone-off garbage. She was in the sewers if she had to guess.*

She was hungry, exhausted and scared. But mostly scared. Not for herself, but for her children. What had happened to them? Were they down here somewhere in the dark? Scared and alone like she was? She tried to call out, but all she could manage was a muffled moaning. That was no good. If they could hear her, that would only terrify them more. She strained her ears to listen for them. The steady drip, drip, drip *was the only reply.*

What if they were dead? Slaughtered and left behind while only she was deemed worthy enough to be taken? The thought turned her insides over and gripped her heart. Not her babies. Do anything to her, but not her babies.

She had to know. If they were down here, she had to find them. She dragged herself up so she was on her side and could turn her head. Her hands and feet were bound behind her, and the effort of getting onto her side was excruciating. Blood creeped into her hands and feet, like tiny needles being pushed in. She shouted 'Fuck!', but it came out as a low howl.

She needed to undo these ropes. She was going nowhere bound up like this. She could still see nothing. Not a thing. The creature had gone and left her here, but not for long. It would be back and then the torture would start. She knew what was coming. But more than that, she feared she'd never know what had happened to her boys. They could be two metres from her and she wouldn't know. She needed to go to them. To comfort them. And if she couldn't do that, then she had to be next to them. To know.

She shuffled on her side. This couldn't be some great wide never-ending chasm. There had to be an end to it. A wall. And perhaps she'd be able to use it to rub at these ropes. Perhaps to break them? She shuffled along the cold wet floor on her side. It was slow progress as she inched her way along. She tried to go in a straight line, but it was hard when she couldn't see.

The pain in her hands and feet was like they were being sawed off every time she moved. The ropes seemed to be getting tighter and she feared the blood supply would be cut off. But she didn't care if she lost her hands and feet. What she needed to do was get these ropes off at any cost. She was dead as long as they stayed bound around her wrists and ankles and she was no good to her children if she was dead. She prayed they were still alive for her to save.

Chapter 36

The safe house was as Loxton had dreaded, in the middle of deepest darkest Kent, hidden far away from any help.

'Is this it?' she asked. Philip had parked in front of a little cottage down a single lane from a main road. She was convinced it was a holiday home and that they would find a family inside in the middle of their dinner.

Philip put the key in the door, unlocked it and walked into the large living room. He insisted on walking around the cottage first, with her following. He pointed his Glock 17 pistol into each room in turn. She couldn't get used to being so close to a firearm. Once he'd done a walk-through he seemed to settle down.

'If you hear anything odd, get down on the floor and cover your head with your hands,' he said. 'Never answer the door, leave that to me. This cottage might look quaint, but it has bulletproof windows and reinforced doors. You'll be safe here.'

Loxton glanced again at the cottage in surprise and saw that the wooden door was thicker than you'd expect. The windows were double glazed – the wooden frames were only for decoration, with strong steel underneath.

'I'm not allowed to leave, right?'

'Right. The kitchen will be fully stocked, so there's no reason for us to go out.'

'And how long could we be here?'

Philip shrugged. 'As long as it takes for your team to find this killer.'

She nodded, although she felt like screaming. 'Won't you have someone to replace you?'

'It would attract too much attention, the movement to and from the house. That's the trade-off. I've set the alarms. There's no way someone can get in here without setting them off and then they'll have me to get through. Plus no one knows you're here.'

She nodded. 'I'm just going to check out my room.'

'Yours is the one at the end of the corridor, furthest from the front door.'

In the bedroom was a wardrobe, which had several sets of jeans and jumpers from size 10 to 16. There were sets of underwear still in packets in the chest of drawers. Several books were neatly stacked on the bedside table to keep the occupant entertained. They'd thought of everything.

She lay down on the bed, suddenly tired. How long would she be trapped in here? And would Philip really be able to keep her safe? He'd been careful on the drive up here. He'd doubled back on himself and she knew that a team had been following them, to make sure no one else was. They'd peeled away about fifty miles from their end destination. She should feel safe, but she didn't.

'Alana, I'm going to eat.' She could hear Philip clattering about in the kitchen. 'Do you fancy anything?'

'Sure. I'll be out in a minute.' She was hungry, and although sleep was calling, her need to eat was stronger.

And in that moment, she wanted to be with another human. Someone to distract her from the dark thoughts that were circling in her mind, waiting to drag her down.

She went to the kitchen and saw that Philip had already put the kettle on. He held up two ready meals, one lasagne and one a chicken pasta dish. 'Five minutes in the microwave. Which one do you want?'

'I'll go chicken pasta,' she said. The kitchen was tired-looking but well stocked, she thought, checking through the cupboards. There was enough food for them to be here for a month, and then she noticed with growing alarm the UHT milk. It didn't look like she'd be leaving the house for weeks, and she tried to shake the feeling of being a prisoner while her team struggled without her.

Philip turned the TV on and ate his meal in silence, watching the news intently. Loxton followed suit. Although their conversation had been minimal, she felt comfortable in Philip's presence. He was always alert, the volume of the TV low, so that he could hear any noises from outside. She had been listening for any noises too. She washed up the plates and crockery and tided up the kitchen.

'I'm going to bed,' she said.

'I'll be up a bit longer,' he said.

'Should we do shifts?' she asked.

'I only need four hours and there are sensors on the outside of the premises. If anything moves out there, I'll know about it. I've got alerts and cameras set up.'

She nodded, not sure if she felt better or worse for this new information. The Met was taking the threat seriously and she tried not to let it scare her.

She headed to the bathroom to get ready for bed. Alone in the unfamiliar bathroom, she found her eyes drawn to the large bathroom window. It had frosted glass, so no one

would be able to see in properly, but she wished it had a
blind. All she could see was the darkness outside; someone
could be stood right in front of the window and she would
have no idea. She strained her ears, but the only thing she
could hear was the murmur of the TV in the kitchen. She
wasn't sure how long she'd been stood facing the window,
peering into the dark, wondering if anyone was out there
watching her. Suddenly she didn't want to linger and she
quickly got ready.

Once she was back in her bedroom, she peered into
the night but could only see the treeline, which started a
few metres from the cottage. She shivered at the thought
of being on the ground floor, so easily accessible for an
intruder. Philip was confident in his alarm system and
Loxton wished she had his assuredness. She reminded
herself that he had done this hundreds of times and knew
what he was doing.

She checked the window was locked and then pulled the
curtains firmly closed and changed into a plain set of white
pyjamas. Then she climbed into bed, pulling the duvet up
around her, as if it could protect her somehow.

She was exhausted from the hectic pace of the past few
weeks, and as her head rested on the pillow, she found
herself drifting without even trying to. The murmur of
the TV in the other room was hypnotic and it was a relief
knowing Philip was there. But she still felt vulnerable and
she eyed the window suspiciously. Finally, she couldn't
fight it anymore. She needed to sleep, regardless of whatever nightmares came.

She woke on Friday morning to the low murmur of a TV.
She rubbed her eyes and stared at the unfamiliar ceiling
and beige walls. And then her eyes fell on the large window

with the curtains drawn and she remembered where she was. The cottage.

She sat up in bed and checked the clock on the bedside table. It was nine in the morning. She could have slept for longer, but hunger gnawed at her stomach, and the smell of fried eggs and bacon coming from the kitchen was too inviting. She got herself up and pulled on a white dressing gown that was hung on the door and walked to the kitchen.

'Morning,' Philip said, and then turned back to the frying pan. 'I hope you don't mind, but I'm starving. There's enough for two. It'll be about five minutes.'

'Thank you, I'll just go and get ready,' she said, feeling self-conscious in her dressing gown. She went into the bathroom to freshen up and dress. She peered through the frosted glass again, but all she could see was a grey blur that she guessed was the sky and green blobs, which she took for the treeline.

Philip was serving up by the time she came back in and she was surprised at how good everything was.

'I worked in the army before the police. You soon get used to cooking fry-ups when you work in the military. Anything else, I'm useless.'

'I can live with a fry-up every day.' She sat opposite him and tucked in gratefully. Philip sipped his coffee and then ate his food with the precision of a surgeon and Loxton realized that breakfast was a sacred ritual for him.

'How long will we be here for?' she asked.

He shrugged his shoulders as he dipped his toast into his fried egg. 'No idea. Each assignment is different. It's impossible to say.'

She nodded, feeling guilty that she was sat here eating breakfast while her teammates were probably rushing around snatching whatever they could on the run.

'This is really good,' she said appreciatively. 'I was thinking of going for a walk after I've sorted out the dishes.'

Philip looked up at her, swallowed his food and sipped his coffee. 'I'm afraid that's not possible, Alana. We're not leaving the cottage for the foreseeable. It's too dangerous. I hope you can understand. This will all be pointless if your cover is blown.'

'But what about just outside, to get some fresh air?'

'Not for now,' Philip said. 'The first few days are the most critical. If we're going to be compromised it will be then. But if you want fifteen firearms officers here within twenty minutes, be my guest.'

'How often has a safe house been compromised?' she asked.

'On my watch? Never. But there's always a first time.'

It was as Loxton suspected. In the cold light of day, this all seemed like a massive overreaction.

'Look, we never normally get a break in our line of work. Why don't you take the time to catch up on some TV, some reading? And finish your breakfast. You look like you haven't eaten in weeks.'

She sighed. It wasn't his fault; he was just doing his job. And then she thought of all the times people had said that to her in her role as a detective. It felt very different when you were on the other side.

After she'd washed up, she sat at the kitchen table with another coffee and watched the rain hitting the window. They were all frosted to some degree or another. She wondered if the local residents knew about this place, or if it was a well-kept secret even from them. They must question why a cottage had frosted windows, but then it was deep in the woods, perhaps no one even knew it was here.

She was used to having her morning coffee with

Kowalski, and it made her realize how much she missed him. She couldn't even call him to see how he was getting on. How the case was going. Anything could be happening while she sat here, waiting it out like a scared animal. She saw a movement reflected in the window and turned around. Philip was stood behind her watching her with a worried look.

'What's wrong?' she said.

'Nothing,' he said.

'Why the face?' she asked, her mood getting the better of her. Had he heard something outside?

He sighed as she continued to stare at him. 'It's that look in your eye, that's all.'

'What look?' she asked.

'The one that tells me you're going to try to make a break for it. But it isn't going to help. It'll just waste resources while we're out looking for you and distract your team. You need to stay here, where you're safe.'

'I'm not going anywhere,' she said.

He shook his head roughly. 'You've still got that look in your eye. It'll only be a matter of time.' He sighed and left the room, leaving her alone. Loxton realized Philip was good at his job – he could read people better than she could. Probably better than they could read themselves.

Chapter 37

The silver moonlight from the window cast an eerie light into the room, with the shadows of the window frame throwing bars across her bed, making her feel as if she were in a cage.

She felt groggy and confused as she remembered where she was. Not at home, but in this strange place. There were noises, shouting, and then Philip burst into her room. Her heart raced and she scrabbled away from him, sitting herself up on the other side of the bed. He leaned over and grabbed her arm, wrenching her from the bed. She realized in horror that she'd followed a complete stranger into the wilderness.

Then the smell hit her – smoke and burning petrol, acidic in her throat.

'The cottage is on fire. We've got to get out.' Philip dragged her to her feet, his Glock 17 in his other hand. She nodded, staggering towards the door.

Philip opened it and she was shocked at the smoke in the corridor. She turned back to her bedroom. 'The window.' She pointed at it.

'None of the windows open. The front door is our only chance.' He pulled her back towards the smoky corridor, ducked down and ran towards the living room. She followed suit, keeping her head low.

The fire was raging in the living room, strongest near the fireplace, and the smell of burning petrol and chemicals was overpowering here. Had they poured petrol down the cottage chimney or were they behind her, somewhere inside the building?

She felt lightheaded; she could barely breathe. Panic was taking hold, but she pushed it down, trying to rub the black chemical smoke out of her eyes and keep up with Philip.

'When we get out of here, run to the car,' he said. He pushed the car keys into her hand, then turned to the door, drawing back the bolts and unlocking it. Her coat was by the door and she pulled it on. Inside one of the pockets was her pocketknife – better than nothing.

Philip flung the door open, which only served to fan the flames in the living room behind them, and the fire leapt higher. The heat on her back was extraordinary as she ran into the cold night air.

Philip was in front of her, his Glock 17 held out in front of him as he swung it at the treeline, looking for danger. Dark smoke billowed out of the cottage and surrounded them. She couldn't see anything.

She knew where the car was, even if she couldn't see it; they'd parked it just to the right of the cottage. She sprinted to it as she heard a gunshot ring out, and then another. She unlocked the driver's door and flung it open, getting inside and locking the door behind her.

Another three gunshots rang out as she turned the engine on. Philip came staggering towards her, his pistol swinging wildly in her direction, and alarm took hold of her for a second.

His other hand was clamped around a knife protruding from his neck. He sank to his knees and waved the gun at her, as if telling her to get away from him. He fired his gun into the treeline again several times.

Loxton put the car into reverse, but she couldn't get near him because he kept firing his pistol. Once he'd emptied the chamber, another knife flew from the treeline, smashing into his neck, this time into the right side. His arm dropped and his face paled horribly. Blood spurted out from his neck at an alarming rate.

Loxton reversed the car and shielded Philip from the woods. She unlocked the car and leaned across to open the passenger door.

'Get in!' she shouted.

He held out the gun to her. She grabbed it and shouted again. 'Get in, now!'

His eyes met hers, and she knew it was useless; the blood oozing from his neck meant he'd be dead within a minute. He grimaced and his eyes rolled backwards as he fell onto his side on the ground. A knife hit her window, but it didn't even leave a scratch, bouncing harmlessly off the bulletproof glass. She crawled over the passenger seat and saw that he wasn't breathing. He was dead.

Another throwing knife hit the window. She had to get out of here. She checked the magazine of the handgun, but it was empty, and her pocketknife wasn't going to save her. She crawled back into the driver's seat, slamming the passenger door shut behind her, relieved as the doors automatically locked.

She slammed her foot on the accelerator, the car skidding with the force forward, and for a horrible moment it careered wildly. She quickly managed to gain control and drive down the lane towards the main road, but then she heard a rhythmic thudding coming from the wheels. They'd been slashed. She had no mobile and the vehicle was slow. Her life was in the balance.

Chapter 38

Loxton drove down the A-road, praying that she would be able to lose the attacker. She kept checking her rear-view mirror, but she saw nothing coming out of the lane behind her. Perhaps the killer thought she had a loaded firearm, or they'd parked a distance from the cottage and had been slowed down getting back to their car.

She tried not to think of Philip. She couldn't help him now. How had the killer found them so quickly? Had they been followed?

She saw a petrol station up ahead. Should she risk it? It was four in the morning. There was no one else on the forecourt. She pulled into the station, driving around to the back of the shop so that no one could see her from the road. She pulled up next to an old dented Nissan Micra.

The teenage attendant appeared a few moments later, a cigarette hanging out of his mouth. A frown lined his tired face. 'You can't park there. That's not for the public.' His voice faltered as he looked at her face, covered in grime and smoke, and he spotted the Glock 17 on the passenger seat. He backed off, putting his hands up.

She must look a sight in her pyjamas and coat with blood

on her hands from when Philip had handed her the firearm. The teenager's scared eyes didn't leave the gun.

She wound down the window. 'I'm a police officer. I'm not going to hurt you. Please, just give me your mobile. I need to make a call; it's urgent.'

The attendant nodded dumbly, pulling out his phone and handing it to her. She could tell he didn't believe that she was a cop, that he was frightened for his life. She took the mobile and turned slightly from him. He was no threat. She watched the corner of the building to see if any car lights pulled into the forecourt. A few cars passed by, but so far so good, and she sighed with relief.

No one would be able to see her parked behind the petrol station. There was CCTV here and a witness, and she hoped that would put the killer off pulling into the petrol station to search for her. Hopefully they'd think she'd kept driving.

She punched in Kowalski's mobile number. 'Dominik, I'm in trouble.'

'What's happened?' Kowalski's voice was strained.

'Philip's been killed and I'm in a petrol station in Kent. The safe house is on fire. I'm driving back to Walworth. I'll meet you at your favourite café, then we can go back to Walworth station together.'

'Shit,' Kowalski said. 'Okay, I'll see you there.'

'Don't tell anyone else you're meeting me there.' She hated to think of her colleagues in this way, but she was convinced that one of them must at least be selling information to whoever was doing this. 'I'm in a Nissan Micra, index M409 BNN, in case I never show.' The teenager's face dropped; she must have guessed right that it was his car. 'Tell Winter I'm not going into police protection again. Fuck that. I'm not letting more people get killed because of me.'

'Alana, you need to calm down. We'll talk to Winter together.'

'I need to get the fuck away from here. Get Kent police to go to the safe house. And I'll see you at the usual. It should take me three hours max to get there.' She hung up on him. She didn't have time to explain things to him. The next few minutes could decide whether she lived or died.

'Give me your car keys,' she said to the attendant.

His face was stricken and he didn't move.

'Give me your keys.' She held out her hand. He put his hand reluctantly into his pocket and handed her his car keys. She got into the Micra, taking the firearm and his mobile with her.

She wasn't going to wait here. The killer had found her, despite her being in police protection. It could be that they'd followed her, but she had a growing suspicion that they had access to police databases, including special protection. They'd got Sarah in the middle of an operation and they'd found her in the safe house within hours. Or they'd somehow bugged her. She checked her coat pockets and inside the top one she never used she found a small black plastic fob-like device. Was it a tracker of some sort? Only other police officers had access to her coat. But then she remembered her door being off the latch. Suspecting someone had been in her flat. Could they have planted it then?

She took a photo of the device on the boy's mobile and then threw it out of the car. She wasn't going to wait for Kent police to arrange a firearms unit to come here to meet her. That could take twenty minutes, and who knew who would get to her first? She was going back to her own police station. Back to her team.

She wasn't going to run anymore.

Chapter 39

Mamuska was busy, as she hoped it would be. She settled into a corner table at the back of the restaurant and ordered a coffee. Her eyes scanned the room, but everyone seemed legitimate. With her coat buttoned up and her hands hidden in her pockets, no one paid her any special attention, even though she had only pyjamas on underneath her coat and she was barefoot. They were busy chatting or tucking into their food. She watched the door. She'd thought Kowalski would already be here waiting for her, but he was nowhere to be seen.

Her eyes were blurry; she was so tired. The past few hours seemed like some sort of weird nightmare and she wondered, if she called the cottage, whether she would hear Philip answer and ask her where the hell she had got to. Was she losing her mind? This all seemed so insane. She'd heard of cases like this. Police officers being targeted, hunted down with their houses set alight, always on the run. But that was always organized crime, an unhinged crime boss trying to seek their revenge and intimidate the police. Not serial killers from prison seeming to have an incredible reach, able to pluck officers from surveillance operations or attack them in safe houses.

Her coffee arrived. She thanked the waitress and waited for her to leave, then used the serviette to wipe away the worst of the blood and dirt from her hands. She took a grateful sip. The coffee was always strong in Mamuska; it was why it was Kowalski's favourite, as well as the obvious links to back home.

Where was he? She felt uneasy. What if it hadn't been Kowalski that had answered his mobile? What if the killer had intercepted his number somehow and replicated his voice? She remembered the synthesizer from the 999 call about Sarah's body. As crazy as it sounded, she desperately wanted reassurance that it was really Kowalski she'd spoken to and not someone else.

She pulled out the mobile she'd taken off the kid and scrolled to the last dialled number so she could call Kowalski again and check it was really him. She shook her head in frustration at herself. It wasn't some sort of trick; it had been Kowalski. She was losing the plot. Though that was no wonder considering what she'd been through.

Kowalski walked into the café, his eyes frantic until he spotted her. She felt her body relax as she started to feel a bit safer at last. His eyes scanned the crowd and, reassured by what he saw, he strode over to her and wrapped her up in a quick hug and then sat down heavily opposite her. 'Sorry I'm late. I was liaising with Kent.'

'For three hours?' she asked. That was how long it had taken her to drive here.

'I knew you'd be a while, and judging from the level of your coffee I'd say I timed it quite well. It was hard to slip out without anyone noticing me. If I left too early, they'd have started to wonder what I was up to, and I wanted them all to think you were coming straight to Walworth and not meeting me anywhere else.'

She couldn't argue with that, but all the same she felt strangely let down. Her nerves were on edge since the attack. 'Did they find Philip?'

'Yes, I'm sorry. Kent have got forensics combing the area, but it would help if you could tell them exactly what happened. That way they would know what areas to focus on. They've got a vague idea, but they don't want to miss anything. I know you must be exhausted.'

She nodded roughly. 'I'm fine. I'll call them when we go back in, I just need a minute.'

'Of course,' Kowalski said. The waitress came over and he ordered a coffee too. 'When you called and told me what had happened. That you could have been killed ...' He trailed off, his face strained.

'I'm okay,' she said, not wanting to dwell on how close she'd come to being the next victim. 'Thanks for meeting me. I'll feel safer going into the police station with you next to me.'

'You'll be safe in Walworth.'

'Maybe not, Dominik. Think about it. They left Emma's body in Camberwell Police Station, missing every CCTV camera in the process. They took Sarah from a police operation and they found me at the safe house. I had this tracker in my top pocket.' She showed him the photo on her phone. 'It *has* to be a police officer.'

'Are you sure that's a tracker?' he said. 'It looks like a fob to a building.'

'I don't know, but it's not mine. I left it in Kent to be safe.'

'Winter and Lena talked to me about it being an officer,' Kowalski said. 'You forget that Harding broke into Walworth station and hacked into our HR records, but maybe that's not all he did. Maybe he somehow got access to all our systems. Our addresses were just a diversion. And he was a cleaner in police stations for a few years, with access to them on his own late at night when it's quiet. Maybe he hacked in a long time ago. Maybe breaking into Walworth was to plant that device in your coat.'

'Maybe.' Loxton remembered she'd gone looking for Kowalski, leaving the office empty. Harding could have put the tracker in her coat then.

'He's ex-military. He's taken his tag off and evaded the surveillance team. Winter got some more on his service record. He worked in the SAS all right – in their intelligence unit. He was one of their best, but he lost the plot. On the field and back at home with his girlfriend. They had to reluctantly let him go. The army doctors thought he had severe PTSD, but Harding wouldn't accept it. That's as much as Winter could get from his old mates back in the military. Harding is our man. We've just got to keep you safe from him. Even if it takes an army, we'll do it.' Kowalski reached across the table and gave her hand a squeeze. 'I promise you.'

'I know you will,' she said, but it was more to reassure him than because she actually believed it.

Loxton had changed into her spare suit and ankle boots before walking into Walworth CID. She was momentarily stopped by the complete chaos, and it reminded her of the morning when she'd found out Emma was missing. There was the same nervous energy and feeling of dread. The universe had shifted and was out of kilter.

The whole room hushed, and Winter, who had been leaning at a computer, stood up straight, staring at her as if she were a mirage. Then he strode across the office and hugged her tightly. 'Thank God,' he said, holding her at arm's length, as if checking again that she was real. He released her and led her towards his office.

It seemed to break the silence, and officers called out to her, grateful that she was all right. Patel was smiling at her. It felt surreal as she stumbled after Winter. Kowalski hovered on the periphery and Winter beckoned him into the office. Kowalski closed the door on their small party.

'Alana, I'm so sorry,' Winter said. 'You could have died.'

'Philip *did* die,' she said. 'Sir, none of this is your fault. This is like nothing we've ever dealt with before.'

He nodded. 'DI Meyer wants you straight back into police protection.'

'I'm not going into police protection again,' she said. 'I need to be here.'

Winter closed his eyes briefly. 'Against all my better judgement, I agree with you. I'd rather you were here helping us catch this bastard than a sitting target some-where. We can't trust special protection; they've been compromised.'

Kowalski nodded. 'Alana's better here with us. I won't let her out of my sight.'

'At this point the fewer people we trust the better,' Winter said. 'Let's decide where Loxton goes and keep it between the three of us. Not on police records, not written down anywhere. Just us three know. Verbal communications only.' Winter pulled out three burner phones from his drawer and handed one to Kowalski and then Loxton, keeping one for himself. 'I thought these might come in handy. They've got each other's numbers pre-programmed in.'

Kowalski looked relieved. 'We'll get you in a hotel under a different name, Alana. I'll stay with you. Let's just keep where you're staying off the record. Then Harding won't be able to find you.'

Winter looked thoughtful. 'It might work. Obviously I'll deny all knowledge, say you've gone AWOL.'

'Of course, sir,' Kowalski said.

'Did you see who attacked you?' Winter asked Loxton.

'No.' She felt useless, not even being able to identify Philip's killer. 'There was a fire. We went outside and it was dark. There was smoke everywhere. Then they started throwing knives from the treeline. Philip had a gun but he didn't stand a chance. He drew them off while I got in the armoured car.'

'Knives?' Winter shook his head. 'They went up against an armed officer with *knives*? Was there more than one person?'

'I don't know but they must have known it was just Philip there. I don't understand why they didn't just slit my throat if they got into the cottage to start the fire.'

'They didn't get in the house,' Kowalski said. 'They disabled the alarms and then climbed onto the roof and poured petrol down the chimney stack and then threw down a bag of lit firelighters. The blaze took hold in minutes. You were lucky to get out alive. That's what the fire brigade in Kent said.'

'Kent want you to call them back via video call,' Winter said. 'Summarize what happened at the safe house to assist their forensic examination. And then we're going to need to take your full statement. I know you must be exhausted, but we need it now. An officer was murdered and you're the only witness.'

'Of course,' she said, although she felt her mind drifting in and out of focus. All she could think about was Philip's kind eyes and the smell of cooked breakfast. His family would have been told what had happened by now, and she closed her eyes for a moment, the grief too much.

Winter's radio crackled into life.

'Calling DCI Winter,' said a male's voice.

Winter picked it up. 'Winter here, go ahead.'

'DCI Winter, it's PC Nicholson here. Another body's been reported. It's a female. We're with the body now. It's on Thurlow Avenue, not far from the nick.'

'Another body?' She felt her stomach clench in grief. Who was it? She shook her head, willing the tears not to come as her eyes welled up anyway.

'Repeat, Thurlow Avenue, halfway down the road,' the young officer's voice said.

'What number?' Winter asked.

'The body's on the street, sir. There is no number. It's just halfway down, by the communal bins – dumped there.' The officer sounded defeated and Loxton felt a vast emptiness opening up inside her. For a moment she felt dizzy.

'We'll head over now,' Winter said. 'You've set the cordon up? I want fifty metres at least.'

'We're trying, sir, but there are only a couple of us here.'

'Well get more of you there!' Winter's voice was raised and angry. 'I want that scene closed down.'

Loxton had never seen him shout on the radio before; he was always so calm. DI Meyer came into the office. 'Have you heard?' He saw Winter's face and nodded as if to answer his own question.

'You're to stay here, Loxton,' DI Meyer said before glancing behind him and spotting Lena, who had followed him in.

'Alana, you're all right,' Lena said, relief flooding her face. 'I thought you might be hurt.'

'The profiler will stay here with you, DC Loxton,' DI Meyer said.

Lena pulled a confused face. 'Sarge, if a protection officer couldn't keep her safe then how do you think I'm going to manage it?' Lena asked, not even trying to hide the sarcasm in her voice. 'I don't even have a gun; we'd be dead in about ten seconds.'

'She's right, it's best DC Loxton comes with us for now,' DCI Winter said. 'Most of the station will be at the crime scene. She's safer that way.'

DI Meyer shook his head. 'It's against protocol.'

'We're way beyond protocol,' Winter said. 'Loxton, you're in my car. No arguments. Kowalski, you go with Lena. And Kowalski, remember what we talked about. I want you to make sure that action happens.'

'Will do, sir,' Kowalski said, dropping his burner phone into his pocket. Loxton nodded at Winter too as he rushed to the door.

'Come on,' DI Meyer called to one of his detectives who was sat in the office. 'We don't want them messing up our scene. Winter, I'm in charge, remember.'

'If you say so,' Winter said as he strode out of the CID office first not looking back at Meyer.

Chapter 40

Thurlow Avenue was chaos. Police officers were shouting at one another, the panic beneath the surface palpable. Winter pulled up and his mobile rang. 'It's the borough commander,' he said. 'Just what I don't need. Lena and Kowalski are just up ahead.' He pointed them out to her.

'Thanks for sticking up for me back there.'

'I'll be watching you from the car,' Winter said. 'I won't be long.'

She nodded. There were about twenty uniformed officers and several detectives that she knew, all turning up now, making the chaos seem larger.

She reached the police officer on the external cordon. 'You need to widen the perimeter,' she said to him. 'This is too small. DCI Winter wanted at least fifty metres.' It was easier to work through this, to push her feelings downwards, to put on her police mask.

'We're trying to widen it,' the officer said, getting on the radio to advise his supervisor. She showed him her warrant card and he jotted her name down on the scene log and let her through.

Loxton expected it to be a similar scenario to Emma

and Sarah. The victim killed somewhere else. Transported here in some sort of vehicle. No forensic evidence left. But she couldn't take the chance. Maybe he'd brought her here on foot. And once the scene was closed, the police wouldn't come back; any evidence missed would be lost forever. She wanted the net as wide as possible. She didn't want to miss a thing.

All they needed was for the killer to make one tiny mistake, as small as a head hair left behind, and then they would be able to identify him. She couldn't believe this person wasn't in the system for something.

As she moved from the outside to the inner cordon, she saw a young woman being dragged back by officers. She was shocked when she recognized who it was.

'Rosa, you can't be here.' Loxton tried to hold her back, helping the other officers. Rosa flayed her arms at them, striking out and catching Loxton on the cheekbone.

'She's my sister!' Rosa was screaming at them, straining to get past Loxton and the other officers. 'I need to see her!'

Kowalski joined Loxton, his face full of confusion. 'Rosa, what are you doing here?'

'I want to see her.' Tears ran down Rosa's face. She covered her eyes with her hands.

'You can't, not yet. Not like this,' Kowalski said. 'We don't even know if it's her.'

Kowalski wrapped his arms around her. 'I'm so sorry, but you'll have to wait, Rosa.' Loxton felt like her heart was breaking, watching Rosa fall apart. She caught Lena watching carefully as well, her face for a fraction of a second looking darker – concern etched in her eyes. Lena didn't know that Kowalski had dated Gabriella. She thought he was being inappropriate. Their eyes met for a second and Loxton looked away from Lena. She should have told her about Kowalski's involvement with the murdered detectives. She would tell her later, when she got a chance.

Rosa was crying heavily into Kowalski's shoulder. 'Come on, I'll get someone to take you somewhere safe, kiddo.'

'Gabriella.' Rosa's voice broke as she whispered her sister's name.

Loxton heard the faint crackle of voices from a police radio coming from Rosa's bag. 'Rosa, what's in your bag?'

Rosa handed it to her, her eyes staring blankly through Loxton. 'Here, I don't need it anymore.'

Loxton looked inside Rosa's bag. There was a police radio inside with a sticker on the back which had '*Gabriella Caselli*' written across it. That's how she'd known about the body. She'd been listening to the police channel, probably ever since Gabriella had gone missing.

Kowalski led her away. 'I'll take her to my car and get her into police protection.' His face looked strained. 'Can you both handle things here? Lena, don't let Alana out of your sight.'

'Not a chance,' Lena said.

Loxton nodded and tried to hold back the tears as she watched Rosa being walked away. The crime scene had frozen, forensic officers in their white garb stood staring at Rosa as if she was from another planet. Something that definitely shouldn't be here. Something they didn't want to have to see. Loxton understood why. It was hard enough to deal with the dead without the living reminding you of everything the dead had lost. The wreckage that their passing had left behind. There was no pretending with this one. The pain was palpable, and they couldn't unsee it. It made the work unbearable.

With Rosa gone, the crime scene's rhythm started up

again and Loxton could lose herself in its morbid harmony. Lena led Loxton to the forensic tent, which was erected next to the communal bins. Inside that tent was her old friend.

Lena handed her a forensic suit and began garbing up herself. Loxton silently pulled hers on, then the gloves and finally affixed the mask, covering her face. She glanced at Lena's grey eyes. Lena seemed to pull a pained face, but for all Loxton knew she could be smiling under the mask.

'I'm so sorry,' Lena said. 'I can't imagine how hard this is for you. If you want, you can stay out here? There are plenty of officers here; you'll be safe.'

'I need to see.' Loxton couldn't explain it any more than that. There were other people who could do the work instead of her, but none of that mattered. She needed to see for herself, otherwise she wouldn't be able to think like the killer. And she needed to know how this killer's mind worked.

Loxton pulled the tent flap back and stepped inside. The crime scene manager was crouched by the naked body and looked up at her. She could only see his eyes. His face was covered with the mask, the hood obscuring as much of his face as hers. There was horror in his eyes, not the calm, detached expression she had come to expect. Horror in her colleagues' faces was becoming all too familiar.

She looked down slowly at the body. It was Gabriella Caselli all right, her face contorted in agony. Her naked body was a red mess, ripped to pieces as if by a wild animal. Loxton's stomach tightened and she tried to steady her breathing, burning acid rising up her throat. She looked back at the crime scene manager's eyes.

'It's bad.' He shook his head. 'It's the most violent murder I've ever dealt with.'

She crouched down next to her friend's body. The viciousness of the attack was staggering. As was the sheer energy and force that would have been required to carry it out. Lena stood beside her, briefly putting her hand on Loxton's shoulder and squeezing. Then she too crouched down next to Gabriella.

Lena tilted her head to the side to study the body. 'Frenzied yet controlled.'

'Controlled?' Loxton frowned; she couldn't see it herself.

The crime scene manager leaned backwards for a moment. 'I see what you mean. The stab wounds are all hitting the major organs. It's hard to see because there are so many of them. But you're right; it doesn't look like they've missed the target once. And there's not much blood, which suggests they were inflicted after death, unless he cleaned her afterwards.'

Lena nodded and Loxton forced herself to look at her friend's body again. There must be thirty stab wounds, but they were all targeting some vital part of the body – the heart, lungs, liver, stomach, uterus ... None were wasted. There were no blows glancing off the rib cage; no cuts to the side of the body where the knife had missed its target. Gabriella's legs and arms were untouched. Likewise, her face and neck had not been stabbed. It was like nothing she'd ever seen. The image of the throwing knife piercing Philip's jugular flashed into her mind. The precision.

'I'm not sure it's the person who killed Emma and Sarah,' the crime scene manager said.

Loxton forced the emotive side of herself to shut down. Instead, she leaned towards Gabriella's neck, gently feeling the windpipe, and then stared into Gabriella's opened eyes. 'The strangulation is consistent with Emma and Sarah's murders. The windpipe's crushed, with more bruising on the left side again. I'd say it is the same killer. See the rope marks on the wrists and ankles? It's the same patterning. We'll have to see if the pathologist agrees once the post-mortem's completed.'

'Perhaps there was someone else assisting this time?' the CSI asked. 'To account for the amount of stab wounds and the escalation in violence?'

'I don't think this killer plays well with others.' Lena threw a nervous glance at Loxton. Satisfied by Loxton's nod of her head to go on, Lena continued. 'I doubt he's been able to find himself a new replacement so quickly after failing to get Barratt out. This feels like he's trying to up the ante of each killing. As if he's working himself up to a grand finale. The stab marks are rage-fuelled, but also measured. He feels like he's justified because he's dishing out a deserved punishment. The crime that he believes these women have committed, well, it makes him furious, but he's a man who's used to exacting his revenge carefully. He takes his time. He doesn't want to risk making mistakes. It's a cold fury. Calculated. He obviously didn't rape and kill her here. We need to look at the victims again. Try to work out why the violence is intensifying. Whether there's a pattern we can see. It could be he's sending a message to us.' Lena stared at Loxton, willing her to decipher it.

Loxton closed her eyes briefly, trying to control her rapid breathing. She forced her eyes open and stared at Gabriella again. It looked like he'd raped and strangled her first, crushing her windpipe, then inflicted the stab wounds. Loxton prayed the CSI was right and that was the case. If the stab wounds had come first, before the crushed windpipe, Loxton shuddered at the prolonged agony her friend would have suffered in death.

She found it hard to see the message as she looked at her friend's wrecked body. But she needed to see it to decipher who was sending it.

Gabriella had been instrumental in putting Barratt behind bars. Was this why the violence had increased to such a level? It was Gabriella who had linked the Barratt murders together to make them into a linked series. Jane had spoken to the sex workers who knew the victims, trying to identify how he was choosing targets. She had recognized a type, which was circulated through the media. But it was Loxton herself who had been the one to nail Barratt. He'd been careless at one of the murder scenes, disturbed by a pimp who was keeping an eye on his workers, worried about the recent spate of killings.

Loxton had walked the victim's route and found a stray hair off the path that came back to Barratt. One discarded hair that had linked him to the crime scene. The rest had been sheer hard work. A team effort.

Winter came into the tent and took in the scene quickly, his mouth twisting into a grimace for a brief second. He seemed to gain control of himself. 'I haven't seen anything like this since Iraq.' He shook his head, as if trying to clear his thoughts. 'When do you think this happened?'

The crime scene manager shook his head. 'Not long ago; rigor mortis hasn't even set in yet. The internal temperature is still quite high. Less than twelve hours. My personal guess, less than five, but that's not evidential.'

Winter looked perplexed. 'Is it the same person who killed Emma Robins?'

Loxton nodded. 'It looks like the violence is escalating along with the importance the officer played in the Barratt investigation.' She motioned towards Gabriella's body.

'This murder is exactly like a Szymański killing,' Lena

said, her full attention on Loxton. 'Did Barratt use a knife on his victims?'

'Yes, but not to this extent. This is something else.'

'Szymański's violence increased to this level as his killings went on,' Lena said. 'Szymański is definitely the inspiration, but this killer is doing it to avenge Barratt. Kevin Harding is obsessed with both of them. He's Szymański's Avenger.'

'We'll find him,' Winter said. 'We're putting out a medial appeal to the public that he's wanted.'

Loxton felt herself withdrawing from the scene as if it wasn't real. Gabriella couldn't be dead. Gabriella, so full of life, who could drink anyone under the table. Loxton tried to keep it together.

Meyer came into the tent and glanced at the body and then at the people gathered there. 'DC Loxton, you're going back into protection now,' he said. 'I'm going to get that arranged. DC Trawinska, can you step out here and tell me your thoughts on the killer?'

Lena nodded in a daze and moved out of the tent with Meyer to a quieter spot, leaving Loxton and Winter with Gabriella.

'The specialist protection team can't protect me,' she said to Winter. 'We didn't even make it to forty-eight hours.'

'Alana, Meyer's taken it out of my hands. He called the borough commander when we left Walworth. That's why he was late to the scene. The borough commander was quite clear that this is no longer my case. It's Meyer's call. They think the killer must have followed you and Philip to the safe house, there was that device in your coat. It could well have been a tracker put there when Harding broke into Walworth. They're saying Philip and his team fucked up and it won't happen again. You'll be getting a different team. I'm sorry.'

'I shouldn't be hiding.' She tried to hold back the angry tears. 'We need to find him – *stop* him. Don't you get it? Unless we stop him, I'm going to die.'

'We will stop him, Alana. Just not you.' Winter's voice was softer than she'd ever heard it before. 'The team will pick you up at Walworth. DI Meyer's calling them now. Are you okay here? I'll just get Kowalski so he can take you back to Walworth. Lena and I will stay at the scene.'

Loxton nodded, not trusting herself to speak. It was out of his hands; there was no point in arguing with him anymore. But she couldn't go into protection. Jane was out there and Loxton believed she was still alive, that there was still a chance to save her – to save herself.

Winter left her in the tent alone. The others treated Gabriella as if she were just sleeping and they didn't want to disturb her. But Gabriella didn't look like she was asleep one bit. Her mouth was contorted in a scream and her eyes were wide open. They were blood shot, all the capillaries in them burst, leaving strange, almost snowflake-like bright red patterns on the whites of her eyes. Her neck was at a horrible angle. Loxton screwed her eyes shut for a moment. When she looked again, she found herself leaning closer towards Gabriella's opened mouth. There was something there – a white object lodged painfully at the back of Gabriella's throat.

She stepped outside of the tent and called the crime scene investigator back. Lena and Winter were both stood nearby; she could hear them talking about Kowalski. They couldn't get hold of him to take her back. She saw them both notice her and then glance nervously at each other, as if they were keeping tabs on her.

The CSI came into the tent with her. 'What is it?' he asked.

'There's something in her throat.' Loxton's voice sounded strange and quiet.

'What?' The crime scene investigator glanced at her.

'In her throat.'

The CSI hurried forward and peered into Gabriella's throat. He pulled out long tweezers and Loxton flinched when he inserted them into Gabriella's mouth. He retrieved the object and carefully opened it up.

Loxton saw that it was another note in his gloved hand. She stepped outside and called to Lena and Winter to come over.

The tent was crowded as they all stood together.

Lena leaned closer and read aloud the typed text: '*If you take Alana off the case again, you'll be sorry. More people will die than need to.*'

Chapter 41

'I can't get hold of Kowalski,' Winter said. 'I don't know where the fuck he's got to. Uniform took Rosa to Walworth to meet the protection officers, so he's not with her. I'll have to take you back to the station.'

'He's okay, isn't he?' Loxton asked. 'Harding took his address as well, remember.'

'I hope so,' Winter said.

Loxton's mobile rang with an unknown number and she picked it up with relief. 'Dominik, where are you?'

'DC Loxton, it's Kevin Harding.' Loxton's hand tightened on her mobile. Was he calling to taunt her? Was Jane with him? She left the tent, not wanting to be near Gabriella while she talked to him.

Harding's voice sounded panicky, his words tumbling out in a rush. She frowned and put him on loudspeaker, motioning for Winter to come over and listen.

'Kevin, slow down.' She moved over to Winter, who was frowning in concern.

'I want to talk, but I'll only speak to you. No one else.' Harding's voice was panicked on the phone.

'Well, I'm listening,' she said.

'No, not like this.' Harding sounded angry. 'In person. I only trust you.'

Loxton looked at Winter, who frowned and shook his head. He would never agree. Harding was their main suspect, and now he seemed desperate. If he was the killer, she'd have expected him to be cleverer than this, though. It didn't feel right.

'Can't you just tell me over the phone?' Loxton asked. 'It's just me now.'

'I don't know who's listening in; you don't either. My mobile could be tapped. My life's at risk here. You need to come over right now.' His voice was shaking and he sounded hysterical. Had he been drinking?

She had to keep Harding talking, get as much information as possible. 'Okay, but you need to calm down. Where are you?'

'You know where I am. I'm in my flat waiting for you,' Harding hissed.

'Kevin, I know you took off your tag and left your flat. Why did you do that?'

'Szymański's Avenger can track me using that tag. He's going to kill me. I had to go on the run. I've only come back to the flat to meet up with you. You've got to come quick; I can't stay here long.'

For a brief moment she believed Harding. He was utterly convincing. He seemed terrified of something. He seemed to share her belief that the killer had infiltrated the police. 'Look, I can't just come over on my own,' she said. 'I need to get it authorized first.'

'Please, I need police protection now.' Harding's voice was urgent. 'You're supposed to be getting me protection.'

'Let me send a unit to you; they'll be with you in a few minutes.'

'No police, that will make it worse. Just you.'

'*I'm* police, Kevin.' Harding was hysterical; he wasn't making sense.

'You're different,' he said. 'Szymański's Avenger is trying to kill you too, so I know I can trust you. Your name was on the list.'

List? So he *was* involved. And now he was trying to trick her, by pretending they were in it together – that both their lives were in danger. Attempting to make a connection was classic manipulation; she did it herself with suspects, but this was something else.

'Get out of your flat,' she said. 'Go to a public place. A café. You'll be safer there. I'll be with you as soon as I can.' Loxton didn't like the fear in his voice. It was real. Winter raised his eyebrows in warning and Loxton put her hand out to placate him.

'I'm not leaving my flat now. No way. It's too dangerous. They could be in the corridor outside. I'll be here. I've been on the phone too long.' Harding hung up.

Loxton let out a long breath, her adrenaline levels high, as if she'd contracted Harding's fear through the phone.

'What game is he playing?' Winter said. 'As if I'd let you go there on your own, when he's our main suspect. He's insane.'

Loxton shrugged; she had no idea. 'He sounded genuinely scared, sir. I think he's being serious about his life being in danger. And when people are frightened, they make mistakes. This could be our only chance to catch him. To stop this.'

'You need to go to Walworth to meet the protection team. DI Meyer is adamant.'

'Protection didn't work out so well last time, sir. And you read the note. More people will die if you take me off the case. It's *my* life. Let me make the choice. If you go there without me and Harding sees that I'm not there, he won't talk. If I'm there he might tell me where Jane is. And if there is someone else involved, this Szymański's Avenger, they could kill her while we waste time.'

Winter considered this and then closed his eyes for a brief moment. When he opened them, she saw a flare of anger there. 'Fine, but you're to stay right by my side, whatever happens,' Winter said. 'This feels like a trap, Alana. Kowalski's gone missing now. We're having uniformed units go with us. I'm not taking any chances with any more of my officers.'

She knew what he meant about a trap, but what choice did they have? The note was clear: more lives would be lost if she wasn't on the case. This might be their only chance to get Harding talking and find out where Jane was being held. And two could play at setting traps.

Chapter 42

Winter banged again on Harding's door; there was no answer. He tried the handle, but the door was locked. In his other hand was his drawn baton. Loxton stayed back but made sure she could be seen through the spy hole, so it looked like she was the only person there.

'Kevin, open the door,' she called out.

The uniform were behind the corner, out of view.

Winter shook his head and lowered his voice to a whisper. 'Harding could be stood behind that door with a knife.'

She nodded back in silence, drawing her own baton too. He motioned for the uniform to move forwards with the enforcer. Loxton stepped away to let them through. The largest officer swung the enforcer back in silence and then sent it full force into the door. The crash was deafening, and splinters of wood showered back at them. He then swung it into the door again. The thin council door smashed open and another officer ran forward with a riot shield. The other uniformed officers charged after him.

Winter was next to Loxton, and she realized his only concern was for her. One uniformed officer kept watch and nodded for them to go in while he stayed outside as guard.

Inside the flat, they were met with disarray. A side table in the corridor had been knocked over, a smashed bowl was on the floor, its contents spilled across the cheap linoleum flooring. She saw spatters of blood on the floor.

Winter and Loxton raised their batons high and followed the trail of blood and disaster into the living room, as if someone had run through here, desperate to escape something. The officers were checking all the hiding places, searching everywhere for danger.

The two-seater sofa was shoved to the side. She saw a door leading off from the living room and knew from the previous search that it was the kitchen.

'In here. Suspect's dead,' called a uniform officer. She headed towards the voice, dread filling her heart. Winter caught her, shook his head, and stepped in front of her. She followed him into the kitchen and saw Harding sprawled on his front across the kitchen floor.

His neck was at a strange angle, his face turned to the side, but too far to be normal. Winter checked Harding's pulse before allowing her near. Satisfied Harding was dead, he motioned her over.

One of the uniformed officers put down a bag full of equipment and started handing out forensic suits and masks. This had gone from a welfare check to a crime scene. Loxton pulled a suit on, gloves and fixed her mask in place before crouching down next to Harding.

She was drawn to his eyes, which were wide with disbelief. It was as if, at the moment he was killed, he couldn't believe it had all gone so horribly wrong. There was a kitchen knife a couple of inches from his outstretched hand, his fingertips almost brushing the handle. The tip of the knife had a little white piece of paper stabbed through it.

She glanced at Harding's knife block, which had been

dragged towards the edge of the kitchen counter, and saw the same style of kitchen knives neatly stored there.

Except one knife was missing.

Harding must have run to it and tried to grab the knife to protect himself, but before he could turn around and use it, he had collapsed from his injuries.

She crouched next to the body and saw that there were multiple stab wounds in his back, blood still oozing from them. There were no stab wounds on his front. His neck had red marks on it, where the killer must have remained calm, strangling him to complete their ritual.

She suspected Harding had been a challenge. She imagined him letting his killer in and turning his back on them for a moment. A fatal mistake.

Winter interrupted her thoughts. 'The rest of the flat's clear,' he said. 'The killer's gone.'

'We were too late,' Loxton said. She felt frustration and guilt heavy in her chest. Harding had called her for help, no one else, and she hadn't been able to save him. She hadn't been able to save any of them. She shivered. If Harding, a trained killing machine, couldn't protect himself, what chance did she have? Or Jane?

'He was on bail for murder and he gets killed after requesting police protection,' Winter said. 'We had it all wrong.'

'No one could have predicted this was going to happen,' Loxton said. 'And we got here as quickly as we could. Why did he come back to his flat? He must have known how risky it was. It was like he thought I'd told him to come here.' She felt sick thinking that the killer must have only just left. If Harding had called five minutes earlier, they might have got here first, and he might have told them something vital – something to help them save Jane.

Winter rubbed his hand across his face and then radioed Control and updated them, requesting Forensics. She stared at the dead man and couldn't help imagining Jane in his place. She blinked rapidly, but the image remained – Jane's hand reaching for the knife instead of Harding's. Jane stabbed to death before she could defend herself. Loxton shook her head, trying to dislodge the picture from her mind.

She heard voices from the corridor and called out. 'We're in here.'

Lena and Kowalski walked into the kitchen with full forensic suits on and joined them by Harding's body.

Winter looked relieved when he saw Kowalski. 'I thought something had happened to you. I couldn't get hold of you.'

'I was on the phone sorting out police protection for Gabriella's sister and then Meyer got me to arrange a team for Alana.' He looked guiltily at her, as if he'd betrayed her.

'It doesn't matter, Dominik,' Loxton said. It wasn't his fault.

She looked back down at the body and carefully picked up the note with tweezers and held it up so the others could read it at the same time. The first few words didn't make sense to her and she wondered what language it was written in: '*Wczoraj bracie. Dzisiaj wrogu.*'

Kowalski leaned towards the note and went grey as he read out loud. '*Wczoraj bracie. Dzisiaj wrogu.* "Yesterday a brother. Today an enemy." *Alana, it's your turn to disappear next. Better run, they can't save you.*' Kowalski's eyes met Loxton's and she saw the horror contained in them. For an awful second, she had thought Kowalski had been talking directly to her, that *he* was the killer. But then she saw the address to her on the paper. If she were in any doubt before, she now knew it was their killer who had murdered Harding.

It was the first time he had written in a different language, though. And instead of the carefully crafted printed-out letters, the note had been handwritten, as if he was in a hurry.

'Harding was going to talk,' Lena said. 'He knew who the murderer was, assisted them. Somehow the killer preempted Harding's betrayal and silenced him.'

Winter sighed and looked down at Harding's face. 'If we'd just got here quicker.'

Loxton wanted to reach out her hand and squeeze his shoulder. She saw the guilt she felt reflected in his face, but he was responsible for the whole investigation. He was in charge.

She looked at Kowalski and Lena. They threw each other a worried look. 'What is it?' she asked.

'It's Polish and I ... I recognize the handwriting,' Kowalski said.

'Care to share?' Loxton glanced from Lena to Kowalski.

'It looks like Szymański's handwriting.' Kowalski shook his head in disbelief. 'It's almost an exact match.'

'But it can't be,' Lena said. 'You know that's impossible. I saw his body. I touched his skin to make sure he was cold.' She looked embarrassed by her admission.

'What part of Poland was he from?' Loxton asked. 'It might help us reduce our search. People often write in a similar way when they're from certain areas and generations.'

'He was from the same area as me,' Kowalski said. 'Near Poznań. But Szymański's handwriting is unique. No one else writes quite like that. Sure, there are similarities to people from Poznań, but it's the neatest handwriting you'll ever see – obsessive. It was part of our evidence in the trial;

we had a handwriting expert. Szymański left notes like this at all his crime scenes. Everyone's handwriting is unique; even a good forgery will not be exactly the same. But this looks perfect.'

Lena nodded in agreement. 'I've never seen anyone write like Szymański either. It's so unusual.'

Loxton studied the writing. It was tiny and perfect, almost beautiful in its delicateness.

Winter took charge. 'Kowalski, I want you to make contact with the Poland murder squad who dealt with Szymański. Get a photo of the handwriting sent over. Maybe he has relatives. Maybe a twin. I don't know.'

Kowalski looked perplexed. 'He only had his mother and she's in a home now with dementia.'

'As Loxton said, it's not uncommon for people from the same generation and area to write similarly,' Winter said. 'It might be unique to the way his teacher taught him; maybe others from his class write like him.' Loxton admired Winter's positivity. He was trying to keep them going.

Kowalski took the sample. 'All right and I'll get it to the lab for them to check for any trace evidence too.' Kowalski carefully packaged the note in a brown evidence bag and left the scene.

'It's something,' Winter said. 'But why is the killer recreating Szymański's MO, yet targeting the investigation team that caught Barratt? And why only the female detectives? It doesn't make sense.'

Loxton shook her head and saw that Lena was as confused as her.

'My profile was wrong,' Lena said. 'Harding fit it perfectly. I think the killer was trying to set him up, get him to take the fall, but Harding changed his mind. I've been an idiot; I fell right for it.'

'It's not your fault,' Loxton said. 'The profile made sense to me too.'

'Yes, but it was a distraction, and we've wasted so much time on it and look where it's got us.' Lena's gaze dropped to Harding's body.

'The forensic team are here, sir,' a uniformed officer told Winter, who nodded to allow them access.

Dr Reynolds, the pathologist, was with two forensic officers. He looked more stressed than Loxton had ever seen him. Because Harding was on bail, this was going to be classed as a death in police and court custody. Harding had also called police minutes before his murder asking for protection. There would be a police inquiry. Meyer was not far behind, his face dropping when he saw for himself that Harding was dead.

'I've been trying to call you,' Reynolds said to Winter. 'Where's Kowalski?'

'I've been dealing with this scene,' Winter said. 'Kowalski's just left to take evidence to the lab. The body's here, Doctor.'

Reynolds didn't move. His eyes met Loxton's. He looked pained.

'I'm sorry, Alana,' Reynolds said. 'I found DNA on all of the bodies. We know that what we found on Emma's body came back as Kowalski's, which could be written off as accidental transmission on his part. But there's been a DNA match on Sarah's and Gabriella's bodies now, too. The DNA was found on their necks, just like on Emma's. It matches Dominik one billion to one. The Kowalski I know was never that sloppy when investigating a crime scene . . . unless his DNA was already there.'

'What?' Loxton shook her head in disbelief. 'There must be some mistake.'

'Are you sure?' Winter asked, his face shocked.

'I've run it three times now,' Reynolds said.

'Did he attend the post-mortems?' Winter asked.

'No, Meyer's team did. Because of Kowalski's personal involvement with each victim.'

'Kowalski didn't have personal involvement with them,' Winter said, looking confused.

Loxton closed her eyes. Winter didn't know about Kowalski's previous relationships. 'Kowalski dated Emma and Gabriella a few years back,' she said, filling him in. 'And he'd slept with Sarah.'

Lena stared at Loxton. 'He hasn't said a word about it to me.'

'Or to me.' Winter's gaze flicked from Reynolds to Loxton, then back to Reynolds. 'Are you sure about this?'

'I knew about Emma Robins,' Reynolds said. 'Alana's clearly found out about Gabriella and Sarah.'

'Why didn't you tell me?' Winter said to Loxton.

'Dominik said you knew.' She closed her eyes for a moment, wondering how she could have been so stupid.

'And I'm guessing Jane has been close with him too?' Lena said.

'Maybe, but then it still doesn't make sense,' Loxton said. 'Why would the killer target me?'

'Alana, I hate to ask,' Winter looked at her. 'But are you and Dominik romantically involved?'

Lena looked away, embarrassed on Loxton's behalf.

Loxton felt her cheeks colour at the suggestion. 'No, not at all. Never.'

'If you ever have been, I need to know,' Winter said.

'And I said *no*,' Loxton said. It embarrassed her that Winter would even think that she would lie about it.

Winter nodded roughly. 'Okay. I'm not taking any more

risks. I'll get a safe house arranged for you, but in the meantime, I want you away from this investigation and somewhere safe. Go with Lena and get out of London. I'll send officers to find Kowalski.'

'Sir, I'm not going to another safe house.' She shook her head resolutely. 'I've told you that. I need to help with the investigation. Dominik can't be the killer.'

'This is why you have to go. You're too involved. You've been attacked once already. Lena, get her out of London and then the protection team will tell you where the new safe house will be.'

'And when I'm killed, you'll be able to blame the protection officers and not yourself.' Loxton couldn't hide the anger from her voice.

'Alana, enough,' Winter's voice was sharp. He turned to Lena. 'Don't tell anyone where you're going, not even me. We don't want Kowalski finding her.' Winter's voice was hard as he said the words.

Lena's eyes met Winter's and he held her gaze. 'Understood,' she said.

Loxton felt sick. 'But it can't be Dominik. He's been with Lena for the past hour, and Harding was only killed within the past *half* hour. I spoke with Harding myself.'

Lena frowned at Loxton. 'Dominik wasn't with me. He met me outside the block just before I came in. I thought he was already here with you and DCI Winter. He gave that impression, anyway.'

Winter and Loxton exchanged glances.

'He said he was delayed arranging police protection for Alana,' Winter said.

'That only took five minutes,' Meyer said.

Loxton felt her heart sink at the realization that Kowalski had been missing for nearly an hour.

'I'll let the officers with Rosa know that Kowalski is not to go near her,' Lena said. 'I'll be five minutes.'

'I'll have to rearrange a protection team for you,' Meyer said to Loxton. 'I can't trust anything that Kowalski has arranged now that we know he's involved in all of this. I knew something didn't add up about this case.'

Loxton felt like she was going to scream, as they all just accepted that Kowalski was their killer.

Lena came back into the room. 'Rosa's fine; the uniform said she's with the protection team now.'

'I'll call you with details of where to meet the protection team,' Winter said. 'But for now, get Loxton out of London, Lena.'

'I'll take good care of her,' Lena replied.

Winter nodded and watched as they left the flat. Lena led Loxton to the car. 'I'll drive,' Lena said. 'You navigate us out of London.'

Loxton felt like the world was out of kilter as she climbed into the passenger seat. 'This is all wrong. I can't believe this is to do with Dominik. It doesn't make sense. Harding took both our addresses. Maybe he planted Kowalski's DNA on the bodies?'

'That's possible,' Lena said hopefully. She turned on the ignition and locked them inside the car, casting a wary glance around the street. 'I can't believe your DCI took us off the case, right when it's breaking. And to have Kowalski as the only suspect? They're not thinking straight.' She pulled the car out and got them moving.

'We need to find Kowalski,' Loxton said. 'Talk to him. Warn him that Winter has the wrong idea. Let's head to his place; he might be there. We're not far.'

'You know the way?' Lena asked.

'He doesn't live far from me,' Loxton said. 'I've dropped him off a couple of times after late finishes.'

Lena arched her eyebrow at Loxton. 'I see,' she said pointedly.

'Not like that,' Loxton replied, her voice coming out harder than she intended. Everyone was convinced that because she'd been targeted it meant that she and Kowalski had slept together, but they hadn't. 'We're friends, that's it.'

Loxton's phone rang.

Winter's voice came on the line, urgent. 'Kowalski's not taken the note to the lab, and he's not answering his mobile or radio. We can't find him anywhere.'

'He could have been intercepted by the killer,' Loxton said putting the call on loudspeaker.

'Kowalski is our man.' Winter's voice was angry. 'The Szymański/Barratt element was a red herring to send us off track. Forget about that.' Lena shook her head in disbelief and put her foot on the accelerator, speeding up the car.

'You're wrong,' Loxton said, but as soon as the words were out of her mouth, she knew that she sounded crazy. Everything pointed to Kowalski. His DNA was on Emma's, Sarah's and Gabriella's bodies. He'd sent her in the wrong direction when Harding had escaped from Walworth station, letting Harding get away. He'd been missing when Harding had been murdered and now he was AWOL.

'If it wasn't him, why has he run?' Winter said. 'He isn't the first serial-killer cop and he won't be the last. There's no other explanation for the DNA. He's our killer. I'm sorry.'

Loxton shook her head.

'I'm sending two firearms units to his flat,' Winter said. 'Kowalski's dangerous, Alana. You're not to go there.' It was as if he'd read her mind.

'We're almost there, sir,' Loxton said.

'You never listen,' Winter said, the frustration clear in his voice. 'Loxton, you're too involved. Both of you are friends with Kowalski. You won't be objective. You'll get hurt. Stand down. Kowalski knows all our tricks; it makes us vulnerable.'

'I'm sorry, sir, but this is Dominik you're talking about, and he's not a killer.' Loxton hung up on him. She glanced at Lena, but she didn't look as sure anymore.

Chapter 43

Saturday 5 February, 10:20

There was no sign of any of the other units as Loxton and Lena arrived at Kowalski's block of flats.

'Come on,' Loxton said as she climbed out of the car and ran to the communal doors. 'If he's there we can talk him down before the firearms officers arrive. Once they turn up then who knows what will happen.'

Lena raced after her. Loxton pulled out her fireman key and used it to unlock the communal doors. She ran up the flight of stairs to the third floor. She could hear Lena clattering behind her.

Kowalski's door was locked but Loxton knew there was a spare key under the mat; she'd seen him use it often enough when he'd left his keys at the office. She fished it out and unlocked the door.

They stayed together and it took them less than a minute to rush through the small empty flat.

'He's not here.' The fear that had been gnawing at Loxton choked her words, so that her voice came out as a croak. The place was a mess. Clothes thrown on the double bed and floor. Cupboards left open. It was like it had been ransacked.

'Shit,' Lena said. 'I've got a bad feeling about this.'

'There are no obvious signs of injury. There's no blood, nothing smashed. And the door was locked.'

'It was pretty easy for us to get in,' Lena said. 'It does look like he's left in a hurry, though. Maybe Kowalski realized we'd be on to him soon and came here to grab a few things for his escape.' Lena looked guilty even entertaining the idea.

The flat reminded Loxton of searching Emma's place; she felt the same strange foreboding that the occupant wouldn't be coming back. The image of Emma's lifeless body in Camberwell station came back to her, accompanied by the cleaner's frantic screams. What if Kowalski hadn't arrived at the lab because the killer had got to him? The thought was like a punch to her diaphragm, knocking the wind out of her, and she had to try hard to steady her breathing.

She had to keep a clear head. To think. She couldn't let her emotion get the better of her. She couldn't afford to miss something that might be crucial.

'Can you try and find Kowalski's car on ANPR?' she said to Lena. 'I'll get Forensics down here to check for blood traces. When the firearms unit and uniformed officers turn up, they can try the neighbours, see if they saw or heard anything.'

Loxton realized she was pacing up and down the small living room flat as she made frantic phone calls to arrange everything. She stopped and looked at Lena. 'Any joy with the car?'

Lena was on her mobile to the ANPR bureau. 'His car's last known location was on Oakdale Road.'

'Where's that?' Loxton asked.

Lena pulled up Google Maps. 'It looks like a quiet

residential area with an industrial estate behind it. Not too far – about twenty minutes' drive away.'

'It could be significant,' Loxton said. 'We should check it out.'

'Maybe.' Lena didn't look convinced. 'Winter wants us off the investigation. He's furious right now.'

'He wants *me* off the investigation, but that's not happening. Winter thinks Kowalski's guilty, but he's wrong. It's like Harding all over again. It's a set-up, and we're going to make a terrible mistake if we go down that line of investigation.'

'You're right,' Lena said.

'Let's just check out the ANPR hit on his car. The uniform can take over here and there are other detectives on the way.'

'I think it's pointless going to Oakdale Road, though,' Lena said.

'Why?' Loxton said, trying not to lose her patience. She wanted to get moving, to help Kowalski.

'Well, Dominik's a cop. He knows how this works. The first thing we'll do is put a trace out on his car. He's probably dumped it on a side road around there hoping it would lead us the wrong way and he's hired a car under false details. Or he's leaving London and he just drove through the area, trying to miss cameras and police, so he's been taking a side route off the main thoroughfares.'

'Why are you so sure?'

'Because it's what I'd do.'

Loxton hated to admit it, but Lena was probably right. 'Well, then, there's no risk to us, so we might as well go there while we're waiting for the address of the safe house. And we still need to check it out. We'll see what CCTV is there and if anyone from the industrial site saw anything unusual. And it's worth searching the warehouses. He could be hiding in one of those.'

'You're very thorough.' Lena shook her head in amazement. 'How do you manage to work with Dominik so well? He used to be so impulsive.'

Loxton smiled despite herself. 'I think we balance each other out.' Then she thought of the past hour and her heart sank.

Lena seemed to read Loxton's mind from the expression on her face. 'Let's just be careful if we find him.'

Loxton nodded roughly, trying to keep her emotions in check. She heard a car pulling up outside and looked out of the window. 'Come on, the firearms unit has pulled up. This check shouldn't take long and by then we'll have the safe house address. And Winter can have his way and have me off the case.'

Chapter 44

'There's his car.' Loxton pointed, relieved that it was there. Somehow seeing Kowalski's Audi safe and well was reassuring.

Loxton scanned the area around them. There were a dozen warehouses and they needed to check them all out.

'This is going to take a while.' Lena shook her head.

'We've got nothing better to do while we wait for the safehouse,' Loxton said. She called in Kowalski's car to Control, requesting a full forensic lift. Control told her the pickup truck would be about three hours; it was taking a burnt-out van to the pound. The forensics team wouldn't be much quicker, they were still tied up at Harding's flat. She hoped Winter was too distracted at the Harding scene to hear where she was. As soon as an address came through for a safe house, she'd go, but until then she felt the need to finish what she'd started.

'We can't wait for Forensics; we need to check the boot. Just in case.' Loxton climbed out of her car, imagining Jane trapped inside, her face deathly pale, her eyes unseeing. They both gloved up quickly. Loxton tried to open the boot and was surprised to find that it sprung open.

Lena shook her head. 'Kowalski must have been in a rush to leave the car unlocked like this.'

Loxton lifted the boot door upwards, bracing herself for whatever was inside.

'*Gówno*.' Lena shook her head.

Loxton stared in disbelief. There were ropes, a professional set of chef's knives in a bag, heavy-duty masking tape and a large roll of plastic sheeting normally used for decorating. There were several police forensic suits, gloves and masks still in their plastic bags. All laid out in the unlocked boot.

All the items could conceivably be explained away and put down to Kowalski being a diligent officer, except for the chef's knives, which gleamed at her. And Kowalski was not organized. He wouldn't have put extra police supplies in his own car boot neatly stacked for work. He barely knew where his radio was half the time. This didn't seem like Kowalski at all.

'This is a set-up,' Loxton said. 'If Kowalski was the killer, his DNA wouldn't be on the victims. Look at all this kit.'

Lena knelt down next to the car and taped her mobile to the underside.

'What are you doing?' Loxton asked.

'I doubt Kowalski will come back to this car, but just in case. That phone's GPS is on, so if this car moves, we can track it. I have a "find my phone" tracker on it and I can use your mobile to follow it.'

'Aren't we staying with the car until Forensics get here?' She regarded Lena curiously. Obviously they did things differently in Poland.

'There's no one around and this car's been here for a while by the look of it. We can search these warehouses in the time that pickup truck gets here. And if Kowalski does come back for the car, then we can follow him to where he's operating from. Time is of the essence. You said so yourself. Come on, we need to try to find Jane.'

Loxton nodded. Lena was right. Jane didn't have much time. The police work could wait.

Lena logged on to the 'find my phone' app using Loxton's mobile and handed it back to her and they headed to the warehouses.

When the security man had checked their warrant cards, he insisted on calling Walworth Police Station to confirm who they were. Loxton had tried to keep her patience throughout the call. She hoped Winter and Meyer were still too busy dealing with the consequences of Harding's death to notice.

'I'm sorry, but you can't be too careful.' The security man studied them both, as if still not convinced that they were really police officers. 'These warehouses are all operational. There's no way there's anyone using them to stash anything; someone would have noticed.'

'We appreciate that.' Loxton tried to keep the impatience out of her voice. 'We just need to check and then we'll be out of your way.'

The security man nodded. 'Well, I have to stay on the gate. There's a delivery scheduled any time now. Here's the keys; they've got numbers on that correspond with the warehouses. But I check them every night regular and there ain't anything unusual in them. And if there were, Reggie would tell me.' He patted his Rottweiler's large head while it regarded Loxton with wild eyes.

'Don't worry,' he said, obviously noticing Loxton's wary expression, 'he's all right, aren't you boy?' The security man stroked Reggie affectionately.

Loxton didn't fancy testing the theory. 'Thank you for your help.'

They headed to the first warehouse in the gloomy winter morning. There was a large sliding garage-type door but there was also a normal door to the side of it for them to use. Lena fiddled with the stack of keys until she found the right one and they went inside.

It took Loxton a moment to find the light switch and she was reminded of a large cave, just as the strobe lighting jerked to life and hummed above her head. There were rows and rows of shelves, some empty and some filled with boxes that went almost to the ceiling.

'Perhaps we could have done with Reggie,' Loxton said, taking in the size of the area.

'Let's start in the middle and split up; we'll cover the ground quicker.' Lena set off in one direction.

'I'll meet you back at this door once you've finished your half.' Loxton headed down the first aisle, peering up at the shelves high above her. The only noise was from the hum of the lights, her own footfall and Lena's footsteps getting further and further away.

The warehouse sent a shiver through her and she drew her baton. It was cold and sterile in here, and it felt like she was the only person on the planet. Her footsteps echoed down the aisles and back at her, making her doubt for a second whether she really was alone.

Nothing seemed out of the ordinary. There was a yellow forklift truck parked to the side of the aisles and a tower of navy pallets ready to use. She wondered what was inside all of the boxes, but the labels only contained long serial numbers and barcodes.

She heard a strangled shout back from where she had come. She turned and sprinted towards the noise, her heartbeat racing. As she ran, she cracked open her baton, ready.

'Lena!' she called, her voice high and panicked.

'Over here.' Lena's voice sounded strange – unsure of herself. She flew around the corner of an aisle, stopping short of where Lena was. 'Are you all right?' she asked.

Lena gave her an apologetic smile. 'I'm fine. This rat not so much.' She motioned with her baton towards the prone figure of a lifeless rodent.

'You killed it?' Loxton asked.

'No, innocent.' She grimaced, placing her hand on her heart. 'I reckon they must put poison down.'

'And the shout?' Loxton raised her eyebrows at Lena.

'That was me.' Lena shuddered as she studied the dead rat. 'Sorry. I hate those things.'

'Don't worry about it.' Loxton regarded the animal on the floor. 'This warehouse is clear. Let's try the other ones.'

It took over an hour to check them all and Loxton was cold afterwards, the chill getting inside her bones. The security man saw them off the premises but stopped Loxton just before she walked away.

'Have you thought about the sewers?' he asked. 'I'm not sure what you're looking for, drugs or whatever it is, but if I wanted to hide something around here that's where I'd go. They're behind this industrial site. That's why the warehouses got built here in the first place. No one would want the whiff of the sewers in the summer, so they couldn't build houses here.'

'Do you know if there's an access point nearby?' Loxton asked. She thought of Kowalski volunteering to take on the coordination of the search of the sewers. Now that she thought about it, Kowalski hadn't mentioned how the search was going recently. Had he even got the POLSA searching or was it all a lie.

'Follow the perimeter fence,' he pointed out the direction. 'You'll turn a corner and then you'll see it. There's a manhole around there somewhere with a ladder leading down into them. They did some work on the sewers a couple of summers ago, the smell was dreadful.'

'Thank you,' Loxton said, and they followed the fence round.

'Great,' Lena said. 'More rats.'

'Maybe the rats can't bear it either,' Loxton said.

'I hope you're right,' Lena said. 'I still can't see Kowalski operating so close to where he abandoned his car. It's a complete giveaway.'

'I agree, but it feels like someone's trying to frame him and they're showing us exactly where to go.'

'So *should* we go?' Lena asked. 'Is it a trap?'

'All I know is that Jane might be down there. We've got to try to find her.'

There was an overground railway line and under one of the arches a large manhole big enough for a person to fit through.

'You've got to be kidding,' Lena said.

'I reckon I can use my baton to get it open,' Loxton said, crouching down.

She got to work, grunting with the effort, sweat forming on her lower back as she braced against the metal. Lena pulled out her baton and joined her. Eventually it moved an inch, but with further work it started to turn more easily. They took a handle each and heaved the lid backwards.

Loxton felt drained, her arms shaking from the effort, and she caught her breath for a moment. Lena stepped forward and peered down the hole.

'Ja pierdolę!' Lena shook her head.

Loxton moved over and saw a ladder leading downwards into oblivion. 'How far does it go?' Her voice sounded quiet, as if it was being swallowed by the vastness of the space beneath them.

'No idea, but I bet there are loads of fucking rats down there.' Lena shook her head. 'I'm not keen on this one. There's no way anyone went down there with a body. This feels like a dead end and a whole waste of time. We should get going to the safe house.'

Loxton crouched down next to the hole. 'The rope marks on the bodies suggested they were bound. This would explain it. Whoever the killer is used ropes to lower them down there. You can see someone has opened it recently; these groove marks are new.'

'We could ring Thames Water. See if they've been doing work here?'

Loxton felt something pulling her towards the ladder. 'I don't mind heights,' she said. 'I'll go and take a look. It won't take ten minutes and we're here now.'

'I really don't like this, Alana,' Lena said. 'It doesn't look very safe.' She peered down the hole as if expecting something to leap out at them.

'Trust me, I'm a climber.' Loxton smiled at Lena and sat down next to the hole, taking hold of the first rung with both hands, and then letting her leg dangle until it found a lower step. She swung her body out into the open space, using her hands to hold onto the rung, and her weight landed on the foot balanced on the ladder. Her other foot found purchase and she began the long climb down.

She could hear Lena grumbling above her. 'Rats and heights, what's next?'

'Don't worry, I won't be long. Call it in to Control. And give Winter a call on your radio. He needs to get POLSA down here.'

'Doing it now,' Lena said, and she turned her radio up, the chatter of the operator now far above Loxton.

It grew colder as Loxton climbed down the ladder and

she paused to look up towards the circle of light above her. When she looked down, she couldn't see the bottom and wondered how far it went. She paused for a second, hooking her strong arm around a rung, and then fished out her torch from her pocket with her left hand. She clicked it on and pointed downwards. The metal ladder seemed to go on forever, disappearing into the darkness.

She'd read about the London sewers. They could be as deep as fifteen metres, roughly the height of two houses. She'd scaled taller climbing walls, although she'd had ropes. She turned the torch off and pocketed it again.

'How's it look down there?' Lena called.

'I can't see anything. It goes down too far. I'm just going to climb to the bottom, okay?'

'I'm coming too,' Lena said. 'I'm not letting you go down there on your own.'

'You don't need to do that,' she called up to Lena, but it was too late. She saw the circle of light obscured and suddenly she was plunged into darkness. For a horrible moment she imagined that Lena had closed the manhole up, leaving her stranded below the cold earth, but then she saw Lena's slim silhouette eclipsing the circle of light.

'We'd better not get stuck in here,' Loxton said.

'I told control; they're sending POLSA units with ropes in case we find anything. And I've left a note on the manhole.'

Somehow the note didn't reassure Loxton. 'Take your time,' she said. 'There's no rush.'

'I intend to,' Lena said. 'And don't bother saying "Don't look down"; I can't see a thing anyway.'

Loxton smiled despite the surroundings and the stench that was getting stronger with every rung she climbed.

Chapter 45

Loxton paused to shine her torch downwards and saw the light glimmering back at her from far below. Water. But how much? She was too high to tell if it was moving, so she clicked the torch off and made her way further down.

'We're nearly at the bottom,' she called up to Lena.

'Thank God,' Lena replied, her voice tense, and Loxton knew she was pushing herself to keep up.

Loxton strained her ears in the darkness and could hear the *drip, drip, drip* of water but nothing else. She estimated thirty more rungs, so when she got to twenty-five, she stopped. The torch illuminated the water below her. It was still. She couldn't tell how deep it was, so she pulled out her baton and extended it.

She climbed the last five rungs and then lowered her baton into the water. It hit something hard. She tested the area below her. The water was only an inch or two high. The smell wasn't as bad as she'd expected – more like stagnant pond water than anything else, and she was surprised. She put one foot slowly onto the floor and then the other, glad she was wearing her ankle boots and that it was winter.

'It's fine.' She looked up and saw Lena steadily making

progress above her. She moved away from the ladder, swinging her torch left and right. The tunnel was wider than she'd expected, big enough for a train to pass through.

Would the killer have brought someone down here? It was a perfect area to destroy any forensic evidence. Water washed DNA and fingerprints away, even this small amount, and maybe at different times of the month the water was higher.

Lena hesitated on the last rung. 'What's in there?'

'It's just water. I wouldn't drink it, but it's fine to walk through.'

Lena lowered herself down and carefully put her feet into the water. 'Do you really think Kowalski would have been able to bring someone down here?' She looked up towards the circle of light, impossibly high above them.

'He's strong enough. Or anyone would be able to lower a body down with ropes.' Loxton imagined climbing ropes. If you knew how deep the drop was, it wouldn't be too hard to do. In fact, the rope marks on the body made her sure that the sewers were the right place to look.

Lena didn't look convinced and she turned on her own torch. 'We could split up. I go left, you go right?'

Loxton pulled out her radio and turned up the volume. There was nothing. She couldn't hear the main channel. The radio signal was non-existent. 'We should stick together. Otherwise we'll be completely on our own.'

'Good point,' Lena said.

'Let's go left,' Loxton said.

'Why left and not right?' Lena asked.

'Reynolds suggested the killer might favour their left hand from the way the victims were strangled. If that's the case they would instinctively favour their left, so would be more likely to go that way,' Loxton said.

'Interesting theory.' Lena said. 'I'm ambidextrous; which way would I go? Do right-handed people always go right?'

'It's a fifty-fifty chance,' Loxton said.

They moved through the tunnel. Loxton scanned the water in front of her, sweeping her torch across the surface, not sure what she was looking for. It was impossible to know if anyone had been here recently or whether this place had been deserted for years.

'There's no way this water is going to get any higher?' Lena asked. 'I mean, it's not linked into the Thames tide, is it?'

Loxton shone her torch on the walls. They were dank and dripping, but the highest water mark was only knee high. 'It doesn't look like it gets too high. We'll just go down here for a bit. Then try the other way. Really we're going to need dogs to search this area.'

'I doubt the dogs will be able to pick anything up through this stench.' Lena wrinkled her nose. 'I really don't think this would be the place the killer would operate out of. And there's no way Kowalski would leave his car so close.'

'I don't think it *is* Kowalski. I think he worked out where the killer was operating from and came here to look around. Then maybe he came across the killer and is still down here. Perhaps the killer didn't know Kowalski had come here by car and that it's parked so nearby. We can't rule anything out.'

'You're right,' Lena said, but in the torchlight she didn't look convinced as she checked fearfully around her. 'It doesn't explain the knives in his boot though.'

They moved in silence until Lena stopped still. 'What's that?' She pointed her torch into the water.

Loxton followed the beam and saw something glinting under the water's surface. Silver. She scooped the object out of the water. It was a bracelet, the clasp broken, but she could make out decorative words on it. '*Aaron and Joseph*'.

It was Jane's bracelet.

She turned towards Lena, but before she had a chance, something cracked into the side of her temple. The force spun her sideways, her head swimming from the blow, and she lost her footing, landing heavily onto her hands and knees in the cold water.

She tried to raise her head. Her vision swam and she felt sick. The pain came again, hard into the back of her skull and she fell forwards, her face crashing into the black water and drowning everything else out.

PART 5

ALANA

Chapter 46

Saturday 5 February, 12:55

Loxton blinked rapidly, but she couldn't see anything. She seemed to have gone blind. She must be dreaming. It felt like she was in a cavernous space, with darkness all around her.

She could hear the slow *drip, drip, drip* of falling water. It was cold in the cave, the air icy, shrinking her skin and making it tight across her face and hands. Her left side was wet, and she realized she was lying in water. She pushed herself upright using her left upper arm and leg, managing to find purchase, ending up in a sitting position.

Her back and neck muscles screamed in protest as the blood sluggishly began moving through them again. The pins and needles were incredible, and her calf spasmed in pain.

She couldn't feel her hands and she could barely move them or her legs. She strained against an invisible force. She peered at her wrists but she couldn't see anything. She could feel that they were bound in front of her, the bonds cutting deep into her flesh.

She clenched and unclenched her hands into fists to try to get the blood moving through them. She scanned the area around her, but it was so dark, she couldn't see anything.

A bright white light flashed on, burning her eyes, so that she had to shut them tight.

When she managed to open them again, all she could see was painfully bright light. 'Who are you?' she asked. 'Why are you doing this?'

Her eyes began to adjust to the white light and she saw there was a figure behind the tripod, angling the light so that it captured Loxton completely.

'Why go to all this effort?' she asked. Shadows danced in the corners, cast by the artificial light.

'This is your worst nightmare, right?'

Loxton recognized that voice, but it didn't make sense. Nothing made sense.

'I wanted to make it perfect for you.' Lena stepped forward and crouched down in front of her.

'It can't be you,' Loxton said, her voice small in that cold, empty chamber.

'Not quite how you imagined your worst nightmare, is it? But it's close enough.'

'How do you know what my worst nightmare is?' Loxton had to keep Lena talking. She had to try to make sense of this.

'I've read your diaries, Alana. All of them. Edward Barratt's the man who scared you the most, out of all the killers you've hunted. That's why I copied him for you.' Lena stroked the knife across Loxton's neck.

'You've been in my flat?'

Lena lifted the knife and pressed the tip of the blade against Loxton's skin, just above her collarbone. 'More than you have in the last few weeks. I waited for you, but you never came. That wasn't very kind of you. Getting you on your own has been impossible, until today.' Lena pushed the knife in deeper. 'Say sorry.'

Loxton clenched her jaw to stop herself from crying out. Lena smiled, twisting the blade, and Loxton drew in a painful breath through her gritted teeth. She glared up at Lena. She was going to die, but she wasn't going to give Lena the satisfaction of a scream. She wouldn't shed a tear. Instead, she pushed away the fear and focused solely on her rage.

Lena's eyes darkened; no humanity of any kind contained in them. She leaned towards Loxton. 'Say sorry, or it'll be your cunt next.' Lena dug the knife in deeper.

'Fuck you,' Loxton grunted as the pain heightened beyond anything she'd experienced before.

'You're more stubborn than you look.' Lena pulled the knife out in one swift motion.

Loxton winced in agony. She felt warm blood from the wound. 'Why are you doing this? Was it Harding's idea?' Loxton managed to ask.

'Harding?' Lena laughed. 'I plucked him from Barratt's fan base months ago. He was so unhinged, with his fierce hate for the world and his huge ego, so easily manipulated online. He took your addresses to prove to me that he was who he claimed to be, ex-SAS. But really I just wanted him to incriminate himself. He was always supposed to be the fall guy, although he didn't know that. When I asked him to sacrifice himself for the cause, he agreed, but in the end he chickened out. Getting arrested and the prospect of a lengthy sentence made him panic. Not such the elite warrior to the cause after all.'

'You killed him? How?'

'I called him. Told him to wait at his flat, that you'd see him there and get him into police protection. Then, when

I arrived, he was so relieved; he thought he was safe. He never saw the knife coming.' She smiled, proud of her own achievement.

'So this was all you?' Loxton stared into Lena's grey eyes. 'Why?'

'Sometimes I wonder myself,' Lena said. 'But really, I was just like you, plodding along in the police, working hard to prove everyone wrong. That I was just as good as them. That I belonged. Scrabbling for promotion, for purpose, for acceptance, for some sort of justice in the world. Dealing with the never-ending domestic murders, where wives had been battered to death by their husbands, all because they'd overcooked the dinner or looked at another man the wrong way. Then *he* happened.'

Loxton felt her shoulder throbbing, deep down, and wondered how much blood she was losing. 'Kowalski?'

'No, not him.' Lena laughed. 'Kowalski was a friend, nothing more. Just an ordinary man in the end, nothing special. Szymański, however, was no ordinary man. The police were thrown. We'd never come across anything like it. He was fascinating. Something unique in all the mindless violence and death. He was a meaning in the madness.'

'But you were on the team that *caught* Szymański,' Loxton said, confused.

Lena smiled. 'Actually, it was the other way around. He caught *me*. He came to my flat one evening, walked right in as I was having my dinner. It was the shock of my life. I thought he was going to kill me. But he didn't. He'd seen me investigating the case, was as intrigued by me as I was by him. He said we had a lot in common. We worked the same. Disciplined. Both had an interest in psychology and philosophy. Of course I thought he was abhorrent back then, but he said he'd let me live on the condition that I didn't tell anyone he'd been to visit. He wore a mask. I was going to call Kowalski, but before I knew what was happening I felt giddy and euphoric. He'd drugged me, put something in the food while I'd been out of the house, and I'd unwittingly cooked myself a poisoned meal. He talked some more, the hours flew past, and then I fell asleep. I woke in the morning, asleep on my sofa. I didn't know if it had been a dream or if it was real. My plate and cutlery were washed and put away. I didn't know what to think.'

'You didn't tell anyone?'

'We'd been working long hours and I was fairly new in the job. I'd be mocked for being hysterical, not able to cope with the case and probably taken off it. So I put it down to a dream. It *felt* like a dream. But then he came again. Another night. He let me see his face. I felt sorry for him at first. He'd had a terrible life. But then the pity turned to something else. His was a life less ordinary. An extraordinary man. He'd been abused by his father and his mother hadn't stopped it. She was indifferent to it. That had changed him. He'd seen what humans really are. I listened. *I* wasn't indifferent.'

Loxton shook her head.

'If you think about it, life is so short, so often inconsequential. Nothing happens. We're born, we work, we may have children and then we slowly decay year by year. We become shells of ourselves. Our children come to despise us. And then we die. In a couple of generations we're forgotten, might never have existed. But not Szymański. He'll live forever. He has become a legend in people's minds.'

'And you? Are you a legend?'

'It was enough for me just to love him. But that was taken away from me when Kowalski captured him.'

'But you were on the same team?' Loxton said again, staring at Lena. She was insane.

'I tried to protect Krystian. I tampered with the evidence when I could. Ensured anything potentially incriminating at the crime scenes got destroyed before it was spotted by the forensic team. But Kowalski became suspicious that there were two people involved, possibly one in the forensic team. It became harder for me to cover Krystian's tracks. Kowalski insisted Krystian's house be forensically searched again and a piece of one of the victim's skin was recovered from his shower. Krystian was convicted and I couldn't risk seeing him in prison. And then he was murdered.'

'So why not go after the Polish police? Why target my team?'

'The targets weren't my idea. They were Dominik's. He chose the victims.'

'Dominik?' Loxton couldn't hide the horror from her voice. 'He isn't a killer.' She shook her head vehemently, trying to keep the pain she felt from her face. She didn't want to give Lena the satisfaction.

'He worked out Krystian couldn't have been working alone. Not towards the end anyway. And then he discovered it was me. I'm like a sister to him. He loves me. And love is a powerful thing, Alana. It can make someone do terrible things. He couldn't betray me and eventually I convinced him to join me.'

'You're lying,' Loxton said. She couldn't believe it.

'Believe what you want to if it will help you sleep at night, little sheep. Not that you'll be needing to worry about that anymore. Just think, Alana – I'm giving you a gift. No more striving, no more disappointment in your fellow man. Just rest. And fame. To be remembered generations from now.'

'You're insane,' Loxton said.

Lena laughed. 'Of course I am, little sheep.' She tilted her head sideways as if appraising Loxton for the first time. 'But does that mean you don't like me? I thought you did?'

Loxton thought of her friends, dead at Lena's hands. 'You're not human,' Loxton replied.

'You're just like me all those years ago. Holding on so tight to the idea of right and wrong, as if any of it matters in the end. Desperate for some sort of meaning before you take your last breath. I think you *did* like me. I like *you*. We could have been friends. I could have shown you the other side, a world with no constraints, no rules. But you're not ready for that, are you? And now it's your time to die.' Lena's eyes looked sad.

Lena slashed Loxton's upper chest, causing blood to soak through her shirt. 'You look good in red. That's definitely your colour.' Lena plunged the knife into Loxton's right shoulder so fast Loxton didn't have time to brace for the blow. Her screams echoed around the empty chamber, the knife only stopped by her shoulder joint.

'I didn't expect you to start screaming already.' Lena shook her head in disappointment. 'You started off so well. I thought you'd be harder to break. Dominik usually goes for strong women. They're the ones he really likes. And so far they all proved a challenge – until you. You just trotted along beside me like a stupid little bitch, oblivious to its master's world.' Lena was panting now, the effort and excitement making her jittery. The knife was sticking out of Loxton's shoulder, the pain excruciating. Fear crawled up Loxton's chest, clutching tightly at her heart, choking her throat. She was going to die down here.

'I'm sorry about this next bit,' Lena said, her eyes genuinely apologetic. 'I don't enjoy it. But this little trick has been working well for me. They're convinced it's a man because of the rape element, which suits me just fine. Dominik is willing to take the blame now, since Harding let us down.'

'You're disgusting,' Loxton said.

'I'm sorry we won't be able to be skin to skin for the next bit. Forensics is a bitch.' Lena stroked Loxton's cheek with her gloved fingers, brushing Loxton's angry tears away. 'I'll just get some extra protection for me and my instrument. Don't want them finding my DNA in any strange places on your corpse, do I? That would never do. I'm not going to be making Szymański's mistake. He taught me well.' Lena looked sad and turned away, leaning down to a black sports bag where she pulled out a forensic suit, gloves and a mask. Loxton saw glinting knives and a glass implement.

There was a faint splashing noise and Loxton feared that Kowalski was coming. She couldn't bear it. Lena frowned and paused to listen. She picked out a couple of knives from her bag and headed out of the chamber. She turned back briefly and said, 'Don't go anywhere; I won't be long.'

As soon as Lena was out of the room Loxton bit down on the handle of the knife and yanked at it, but it didn't budge. The pain pulsed through her whole body, making her vision blur. She bit down harder so as not to scream out. She was sweating and cold. She tried again and her vision swam, but she felt the knife move a fraction of an inch. The pain seared through her. She couldn't tell if the knife was going in deeper or coming out but there was nothing else to try.

She breathed heavily through her nose, fast and hard at the pain and effort. Her next attempt pulled the knife out a good inch and she daren't let go of the blade with her teeth in case it fell.

On the next go she drew the blade clear of her muscle and skin. Her shoulder throbbed and she felt warm blood oozing out of the wound readily. Her jaw ached as she kept her teeth clenched down on the handle, terrified she would drop it, and her only chance of survival along with it.

She leaned forwards to her right wrist and sawed at the rope, wriggling her hand until the rope became loose. Then she took the knife with her freed hand and cut at the bonds on her left wrist. Finally, she leaned down and cut the ropes from her ankles.

She wasn't going to die without a fight. She tore the sleeve of her blouse and stuffed the material into the stab wound to compact it, and then wrapped more material around it to slow the bleeding. She did the same to her other shoulder. She checked her pockets but her radio and mobile phone were gone, Lena had taken them.

She crept as fast as she dared towards the opposite entrance that Lena had just gone through. She needed to get as far away from her as possible. She felt weak and lightheaded, and her right forearm and hand were tingling and numb. Her left hand seemed okay, so she swapped the knife to it.

She needed to get help. There was no doubt in her mind that Lena hadn't told control their location. No one was coming to help her. She was on her own.

Trying to take on Lena alone was madness. Lena was unharmed. She was also clearly insane, and that brought with it a special type of strength. The tunnel ahead was dark, and Loxton stumbled into the blackness.

She kept to the wall, using her right hand to trail along the rough stone, looking for any side exits. As soon as Lena saw she was missing, she'd come storming up this tunnel and Loxton would be an easy target.

She had no idea which way was out, the whole network a winding mystery to her. It was massive, a large proportion built in the Victorian era, with abandoned tunnels and dead ends. She could be lost in this maze forever.

She wished she'd never come down here. Then she wouldn't have learnt the truth about Kowalski. How the last few months had all been a lie. He wasn't her friend; had never cared about her. All the time he had been planning to kill her friends one by one until it was her turn. She shivered in the blackness. She needed to focus. To get out of here.

The smell grew stronger as she ran forwards through the flowing water. The darkness deepened and she glanced backwards towards the chamber she'd come from. A soft glow emanated from it and she used it to gauge her progress – not far enough.

She had to get away.

She'd still not come across any side exits on her right. It was pitch black now, so that if there was an exit on the left wall, she'd walk straight past it and never know.

It wouldn't be long before Lena returned to the chamber and found her missing and then it would be over. She tried to push down the overwhelming panic. Not to think of what Lena would do to her when she found her.

She focused on the water flowing around her ankles as she waded onwards. It seemed to be choppier. She stopped for a moment, listening in the dark. All she could hear was the running water, but then something else. Squeaking. It was ahead of her, but it seemed to be coming more from her right. She stumbled forwards quickly towards the noise. Was there a side tunnel?

Sure enough, she felt as if the space had opened up. The flow of water seemed different around her feet now, faster. Her fingertips trailed the wet brick and then found nothing – empty space. She checked in all directions. It seemed to be some sort of crossroads, but she wasn't sure. It was so black.

A howl far behind her – Lena had realized she was gone.

She stumbled right, towards the squeak, which had now scuttled away from her. She moved quickly through the water, running forwards into the darkness. She heard Lena's feet some way away, sloshing up the tunnel as she charged after her. Loxton forced herself to slow down, to creep forwards and make no noise in the water.

She moved along the right wall and ducked down, pressing her back against the cold stone, praying Lena wouldn't see her. Lena was shouting to herself in Polish. She heard a movement to her right, further back, and she shuffled further along the wall. There was some sort of alcove and she backed into it as slowly as she could, making herself as small as possible.

Loxton's hand tightened around the handle of the knife. She tried to steady her breathing. There was a movement beside her; the animal shifted its position for a moment, as if it too was hiding with her.

She felt behind her but there were bars blocking some sort of opening.

Light bounced crazily off the walls and she heard the footfall come to a halt. Lena was at the crossroads. Would Lena go left or right or keep straight on? The light grew stronger on the wall opposite her as she heard Lena splash towards her. Loxton felt her body tighten as panic coursed through her veins, making her heart race. This was it.

Then Lena stopped short.

Lena was listening for her. Loxton held her breath, pushing her lips together, praying. It seemed like time had stopped. She could hear her heart thudding in her chest, so loud she was convinced Lena would hear it too.

The water began to wash around her as Lena waded through it. The light danced against the wall opposite as her torch moved.

Loxton closed her eyes briefly, promising Jane she wouldn't go down without a fight. Then she opened them, lifting the knife silently higher. The splashing continued but it was getting quieter, the light sweeping away. Lena was checking the other way. Loxton allowed herself a moment to relax before suddenly the splashing grew louder again and then reached a crescendo as Lena ran back to the crossroads. Loxton's hand tightened on the handle as she prepared to strike Lena's jugular in an upward thrust.

She braced herself, but the water crashing against the stone walls around her became calmer. Lena had gone straight ahead, guessing that Loxton hadn't found the turnings. It was logical. It's what Loxton would have done. It wouldn't take Lena long to realize she hadn't taken that route, and then she'd be back again, trying each way systematically.

Should Loxton carry on in this direction? Or was the tunnel to the left the way out? Even if there was a ladder to a manhole above, she'd never see it unless she walked into it. She couldn't see anything. And she wasn't convinced she'd be able to climb up it with her wounded right shoulder. Her hand still felt numb and there was a strange tingling sensation and a coldness now spreading from her shoulder down her arm.

Loxton slowly got up, her legs aching as the blood flowed freely into them again. She couldn't stay here. If she did, she'd die. She had to make a choice.

She carried on in the same direction, praying this would

lead her to a way out, though for all she knew it would lead her in a circle back to the chamber. Progress was slow, and in the darkness and cold her mind kept going back to Kowalski. He'd betrayed them all. She didn't want to believe it, but his DNA had been on all of the bodies. And he'd been so keen to get Lena on board with the investigation as the profiler. Now she knew why.

Kowalski and Lena had been working together, targeting his ex-lovers in some twisted deadly game. But why had they targeted *her*? Perhaps it had evolved from being simply about his ex-lovers to avenging Barratt as well, which meant adding Jane and her to the list.

From the beginning, Kowalski had befriended her and worked hard to gain her trust, just so that he and Lena could finish off what Barratt had threatened to do.

Kowalski had been playing her since he met her five months ago. None of it had been real. She tasted salt water in her mouth as tears rolled silently down her cheeks. But she kept moving forward. She didn't stop. She had to get out of this alive.

Chapter 47

As she waded through the water she heard a noise in the tunnel ahead. Splashing water. Torchlight. Lena was behind her, wasn't she? Could she have got ahead, done a full loop of tunnel, or was Loxton completely disorientated and had somehow headed back towards the chamber?

Loxton stepped backwards and then turned around, hurrying back the way she'd come. The person behind her cursed to himself – it was a man. And he'd cursed in Polish. Her heart clenched in fear.

Kowalski.

He was going to kill her.

Rage filled her. If she didn't survive this there was a chance that Lena would get away again, another accomplice sacrificed so that she could continue.

Loxton slipped the blade of her knife up her sleeve and obscured the handle with her palm. She was bleeding, and escape seemed impossible. It was time to finish this.

She took a deep breath and tried to hide the fear she felt, calling in a steady voice. 'Dominik, I'm over here.'

'Alana?' The splashing grew louder as he raced forwards, the torchlight bouncing off the wall and ceiling, growing stronger. 'You're alive.' His eyes were full of relief.

For a moment she hesitated. She knew this was going to be hard, but he was pretending to be *her* Kowalski and it killed her. 'Where have you been?' she asked.

'Someone's set me up. Lena called me on my radio, told me that I was the main suspect, that my DNA was on all of the bodies. She told me to come here and she'd meet me. She'd studied the sewer maps and felt like this access point was at the centre of it all. I checked the search record and it hadn't been explored yet. I thought I could find the killer before it was too late for Jane and for you.'

'Why didn't you call me?' she asked.

'Lena said they were tracking my phone, that as soon as I called anyone they'd be able to trace where I was. So I got rid of it and my radio. I headed straight for the tunnels. If I was arrested, then there would be no one to try to stop the killer getting to you. The police would even stop looking. You'd be a sitting target.'

'But I was in danger. You left me up there alone.' He had almost convinced her, but she knew that falling for his lies would be fatal.

'You had Lena,' he said. 'She was with you.' And there it was. He was testing her. Seeing if she had figured it out yet.

'She didn't do a great job of protecting me.' Loxton showed him her shoulder, the blood seeping through the hastily made compact she'd applied. She needed him to think she was weak and vulnerable before she struck.

Kowalski's face twisted into concern and he stepped towards her. 'What happened?'

'I was attacked.' She kept the knife hidden and it was all she could do not to lean away from him. 'Where's Jane?'

'I haven't found her; I've been searching the tunnels for

hours now. I haven't seen any evidence of anyone down here until I came across you. Who did that to you?'

'I didn't see their face; it's so dark.' She hoped he was fooled by her lie. She needed him to be off his guard when she attacked. 'We have to get out of here. Do you know the way?'

'I thought I did, but I'm not sure anymore.' He pulled out a map. 'These are the blueprints of the sewers. We need to get you out of here.'

'I can look at the map,' she said. 'You keep a look-out in case the killer comes. He was chasing me, but I lost him.'

'Have you got any signal down here?' Kowalski took up position, facing away from her and watching from where she'd come.

'When the killer attacked me I lost my radio and mobile. You?'

'No phone or radio either, remember.' He sighed. 'Can you say anything about what the killer looked like?'

'I didn't see him, it was completely dark,' she lied again. She reluctantly glanced at the map, wanting to keep her eyes on Kowalski at all times. Without knowing where they were, it was impossible to work out which way to go. 'Where are we?'

He turned to her and she tried not to shrink away as he leaned towards the map. 'I think we're about here.' He stabbed at a point on the map. 'There are numbers on the walls at interchanges which correlate with the blueprint, like on a motorway.'

'Okay, I think it's straight on. You go first, you've got the torch. I'll direct as we go along.'

He headed down the tunnel. 'Was it just one person who attacked you, or two?'

'Just one, I think, but it was pitch black,' she said. 'They stabbed me and I just ran.' She prayed he didn't wonder how she'd managed to lose her mobile and radio. If he did, he'd know she was lying.

'Good that it's just one,' he said. 'We should be able to overpower them. I've got a Taser on me.'

Panic rose inside her. He had a Taser gun. If she aimed for his jugular now and missed, he'd be on top of her. She only had one shot at this. She followed him closely, staring at the point on his neck where she thought his artery protruded and was easiest to sever. Her stomach squirmed in repulsion at the thought of stabbing Kowalski. There was still that small niggle of doubt that she was wrong. That Kowalski had been set up and Lena was lying. That he was telling the truth.

'How did you get here?' she asked.

'I drove. Left my car a few roads back.' So he *had* driven his car here, which meant the knives in the back were his.

'Did you ever sleep with Jane?' She kept her eyes on the point on his neck.

'I know this is going to sound weird, but yes, I did. When I first got here from Poland, I was a mess. Most of my Polish colleagues had turned on me, fed up of my theories on Szymański. It was only ever Lena who didn't turn on me. I arrived in London on my own, an outsider. I got to drinking and partying hard. We all drank a lot back then. We were younger. Jane was just a fling and I was the same for her. It didn't mean anything to either of us. She met her husband soon after.'

He'd slept with every woman murdered on this case. There was no set-up. It had been Kowalski all along. Now it was his life or hers.

'Why didn't you tell me?' she asked, trying to keep him talking and distracted.

Kowalski hesitated. 'I was worried that I'd get taken off the case and I wanted to find Emma's killer. But I should have told you. I just didn't want you to think less of me, stupid I know.'

'And Szymański. You had to leave Poland. Why?'

'I told you. I always thought he was working in a pair. Some of the timings of the killings were almost impossible for just one person to complete. He was either the luckiest man on the planet, or someone helped him. But the bosses didn't like it and Szymański denied it. My superiors thought I was confusing things. Catching the killer and closing the case was better for their careers. I was a thorn in their side ruining their great success. They made things very difficult for me.'

It was a brave move. Insist that Szymański had been working in a pair after you discovered it was Lena. Let other officers see the senior ranks turn against you, so that no one else would want to venture there.

What she couldn't believe was that her Kowalski would do this. She thought she'd known him. And it felt almost impossible that two police officers had become serial killers together. But she'd read somewhere in her studies that there was a disproportionate number of psychopaths in the police and perhaps they were naturally attracted to murder in an unhealthy way. And then, with a little persuasion, they were easy to corrupt.

Kowalski stopped and turned towards her. 'Do you hear something behind us?'

She strained her ears, but she couldn't hear anything. She shook her head at him. She didn't want to turn her back on him.

'Just behind us.' He nodded behind her. 'I think someone's coming.'

She was losing her opportunity. 'I can't hear anything; let's keep going.' If Lena was behind them, she didn't want her catching up with them.

Kowalski put his hand up to signal for her to wait. 'There. Did you hear it?'

She could hear it, faint but growing stronger. Splashing.

Kowalski's eyes met hers. He pulled out his Taser and pointed it down the tunnel. She was in his sights. 'He's coming. Get behind me, Alana. You said he throws knives.'

Loxton stared into his blue eyes. This was her only chance; he wasn't pointing the Taser at her, but past her. If she didn't strike him now, when Lena arrived it would be two against one and she wouldn't stand a chance.

Chapter 48

'What's wrong?' Kowalski stared into her eyes, confusion and concern inside them.

She couldn't do it. She couldn't attack him first. She didn't have it in her. There was the tiniest doubt inside her, and she realized she'd rather die than risk hurting her Kowalski.

'Nothing. Nothing's wrong.' She moved to the side of him to face Lena. He'd seen something in her eyes, would be wary of her now, but she didn't care. She couldn't make the pre-emptive strike.

'Dominik, so nice of you to join us.' Lena smiled at him. 'As you can see, Alana and I were just getting better acquainted.'

'What's going on?' Kowalski asked, confusion spread across his face – and something else: a growing horror.

'You don't have to pretend anymore, Dominik. Alana's a clever girl; seems she's worked it all out.'

Kowalski glanced at Loxton. 'What's going on?' he asked again.

'Lena attacked me,' Loxton said angrily. 'She's the killer.' Loxton prayed that Kowalski wasn't involved.

Kowalski shook his head slowly. 'No. Lena, it can't be you.' Kowalski's voice was so quiet that Loxton barely heard him.

'I'd have thought you'd have killed Dominik by now, Alana. You had your chance to get rid of one of us. Why not take it? Now you have two of us to take down.'

Loxton glanced at Kowalski and he stared at her. 'Alana, you know me.' He put his hands up in surrender. 'You know I didn't kill them. She's lying.'

Lena laughed. 'Alana, you know me, and I bet you didn't think I was capable of murder. Dominik, you can drop the act. She's not an idiot. Now Taser her and I'll let you make the first cut.'

Kowalski's face changed to one of pure hate and for a moment Loxton was taken aback by it. He lifted the Taser towards her and then moved it past her, swinging instead to point towards Lena.

Loxton stayed by his side, facing Lena. Logically she shouldn't trust Kowalski, but in her heart she did. And although following her heart in the past hadn't worked out so well for her, she didn't care. Kowalski was worth the risk. Was worth her life.

Lena pulled a knife from her back pocket and hurled it at Loxton. The knife was so fast, Loxton barely managed to turn her body sideways to escape its full bite. The knife sliced past her left shoulder and she winced in agony as her skin yielded to the passing blade.

Kowalski glanced at her but was then forced to face Lena as she charged at them. He fired his Taser, but Lena zig-zagged towards them and the prongs missed her by millimetres, splashing uselessly into the water, the five second charge dispersing in the water harmlessly.

'Get the knife,' Loxton called to him, knowing that

his Taser would be useless now that it had been in water. Then she charged forward towards Lena, who had her knife held high. Loxton kept her hands low. Her intention now wasn't to get out of here alive, but to kill Lena. She just needed one chance. Making sure Lena was dead was all that mattered.

Before they collided, Lena pulled up short, hanging back, her body swaying as if it were a snake ready to strike, and it took everything Loxton had to not run into her blade.

Loxton realized too late she'd never wielded a knife before. Had never stabbed another human being. Her mind recoiled from the very thought of it. She kept the knife hidden, praying Lena underestimated her, and that she would get her chance before it was too late.

Lena aimed for Loxton's wrists, slashing forward then pulling back so that she didn't leave herself vulnerable. She never stopped moving. Loxton stumbled backwards, dodging away from the blade, terrified of what it could do. Her shoulder and arm throbbed, and she felt the rising panic taking over. She had to focus. She could tell Kowalski was behind her, trying to get around her to fight Lena, but he didn't have a weapon.

'Get the knife Lena thew,' she told him again. He shouted something behind her, but then she heard him splashing through the water wildly, looking for the knife.

Lena grinned and lunged forward, but it was just for show, just to frighten her. Lena made to throw the knife at Loxton's neck and Loxton screwed her eyes up involuntarily, raising her arms in front of her face to stop the flying knife. At that moment Lena was upon her instead, and it felt like she was being punched repeatedly in the sides, even though Loxton knew it would be the blade causing the damage.

Loxton let the knife drop from her sleeve and caught the handle in her hand and pushed the blade upwards, towards Lena's neck. Lena reacted instinctively, moving away and raising her arms to protect her neck. Loxton's blade rebounded off Lena's forearm as the point collided with Lena's bone.

Lena lunged forward, bringing her elbows down onto Loxton's raised hands, knocking the knife out of them. It fell away to the side of Loxton, disappearing under the water before she could grab it, and she realized in horror that Lena had managed to keep hold of her own blade.

If Loxton turned and looked for the knife now, she'd be completely open to Lena's next knife assault, and she wouldn't survive that. All she could do was try to protect herself by keeping her arms up to ward off any blows that might hit her major organs.

'I've found it,' Kowalski called, and Loxton turned briefly towards him. He was behind her, holding up the throwing knife that Lena had hurled at Loxton earlier. He held it out towards Loxton handle first. She turned and ran towards it, Lena right behind her, and grasped for the knife, managing to grab hold of the handle and spin around, slicing an arc around her.

Lena's eyes widened in shock just before the sharp blade sliced into the side of her neck. As it hit her muscle and vertebrae, it stopped, the jar reverberating up Loxton's arm. Lena moved the knife she was holding back and forth into Loxton's side, but her movements were slower, sluggish, the punches weaker.

Loxton twisted her knife as she pulled it out and then plunged it in again. Something snapped inside her. The punching stopped as Lena sank to her knees. Blood oozed out of Lena's neck. The only thing slowing the flow was the knife still stuck in the side of her neck. Lena dropped her own blade into the dark water and with her hands covered around the knife hilt, trying to stop the flow of blood from the wound.

Her face paled and her eyes seemed to lose their fire as they locked onto Loxton's and then looked past her. Loxton turned and saw Kowalski beside her. He knelt down in front of Lena and cupped her face in his hands.

'Lena, what have you done?' His voice shook with horror. Lena kept her eyes locked onto his. She tried to move her lips, but the pain seemed too great for a moment, and she grimaced. Kowalski gathered her to him as she began to fall backwards. He cradled her in his arms, staring into her eyes. Nothing would save her. Loxton knew Lena would be dead within minutes.

Loxton felt dizzy, her head spinning, and she used the wall to slowly lower herself to a sitting position, facing the pair locked in their final embrace.

'You told me a load of shit back there, didn't you?' Loxton said to Lena.

Lena grimaced. 'You are clever,' she managed to say. Blood tricked from the corner of her mouth.

'Why did you do this?' Kowalski asked.

Lena locked eyes on him. 'I wanted you to feel the pain ...' She took a painful breath. 'The pain I felt when Szymański was murdered. It was your fault he was in there.'

Kowalski shook his head at her, as if he couldn't accept what she was saying.

'You were meant to rot in prison, everyone you ever loved dead, and in their last moments thinking you were part of it.' She coughed violently, struggling to catch her breath.

Kowalski's face twisted in disgust and he leaned away from Lena, as if she were poisonous.

'Why did you try to kill *me*?' Loxton asked. It infuriated her that Lena's story didn't make sense. She'd already lied once and Loxton wanted the truth. This was their only chance.

Lena tried to laugh, but a horrible gurgling, bubbling sound came from her throat. 'Maybe you're not so clever after all.' She glanced from Kowalski back to Loxton, tried to say more, but she couldn't. Her face twisted in pain. Her lips had a blue tinge and her skin was ghost-white.

Kowalski stared into Lena's eyes. 'I should have seen this. I should have stopped you.'

Lena looked up desperately at him, as if she wished he *had* stopped her, but she couldn't speak anymore. Her body stiffened and then convulsed briefly. Finally, she slumped backwards as she became a dead weight.

Kowalski lowered Lena into the water. Her eyes were partly closed, and she looked strangely peaceful before the water flowed over her. Kowalski turned to Loxton, and for a brief moment Loxton felt afraid, but then she saw the look in his eyes – the fear for her.

Lena had thought that Kowalski had feelings for her. Loxton felt a pang of shame that she'd ever doubted him. She wanted to reach out to him, but it felt like there was an impenetrable wall between them now. Kowalski was in a place she didn't know, his face wracked with grief and horror at Lena's revenge against him.

She tried to stand but her head felt light and her vision blurred. She blinked rapidly to try to focus.

Kowalski moved over to her. 'Let me see.'

She gingerly lifted her shirt so that he could see the damage that had been done. She turned her head away.

She didn't want to see. He pulled off his shirt and twisted it into a bandage. He wrapped it around her waist and tied it tight. She grunted at the sharp pain as he finished the knot. Kowalski watched the bandage for a moment and then his frown increased. She looked down and saw dark red beginning to seep through the material.

'We've got to get you out of here. Do you think you can walk?'

'I can try,' she said.

He unbuttoned her shirt, gently taking it off and twisting it into a second bandage to put around her midriff. He wrapped that on top of the first and tied it even tighter. She winced in pain, taking in a sharp breath. The pain radiated through her abdomen and lights swam in front of her eyes.

'Ready?' he asked.

'Just give me a moment,' she managed. She wasn't sure if she could even stand. She didn't think she would be getting out of here alive.

Kowalski looked down at Lena's dead body in disbelief, as if his mind were unable to process it all. 'She was a good person once,' Kowalski said. 'This was Szymański. It was him.'

Loxton saw all the good memories of Lena etched on his face. And in the end, it had come to this.

'Szymański's dead, Dominik. Lena did this all on her own and I'm glad she's gone.' It was all Loxton could do to stop herself from screaming with rage at the woman who was broken and dead in the water. Loxton would be joining her if she didn't get out of this place soon. Her shoulder throbbed, her sides were swollen and sore, and she was dizzy and growing weaker.

She had come so close to suffering the fate that Emma, Sarah and Gabriella had. She thought of the fear they'd

felt, the fear that she'd now experienced. She couldn't pretend anymore. The terror and the pain they'd undergone
with Lena's cold eyes watching them, full of hate. Had
Jane died down here too, or was she tied up nearby, scared
and alone?

'Jane could still be alive,' Loxton said. 'We need to
find her.'

'We need to get you out of here,' Kowalski said. 'You've
lost a lot of blood. And I've been searching these tunnels
for hours. I haven't found her. We need to get you out.
They'll get search dogs down here.'

'Please, let's just check the area where Lena planned to
kill me. There was another chamber behind where I woke
up. I know the way from here. And the entrance I came
in can't be far from here.' She tried to stand, but her arms
shook as she tried to push herself up.

'Let me help you.' Kowalski crouched next to her. He
put his hands under her arms and pulled her upwards. The
pain was extraordinary and she gasped involuntarily.

'I know, I know,' he said gently.

She was standing, but only just. He wrapped his arm
around her back, and she slung her arm over his shoulders,
using him to keep herself standing up.

They made their way painfully back towards the chamber Loxton had woken up in. Her ragged breath and the
splashing of their feet were the only sounds. Could Jane
have been so close to her? And was there any chance she
was still alive? Loxton couldn't bear the thought of leaving
her alone down here.

They reached the chamber and Loxton recognized it
immediately. It was larger than the others, with a curved
tiled ceiling above her. On the floor was a discarded black
sports bag and inside she caught a glimpse of surgical

wipes, ropes, a glass dildo, plastic gloves and a forensic suit. She felt the bile rise as she thought about how close she had come to being violated and killed.

'Christ,' Kowalski said, his voice echoing around the chamber.

'She went back there.' Loxton pointed towards the narrow tunnel Lena had gone down and they made their way through the water. It felt colder here, darker.

Kowalski spun the torch around the cramped side chamber they found themselves in. There were no other exits; it was a dead end. A tiny square was chiselled into the rock and she wondered what purpose this room had once served. She saw some bloodied torn ropes floating on the surface of the water.

Kowalski leaned her against the wall and then he crouched down to examine the ropes. 'They look roughly cut, not by anything sharp. Are they yours?'

Loxton shook her head and stared around the small space. Is this where Jane had been hidden until it was her turn to be moved into the killing chamber?

Kowalski frowned at Loxton, shining the light into her face. She blinked into the blinding white, putting her hand up to shield her eyes.

'You don't look so good,' he said. 'Come on, that's it. Let's find the entry you came through. It can't be far.' He put his arm around her back and she used him to prop herself up as they headed back out into the large cold chamber. She shivered with blood loss and the horror of what had happened here. She was glad to be leaving.

It felt like they had been stumbling through the tunnels in silence for hours, but the truth was it had probably only been minutes. Kowalski kept stopping at numbers scrawled on the walls and to check the map, but she couldn't focus, everything was dancing in front of her eyes.

She felt her energy waning and the darkness seemed to grow with every step they took. Despair began to take hold. If they couldn't find their way out of this maze soon, she would bleed to death. She knew Lena hadn't called for backup or told Winter where they were. She'd been an idiot to trust Lena when she'd climbed down that ladder. And now no one was coming to save them – to save her.

She staggered forward, nearly losing her footing as her feet went numb and her hands tingled. She struggled onwards, one hand in front of her, but there was nothing to hold on to but blackness. She felt her legs going underneath her. Kowalski pulled her closer, keeping her upright.

'Dominik . . .' She felt the world tip and everything rotate.

'I've got you,' he said. 'Don't worry, I've got you.' He lifted her up into his arms. She was being rocked gently backwards and forwards and she felt so tired. It was so hard to stay awake. She couldn't tell if her eyes were closed or open. She could hear his voice, but she couldn't make out the words. Everything felt so hard, too hard, and she didn't want to fight anymore. She let herself go. It was time. All she wanted to do was sleep.

Shaking. The earth was shaking. She thought of an earthquake and tried to look around, but the world was pitch black. Perhaps she was dreaming?

'Alana, wake up!' Kowalski sounded panicked. The shaking grew more violent and she moaned. She just wanted to sleep.

'Alana, you've got to stay awake. It's important.'

She mumbled, 'Dominik.'

'Please. I can't lose you too.' His voice was urgent.

'I'm right here.' She couldn't understand why he was so worried or why it was so dark. She tried to stay awake for him, but it was so hard. It felt impossible.

Chapter 49

Loud, rasping sobs echoed in her head. Desperate. She forced her eyes open and she saw Kowalski's face near her, the torchlight exaggerating his forehead, nose and jaw, making his face look skull-like.

He had balanced the torch against a cold, ancient wall, so that it cast its light upwards. It was like they were gathered around a campfire about to tell ghost stories. There was someone with him – someone crying.

'Who ... who is it?' Her voice croaked and she felt the coarseness in it. She was so thirsty; it was painful to talk.

'Alana.' Kowalski rushed to her side, crouching down next to her. 'It's Jane. We've found Jane.'

Loxton peered into the darkness and the figure moved towards her and into the light. Jane's crying rose when she saw Loxton, the pain and panic turning into horror. 'Oh my God, is that Alana?'

Loxton wasn't sure who else Jane thought it could be, but she didn't question her friend. She didn't have the energy to ask what she meant.

'I saw Alana in the chamber with a woman, Alana had a knife in her neck. And then that woman came after me, so I had to run. She had a knife. I thought Alana was already dead.'

Loxton wanted to say thank you. That Jane had actually saved her life, drawing Lena away from her so she could escape. But she couldn't form the words.

'We've got to get her out of here.' Kowalski had lowered his voice, but Loxton couldn't tell who he was trying to stop from hearing. 'She's in a really bad way.'

'Is that woman close?' Jane's eyes were wild. 'We need to turn that fucking torchlight off.'

'It's okay.' Kowalski put his hands on Jane's shoulders. 'Alana took care of her. She's dead.'

'Are you sure?' Jane whispered. 'We need to be sure.'

Kowalski nodded. 'I saw for myself. She's dead.'

Jane broke down again, tears wracking her body. She tried to steady her breathing. She seemed to gather herself. She looked dreadful. 'I've been trying to find a way out.' Her voice sounded funny. 'But it all just leads in circles.'

'How did you get away?' Kowalski asked.

'She'd tied my ankles and feet together. Left me in a small chamber. Said she'd be back. I managed to crawl to a wall and rub at the ropes. It felt like hours. Once my hands were free of my ankles I could crawl, and I just started going. I couldn't be there when she came back. I crawled for as far as I could and then stopped to free my ankles. Then I could run. I've been running ever since.'

'How did you hide from her?'

'The tunnels are long, and when I heard her coming, I moved quietly, always keeping ahead of her. There's not too many cul-de-sacs around here; it all seems to go on forever, but then I keep ending up near the chamber. It's like a nightmare I can't wake up from. I thought I'd learnt all the routes but then I can't have, unless it all goes in a circle. There were a few close calls when I saw the light from her torch, but I knew where the crossroads were. How long have I been down here for?'

'Forty hours, give or take.' Kowalski shook his head. 'Maybe a little longer.'

She nodded in the gloom. 'I thought I'd been here for days. I've not slept. I kept thinking she'd done something to my boys. They are all right, aren't they, Dominik? You said they were okay.'

'They're okay, I promise,' Kowalski said. 'What about water? Alana needs some.'

'There are places where water's trickling down the walls. I'll show you. I've been drinking that, from as high up as I can. I didn't want to risk the water below.'

'Can you show me? We can bring some back for her.'

Jane looked at Loxton and she nodded, not saying any more. Loxton wanted to go with them, but she couldn't lift her head up. Minutes later they were back, and a strip of wet cloth was put against her mouth. She sucked at the water greedily.

'I've been struggling to find the way out of here in the dark, but if you give me the torch, I'll be able to find the tunnel I've been missing.' Jane put her hand out.

Kowalski hesitated. 'I'm stronger than you are. You've not eaten anything or slept.'

'But I know the paths, Dominik. I'll be quicker.'

'We should go together,' Kowalski said. 'I can carry her.'

'You'll slow me down, and should you really move her?' Kowalski's eyes met Loxton's.

'You should both go,' Loxton said. Her throat felt like sandpaper. 'It's our best chance. *My* best chance.' She knew that when they left, she'd probably never see them again. She didn't have long left, maybe an hour, maybe just minutes. But the thought that they would be getting out, back into the light, eased the realization that she was going to die down here. For a moment she let herself imagine Jane's children seeing their mother again. Ben's face when he saw her.

'I don't want to leave you,' Kowalski said.

'And I don't want to die. This is my best chance. If Jane goes but can't make it out, then you won't be sat here waiting for us to be rescued; you'll be sat here watching me die. You know it, Dominik.'

Kowalski stared at her hard, frowning. His face cracked. 'All right. What blood type are you?'

'A rhesus-positive.'

'We'll be back. Just hold on.'

She tried to nod but the effort was too much. She watched the light receding. Watched Kowalski and Jane moving away. Jane was safe. Kowalski was safe. It was over. She felt tears well in her eyes. Nothing mattered but that Kowalski was safe. He would go on. She hadn't made a terrible mistake in these dark tunnels.

Chapter 50

Saturday 5 February, 15:01

Loxton shivered as she lay on the damp floor. The tiny patter of paws grew closer and she felt something brush against her arm. She managed a strangled moan and the animal skittered away. It wouldn't be long before her moans stopped working. The blood on her arm was too tempting and she was growing weaker. Tiny eyes watched her. They could sense their time was coming.

She didn't know how long she'd been laid there on her own in the dark. She'd been dreaming of her mother in the garden, hanging washing out while Loxton played at her feet. Her mother had been singing, but Loxton couldn't remember the tune now. Then storm clouds had covered the blue sky above them, her mother oblivious, and the heavens had opened. A torrent of rain, the water hammering her head, soaking her as the temperature dropped. She shivered as she sat on the grass, her toys abandoned. The rain splashing against her head and bare legs, the noise deafening. All the while her mother didn't seem to realize that they were getting soaked. That she was freezing.

Splashing. And voices shouting. She shivered in the cold. She wanted to call out to them, but she couldn't. The darkness was so complete around her. But then she saw it. The light dancing wildly in the black.

'Alana!' Kowalski's voice called to her. 'Alana, we're coming!'

She saw dark figures rushing towards her, growing bigger and bigger until they were nearly on top of her.

'Thank God,' Kowalski whispered.

Paramedics knelt in the dirty water next to her. A bright white light burnt into her eyes. 'Alana, can you hear me?'

She couldn't even nod her head, but she kept her eyes open, even though the light sent a searing pain sharp into her brain.

'She's lost a lot of blood.' The paramedic lifted a bag of it off the stretcher. 'A rhesus-positive, correct?'

'That's right,' Kowalski said.

The other paramedic took her arm and she felt a sharp pain, which was then dulled by the throbbing in her shoulder. One paramedic handed the bag to Kowalski. 'Hold it a little higher and gently squeeze it. That's it. Keep that up while we try to stop the bleeding.'

They untied the bandage around her shoulder and a new wave of pain hit her, making her head dizzier.

'Still bleeding. Try the cold compress and let's bandage her up again and get her on the stretcher.'

Loxton felt the cold on her skin and for a moment there was relief, but that was soon replaced with searing pain. The paramedic's rough hands wrapped a bandage tight around her shoulder and she gasped. Then they lifted her onto a stretcher. She moaned in agony and the paramedic looked relieved. 'She's picking up. Come on, let's get her out of here.'

Kowalski handed the bag to the smaller paramedic and took hold of the stretcher. 'You hold on, Alana. You're going to be okay.'

She didn't think she'd ever be okay again, but before she could tell him, the darkness folded in around her.

Chapter 51

'Alana, how are you feeling?' Winter smiled at her.

It was strange seeing him in a jumper and jeans. She wasn't sure it suited him. She coughed as she tried to answer.

'Not great,' she admitted, her voice hoarse. 'My throat's killing me.' Her shoulder ached and her arm too. She grimaced as the pain radiated down her sides. Her head was banging as if something was digging inside it and the sockets of her eyes throbbed worse than any migraine, the hospital lights too bright.

Winter poured her a glass of water out of the plastic jug and held it out to her. She took it gingerly and sipped.

'How's Jane?' she asked.

'Recovering well. Her husband and children were thrilled to have her home. She didn't need to stay in long, just dehydrated, sprained wrists and ankles, but it'll all heal. Nothing serious. How are you doing?'

'They say no major ligaments or nerves were damaged so I should make a full recovery.' She thought of Emma, Sarah and Gabriella. There was no recovery for them. 'Is Dominik all right? He hasn't come to see me.' It bothered her more than she wanted to admit. She'd expected him at her bedside when she woke up, but instead he'd been absent the whole time she'd been in here.

'He's suspended. We've told him he's not allowed to see you. I'm sorry, but you understand what a mess this is. He didn't disclose the relationships with the victims. And there are real question marks about his involvement with Lena Trawinska. He brought her on to the case.'

Loxton sat up straighter, wincing as she did so.

'I know, I know.' Winter put his hand up as if to placate her. 'I'm sorry, at the very least he's made some serious errors of judgement, and at the worst ... Well, the investigation is ongoing.'

Loxton shook her head in frustration. 'You're wrong about him, sir. He didn't know what Lena was. She admitted she was avenging Szymański's death; she blamed Dominik for catching him and sending him to prison. We can't let her win. Without Dominik I'd be dead. Jane would be dead too.'

'Look, it's too early to talk about that now. We have to let the Department of Professional Standards carry out their investigation. I understand your loyalty to Dominik – I feel the same, but it's a professional matter.'

'Lena confessed. Doesn't my statement count for anything?' She shook her head, her shoulder aching. 'I want to see him; you can't stop me seeing him.'

'I'd rather you didn't while the investigation is ongoing. We have to let them do their job.'

'If we'd let homicide do their job, who knows if I'd still be alive,' she said.

Winter hesitated for a moment. 'They got side tracked by Pearce but they were doing their best. It was a unique case. Lena had access to everything, it meant she could tamper with the evidence, manipulate us all.'

Loxton knew it wasn't fair to take it out on him, but she hated how Kowalski was being treated.

'I need to talk to you about homicide, actually,' he said. 'They're recruiting next month and they've asked for you to apply. They're going to offer you a position. DI Meyer was impressed with how you handled this case and the work you did in the past on Barratt. You don't have to do the application until you're well enough, but they'll keep a space open for you, off the record. Murder's what you excel at, Alana. You deserve this.' He smiled at her. 'We'll miss you, of course, but I'm happy for you.'

'Thank you, sir.' She'd been desperate to get back to murder. It's all she'd ever wanted to do. But somehow the joy had gone from it.

'And I've got some more good news. Luke Pearce was sentenced to three years for dangerous driving. It's not the full five years he could have got, but it's something. The motorcyclist is out of the coma, although he'll never walk again.'

She nodded absently. Three years' imprisonment seemed small compensation for the motorcyclist.

'I'd better let you rest. Let me know what you think of the murder squad's offer when you've had a chance to mull it over.' Winter picked up his coat, ready to leave.

'What about Dominik?' she asked. 'His promotion?'

'He can forget about that for a while. You can't be promoted while you're suspended, so he'll miss being posted and then he'll have to start the process again. With what's gone on, he needs to focus on getting back on his feet again first.'

'Dominik's going to need his friends around him.'

'He's a good officer,' Winter said. 'I'll do what I can, but we have to let the DPS do their job. Now get some

rest. Take as long as you need. Your new role can wait.'
He patted her arm and left her.

She thought of Dominik, the pain he must be feeling,
the confusion, and she wished more than anything that
she could see him.

Chapter 52

The building was the colour of wet sand, with a large chimney stack rising from it, dominating the skyline. It could have been mistaken for a practical church, except for the lack of any cross. It sat squat and functional in the bare grounds. There was no one around, the only noise the crunch of Loxton's shoes through the gravel path as she made her way inside.

The hall was plain, with nothing on the walls. There were seven neat rows of cheap plastic chairs. At the front was a set of navy curtains, part-way open, reminding her of community theatres she'd been to as a girl. Peeking through the curtains was a simple pine coffin, which sat on a conveyor belt, waiting to be pulled away.

Kowalski was stood at the front of the room, the only attendant, staring through the gap in the curtains at the coffin that contained his old friend. The priest stood at the front facing his congregation of two, reciting the Lord's Prayer quickly, clearly wanting the service to be over with. He threw nervous glances at the coffin and the entrance, as if anxious that angry family members of the victims would arrive, or, worse, that Lena would rise from the dead.

It was so different from the recent funerals of Loxton's friends, where she and Jane had clutched at each other's hands to stop from screaming. Emma, Sarah and Gabriella – each funeral unique, but somehow chillingly the same. The churchyards had been full to bursting with family, friends and police officers gathered around the graves, people having travelled for miles to see them off.

Here, it was just Kowalski and Loxton. She stood beside him, took his hand in hers and squeezed it tight. He squeezed back and they stayed that way as the priest finished the prayer and finally the box was pulled along the conveyor belt away from them. Once the coffin had passed the curtains, which swung clumsily closed, she felt finally free of Lena.

Outside, the air was biting, and grey clouds raced each other across a dull white sky. Her shoulder throbbed as the cold seeped into her bones.

'What will you do now?' she asked him, wrapping her arms around herself to try to keep warm.

'I'll take her ashes back to Poland. I'll scatter them on her parents' old farm. They're not too far from the main town, on a hill overlooking a lake. Her parents would have appreciated that if they were still here; they were good people. And she used to tell me it's where she was happiest.'

She nodded, words failing her. All she felt was the burning rage as she thought of her friends, brutally murdered by Lena.

'Police work destroyed Lena,' Kowalski said. 'Szymański destroyed her. The lines between protector and predator became blurred. And because of that, Emma, Sarah and Gabriella are dead.'

'She was ill,' Loxton said. She had to believe that. The

idea that anyone could be so easily corrupted was too much to accept.

Kowalski closed his eyes for a moment, lost in thought.

'When's the misconduct hearing?' she asked, desperate to pull him away from thoughts of the past. And secretly she couldn't bear to hear him talk of Lena. It was too raw.

'In a couple of months. I guess I'll be seeing you then; I'm afraid they're going to call you. That's what my federation representative told me.'

'I've talked to Winter about this. I want to come with you for the whole hearing.'

Kowalski looked away. 'Can you do that?'

'Yes, if you don't mind? The board has agreed. None of this was your fault, Dominik.'

Kowalski focused on the passing clouds. He wouldn't look at her. 'If Emma and the others had never met me, then they'd still be alive now. Lena had been asking people about me. Finding out everything about my life here, who I'd been involved with. If I'd made the connection between her and Szymański back in Poland, realized that she was sick, then they'd still be alive.'

'You told me once that we can't worry about the what ifs and the maybes in this job. Reality keeps us busy enough. This is on Lena – no one else. She became unhinged after meeting Szymański. You're a good detective, you've done good things, and we're not going to lose you.'

He nodded, keeping his eyes away from hers. 'I wanted to say thanks, for keeping in touch with me. I appreciate it. I'd understand if you didn't want to.'

'Dominik, we don't give up on each other. Ever. You told me that.' Loxton smiled at him.

'Do you know which murder team you're going to be

posted to? I'm glad you're going back. I know it's what you wanted.'

'I'm not going.' Now she couldn't look at him. 'I turned them down.'

'Why?'

'I'm not finished with Southwark yet. And after everything, I think I need some time away from murder. To recover. I'm not ready to go back yet. We lost a lot of friends. Good friends.'

He nodded and swallowed hard. 'Too many. I don't know how we'll ever go back to how we were before.'

'We won't, Dominik. But that will have to be enough. Some things you don't get over; you just get through them, and this is going to have to be one of them.'

He nodded. 'Thanks for coming today. I didn't expect you to under the circumstances. You'd best get going. I need to collect her ashes later when they're ready.'

'I passed a pub on the way here. I'll wait with you. We can sit in there together.'

'Are you sure?' He looked at her in surprise.

She gave his hand another brief squeeze and looked him in the eye. 'More than I've ever been before.'

Acknowledgements

Normally I start by thanking readers, but as I sit here writing this, we are in the middle of the Covid-19 global pandemic. So instead, it feels fitting to start by thanking all the NHS workers, supermarket staff, teachers and essential workers who risked their lives during Lockdown to keep us going. Without them, we would have all been lost.

I want to thank the readers, bloggers and reviewers, because without you there would be no books! I'd like to say thank you so much for taking the time and energy in these difficult times to read this one.

Thank you to Camilla Bolton, the best agent in the world, for your faith in this book and for championing DC Alana Loxton and for all of your advice. To Jade Kavanagh for the encouragement and puppy pictures! And thank you to everyone at Darley Anderson for their continued support in the most trying of times.

Thank you to my incredible editor, Bethan Jones, for the brilliant title and for making this book so much stronger. To Victoria Godden, my copyeditor, who once again did a fantastic job. To Jessica Barratt for your hard work and for so successfully spreading the word about this series. And thank you to everyone at Simon & Schuster for your endless enthusiasm and expertise, despite everything that is going on in the world.

To my police colleagues in the Met Police, it was a privilege to work alongside you, and thank you for all the hard work you do every day.

Thanks to my teachers on the City University Master's course where it all began for me: Claire McGowan, Laura Wilson, William Ryan and my mentor, Alex Marwood.

I'm so grateful to the other writers on the City Crime Writing MA I got to meet who have become firm friends, but especially to: Finn Clarke, Vicki Jones, Jane Phillips, Paul Durston, Fraser Massey and Sian Williams. Thank you for our virtual writing get-togethers that have kept me sane in these strange times.

To all of my friends and family (you know who you are), for your patience, encouragement and support. But especially to: Andy Niewiarowski (Grammar Panda), Tom Chambers, James Rollinson, Lucy Howard, Joanna Glenn, Elly Savin, Kalynda Bradley, Pete Bradley, Adrian Wallett, Sheila Wallett, Alan Frost and Bernard Wallett for spreading the word about the book. And to Rosie White, Mel Wilson, Lauren Koegler and Alison Niewiarowska for still being the best cheerleaders a girl could wish for.

To my mum and dad, Sylvia and Charles Richard Bradley, for all the sacrifices you made for us and for passing on your love of reading.

And last but not least, thank you to my husband, Mike. For all of your encouragement, patience and humour in Lockdown and for being a great co-worker (even if you did steal my writing office). And for making every day with you amazing; I couldn't have gone on this writing adventure without you.

Do you want to read more from Vicki Bradley?

Then don't miss

Julia is nervous and it's not just because she's about to get married. There's a lot that her soon-to-be husband, Mark, doesn't know – and she is determined to keep it that way.

As she walks down the aisle, spotting Mark in his tailored suit, she knows she is taking her first steps to happiness – her past can't catch her now. He turns to face her . . .

But it isn't Mark in the beautiful suit – it's his best man.

Because Mark is missing.

And Julia's past is closer than she thinks.

Keep reading to enjoy an extract now.

Chapter 1

Julia Talbot

Sunday

My hands were shaking. I was terrified, but also elated by the promise of a new future: like waiting to be called for a job interview, but much, much more intense.

Outside, the summer sun was trying to push through the white clouds, and I willed it on, as if the light would bring me luck. The hotel grounds looked peaceful, not a single person around, but the surroundings did nothing to calm my nerves.

My palms were sweaty. Panic was building up in my stomach and rising to my chest. I took a long breath in, held it, and then I let it go. It was what my therapist had taught me to do.

'Not long to go,' Lucy said. She looked beautiful in her bridesmaid's dress. I'd asked her to make sure everything ran smoothly, and the pressure was showing. She was like a coiled spring ready to explode. She wanted everything to be perfect for me. It wasn't helping my rising anxiety.

'We're both ready,' I said.

Lucy nodded and then fussed with a loose strand of my hair, which had come free from my chignon and framed my face. She kept trying to tuck it back in, but it wouldn't stay. She knew my fine hair was unmanageable, but today she was refusing to give up.

'It's okay.' I moved away from her.

'Sorry.' She clasped her hands together. I wasn't sure who was more apprehensive: her or me.

I surveyed myself in the hotel mirror, checking every last detail, and smiled. My long blonde hair was staying up, a few delicate white pearls sprinkled throughout. My white dress fit perfectly, cascading around my feet. Lucy was reflected behind me in the glass, her brow creased with the strain of concentrating as she checked every detail too.

I smiled at her and made tiny adjustments to my flowers and dress. I took my time. I touched up the pink gloss on my lips; the colour made them fuller. This was my moment of transformation. No one was going to hurry me. I needed to get this right. Everybody would be watching me, including Mark's family. I had to be perfect.

'How do I look?' I grinned at her.

Lucy's brow creased and her lip wobbled.

'Come on.' I gave her a quick hug. 'We promised each other we wouldn't cry.' She was meant to be supporting me, but here I was having to carry her, on today of all days.

'I'm sorry.' She dabbed at her eyes, trying not to smudge her mascara. 'You look incredible.'

She composed herself and then wrapped her arms tightly around me, her auburn curls brushing against my cheek. I untangled myself and held her at arm's length.

I couldn't help but smile. Her curled auburn hair tumbled around her shoulders and her peppermint bridesmaid's dress made her green eyes glow.

'You look beautiful,' I said. 'It won't be long until it's your turn.'

'It's only been six months,' Lucy said, but a huge grin appeared at the mention of her boyfriend, James. I was glad to see her so happy. She'd had more than her fair share of pain over the years. 'Sorry he couldn't come today,' she said. 'He really did try, but he couldn't get out of the Dubai work trip.'

'Don't worry,' I said. 'You're here and that's what matters.' I gave her a twirl and she let out a little sob. Part of me suspected that her tears weren't all joyful. She'd never been sure about Mark and had been very vocal about it at the beginning. When she realized that I wouldn't give him up, she'd toed the line, but her concerns had always left me with a niggle of self-doubt. She'd known me my whole life; knew me better than anyone. I had found myself asking the same question over and over again. Was I making the right choice? But then Mark's lopsided grin would come into my mind and I told myself I'd never find anyone like him again. The day I'd met him I knew we were going to be married and live happily together, always.

'Come on, Miss Time-Keeper.' I tapped my wrist as if I was wearing a watch. 'Don't we need to get going?'

Lucy moved away. 'Sorry. Yes. They'll be here soon.' She wiped under her eyes with tissue and touched up her foundation before picking up her bouquet; it matched my larger bunch of peach and yellow roses.

I turned towards the door. As if on cue, there was a knock. A middle-aged man in a black suit marched into the room. He looked every inch the police detective, with his composed presence and the way he took control of the space. It made my heart stop.

'Miss Talbot, my name is Henry.' He thrust his hand towards me and I stared at it blankly. 'I'm going to be

your registrar for today.' His hand hovered in the air
uselessly and he tilted his head at me, a look of concern
on his face.

'Of course, thank you.' I grabbed his hand gratefully,
but shook it too fast in my relief. I caught a glimpse of
my reflection glaring back at me from the large mirrors
on the walls. I was frowning, and my shoulders were
tense. I tried to relax. I was being ridiculous. Of course
he wasn't from the police.

'First off, I need to check that you are Miss Julia
Talbot,' the registrar said.

'I am.' I smiled at him.

'And have you ever been known by any other name?'

'No.' My skin prickled as I told the lie. Lucy's face
didn't change but she gave a slight nod of approval. I
could always rely on her.

'It's nothing to worry about,' the registrar said chirpily.
'Just part of the legal process. One always has to satisfy
the law.' I suspected that he'd never been on the wrong
side of it.

'I'm sorry.' I tried to relax. 'I'm all over the place today.'

'I've yet to meet a bride who hasn't suffered with
nerves.' He patted my arm kindly, like a father would,
and I felt pain needle sharp in my heart.

'Will anyone be walking you down the aisle?'

'No. I'll be walking down the aisle by myself.' My
dad's face came into my mind, the last time I'd seen him.
He was cradling his head in his hands, his whole body
shaking with sobs.

'Right . . .' The registrar was flustered by my answer.
'And you've got one bridesmaid here.'

'Yes, that's me.' Lucy nodded at him. With Lucy stood
beside me, I could do this.

'And who is your witness for the signing of the register?' he asked.

'Witness?' I looked at Lucy.

'When you and Mark sign the register, you'll have two witnesses,' the registrar said. 'I believe Mark has chosen his mother.'

'I thought his mother and father were going to be the witnesses?' I said. 'They both wanted to be involved in the ceremony.'

'Sorry, tradition dictates one witness should be from the bride's side.' The registrar shook his head at me and smiled. 'And I'm a stickler for tradition. What about your friend here?'

'Oh. Yes, Lucy.' There was only Lucy left on my side to be my witness.

'Or maybe a sibling, to get them a bit involved?' He clasped his hands together, waiting.

My chest felt tight and a sudden wave of dizziness hit me. I heard Rachel's childish laughter pealing through the trees, saw sunlight filtering through the woods.

I had to sit down or I'd fall. Lucy grabbed my arm. She guided me to the plush sofa in the middle of the room. My legs buckled under me and I collapsed onto it.

'Are you all right?' The registrar rushed forward; his already wrinkled brow was furrowed deep. He seemed at a loss as to what to do.

'She's fine.' Lucy bent over me, peering into my face. She turned to him. 'I can be the witness.'

'Do you need some water or something?' He shifted his weight from one leg to the other, not sure where to go.

'Great idea.' Lucy rushed to the table where a jug of water stood and poured me a glass.

'I'm all right,' I said. 'A little hot, that's all. This dress is too tight.'

'I have to ask . . .' The registrar leaned closer towards me. 'Is anyone forcing you to get married?'

'No, no one's forcing me to do anything.' I couldn't keep the irritation out of my voice. *Why was he asking me that?* I wished he would get away from me.

His face relaxed. 'I'm sorry – I have a legal duty to ask. It's one of the standard questions.'

'Of course.' I tried to control my breathing.

Lucy handed me the glass of water.

'I'll . . . I'll leave you to it,' he said. 'Thank you.' He hurried out of the room without looking back.

'Drink the water,' Lucy said. 'It's going to be fine.' She squeezed my shoulder gently.

Cool water slid down my throat. 'Do you . . . do you think they know about what happened?' I couldn't look at her as I said it.

'You're being paranoid.' She stood up straight. 'How could they know?' There was a sharpness to her voice.

'You're right. It's just . . . I hate being the centre of attention. Everyone staring at me again.'

She gave a brief nod but said nothing. We never talked about our past; it was our unspoken rule.

'We need to get going.' She handed me my bouquet and smiled at me. 'It's nearly two.'

I smoothed my dress and glanced in the mirror one final time. The colour was coming back to my cheeks. Today my life was going to begin with Mark. He had been everything to me for so long now and soon we would be married. I felt a flutter of happiness at the thought.

*

We waited outside the ceremony room – the point of no return. Once I crossed that threshold, everything would change, my life would never be the same again. I was ready.

But voices rumbled from inside the room; I'd expected silence. I glanced at Lucy, who was hunched over, fussing with my satin train.

I thought of Mark. How we'd talked about this day for so long. Now it was finally here it felt different. Strained, maybe. As if everything was pulled taut and a single thing could rip it all apart.

Lucy stood up and waited beside me. My feet were starting to ache and the underwire of my lacy bra was digging into my ribs. I tugged at my bodice.

Lucy turned to me. 'Shouldn't someone open the doors for us?'

'I would have thought so.' I tried to remember what my wedding planner had said would happen at this moment. The voices still rumbled on through the door.

'I can go in and find out what's happening?' Lucy suggested.

'No, everyone will see you. Let's give it a couple of minutes. David's probably lost the rings or something. I told Mark he'd be useless, but did he listen?' I'd never liked David. He seemed so superficial and didn't strike me as a good person.

'Tweedledum and Tweedledee.' Lucy muttered under her breath, but then saw my look and realized what she'd said. She knew I hated it when she compared Mark to David. 'I mean . . . you know, for friends, they're very alike. Same haircut, same suits. That's all. I didn't mean . . .' She blushed and looked downwards. I decided to leave it. Now was not the time to start arguing with my only bridesmaid.

'Sorry,' she said.

'It's fine.' It wasn't and she knew it. We waited for a few more minutes. 'I put one-thirty on the invites. They'll all be sat there waiting. This is embarrassing.'

'The bride's always late,' Lucy said.

'But I'm not late. I'm ready.' My patience was wearing thin. I'd never understood that tradition. 'Maybe you're meant to open the doors?'

Lucy peered through the tiny gap in the oak double doors, which were festooned with white ribbons and peach roses. 'They're all just sat there waiting.'

'Well, I can't stand here for ever. Open the doors.'

Lucy was still trying to peek through the doors, stealing nervous glances back at me. She turned to me. 'Surely someone should come out and open the doors for us?'

I wasn't going to stand here any longer. I set off towards the door with Lucy trotting behind me. She hurried in front of me and pulled open the doors, and then fell in line behind me.

The ceremony room was not as I remembered it. People filled the room, mostly sitting, but a few were on their feet. They weren't looking my way, and some were even blocking the aisle.

Mark was at the front, speaking with the registrar, his back towards me. I remembered the first time I'd met him, when he'd come into my little jewellery store. I'd known he was different. I couldn't stop watching him. He had a good eye for jewellery, selecting one of my favourite pieces for his mother's birthday. I felt at ease with him. When he discovered I was the jewellery maker and owner, he was amazed. Most people see jewellery as frivolous, but he said it was art.

He'd bought the piece and left, but the next day he

came in again. He'd claimed he needed to buy another present, but it became clear he wasn't there for the jewellery. I hadn't been able to stop thinking about him, and I couldn't believe he'd come back. I knew in that moment that one day we'd be married and now here we were.

I waved at the pianist to start playing and he frowned at me and shook his head. I mouthed '*play*' at him and he shrugged his shoulders and began the canon, filling the room with a rising crescendo. All faces turned towards me, but no one was smiling.

Gemma, a colleague of Mark's, loomed in front of me, blocking my way. 'Julia, you shouldn't be here,' she said. 'Elizabeth was supposed to talk to you.'

'What do you mean? Of course I should be here. It's my wedding day.' *Had she lost her mind?*

'Get out of her way.' Lucy stepped in front of me and pushed Gemma aside.

I saw a smirk play across Gemma's face as she shrugged her shoulders and turned away. I'd always suspected she'd liked Mark a bit too much. She'd certainly never been keen on me. Tears filled my eyes. Everything was blurred.

As I stumbled down the aisle, the people around me gawped. One of Mark's cousins put her hand over her mouth.

I concentrated on Mark; he was a few metres away. If I could get to him, everything would be all right. He was in a deep discussion with the registrar, their heads bent towards each other. Those standing were blocking my view. I couldn't get his attention without shouting at him and I wouldn't stoop to that.

Confusion spread through the room. The whispers grew. Elizabeth, Mark's mother, was hurrying down the aisle towards me, a strange look on her face.

Mark turned around to face me – but it wasn't Mark. It was David.

When Mark had joined the gym, David had too. When Mark changed his hair, David had too. I couldn't believe I'd mistaken him for Mark. Of course it wasn't him.

I brushed the tears from my eyes and checked the crowd either side of me, but Mark wasn't there.

David hurried towards me, meeting me halfway down the aisle just as Elizabeth reached me. He was the last man in the whole world I needed right now, but I was stuck with him.

'Your wedding planner was going to talk to you.' His eyes darted from left to right, searching for her.

'Where's Mark?' I grabbed his hands to make him focus on me.

'I don't know.' He pulled his hands from mine. He wouldn't look at me.

'When did you last see him?' It felt like I was free-falling as my stomach flipped in fear.

'Yesterday afternoon.' He glanced at me and then quickly looked away.

'But you were meant to be staying at our flat with him last night?'

'He didn't turn up. I just thought he was with you.' He pushed his hair back and his eyes searched the room, as if looking for an excuse to get away from me.

'You knew he wasn't with me,' I said. 'We told you we wanted to spend our last unmarried night apart. He was meant to be with *you*.' Mark had been missing for twenty-four hours and David hadn't told anyone.

'Sorry, what do you want me to say?' He put his hands up in surrender and moved away from me. 'Look, I'll try to call him again. We'll find him, don't panic.' He pulled out his mobile and put it to his ear.

My heart hammered inside my chest. Mark was gone. So, this is what it felt like. I'd been preparing myself for this for so long, imagined it enough times, but I hadn't expected it to feel like this. As if my insides had been scooped out. An emptiness.

Elizabeth, Mark's mother, was wittering on at me. She was wearing a ridiculous, pink and gold, frisbee-like hat, which was balanced precariously on top of her greying curls. Her dress was white with a matching pink and gold swirling rose pattern, too bridal for my liking.

'I thought you were going to tell her?' Charles, my soon to be father-in-law, was standing up.

'I thought the wedding planner had gone out to do it.' Elizabeth waved her hand towards me dismissively.

My cheeks burnt with shame. They all thought he'd left me. Snatches of gossip rushed at me. I felt my jaw tightening in anger. I wanted to scream for silence, but my voice had stopped working.

Above me there were white angel sculptures flying out of the top of the stone pillars, their shoulders bent under the weight of the oak beams they were holding up. The effect was meant to be ornate, but the angels were suffering under their burden. Their eyes stared down, pitying me.

I had come so close to happiness. I dropped my gaze to the tiled floor. God was getting me back for everything I had done. And I didn't deserve anything less.

Available now in paperback, eBook and Audio